BLACK SUN RISING

BLACK
SUN
RISING

MATTHEW CARR

PEGASUS CRIME
NEW YORK LONDON

BLACK SUN RISING

Pegasus Crime is an imprint of
Pegasus Books Ltd.
148 W 37th Street, 13th Floor
New York, NY 10018

First Pegasus Books edition June 2020

Interior design by Maria Fernandez

Library of Congress Cataloging-in-Publication Data is available.

ISBN: 978-1-64313-424-6

10 9 8 7 6 5 4 3 2 1

Printed in the United States of America
Distributed by Simon & Schuster

For Lara

May the long time sun shine upon you
All love surround you
And the pure light within you
Guide your way on.

The Barcelonians combine the vivacity of the Gaul with the dignity of the Castilian, while their appreciation of music recalls the Teuton. In no town in the Iberian peninsula flows a more vigorous and cheerful tide of life; and none makes so cosmopolitan an impression.

—Karl Baedeker, *Spain and Portugal*
Handbook for Travellers, 1901

But to this day the natural affiliations of the Catalans attract them to the S. provinces of France; and they are always ready for revolt. Barcelona in particular is a hot-bed of anarchy.

—Karl Baedeker, *Spain and Portugal*
Handbook for Travellers, 1913

The city of spies, labyrinth of mines and countermines, of secret rendez-vous, of multiple treacheries . . .

—Victor Serge, *Birth of Our Power*

PROLOGUE
Barcelona June 14, 1909

Hermenigildo Cortéz woke up in the early morning of the greatest day of his life and looked down through the shutters. The sun was only just coming up but already the port was beginning to stir. He saw the wagons and carts bringing fish and vegetables to the market; the factory workers in their caps and blue smocks drifting sleepily through the gray dawn. He heard the clatter of horses' hooves from just outside his field of vision and the blare of a horn coming from the direction of the harbor. Beyond the statue of Columbus he could see the streaks of red spreading across the sky beyond the rows of fishing boats, masts, and funnels. For the next two hours he paced the room or sat in bed, smoking and staring into space. At seven o'clock he began to get dressed. He put on the double-breasted suit, shirt and tie, the scuffed box toe shoes, the false beard and moustache, and finished it off with the fedora hat.

When he was done he paused to examine himself in the mirror. He looked like any other *Indiano*, fresh off the boat from Buenos Aires with nothing to show for it but the clothes he stood up in. He went downstairs to the seamen's café and drank a brandy to steady his nerves before returning to pay his bill. No sooner had he come back to his room than the butterflies began to swirl around in his stomach once again. He took off his jacket and drew the little suitcase from under the bed. Even though there was no danger, his hands were clammy as he laid it down gently on the dressing table.

Once again he lifted the infernal machine from the pile of clothes and thought how much it looked like an iron. He turned it on its side to unscrew the metal casing and looked down on the rows of taped dynamite, and the wires that connected them to the detonator and the timing mechanism. Even though he had already practiced all this various times, he bit his lip as he adjusted the timing mechanism to ten o'clock. Now the clock was ticking and his heart seemed to beat in time as he reassembled the device and put it back in the suitcase. By the time he stepped out onto the street, he had managed to calm himself. He walked alongside the harbor, and saw the fortress perched on the hill beyond the Columbus Monument, and then turned into the Ramblas. In the far distance he could see Mount Tibidabo overlooking the city, beyond the canopy of trees and the beige hotels and apartment buildings with their wrought iron balconies.

Many years ago his grandmother had told him how the mountain got its name from the Latin *tibi omnia dabo*—all these things I will give to thee. These were the words the devil had spoken to Jesus in an attempt to tempt him, his *abuela* said, and she told him that he should think of them every time he looked at the mountain so that he would not give in to temptation himself. Hermenigildo had once been fond of the old woman, but he knew he had disappointed her when she was alive and she would not have been pleased with him now. Her disapproval did not bother him, because he had long since freed himself of all the laws, superstitions, and sentimental attachments that might once have inclined him to seek her approval. And now he was conscious of the power that his freedom gave him as he walked up through the central thoroughfare, past the newspaper stands and terraced cafés, past the gentlemen in leisure suits, canes, and boaters, accompanied by well-appointed señoras in feathered hats, holding fans and parasols.

He passed servants and housewives in long white skirts carrying straw baskets, workers in blue smocks and crumpled caps, army officers in uniform with ladies on their arms, nuns and priests, beggars and barrow boys. There were also police; watching over the daily herd like dogs: Guardia Civil in their three-cornered hats; Mossos d'Escuadra in their English-style helmets, municipal guard dogs with clubs and red capes; militiamen in plain clothes with shotguns hanging from their shoulders and pistols bulging under their coats.

For a moment Hermenigildo imagined that they could hear the ticking bomb, but he knew it was an illusion. There was nothing in his appearance or demeanor to attract attention, and it was impossible to hear the bomb above the sounds of the new century. Even the voices around him were muted by the factory sirens, the tinkling bicycle bells and screeching streetcars, and the occasional roar of a motor car spluttering through the stream of traffic on both sides of the thoroughfare, as though the whole city was nothing more than a gigantic factory machine turning around on invisible cogs.

Hermenigildo took care to match his step with the flowing crowd, because it was not good to seem like a man in a hurry on the Ramblas. He strolled past the cafés; the Central, the Suizo, the Americano and the Oriente; past the Boqueria market and the flower stalls of the Rambla de las Flores. He glanced at the roses and carnations and bright bouquets, the blue-tipped irises and cobalt allium with heads like sea anemones, the children peering at the trilling songbirds, and the flower vendors tying up bouquets or adjusting their arrangements.

It was nearly 9:15 when he reached the watchmaker's shop at the top of the Ramblas and crossed the road toward the floral glass and striped awnings of the Bar la Luna. By lunchtime the café would be packed, but now there were only a few customers scattered around the terraced tables. In the far corner an elderly gentleman was sitting under the awning, accompanied by a woman who looked considerably younger. The man was tall and distinguished, with old-fashioned white sideburns, and a flat-topped hat. He looked English or German. His companion was wearing a veil over her eyes, but Hermenigildo could see enough of her face to see that she was pretty. He ordered a coffee and looked out toward the watchmaker's clock, while the woman sipped at a cup of hot chocolate and the foreign gentleman pored over what appeared to be a guidebook.

At 9:50 Hermenigildo laid some coins on the table. A moment later the woman got up and went inside. The foreign gentleman was still immersed in his book, and Hermenigildo tried not to look at his face or the faces of the other customers, because it was better not to dwell on such things. It was better to think of himself as a shell that had been fired, and had now reached its destination. He pushed the bag under the table and walked out toward the street. Even as he left the café he half-expected to hear someone calling him back, but now he was out of sight of the terrace and walking quickly across the Plaza Catalunya. He was halfway across the square when the bomb exploded behind him. Even from that distance the noise made him jump, and he seemed to feel the hot air blowing toward him. His first instinct was to keep walking, but he sensed that he was more likely to attract attention to himself if he did. Instead he turned and looked back. In spite of himself he could not help admiring what he had unleashed. There was power and beauty in the explosion and its aftermath. It was as if a small volcano had erupted from underneath the city, bursting up through the café in a cascade of fire, smoke, leaves, and debris. For a moment the blast seemed to reverberate through the streets, swallowing all other sounds, and then he heard the first screams and saw the customers running out into the street. Directly opposite the café a tram had come to a halt, and its passengers were staring with horrified fascination as a woman staggered out onto the pavement. Hermenigildo was pleased to see that it was not the woman who had been sitting with the foreign gentleman. This woman was older and stouter and not as pretty. Her face and hair were covered with dust and her dress was stained red.

It was not until she turned toward him that he realized that one of her arms was missing. He thought that he had seen enough now, and as he walked away he could not help feeling slightly sick.

1

From the fifth floor of the Mountview Hotel, former detective-sergeant Harry Pedro Lawton could hear the sound of children's laughter and the sea gently rolling on the shore behind him as he prepared to climb onto the opposite balcony. It was less than three feet away, but he knew that Dr. Morris would have been horrified to see him there. Once again he considered knocking on the door. But Divine & Laws paid only by results and Mrs. Evangeline Watson and her companion were under no obligation to open it to a private investigator. They might even summon the receptionist and have him thrown out, in which case three weeks' work would be wasted.

There had been a time when he would not have thought twice about climbing over, but now the street seemed a long way down, and he knew that if he waited any longer his nerve might fail him. He hoisted one leg and then the other over the edge of his own balcony, and stood gripping the edge with both hands. Turning sideways toward the wall, he reached out with his right hand and stepped out with his right leg toward the opposite ledge, even as he held on to the ledge with his other hand. He ignored the sickly sensation in his belly and pulled himself onto the opposite balcony, shifting his weight as he did so, until he was gripping the ledge with both hands. Now the sounds of coitus became louder as he climbed over onto the balcony, and his palms were damp as he gripped the window sill and climbed in through the rose-patterned curtains.

"Good morning," he said brightly. "Sorry to interrupt."

The two bodies erupted in a flurry of hands, heads, and feet, and Mrs. Evangeline Watson stared back at him in horror. Lawton could not help feeling a pang of guilt at the sight of her flushed cheeks and disheveled hair, as Lieutenant Teddy Rycroft rolled away from her and sat on the edge of the bed.

"Who the hell are you?" he said.

"Harry Lawton, private investigator. Acting on behalf of Divine & Laws solicitors. I'm here to serve Mrs. Watson with her divorce papers."

"You'll do no such thing, you dirty Fenian bastard." Rycroft advanced toward Lawton with his fists clenched and his manhood already drooping.

"I wouldn't advise that, sir," Lawton said. "I have some knowledge of the pugilistic art."

"So do I." Rycroft brought his fists up to his face and took an obvious swing at Lawton's head with his right, which Lawton easily evaded by dropping underneath it and stepping back with his own fists raised. Lawton had never fought a naked man before. He had read somewhere that the ancient Greeks used to do this, but now the confrontation seemed embarrassing and faintly ridiculous.

"This won't help anyone, Lieutenant," he said. "And it definitely won't end well for you."

"Oh stop, Teddy." Mrs. Watson was sitting up in bed now with a sheet wrapped around her. "How much is my husband paying you, Mr. Lawton? I'm sure I can find more."

"Your husband pays the solicitors not me, madam. And I'm not here to blackmail you. Just doing my job is all."

"And what a job." Rycroft pulled on his underwear. "Your mother must be proud."

Lawton shrugged and dropped the envelope onto the bed. "My mother's feelings are no business of yours. Bring these to the solicitors next week. Please don't try to pretend you didn't receive them. My statement will be sufficient proof that you did."

Rycroft gave him a baleful stare as he opened the door and stepped out into the corridor. Behind him he heard Mrs. Watson let out a very different moan to the ones he had heard before. He could not know whether she was crying because of the divorce that would ruin her or the loss of the lover who would certainly abandon her. Either way he felt sorry for her, because Lieutenant Rycroft was a typical army rake, whose career and reputation would remain unscathed by this, but Mrs Watson's husband was a hard-nosed bastard who would crush her in the courts. It was always the women who came off worse in these situations, but the world was what it was and there was nothing he could do about it. He unlocked the door to his own room, picked up his overnight bag, and walked back out into the dark corridor with its creaking floorboards and well-trodden carpets. At the end of the corridor a shifty face stared back at him from a hallway mirror that had not been polished in a long time. The reflection showed a big man, six feet tall and comfortably over the police regulation height despite his hunched shoulders, but in that moment he felt much smaller. He looked away from his own accusing gaze and hurried back down to the street to catch his train.

Divine & Laws had their offices near Great Ormond Street Hospital, close enough to Chancery Lane to maintain a veneer of respectability and just far enough to allow their clients to visit them without losing theirs. Lawton arrived in the late afternoon to find John Divine reading the court report from the *Evening Standard* on the Rainier divorce case to his partner and Donaldson the articled clerk. Mrs. Rainier's attempt to divorce her Jewish husband on grounds of cruelty had attracted a lot of attention in the press, partly because of the juicy counterclaims from her husband regarding her own adultery, and also because Mr. Rainier had enlisted the services of Sir Edward Carson KC, the prominent Ulster Unionist and the *Standard*'s favorite barrister.

Carson had demolished Mrs. Rainier's claims with his usual efficiency, and Divine was reading a letter that Carson had produced in court from

Mrs. Rainier's Austrian lover. "As you well know I do everything in my power to please you," he read. "You have no idea how often I think and dream of you—how often I have you in my arms, kissing you fervently all over your lovely body, your lips, your beautiful eyes."

Divine shook his head in mock disapproval. "*All* over her body gentlemen! If I was her husband I'd want to strangle her if I heard some Jew talk to his wife like that. Good afternoon, Harry. I take it you have news?"

"Yes sir. The papers are served. And well-served."

"Excellent. And I have news for you. You had a visitor this morning. A gentleman. Chief Inspector Maitland—from Scotland Yard. Not in any trouble, are we?"

"Not that I know of sir. I knew Captain Maitland from the army. I worked under him in Limehouse."

"Well he left his phone number. You can call him when you've given your deposition."

Lawton sat down at the clerk's desk and described how he had witnessed the respondent Mrs. Evangeline Watson in the act of sexual congress with Lieutenant Edward Rycroft , in Room 510 of the Mountview Hotel in Brighton at precisely 9:15 A.M.

"How did you get into their room?" Divine asked. "Do tell."

"I climbed in through the window."

"Five floors up!" Laws exclaimed. "Harry, your talents are wasted on us! Perhaps you should have taken up cat burglary."

"I know a lot about it, that's for sure," Lawton said. "But I do have some morals left—just about."

"The same can't be said of Mrs. Watson," Divine said with a sigh. "The women of today! Too much time on their hands and too much freedom. They behave like this and now they want the vote!"

Lawton said nothing. After signing his statement he dialed the number and waited for the exchange to make the connection. A few moments later James Maitland's crisp upper-crust accent came crackling down the line.

"Good afternoon Harry," he said. "Glad to hear from you."

"Captain. I didn't know you were at the Yard."

"I am. And I have some work that might interest you. Very well-paid work—in Barcelona."

"Barcelona?" Lawton said. "In Spain?"

"That's the only one I know. Listen, do you know the Clarence? It's just up the road from the Yard."

"I do."

"Can you be there in an hour?"

"Yes sir. But—"

"See you there then."

Maitland hung up and Lawton put the phone down to find the others looking at him with obvious interest.

"Going on holiday, Harry?" Divine asked.

"On what you pay me?"

Divine laughed. "You can go, you know. We've got nothing for you right now." He handed him an envelope filled with bills and coins. "Barcelona. Isn't it full of anarchists?"

"Crawling with them," Divine agreed. "And even madder than ours. A bomb went off there just last week. In a café. The bastards."

"Do you remember one of them bombed an opera house there some years back?" Laws said. "In the middle of *William Tell* if I remember correctly. Just tossed two bombs into the audience! One of them fell onto a lady's lap and didn't explode. The other did. Absolute bloody carnage."

Divine grimaced and shook his head. "Wild beasts. They need to be put down."

Lawton left Divine and Laws discussing anarchists and infernal machines, and made his way through the stream of hansom cabs, trams, and motorized taxis, omnibuses, milk floats, carts, and drays. He passed a giant billboard painting advertising *The Arcadians,* showing the actor Dan Rolyat in a forest setting, surrounded by a cluster of appealing young women in long white dresses and flowers in their hair. Rolyat looked like a cat with the cream, and no wonder. The musical was the big show in town that year. Even the widow Friedman had hinted that she wanted to go, as if he had enough money to take her to the West End.

Lawton walked on through a haze of smoke, dust, and petroleum fumes. He was surprised how unsettled he felt at Maitland's unexpected call. Maitland had made no attempt to contact him since his illness, and there was no reason why he should. Even when they had worked together in Limehouse, Lawton continued to think of him as an army officer rather than a policeman. Maitland had moved in a more elevated world of gentlemen's clubs, Wimbledon, Lord's, and country houses when he was away from the station. A man like that did not come to the East End except for work or business.

He arrived at the Clarence to find Maitland sitting in the deserted saloon bar, nursing a pint of ale. He was dressed impeccably as always, in a well-cut suit and starched pointed collar, and looked much the same as he had last seen him, except for a few streaks of gray in his handlebar moustache. Even as he got to his feet Lawton saw him once again in his khaki uniform, standing over the five kneeling Boers with a Browning in his hand. He remembered his face shining like marble in the moonlight, and the hard victor's smile on his face as he looked down on the prisoners and said "So gentlemen. What do we do with you?" Even in the darkness, his voice had sounded thick and charged with menace, but there was no trace of that man now, as Maitland smiled graciously and shook his hand. "Harry! Good to see you again! Let me get you some neck-oil my friend."

"I don't drink," Lawton replied. "Not anymore. I'll have a ginger ale."

"Pedro Lawton doesn't drink?" Maitland shook his head in disbelief. "Wonders never cease."

Maitland went over to the counter and returned with a Belfast ginger ale. Lawton had not been inside a pub in more than two years, and the smell of hops and whiskey aroused an old thirst that was best left unrequited.

"Congratulations on the promotion," he said. "When did it happen?"

Maitland smiled modestly. "Last year. It came as a surprise, to be honest. I've been lucky. But the West End is not like Limehouse. Even the thieves dress well."

"I don't doubt it." Lawton sipped at his glass.

"So how've you been?" Maitland gave him a sympathetic look. "Keeping alright?"

"Well enough."

"You know I was at the dentist last week, and I saw your advertisement in the *Mirror*. Not a newspaper I normally read, but I saw your name! 'Private enquiries. All business undertaken. Discretion assured.' Good old Harry, I thought. I presume there's plenty of work around?"

Maitland looked genuinely interested, but Lawton knew what real detectives thought of private investigators, and he doubted whether he would have been impressed to know how he had spent the morning. "It pays the rent. You mentioned some work, sir?"

"I did indeed. Does the name Randolph Foulkes mean anything to you? Dr. Randolph Foulkes?"

"Isn't he some kind of explorer?"

"He is. Among other things. Well it seems he was blown up by a terrorist bomb in Barcelona last week."

"Seems?"

"It's not been confirmed. The British consul says a foreigner was killed, and Dr. Foulkes is missing from his hotel room. The body's a mess, as you can imagine. Poor bugger was sitting right next to the bomb. And now his wife has come to us and said that Foulkes paid out £500 through a Barcelona account before he died—to a woman. She wants us to send someone to find out who it is. We don't have resources to send someone to Spain on suspicion of adultery. But I thought it might interest you. Given that you speak the lingo."

"I haven't spoken Spanish for a while now. And I've never been to Spain. Wouldn't it be easier to get someone over there?"

Maitland shook his head. "She doesn't want a foreigner. Very adamant about that. And she's not poor. You don't have to see me as a gift horse. I'm not doing you a favor here, Harry. I owe *you*."

Maitland gave him a meaningful look, and Lawton shifted uncomfortably. "I'm happy to meet her and discuss it," he said.

"Good. I've arranged a meeting with her tomorrow morning. She lives near Hastings. St Pancras at 9:20 all right with you? We can go together."

Lawton felt a flash of irritation at Maitland's presumption. Even after two years, he still seemed to behave as if the world was at his beck and call, and Lawton was still his subordinate. And yet Maitland also seemed pleased to see him, whereas the captain's presence only reminded him of many things that he wanted to forget.

"That's fine," he said. "I'll be there." There did not seem much to talk about now, and he drank the last of his ginger ale and got up to leave.

"Till tomorrow then." Maitland reached out his hand. "This is a good decision Harry."

Lawton was tempted to point out that he had not decided anything, but even as he left the pub, he knew that there was really only one decision a man in his position could make.

2

The train had just pulled out of Mataró when Esperanza Claramunt saw the balloon coming toward them from the direction of Barcelona. From a distance it looked like a large yellow ball floating above the sea, but as it came closer she could see the basket beneath it and the tiny heads protruding above the rim. Some of the other passengers had also noticed the balloon. Most of them were peasants, bringing herbs, saffron, oranges to sell, and some of them had even brought live hens and chickens that clucked in the luggage racks above them. Many of them had clearly never seen nor even heard that human beings were now able to fly, and one old woman crossed herself as a man and a woman waved at them from the flying basket.

Some of the passengers waved back, and Esperanza heard cheering from the men and women on the roof of the train. She would have liked to wave herself, but she did not want to appear frivolous in the presence of the Ferrers. It still seemed incredible to her that she was sitting directly opposite Francesc Ferrer I Guardia and his wife Soledad. It was little more than a year since Ferrer had been acquitted of complicity in the attempted assassination of the king during the royal wedding procession in Madrid. Esperanza wondered what the newspapers would say if they could see the nation's most famous anarchist sitting in a third-class carriage, while his radiant wife sat fanning herself next to him. Apart from the folded copy of *Solidaridad Obrera* on his lap, Ferrer looked more like a shopkeeper or a farmer than a terrorist with his downturned moustache, linen suit, and straw boater.

"Look Francesc!" Soledad nudged him and pointed her fan at the balloon.

Ferrer looked up and grunted, and returned to his paper.

"Incredible!" Soledad exclaimed. "Wasn't it last year that those Americans actually flew in a flying machine—with wings?"

"The Wright Brothers," said Esperanza.

"That's it!" Soledad exclaimed. "And they say it won't be long before people can fly to every city in the world."

"It won't be long before those machines will be capable of dropping bombs on every city in the world," Ferrer said.

"Ay, Francesc!" Soledad fluttered her fan. "Not everything has to be serious all the time."

"It's an entirely logical development," Ferrer persisted. "The marriage of technology and militarism. Every new invention sooner or later finds a military purpose. Think what Napoleon would have done if he'd had a flying machine at Zaragoza. It wouldn't matter how thick the walls were. And I'm going to make a prediction—one day these flying machines will be dropping bombs on Barcelona, unless we win."

Soledad rolled her eyes and looked at Esperanza, who responded with a faint smile. Once again she was impressed by Ferrer's knowledge, insight, and erudition. There was really nothing he could not talk about, and if he showed no interest in balloons then she would not show any either, at least in public. But even as the balloon flew by, she could not help feeling excited by it. She imagined herself and Pau floating above the world with the blue sky all around them, in perfect silence, with the fields and ocean stretched out below. She felt thrilled to be young in such a century, when even gravity was no longer an obstacle to human progress, when the future seemed filled with possibilities that previous generations had only imagined. The end of poverty, disease, and super-stition; bridges and roads connecting the most far-flung places; flying machines and motorcars; rational education for all; immaculate cities built of towers and glass with parks and sanitation where the workers divided their hours between study and labor—all these things were likely to occur in her lifetime. She and her comrades had spent much of the day discussing the glorious possibilities that awaited Spain and the world, when capitalism was overthrown and the workers took control, and the social revolution brought an end to a society ruled only in the interests of the few. In the mountains that future seemed closer, and the city of slums and policemen seemed to lose its hold on them as they walked through an ancient and more peaceful world inhabited only by shepherds, charcoal burners, and woodcutters.

Even the older members of her affinity group, who had known prison and torture, seemed to walk more lightly as they talked of Tolstoy, Nietzsche, and Malatesta, of rational education, strikes, and the revolu-tion that would soon change everything. Some comrades, like Arnau Busquets, were so poor that they had nowhere to wash in their own homes, and after lunch the men stripped down to their underwear and bathed in a stream. Esperanza had heard of anarchist groups in other countries where men and women took all their clothes off during expe-ditions to the countryside, and she was relieved when Flor and Soledad contented themselves with dangling their bare ankles in the cool water. Now she felt the warm pressure of Pau's thigh beside her and she pictured his dripping hair and shoulders and his slim tapered waist, when she saw Ferrer looking at her thoughtfully.

"I've been meaning to tell you, Miss Claramunt. I intend to reopen the Modern School, hopefully next year."

"I'm very glad to hear it." Esperanza replied. "The city needs it."

"If I succeed I shall need new staff. And I would like to send some of them to Paris for training—funding permitting. Is that something that might interest you?"

Esperanza was so pleased and so taken aback by this unexpected offer that she could not think what to say. "It would be an honor," she replied finally.

"Very good." The train was coming into Badalona now and Ferrer got to his feet and lifted his knapsack from the shelf. "Why don't you and Pau come and visit us in Montgat? We can discuss it then."

Pau said they would try to come next week. Once again Esperanza wished Ferrer's ailing niece a quick recovery, and Ferrer thanked her as he and his wife got down from the train. No sooner had they departed than Ruben Montero and his wife Flor took their vacant seats. Ruben took a swing from a hip flask, and stared at Esperanza with the faintly mocking smile that always irritated her.

"You do know that Ferrer invests in the Stock Exchange?" he said.

"Yes." Esperanza suppressed her irritation. "And he uses the money to pay for the people's education. He plays the capitalists at their own game."

"They say he's a mason," Ruben said.

"A progressive mason!"

"If you say so." Ruben's hooded eyes gleamed, and once again Esperanza sensed that he was playing some kind of game with her. She turned away and stared out the window as Barcelona appeared up ahead and the familiar stations flashed past. The train stopped at the little station halfway down the Passeig de Gràcia, and she expected Pau to continue down to the Plaza Catalunya with the others. To her surprise and pleasure he said he would walk her home. Once again Ruben looked at her with a smirk, and she was relieved to see the back of him as the others continued onward to the Plaza Catalunya. It was not yet dark, but the new electric lights were already beginning to glow as they walked past the scaffolding that surrounded the new building at the corner of the Calle Provenza, which her father's old friend Antoni Gaudí had designed.

Even draped in scaffolding, it looked more like a mountain than a building and there was something faintly ominous about it. Further up on their left she saw the Batlló House, another Gaudí building, which had been completed only a few years ago, and which she definitely preferred. In the dusk it looked even more like a fairy palace with its coral-like mosaics, its curved dragon roof, and seashell balconies.

"I don't like Ruben," she said suddenly. "I don't know why he drinks like that."

"You might drink if you'd spent three years in a penal colony," Pau replied. "Ruben's better than you think. When the time comes, he'll come out alright. Anyway he's married to my sister so I have to put up with him."

Esperanza said nothing, as they crossed the Diagonal and turned into the village. Even though Gràcia was now connected to Barcelona by the Passeig de Gràcia, she still thought of it as a village, despite the new workshops and the electric street lights that had been introduced in some of its principal streets. Most of Gràcia was still lit by the old gas lights, and some streets still had no lights at all.

"Did you enjoy today?" Pau asked.

"I did." She smiled to let him know that he was one of the reasons why she had enjoyed it.

"And now you're going to go to Paris?"

Esperanza laughed. "Would you miss me if I did?"

Pau did not reply. They had nearly reached her street now, when he stopped to light a cigarette. Esperanza noticed a small carriage coming up the street behind them, and she wondered what her mother would say if she could see her standing in a darkened street with a young man.

"I've been meaning to ask you something." Pau shuffled and looked down at his feet. Esperanza looked at him expectantly, and wondered why he suddenly seemed so awkward and uncomfortable. "I—oh never mind, it can wait. Are you coming to the Athenaeum on Wednesday? A professor from the university is coming to give a talk—'Religion or Science: Which will define our age?'"

"That does sound interesting."

"Good. I'll see you there then."

Esperanza was still wondering what he had been about to say to her, when he leaned forward and pecked her lightly on the cheeks. She would have liked him to kiss her on the lips, but that was not the way even anarchist girls behaved, at least not in her neighborhood. She waved at him playfully and walked away. She was just about to turn the corner when she heard a scuffle behind her, and she looked back down the darkened street. The carriage was stationary now, and two men whose faces she could not see appeared to be dragging Pau toward it. Pau's head was lolling forward and he was not putting up any resistance as they dragged him into the carriage.

Esperanza watched all this with stunned amazement, as if she could not believe it was really happening. "What are you doing?" she called, in a thin, frightened voice that did not sound like her own. "Stop!"

There was no answer. The driver flicked the reins now and the two black horses came trotting toward her. As she backed against the wall she caught a glimpse of angry, hate-filled eyes beneath the floppy hat and the scarf that covered most of the driver's face, and it was only then that she ran toward it and screamed for help.

Through the open doorway Lawton looked down at the body of Elizabeth Hutten, lying face upward in a pool of blood. Everything was how he remembered it: the red sheets and the bloodstained poker, the blood splashes on the wall just behind the bed. But now the blood was flowing out of the doorway and lapping all around his feet. Even when he backed away it followed him down the stairs and out into the street. It flowed all around the feet of pedestrians and the wheels of carriages and motor cars, though offices and department stores, theaters, and foreign embassies, and down the Strand and the Mall and onward toward Buckingham Palace, Whitehall, Downing Street, and the Ministry of War. Yet no one else but him appeared to see it or react to it. Even when he slipped and fell floundering and sliding in the current, the people in the street continued to walk past, ignoring his cries for help.

He woke up with a start to find the widow Friedman shaking him, and her two youngest children standing at the foot of the bed, their pale faces staring anxiously out of the gloom.

"Harry, vake up. You having a nightmare."

Lawton sat upright as the widow shooed her children away.

"You alright?" she asked.

"I'm fine." He lifted back the sheets. "Go back to sleep."

"It's early. You don't vant breakfast?"

Lawton shook his head. He had not even intended to stay the night, and breakfast would only arouse expectations that he could not fulfil, both in his landlady and her children. The widow sighed and laid her head back down on the pillow as he got dressed and walked downstairs through the café and out into the street. Already a thick curtain of smog covered the city and men, women, and even children were slipping out of their mean terraced houses, their clogs and boots clattering on the greasy cobblestones. Lawton passed a cluster of Jews huddled together in conversation outside the makeshift synagogue, speaking in Yiddish, Russian, and Polish. Some of them were wearing prayer shawls, others wore dark jackets and black Homburg hats, and a few had long locks hanging down their pale cheeks. The Aliens Act was four years old now, and all that was left of the British Brothers League was the occasional tattered poster, yet still more Jews continued to make their way to the East End from the edges of Europe, like the relics of some ancient wandering tribe.

John Divine had asked him more than once how he could stand to live in Jewtown, and Lawton usually replied that his room only cost two shillings a week. It was easier than trying to explain that he preferred to live in a place where he was a stranger, surrounded by foreigners who knew no more about his life than he knew of theirs. The boarding house was just around the corner from the café, and he shut the door of his room behind him and looked around at the narrow iron bed, the worn armchair, the little chair and table by the sink, his father's barbells, and the wardrobe with the broken mirror.

Next to the window stood the table bearing his Victor phonograph machine—his only prized possession—and a handful of twelve-inch records. Some old penny dreadfuls and copies of *Illustrated Police News* and *Reynolds's Weekly* were piled on the floor with a handful of books: Gross's *Criminal Investigation*, *The Hound of the Baskervilles*, *The Riddle of the Sands*, and a few detective memoirs that he still kept. He took off his shoes and jacket and lay on the bed smoking and listening to the warbling pigeons from the roof while he summoned up the energy to perform his morning routine. Once, when he was still on the force, he had gone almost every morning to the gym to lift some weights or do some light sparring, now he preferred to exercise at home. He felt so tired that he was tempted to forego it, but as always the stern voice in his head warned him that any slackening of the will could only lead to further disintegration. Finally he got off the bed and performed his usual set of press-ups, sit-ups, and side bends, finishing off with the barbells for the biceps and some shadowboxing.

Afterward he washed and put on the smarter of his two suits, and went downstairs to the kitchen, where he ate a breakfast of bread, Bovril, and tea. He walked the short distance to the underground, and bought a copy of the *Mirror*. Even as he waited for the train he checked his body and the world around him for any warning signs that might oblige him to retreat from the day. But there was no numbness or tension, no unwanted sights or smells, and the faces around him seemed clear and distinct as he sat on the train and read the paper from cover to cover, from the advertisement offering treatment for alcoholic excess to the society and sports pages. By the time he reached St Pancras he had learned that Bertie was motoring at the Newmarket races; that Lloyd George's budget faced another challenge in the Lords; that Hobbs was on his way to another hundred, and that the suffragette prisoners would now be force-fed.

The paper also reported that the army had perfected its military measures against the Somaliland Mullah. Lawton had learned to take such claims with a pinch of salt. From a distance it was always a pleasure to imagine generals effortlessly moving the empire's armies back and forth like pieces on a board, but he had seen war with his own eyes and so had Maitland. He glanced up at the list of stations and pictured a line of soldiers sweating and cursing their through Somaliland toward some unknown destination in their scratchy uniforms and helmets, weighed down by their knapsacks and rifles. And then he saw himself and his companions standing over the five Boer commandos, who knelt beside their blankets with their hands on their heads. He saw Maitland's face like a smooth marble statue in the moonlight and heard the horses whinnying just behind him, and the rustle of the wind stroking the trees above their heads.

Even in the darkness he saw the anger and disbelief on the faces of the Boers that they had allowed themselves to be taken by surprise in the bush by the English officer with the plummy accent. They were not the only ones to underestimate Maitland. When the young captain took command of their unit that winter, few people had expected much from him. Maitland came to them fresh off the boat, smelling of cologne and exuding an air of the cricket pitch, country estates, and drawing rooms, but he had proven himself to be a tough, brave, and decisive officer who never asked his men to do anything he would not do himself. He was also ruthless. Where some officers had balked at putting Boer women into camps or burning their farms, Maitland had not shown a moment's hesitation. Lawton had not fully realized how ruthless until that night on the veld, when Maitland stared down at the five commandos and said, "Corporal, draw up the firing squad."

Lawton remembered that Maitland had given the order in the same voice that he might have used to give instructions to a servant or the gardener, so that he was not sure if he had heard him correctly.

"Sir?"

"You heard. These men are guerrillas. We aren't taking prisoners."

By that time Lawton had already done a lot of things in the war that he had never imagined doing, and he did not question his orders further. No one knew how many of their men the Boers had killed, and even the notion of taking prisoners seemed like a quaint relic of a different kind of war that had neither meaning nor relevance in a situation like this. Out there in the veld, on that calm moonlit evening, Maitland's order seemed entirely logical, and even the Boers seemed to expect it. They left the five bodies lying in the copse and took their rifles, horses, and ammunition, and it was only afterward when they rode away that Maitland told them that they would be better not to speak about it. And now as the train pulled away from Liverpool Street, it seemed to Lawton that he could still smell the sweet scent of acacia as the oldest of the Boers lay twitching on the ground till Maitland finished him off with the Browning.

In the end they had been forced to speak about it to the military tribunal. At the inquiry, they all told the story they had agreed upon and rehearsed with Maitland, and Lawton had been the first to testify. Once again the scene unfolded before him; the barracks hut where the regimental commander Colonel Phillips sat behind the desk with his two officers, one of whom was taking notes; the wooden chair where Phillips invited him to sit down; the fresh young faces of the newcomers marching up and down the dusty square outside in their khaki uniforms.

"Corporal Lawton, this is not a court-martial. But I would appreciate your frankness. I want you to describe what happened on the night of September 24."

"Our column was carrying out anti-guerrilla operations in the Lichtenburg sector, sir. We were looking for a Boer commando camp, acting on intelligence information."

"And did you find it?"

"We did, sir. We left our horses and advanced on foot. But our presence was discovered. There was a firefight sir. All five commandos were killed."

"But there was a sixth who you didn't find, wasn't there?" Phillips looked at him intently. "And he says that Captain Maitland ordered you and your men to execute the prisoners in cold blood. And if that is true, then it is a very serious matter."

"It isn't true sir. They were armed guerrillas and they were shooting at us."

"Well why do you think this Boer is saying something completely different?"

"To discredit His Majesty's army sir. And make up for the fact that his unit was caught with its pants down."

Phillips smiled faintly. Even then Lawton sensed that he wanted to believe what he was being told, and that he knew, as all of them did, that bad things happened in war that could not be helped, even if the politicians and the public preferred not to hear of them. In the end there had been no court-martial, and the incident was forgotten because it suited everyone to forget it. He had lied, and lied well, and it was because of his lies that Maitland had not ended up in prison or in front of a firing squad, and left the army as a hero and gone on to become a chief inspector at Limehouse station.

It was Maitland who invited him to join the force and Maitland who encouraged him to become a detective. Lawton did not know whether he had acted out of guilt or gratitude, and until yesterday he had not expected to see him again. Now he found him waiting by the ticket office, wearing the same suit he had worn the previous day, and a newly starched collar. No doubt he had a fragrant wife to do such things for him, Lawton thought, and he wondered whether she had any idea what her husband had once been capable of when he wore a uniform.

"I meant to tell you yesterday," Maitland said, as they sat down on the train. "There's an English detective in Barcelona already. Charles Arrow."

"Arrow of the Yard? I thought he'd retired."

"He has. But he's been helping the city with its terrorism problem."

"And he didn't want to take this on?"

"He's not interested. But he might be able to help you if you need it. And one other thing, I've told Mrs. Foulkes that you left the force to become a private investigator—for the salary. If she asks just go along with it. We don't need to give her any more . . . unnecessary information."

"Yes sir." Lawton felt himself reddening.

"No need for sir, Harry. We're not in the army now. I was very sorry to hear what happened to you. All the things we went through in the war. And then this? Damned bad luck."

Lawton did not like sympathy, whether it came from the widow Friedman or from Maitland, and he nodded vaguely and looked out the window as the train chugged out through the suburbs. Maitland briefly attempted to make conversation about their Limehouse days, but Lawton's obvious lack of enthusiasm was such that he soon gave up and retreated behind his newspaper. From time to time he made some comment on what he was reading, as though he were talking to a complete stranger. None of this dispelled the awkwardness between them. Even as Lawton looked out at neat little towns and villages, the soft undulating hills and woodlands, he found himself thinking of the war. He saw his unit riding across the veld in the rain and sun, chasing guerrillas, and blowing up watering holes with dynamite. He saw himself bayoneting sheep and cattle at Boer farms, smashing furniture and setting fire to Boer houses. It seemed incredible to him that he could ever have done such things, but Maitland's presence was a reminder that he had. He was not sure whether war changed men, or whether it merely brought to the surface things that were normally kept hidden in peacetime, but a part of him now wished that Maitland had not come back to remind him of his own transformation.

On arriving at Hastings, they took a motor-taxi to the village of Graveling, and drove out through a landscape of hedgerows, fields and oast-houses.

Twenty minutes later the taxi drove into a tree-lined drive and pulled up in front of a large redbrick house, with a coat of arms of crossed swords and a shield above the doorways. A servant girl in a black dress, white apron, and bonnet ushered them into a large drawing room covered in a wallpaper design of birds and flowers. Lawton stared at the oriental carpets, the paintings and pictures, the long mirrors on either side of the fireplace, the two sofas that faced each other in front of the French windows, and the freshly mowed lawn that stretched out toward the fields beyond.

He also noticed an unmistakably medicinal smell that seemed out of place in such opulent surroundings, and he soon found the explanation for it in the array of medicines, pills, and powders piled on the table next to one of the sofas. Some of them were familiar to him, from Clarke's Blood Mixture, Spasmosedine sedative, Bromocarpine nerve tonic, and Eno's Fruit Salt for the liver, to the strychnine and potassium bromide that he knew only too well. He was still looking through them when Maitland gave a little cough, and a woman in her early sixties appeared in the doorway, holding a stick in one hand and her maid's arm in the other.

Mrs. Randolph Foulkes was wearing a red satin dressing gown emblazed with damask flowers that reached all the way down to her Moroccan slippers. The richness and playfulness of these colors only accentuated her sharp, bony features and unforgiving demeanor, as she sat down opposite the window and invited them to do the same. The maid drew the curtain and Mrs. Foulkes stared disapprovingly at Lawton as Maitland introduced them.

"Well," she said, "I wasn't expecting a half-caste. And what happened to your nose?"

"I used to box in my youth ma'am," Lawton replied. "It was broken on one occasion."

"Really Maitland, I asked for a detective not a brawler!"

"I worked alongside Detective-Sergeant Lawton in K-Division," Maitland replied. "That's Limehouse, ma'am—one of the roughest districts in London. I can assure you there was no better thief-catcher in the district."

Mrs. Foulkes looked only partially mollified. "Yet you left the force for private enquiry?"

"I did, ma'am. For financial reasons."

"And you speak Spanish."

"My mother was Chilean. My mother was part Mapuche."

"What an exotic combination! I'm sure Randolph would have found you fascinating. Amelia, it's time to feed the rabbits."

The maid nodded and left the room. Lawton's face was expressionless, but the widow was not endearing herself to him. "I'm sorry for your loss," he said.

Mrs. Foulkes waved her hand as though a fly had just entered the room. "We all *die*, Mr. Lawton. But this affair requires further investigation. I assume the chief inspector has explained why?"

"I understand that your husband left money to an unknown beneficiary."

"He did—to a woman." Mrs. Foulkes grimaced. "I didn't even know Randolph was in Barcelona."

"He didn't know anybody there?"

"Only Señor Ferrer. He was in London in April. He came to see me with his wife. But Randolph wouldn't have visited him."

"Why not?"

"Ferrer is an anarchist," Mrs. Foulkes explained. "But he's also an educationalist. I write children's books for the Moral Education League and Señor Ferrer wanted to publish one of them. He and Randolph spent an hour yapping in his study. When they'd gone Randolph told me he never wanted to see him in his house again. He certainly wouldn't have gone to see him in Barcelona. As far as I knew he was in Vernet writing a book."

"Vernet?" Lawton said.

"Vernet-les-Bains. In the French Pyrenees. Randolph rents a house there. He goes there every year to write and walk in the mountains. Sometimes he spends the whole summer there when he's writing a book. I've never seen the house, but I used to go to Vernet to take the waters. We stayed in a hotel then. Now I don't go anywhere. I suffer from neurasthenia, you see."

"I'm sorry to hear that," Lawton replied.

"The disease of the century!" she exclaimed wearily. "My doctor says it's because the world is moving too fast. Newspapers, steamships, and trains, and now the automobile. The brain can't cope, he says. Well I don't know why this should affect *me*. I only take the *Times* and I've never even been in an automobile. Yet some days I can't even get out of bed. You'd never believe I used to be on the stage."

"Oh I can very well believe it," said Maitland.

Mrs. Foulkes acknowledged the flattery with the faintest of smiles. "Before your time perhaps. I was at the Lyceum when Mr. Stoker was manager."

"*The* Bram Stoker?" said Lawton.

She looked at him in surprise. "Well, well. You didn't strike me as a literary man."

"I don't read much," Lawton said. "But I have read *Dracula*. A strange tale."

"I knew Mr. Stoker before he wrote it. He used to say my Ophelia was one of the greatest performances he had ever seen. I made grown men and women cry, Mr. Lawton! Now I merely waste away."

She gave them a pained look. It was no wonder she had been on the stage, Lawton thought. "So your husband was writing a book in Vernet?" he asked.

"So he said." Mrs. Foulkes opened a drawer in the medicine cabinet and handed him a postcard of a large pink building with tall white arches and cream façades with the word CASINO emblazoned above the doorway. Lawton read the message dated June 11: *Thought this would bring back memories. Weather marvelous as always. Writing going well. Plenty of walks and good conversation. Keep well, Randolph.*

"My solicitor told me about the payment last week," Mrs. Foulkes said. "The money was requested from Barcelona two days after that postcard was sent, at the Bank of Sabadell. The payee's name was Marie Babineaux."

"Do you know this woman?"

"Never heard of her. That's why I want you to go to Barcelona and find out who she is. After you've confirmed whether Randolph is actually dead."

"I should point out ma'am, that it isn't always easy to identify a body after a bomb blast," Lawton said.

"That won't be a problem. Randolph was one of the pioneers of finger-printing. He has many copies of his own at his laboratory. My secretary will supply you with them. Randolph was also missing two toes on his left foot—from frostbite. There are also photographs—Bertillonage photographs. Another of my husband's interests. Will that be sufficient?"

"I'm sure it will," Lawton replied.

"Good. I want you to leave as soon as possible. Your pay will be £5 a day plus traveling expenses—the first month payable in advance. There will be a bonus of £30 if you find this . . . trollop. I assume that's accept-able to you?"

Lawton suppressed his astonishment. These rates were more than his detective's salary, and nearly twice as much as he received from Divine & Laws. "Very much so," he replied.

"Good. Is there anything else you need?"

"Does your husband have a workplace or study here in the house?"

"He does." She looked at him suspiciously. "Why do you ask?"

"I'd like to look around it," Lawton said. "If there's a possibility of deception it's always good to know something about the person who may have been deceived."

Mrs. Foulkes did not look pleased. "I assure you there's no other pos-sibility, Mr. Lawton. My husband would not have had an extramarital affair. He wasn't the type."

Lawton had heard too many similar claims to take her insistence for granted, but he said nothing as Maitland gave her a reassuring smile.

"As I told you, Mr. Lawton is very thorough. But I must get back to the Yard. I've asked the taxi to wait."

Mrs. Foulkes was about to call for the maid to show Maitland out, but Lawton offered to do it himself and accompanied him to the door.

"Thank you, sir," he said, almost in a whisper. "Appreciate it."

Maitland looked pleased. "Not at all. Glad to be able to help. And this is easy money Harry. If you need anything from me when you're over there, let me know. Good luck."

Once again they shook hands, and as Lawton watched him walk back to the taxi, it occurred to him that for the first time in two very dismal years his luck might have finally changed.

3

On Thursday afternoon Bernat Mata finally took his children to the Barcelona zoo to see the great ape. For weeks his son Carles had been pleading with him to take them to see the monster, now the boy stood holding his father's hand and stared nervously at the white gorilla that glared back at them from the opposite side of the narrow moat.

"Are you sure it can't escape?" he asked.

"Of course it can't escape," Alba rolled her eyes. "It's in a cage."

"I didn't ask *you*," Carles retorted. "And what if it breaks the bars?"

"Then it will eat you!"

Mata smiled patiently. "Alba, please remember that you are eight and your brother is five. I promise you son, that this monster cannot escape."

"He knows we're talking about him," Carles said.

Mata stared back at the ferocious yellow eyes and jutting teeth, and thought that his son was probably right. Since its arrival from the Belgian Congo that spring, a lot of people had been talking about Snowy the gorilla. This was partly due to its size and its color, and also to the sign on the animal's cage that claimed, "there is less difference in size and structure between the well-developed brain of a gorilla and that of the lowest living savages than there is between the brain of such a savage and the brain of a high European type."

This seemingly uncontroversial observation had offended the Catholic papers, which accused the zoo authorities of exposing young children to Darwinism. Snowy had even become the subject of one of Archbishop Laguarda's sermons at the cathedral, in which His Eminence reminded his congregation that man had been brought into the Garden of Eden fully formed, that Eve had been born of Adam's rib, and that any arguments to the contrary were fallacious and blasphemous. Mata wondered whether this was the first time in history in which a gorilla had been mentioned in a sermon. The ape reminded him of the soldiers who had attacked the offices of ¡Cu-Cut! magazine four years ago, because of Joan Junceda's cartoon mocking the armed forces. Those soldiers had shown the same brutish ferocity that day, and it was easy to imagine the gorilla raging through the offices, knocking over desks and smashing typewriters in the street.

The soldiers had accused Junceda and the magazine of insulting the honor of the armed forces, but as far as Mata was concerned, men who behaved like hooligans in response to words and pictures they did not like had no honor to defend. That was bad enough, but instead of punishing them, the government had given in to their thuggery and passed the Law of Jurisdictions, which now obliged every newspaper and magazine in Catalonia to submit to the military censors. And all this had been done with the approval of the bishops and archbishops who lectured the city on the evils of evolution.

"We should go home now," he said.

"But we've only just arrived!" Carles complained.

"Yes. To see Snowy. And now we've seen him. We'll come on a longer visit another time. Right now you need to eat and I have to work."

Mata took his son's hand while Alba skipped along beside him, past the mad puma pacing up and down the same few steps that it would follow till the ends of its days, past the anteater and the armadillos and the Pyrenean brown bear. Outside in the park couples and families were seated on the grass, rowing on the lake, or strolling back and forth between the rows of trees while parrots shrieked and squawked in the trees above their heads. They had just left the zoo when he heard what sounded like an explosion coming from the direction of the Ramblas. It was not as loud as the Bar la Luna bombing two weeks ago, and no one in the park seemed particularly concerned by it.

Mata was not sure whether such sangfroid was a sign of civic strength or weakness. Since Joan Rull's execution last August, the bombings in the city had quieted down. His execution had brought to an end a three-year period in which bombs had gone off all over the Raval. At times there had been an explosion around the Ramblas almost every week and sometimes every day, as large and small bombs went off in alleyways, marketplaces, urinals, and doorways. Even then the population got on with its daily business as if all this mayhem were of no more consequence than a streetcar accident.

According to the prosecutors at his trial, Rull was responsible for most of these bombs, and the lull that followed his conviction seemed to prove them right. Yet Rull had protested his innocence right up until they tightened the garotte around his neck in the Modelo prison. Mata had no idea whether he was telling the truth. Many times during the trial he had glanced over at his mane of combed-back hair and his dark hooded eyes and tried to gauge his reaction to the witnesses and statements, but his expression never changed.

Mata had spoken to the English detective Arrow about the bombings, and Arrow had dropped hints that he did not believe Rull was uniquely responsible for them. Many people had the same doubts, but no one could ever prove them. The state claimed that justice had been done and the minister of the interior boasted that peace had been restored to Barcelona. But now the Luna Bar suggested that such claims were premature. He had witnessed the bloody aftermath of the explosion there and he still felt revolted by what he had seen. Of course no one had claimed responsibility for it, and that was not unusual. It had been the same during the Rull years, and Mata wondered whether the bombing signaled the beginning of a new campaign, as they came into the dirt square that surrounded the Monumental Fountain. He looked at the man in a battered top hat standing by the fountain, playing with a dancing monkey while a child solemnly cranked out a waltz on a barrel organ. That was how the city worked: the monkeys placed bombs while someone else cranked the organ, and only the monkeys ever got caught.

Mata gazed at the waterfall, past the statues of a chariot and horses, Neptune and the Griffin toward the half-naked Leda. Whoever had known that model was a lucky man, he thought, as he noticed a young woman coming toward him from the entrance to the Arc de Triomf. Even from a distance she looked vaguely familiar. As he came closer he looked at the long neck and heart-shaped face, the wide brown eyes and chestnut hair tied up beneath her hat.

"Good afternoon Senyor Mata," she said in Catalan. "Your wife said you would be here. I'm Esperanza Claramunt. Rafael Claramunt's daughter. I believe you knew my father."

Now Mata remembered the little girl he had seen holding her mother's hand at Rafael Claramunt's funeral in 1896. She would have been not much older than Alba, he thought, as he looked at her with an expression of concern and surprise.

"I did," he said. "And your mother, too."

"She suggested I talk to you." Esperanza's eyes flickered toward the children. "On an urgent matter."

"Of course." Mata sent his children to look at the monkey and he and Esperanza walked over to a nearby bench under the shade of a tree. He slumped down like a heavy bear with his hands resting on his cane and looked at the young woman expectantly.

"A comrade—a friend of mine has been kidnapped," she said. "By the police."

Mata raised his eyebrows. He had known Rafael Claramunt mostly through his writings and speeches, and as one of the many tragedies of 1896. He remembered him as a decent man, a moderate republican who had fallen victim to the inquisitorial frenzy that followed the Corpus Christi bombing. It soon became obvious that Esperanza Claramunt had gone on a very different political journey, as she described the kidnapping of the anarchist Pau Tosets.

"I'm sorry to hear this," he said. "But if your friend was arrested, there isn't much a journalist can do about it."

Esperanza's cheeks turned suddenly pink. "The comrades said this would be a waste of time. But my mother said that you wrote about my father. She said you were one of the few bourgeois journalists to question the charges against Ferrer."

Mata sensed that this was intended to be a compliment, but it did not sound like one. "I was," he said. "Because the charges were without foundation."

"Pau's done nothing wrong!" Esperanza insisted. "He's just a printer and a journalist—like you."

"An anarchist journalist. Who works for *Solidaridad Obrera*."

"Is that a crime now? And it's not the police I'm worried about. It's the *Brigada*. You know what they're capable of."

Mata knew very well. The Social Brigade had led the investigations into the Corpus Christi bombing, and its officers were responsible for many of the outrages that followed. Nowadays the Brigada was supposed to be under strict orders to moderate its behavior, but when it came to anarchists and political crimes the collar was easily slipped, and the savage bombing at the Bar la Luna would not have inclined them to remain on the leash.

"How do you know the Brigada is involved? You say you didn't even see who kidnapped your friend."

"I don't know. But if they have arrested Pau and someone asks about him—someone with influence—it might save him."

Mata could not help feeling pleased that she thought of him as a person of influence, and her earnest puppy-dog eyes seemed suddenly difficult to refuse. "I'll go to the castle and ask," he said. "They don't have to tell me anything. But if he is there, I might at least shake the tree and get them to admit it publicly."

"Thank you." Esperanza looked so relieved and grateful that Mata could not help feeling sorry for her.

"I won't be able to go until tomorrow," he said. "Come by my house in the evening."

Mata called his children back, and the four of them walked out of the park along the wide promenade toward the Arc de Triomf. Esperanza chattered to Carles and Alba with the ease of someone who was used to being in the company of children, and Mata was not surprised to hear that she was a teacher at one of the Ferrer schools. On reaching the arch she turned away toward the Plaza Catalunya, and Mata and his children walked on home. Sylvia had lunch ready and the children chattered about the gorilla and the nice lady they had met in the park. Mata did not tell his wife what he had agreed to do. After lunch he took the siesta as usual and then set off to his offices in the Calle Escudellers.

He was tempted to take the tram, but he needed to lose weight and Sylvia was worried about his heart. A walk would also give him time to mull over the column he had already agreed with Rovira on Marinetti and the Futurist movement, whose manifesto he had just translated into Catalan. Half an hour later he arrived out of breath at the offices of *La Veu de Catalunya* to find his colleagues sitting at their desks like galley slaves, while Rovira strode menacingly up and down the aisle between them in his waistcoat and short sleeves. Rovira looked at him in disapproval. Mata knew that Rovira wanted his journalists to look more like businessmen in order to impress the newspaper's funders, and disapproved of his floppy hats, his long frock coat, and his cane pipe, but he also knew that there was nothing Rovira could do about it.

"There you are Mata," he said. "We've just had a messenger from Bravo Portillo. You can save that Futurist stuff for another day."

"Is it about the bomb?" Mata asked. "I heard it earlier."

Rovira clucked his tongue. "That was nothing. Just a coffee-grinder bomb in the Calle Ferran. Blew out a shop window. But now there's been a murder. At the swimming club. Ten more minutes and I would have given it to someone else, but of course the inspector asked for you."

Despite the sarcasm, Mata knew Rovira was pleased with his mutually beneficial arrangement with the chief of the Atarazanas district station, and *La Veu* had often benefitted from Inspector Manuel Bravo Portillo's interest in getting his name in the papers. Such publicity enabled him to uphold the reputation of the Barcelona police force and also to advance his own career prospects, and as long as he saw Mata as his best vehicle for achieving these ends, then Rovira would not send anyone else to report on important stories like this.

Mata had never heard of a murder at the swimming club before, and he wondered what could have happened as he walked onto the Ramblas and caught a cab. Ten minutes later he was sitting in the back of a one-horse carriage moving at a trot around the customs house. As they followed the curve around the port toward Barceloneta he saw the three funnels of the German battleship *Helgoland* looming up out of the ocean just beyond the entrance to the harbor. The arrival of the lead ship from the Kaiser's new class of dreadnoughts in Barcelona had thrilled and flattered some of Mata's compatriots. Some of them saw it as another confirmation of Barcelona's transformation into a European city, but he sensed that its presence had more to do with the Kaiser's attempts to flatter Spain than anything to do with Catalonia. Soon the carriage came alongside the swimming club, and he saw the crowd gathered on the beach just before the upturned boats and nets. Bravo Portillo was standing at the center of the crowd with two uniformed Mossos d'Escuadra, and the mortuary wagon was already drawn up just behind the onlookers.

"There you are Mata," Bravo Portillo said. "Just in time."

Mata threaded his way through the fishermen, sailors, and local women, past a few members of the swimming club who were still wearing their striped one-piece bathing suits and vests with towels around their shoulders. One of Bravo Portillo's officers pulled back the tarpaulin to reveal the corpse of a man in his early thirties. Though he stopped just above the waist for the sake of decency, it was obvious that the victim was naked. Mata stared at the flecks of seaweed in his jet-black hair, and the swirling tattoos that he had seen on certain criminals in the Modelo prison, from the dagger on one forearm and the pistol on the other, to the large gallows that covered most of his bony chest with the words CARPE DIEM tattooed beneath it. The corpse also contained a number of wounds that looked like bites, and there was a large gash in his throat, where a mesh of torn pink veins protruded from a rim of whitened flesh.

"What's this?" asked Mata. "Did he get bitten by a shark?"

"I don't think so." Bravo Portillo rolled the body onto its side to reveal a piece of frayed rope tied around his wrists. "One of the swimmers found him floating in the water. Poor little Hermenigildo. I don't think he expected to leave the world like this."

"You knew him?"

Bravo Portillo nodded and folded back the tarpaulin over the corpse's face. "There wasn't much to know. His name was Hermenigildo Cortéz. Typical rubbish from the Raval. Petty thief and pickpocket. He used to run with Rull's group. A nobody—though he didn't always realize it. Well, he seems to have upset someone."

Mata looked out toward the gleaming ocean that had brought this corpse ashore. In his youth he had been a member of the swimming club and he still occasionally came here with his children. Now he thought that he would not be bringing them here for a while. And he could not help thinking that whoever had inflicted such strange wounds on the nobody from the Raval had more in common with the Barcelona zoo's latest acquisition than with anything human.

Lawton sat smoking and listening to Caruso singing an aria from *Tosca* on the phonograph. From where he was sitting he could see the sunset spreading across the sky in the direction of the Thames like a forest fire, as the great tenor filled the room. Lawton had not bought any new records since leaving the force, but even after two years it still seemed miraculous that science had made it possible for Caruso to sing to him in his own room. He was also grateful, because he had stopped going to concerts or the music hall since his illness. In the half-light, the Italian's voice seemed to weep from the little speaker horn, and even though Lawton did not understand the words, he felt soothed, uplifted, and moved by by the emotion behind them.

The music continued to resonate even after he got up to lift the needle. Beyond the rows of chimneys and clotheslines the sky reminded him of the Great Unexplained Event the previous June. That night the sun had refused to set, and the sky was lit up with a lurid orange glow that lasted till past midnight, so that it had been possible to read the newspaper without even turning the light on. At first he had thought it was another hallucination, but then he heard the excited voices of his neighbors and he realized that everyone else was seeing the same thing.

Some said that war had broken out and that the German invasion was underway. Others claimed that another great fire was spreading through

London, but the next day the newspapers reported that the same ghostly light had been seen all over Europe. No one knew what had caused it. There were reports that a volcano had erupted in the South Seas; that a meteorite had crashed in Siberia and caused a forest fire; that the Kaiser had been experimenting with a new super-weapon. Some God-fearing Christians had even gone out into the West End with sandwich boards declaring that the end of the world was coming and calling for all theaters and music halls to be closed.

Now Lawton wondered how Randolph William Foulkes would have accounted for it, because there was no doubt that Dr. Foulkes was a very learned man who knew a lot about many things. His bookshelves were a testament to the breadth of his knowledge and interests. Many of the books in his collection were written in foreign languages, and Mrs. Foulkes said her husband was fluent in German, Latin, and French, and he could also read Sanskrit. At least fifteen of them were written by Foulkes himself, Mrs. Foulkes said, and some of them had been translated. Foulkes had a degree in medicine from Oxford and a doctorate in anthropology from the Royal Holloway. He was a fellow of the Royal College of Physicians, the Royal Geographical Society, the Royal Anthropological Institute, the Society for Racial Hygiene, and the Society for Psychical Research. According to Mrs. Foulkes, his friends and correspondents included Sir Francis Galton, Gladstone, Conan Doyle, Cesare Lombroso, Ernst Haeckel, and Alphonse Bertillon, some of whom had dined at their house.

Foulkes's study was filled with souvenirs and mementoes of his travels and encounters with famous men. There was a framed letter of appreciation from Signore Lombroso for a lecture Foulkes had delivered in Milan; an African witchdoctor's mask, two crossed spears, and a leopard-skin shield, in addition to various fossils, bones, and glass cabinets containing insects and butterflies. The study also contained a number of photographs of Foulkes himself, including an early daguerreotype showing him receiving his degree in medicine at Oxford.

Even as a young man in his gown and mortarboard, Foulkes looked older than he was, with his high-domed forehead and high cheekbones, his long sideburns and the serious and faintly distant expression on his face as he stared back at the camera, as though he were looking at some point just beyond it. Foulkes had the same frown in a more recent photograph that showed him in a parka, standing outside a wooden hut against a background of ice and snow, with a group of men who were similarly dressed. Behind them was a pile of boxes and bags loaded on sledges, and Lawton noticed that some of the boxes were marked with what looked like a flash of lightning and the single word, EXCELSIOR.

"That was taken five years ago," Mrs. Foulkes said. "The Excelsior expedition to Greenland. Randolph was sixty-three. I told him he was too old to go. He wouldn't listen, of course. He never did."

"Was your husband interested in polar exploration, ma'am?"

"He was more interested in the natives. He took his camera and his measuring instruments with him. Randolph was always measuring people and photographing them."

"I'll need his photograph," Lawton said. "And a copy of his signature."

"Mr. Pickering will give you whatever you need tomorrow. You will also need a passport. I assume you have one?"

"No ma'am. We didn't need one in the army."

"Well you need to get one. And you will also need francs and pesetas." Mrs. Foulkes looked at him dubiously. "I hope you can cope with being abroad, Mr. Lawton. Chief Inspector Maitland seems to have great faith in you."

Lawton was tempted to tell her that he had fought in a war; that he had supported himself with his fists for nearly three years; that he had risen from street constable to detective in less than two years. He would have liked to sit down with her and tell about all the villains he had chased through Limehouse streets and rookeries that were as far removed from the world in which she lived as Africa or the jungles of Borneo. He could have told her how he had once dressed up as a priest in order to catch the Spitalfields confidence trickster who pretended to be a missionary in order to deceive rich women just like her. He could have described how he had used fingerprints and footprints to prove that Lizzie Hutten's husband had cracked his wife's skull with a metal bar and tried to blame it on a burglar—a case that had been featured in the *Police Gazette*. He could have thrilled her with tales of cat burglars he chased across the rooftops in his prime; of the days and even weeks he had spent stalking and following suspects without any of them knowing until it was too late, and all the other villains he had brought to justice and sent to prison or the gallows by using ingenuity, guile, and disguise as well as physical force.

"I'll do my best ma'am," he said finally. "I'd also like to borrow one of your husband's books. I'll return it to his secretary tomorrow."

"What on earth for?"

"It would be useful to have some idea of your husband's interests."

Mrs. Foulkes told him to help himself and pointed out some of her husband's works. There had been a time when Lawton had read books on criminal investigation methods and the law in the station or the public library. Since leaving the force, he read mostly for recreation and distraction. Foulkes's books clearly did not belong to any of these categories. Titles such as *Heredity and Nature,* and *Practical Eugenics* held no appeal. Lawton briefly considered *Narrative of a Traveler in Nyasaland* and *Children of the Sun: Travels in the Sami Arctic,* before settling on *The End of England,* which Mrs. Foulkes said was his most recent book.

Now he turned on the gas light and sat down to read it. Within a few pages the explanation for the title became obvious. The introduction was peppered with statistics about destitute aliens, paupers, drunkards, and moral imbeciles who were filling the nation's slums, workhouses, and asylums. While the unfit continued to breed without any attempt at intervention or mitigation, the birth rate among the more productive sectors of the population continued to fall. According to Foulkes these developments posed a direct threat to the nation's survival, and had left the greatest empire the world had ever seen increasingly vulnerable to its enemies.

Lawton had never heard such ideas before, and he was wondering what Foulkes proposed to do about them, when he felt the familiar sharp pain in his head and he smelled the faint whiff of smoke. He knew immediately that there was no fire. He dropped the book and rushed over to the cupboard where he kept his medicines. He broke a vial of amyl nitrate into a cloth and pressed it against his nose and mouth. Immediately his head swelled up like a balloon as he tried to fill his mind with images of strength, youth, and vigor. He saw himself as a boy, climbing trees in

Donegal. He heard the roar of the spectators from his fairground fights. He saw Corporal Lawton, First Battalion of the King's Royal Rifles, running down Spion Kop with a soldier on his back and bullets whining past him. He saw Constable Harry Lawton sprinting through the streets of Limehouse at night. And then his hands began to tremble and the band around his head tightened once again. He dropped onto all fours and rammed the bit between his teeth, as the flame spread through him like the Holy Ghost descending, and he was no longer able to imagine anything at all.

4

At ten o'clock the next morning, Lawton knocked on the door of a white Georgian house in Goodge Street. He had not hurt himself during the seizure, but he felt raw and self-conscious as a little man in pince-nez glasses and a brown tweed suit opened the door and looked him up and down. He looked remarkably like a model from Madame Tussauds, Lawton thought, and he seemed barely more animated.

"Mr. Pickering? I'm Harry Lawton."

"Ah yes. I've been expecting you." The secretary ushered him into a large room with a bay window overlooking the street. Lawton took off his hat and looked around in amazement. He had never visited a scientific laboratory before, and this was not how he imagined such places to be. At first sight it reminded him of the classroom at the Christian Brothers school, where Father McGuire once kept pickled birds, reptiles, and animal fetuses in jars as examples of God's creative genius.

The shelves and cabinets in Foulkes's laboratory were lined with glass jars containing what appeared to be brains and fetuses, but unlike Father

McGuire's collection, some of them appeared to be human. One wall was lined with rows of human skulls. Another was mostly taken up by a gallery of Bertillonage-style mugshots of criminals, whose wretched subjects stared back at the camera holding cards detailing their crimes. There were also photographs of men and women with Asiatic or Negroid features, taken at the front and the side. Other subjects bore signs of syphilis, cretinism, or other physical deformities.

Lawton peered at the skulls and their explanatory labels: Orsini the Brigand 1884; Congolese pygmy 1865; Sami 1900; Herero 1907; Irishman: County Antrim 1847.

"Quite a collection," he said.

"You're familiar with phrenology?" Pickering asked.

"You mean that bumps-in-your-head malarkey? As a matter of fact I did read one of Mr. Lombroso's books once. I wasn't much impressed by it, to be frank with you. But I hear 1847 was a good year for collecting Irish skulls."

Pickering blinked. "Dr. Foulkes was very enthused by Signore Lombroso's findings—at least initially. But Lombroso's central preoccupation was the elimination of criminal and deviant behavior. Dr. Foulkes was more concerned with heredity and the pursuit of perfection. What makes human beings the best they can be? How can these characteristics be preserved and extended?"

"I read something about that yesterday." Lawton handed him Foulkes's book. "I told Mrs. Foulkes I'd give it back to you."

Pickering looked at the title. "Dr. Foulkes's last book. It was an attempt to explain his theories in layman's terms."

Lawton ignored the little secretary's condescension. Just then his attention was caught by one of the skulls. He leaned forward and read the inscription. "Caucasian female 22 years old. Epileptic: Everdale 1898."

"Where did Dr. Foulkes get these exhibits?" he said, in a hard, clipped voice.

The secretary looked taken aback by his change of tone. "From various sources. Some were collected by Dr. Foulkes during his travels or donated by researchers. Others were donated by hospitals and other institutions."

"From asylums like Everdale?"

"Indeed. Dr. Foulkes was director there for three years, in the late 1890s."

"So this skull came from one of his patients?"

"I assume so."

"With their permission?"

Pickering gave him a pitying look. "The mad don't generally give much thought to what will happen to their bodies after their deaths, Mr. Lawton. But of course it would have been with the permission of the institution. Shall we conclude our business?"

Lawton followed Pickering into another room lined with more glass cabinets, books, photographs. There were also a number of measuring instruments including a microscope, calipers, and a curved silver instrument that looked like a kind of brace. Lawton looked around at the large drawing of a human body with its arm extended, the close-up photographs of ears, lips, and eyes, and a framed weaving of the lightning flash he had seen on the Greenland expedition boxes, with the word Excelsior sewn in beneath it.

"What is that mark?" he asked.

"It's a runic symbol."

"A what?"

"The runic script was used by some Germanic and Nordic language groups before Latin. This one is called the sig-rune—the sun or victory rune. Do have a seat." Pickering handed him a small leather satchel. "You'll find everything you need here. Photographs that Dr. Foulkes took of himself. Copies of his fingerprints. I've also included a fingerprint kit. I assume you know how to examine and compare prints?"

Lawton stared back at him. "Mrs. Foulkes hired a detective not a chimney-sweep."

"Of course." Pickering gave a thin smile and handed him an envelope. "Here's your initial payment. Your expenses will be sent through the Western Union offices in Barcelona once a week. Do you need anything else?"

"Yes. I'd be interested to know why you think Dr. Foulkes went to Barcelona."

"I have no idea. All I know is that the nation has lost a great man. The last of the Great Victorians."

"If he was so great why hasn't he got a knighthood?"

"Great men don't always get the recognition they deserve, Mr. Lawton, at least not in their own time. Dr. Foulkes was consulted as an expert witness by the parliamentary Committee on Physical Deterioration in 1904. Like many of our politicians, he was very concerned about the quality of the national stock, after the Boer War. He thought something needed to be done to prepare us for the next one. Some of his proposals were considered . . . controversial."

"Such as?"

"Dr. Foulkes believed that the morally defective and physically unfit should not be allowed to reproduce themselves. That certain marriages should be prevented, that in some cases compulsory sterilization might be required. He also believed that there were cases in which it might be necessary to terminate lives that were likely to be a burden to the state and society. These ideas were not well received—not by the government or by the national press."

"I'm not surprised. But I can tell you one thing—none of this would have made much difference against the Boers. We fought a war we weren't prepared for. We were led by fools who had no idea what they were doing—at least at first. We fought men who were defending their land and their homes. Anybody will struggle to win a war like that, even the British Empire."

Pickering bridled. "And how would you know that?"

"Because I fought in the war."

"I see." Pickering looked unsure how to reply to this. "Well, sentimental moralists may disapprove. But I believe that posterity will view Dr. Foulkes in a very different light—as a genius and a visionary. And a patriot who loved his country."

"Did he love his wife?"

"I don't think that's any of your business."

"If I'm to find out what happened to him then everything about him is my business," Lawton said. "They had no children, did they?"

"I can assure you that Dr. Foulkes was a very solicitous husband. Despite his wife's infertility."

"I'm sure he was. But husbands can be solicitous when they find consolation elsewhere, can't they? And Dr. Foulkes was often away."

Mr. Pickering wiped his pince-nez. "Dr. Foulkes was not that kind of man."

"Yet there is he is in Barcelona, giving his money away to a woman who no one seems to know. It's a curious thing, don't you think?"

"It is." Pickering looked more perplexed than indignant now. "And I hope you can shed some light on it. Mrs. Foulkes wants you to leave as soon as possible. You'll take the train to Dover for the ferry. From Paris you get the train to Perpignan and Barcelona. Mrs. Foulkes says you don't have a passport. You should go to the Home Office immediately. I've already called them to expedite the process. I've arranged an appointment for you this afternoon."

Pickering got up to show him out. As they walked back into the laboratory, Lawton glanced once again at the skull of the epileptic from Everdale. Great man or not, he did not much like Randolph William Foulkes, and it occurred to him that there was one more place to visit before leaving the country to find out what had happened to him, and he saw no reason to tell Mrs. Foulkes or her secretary about it.

Even as a child Bernat Mata had despised the Montjuïc fortress. He had grown up with his grandparents' accounts of the insurrections of 1842 and 1846 when the Bourbon cannons had bombarded the city from the castle. As a journalist he had witnessed the processions of anarchists and liberals escorted in chains up the hill. In 1896 he had spoken to innocent men who had been taken there to have their balls crushed with pliers or their fingernails pulled out. It was now nearly two hundred years since the Bourbons had crushed the Catalans and taken away their rights and their language, and even now in the twentieth century the fortress continued to loom over the city, the visible symbol of Bourbon power, domination, and corruption.

Mata told the driver to wait for him. He stared bleakly at the waterless moat, the thick sloping walls, and the cannons that still pointed inward toward the city rather than the sea, and walked across the stone bridge to the main entrance, where two soldiers in olive green uniforms and puttees stood rigidly at attention. Mata informed them that he had come to speak to Lieutenant Ugarte from the Social Brigade, and one of the soldiers told him to wait and went inside. A few minutes later he returned to announce that the lieutenant was in his office. As always Mata felt his spirits sink as he walked across the cobbled courtyard and remembered the five blindfolded anarchists kneeling on the ground outside the fortress wall with their hands tied behind them on May 3, 1897, as the firing squad lined up in front of them.

He remembered the soldiers standing in line like figures from a Goya painting, in their red striped trousers, boots, and black caps, while the officer raised his saber and gave the order to fire. He remembered the priests hovering in the background like weird black crows with their rosaries and crucifixes; the satisfaction on the faces of the city's great and good as they watched the first volley; the officer who administered the coup de grâce with his revolver to two of the anarchists who were still alive.

Even then Mata doubted whether any of the men had committed the crimes they were accused of. Esperanza Claramunt's father was the last person who would have thrown a bomb, but he had been arrested and died under torture at the hands of men like Ugarte, for whom liberals were only one step removed from anarchists. It was Rafael Claramunt who had brought him back to the fortress, to carry out this act of charity on behalf of his daughter. Even as he descended the stone steps, he felt as if he were leaving the twentieth century behind and descending into a world where justice disappeared and only the brute power of the Restoration state prevailed, despite the trappings of parliamentary democracy.

He walked down the dimly lit corridor and knocked on the door of the Brigada's offices. Ugarte called him in, in his familiar growl. He was sitting in his chair with his feet up on his desk, reading a French erotic magazine called *Jeunes Filles de la Campagne*. He laid it down and looked at Mata with an expression of mild surprise. "Well, well, if it isn't the voice of Catalonia! To what do we owe this honor? The last time we met you were working for ¡*Cu-Cut!* if I remember correctly."

Mata nodded as Ugarte gestured to the seat in front of his desk. Ugarte had been outside the offices on the day the army smashed them up, and Mata knew that he had enjoyed the spectacle. It was not an acquaintance he had ever thought about renewing. Even now he felt faintly uneasy at the sight of the lifeless black eyes, the puffy cheeks with their smallpox scars, and the thick fingers that seemed to be faintly caressing the photograph of a naked woman posing on a haystack in the half-open magazine. "I came about the Luna Bar," he said. "I wondered if the investigation had made any progress."

"If we had, we would have announced it. You know how these things work."

"I do. But I've heard that someone may have been arrested."

"Oh?" Ugarte clasped his hands and cracked his knuckles. "And who would that be?"

"An anarchist named Pau Tosets. He works for the *Soli*. I thought I'd come here and find out if it was true."

"May I ask how you came by this information?"

"On the street."

"The street." Ugarte's pineapple cheeks creased in the faintest of smiles. "Such diligence on your part—to come all the way up here on the basis of gossip and rumor."

"Well it is my job to separate rumors from facts," Mata said apologetically.

"And on this occasion you've wasted your time."

"So you still haven't found the perpetrator?"

"Not yet. But we will. And until then it might be better to wait for official announcements rather than listen to what foolish tongues are saying."

Mata felt that the visit was not going well. "Of course. That's why I came here to make sure. It seemed sensible to speak to you directly."

Ugarte shrugged. "It would be more sensible to stay out of matters that don't concern you."

Ugarte glanced down at his magazine, and tapped on the young woman's head. The conversation was clearly over, and Mata hauled himself out of the chair and went back out into the corridor. As soon as he felt the sun on his face he took a deep breath as if he had just come up from underwater. Even as the carriage returned to the city, the stink of the fortress seemed to cling to his clothes, and Ugarte's mortuary eyes continued to haunt him. Below him his native city tumbled down like a giant's stairway from the mountains into the sea. To the east he could see the factory towers of Poblenou overlooking the ocean, the mighty Church of Santa Maria del Mar, the spiked Gothic turrets of the cathedral, and between the sun-drenched buildings he could see the darker lines of crisscrossing streets and avenues whose names he knew, and the wide avenue of the Passeig de Gràcia passing through the open fields between Gràcia and the still recognizable pentagonal shape of the old city.

As always the sight of it filled him with hope and pride. One day, he thought, Barcelona would be the capital of an independent Catalan Republic and one of the great cities in Europe. Whatever had happened to Pau Tosets, it would be a better place when men like Ugarte no longer had any power over it. And even as the carriage rode back into the shantytown of Poble Sec and past the theaters, cafés, and music halls along the Parallelo, he could not shake off the nagging suspicion that Ugarte had not been telling the truth.

5

"Do you know how long you'll be in Barcelona, Harry?" Dr. Morris laid the stethoscope on his desk as Lawton put his shirt and jacket back on.

"Difficult to say. A week or two I expect."

"When was the last time you had a seizure?"

"About a month ago. Only minor."

Lawton knew he had no need to lie, and that Morris could not stop him going anywhere, but he still regarded doctors with something of the reverence and respect he had once reserved for priests, and he was reluctant to tell them anything that might arouse their disapproval.

"Well, you're in fine physical shape," said Morris. "But that's not the problem, is it? Remember you need to avoid any mental or emotional strain."

"It's a straightforward job. More like a vacation."

"Well, perhaps the sunshine will do you good. I'll give you a month's prescription just in case. Potassium bromide for the seizures. Nitroglycerin and amyl nitrate for headaches. Remember to take the bromide daily or it won't work. And no drinking. I'm sure I don't have to tell you that."

"No sir." Lawton handed Morrison his fee. "Haven't touched a drop in more than a year."

"Good for you." Morris was looking at him thoughtfully now. "You know, Harry, I was wondering, have you heard of Victor Horsley?"

Lawton had not, and Morris explained that Horsley was a surgeon at the National Hospital for Paralysis and Epilepsy, who had had some success on epileptic patients using surgical procedures.

"With respect, Doctor, I've seen too many field hospitals to allow anyone to look inside my skull," Lawton said.

"Horsley's not some army butcher, Harry. His team have actually stopped some patients from having fits. It's just something to consider, that's all—if things should deteriorate. Of course we both hope they won't."

Lawton gave a noncommittal grunt and Morris made out the prescription. He went directly to the apothecary to have it made up, and then made his way back along Commercial Street and into the warren of streets behind Brick Lane. On arriving back at the house he was disappointed to hear the widow Friedman remonstrating with one of the tenants in the kitchen. He had intended to pass by the café to give her the rent in order to avoid a scene, and he went quickly upstairs before she noticed him. He had nearly finished his packing when there was a discreet tap on the door and he went over to let her in. She was carrying a little basket, and she smiled the tentative, hopeful smile that always made him feel guilty.

"I brought you some blinis," she said, as he shut the door behind her. Her smile immediately vanished at the sight of the battered leather suitcase on the bed. "You're leaving?"

"Just for a fortnight. I'm going to Spain."

"And you don't tell me?"

"I was about to." Lawton reached for his wallet and counted out six shillings. "Here's three weeks rent—just in case."

The widow had a pained look in her eyes now as she looked at his outstretched hand. "You don't need to pay me now, Harry. I keep your room empty for you."

"No, no, take it. Here." Her eyes looked teary now as she took the coins. "I won't be gone long," he said in a softer tone.

"But you're not well Harry. Vot if . . ."

Lawton immediately stiffened. "I have to go. My train leaves at four."

The widow looked as if his imminent departure was one more disappointment in a life that had already produced too many of them. She insisted that he take the blinis, and Lawton fretted impatiently as she wrapped them in newspaper. He sensed that she wanted him to kiss her or make some pledge or promise, but he put on his mackintosh and hat and picked up his suitcase.

"I'll see you soon," he said.

"Alright Harry. You take care."

Lawton smiled tensely and hurried away with a feeling of relief from this unwanted intimacy and all the unspoken feelings and obligations that it imposed on him. It was beginning to rain now, and as he dipped his hat against the drizzle and walked quickly toward the station, the East End seemed suddenly smaller and more claustrophobic than it should have been, and it did not seem like a bad thing at all to be getting out of it.

He arrived in Dover in the early evening and booked into a bed and breakfast overlooking the new port. The next morning he hired a motorized taxi to take him to the Everdale Asylum. It was a clear day and already the first day-trippers were arriving at Dover station as the taxi drove out into the countryside toward Folkestone. Fifteen minutes later he saw the familiar red buildings above the line of trees on the hill. He asked the taxi to wait for him at the entrance and walked into the grounds. Apart from the nurses, doctors, and orderlies, and the distracted-looking people wandering around the grounds under their watchful supervision, Everdale's purpose was not immediately obvious.

Some of the patients were playing bowls and croquet, others were sitting on the lawn chatting as though they were having a day out in the park. The acute wards were a different matter, and he braced himself as he announced his arrival to the duty nurse and told her that he had come to collect Estela Lawton. He stood waiting in the corridor while she went off to fetch her, and looked at the portraits and photographs of Everdale's directors lining the walls. They reached all the way back from the present to the late 18th century. To his surprise there was no photograph or portrait of Randolph Foulkes, even though Pickering had said that Foulkes worked there in the 1890s.

Lawton was still staring at the portraits when the nurse returned with his mother. As always the sight of her filled him with desolation and guilt. She was wearing the same green dress and bonnet that she had worn when he had brought her there, but now it seemed to hang off her as though she had shrunk inside it. Even when she was younger, his father had often taunted her that she belonged in a freak show or a human zoo. Now she looked frailer and madder than the last time he had seen her, as she peered at him suspiciously.

"I know you," she said.

Lawton smiled patiently. "'Course you do Ma. *Soy* Harry, *tu hijo*."

"I don't have a son!"

"I'm afraid you do." He winked at the nurse. "And he's come to take you to the seaside."

His mother looked suddenly frightened. "But I like it *here*."

"You also like the sea," Lawton reminded her. "And afterward we'll come back here."

Estela brightened now and let him take her arm. Lawton had forgotten how light and insubstantial she was, like a bird that could fly away at any moment.

"I have a question about one of your directors," he said to the nurse. "A Dr. Randolph Foulkes. He worked here in the 1890s, but I don't see his picture up on the walls. Just a three-year-gap between 1897 and 1900."

"I wasn't working here then," the nurse replied. "But I can ask about him while you're out."

Lawton thanked her and walked away with his mother. No sooner had they left the building than she gripped his arm and looked at him with sudden intensity. "That woman," she whispered, "would like to drink my blood."

"I don't think so," said Lawton.

"She would!" His mother insisted. "She's a *peuchen*."

Lawton sighed. It was going to be a long day. "This isn't Patagonia Ma. There are no monsters here."

His mother looked unconvinced, but she had cheered up by the time they arrived in Folkestone, and the day passed more easily than he had anticipated. Much of the time all he had to do was nod and humor her more wayward thoughts and fixations, which she mostly expressed in Spanish with a smattering of Mapuche words, as they walked along the beach and promenade to the strains of a carousel and a military band on Victoria Pier. His mother tapped her feet in time to the music, and Lawton remembered the volunteers singing some of the same songs as they marched through Limehouse in 1990 on their way to fight the Boers.

Once those parades had inspired him to seek military glory. Now he found their gaiety jarring and dishonest. The spectators loved them, as civilians always did, because these tunes conjured up images of men in the saddle, of sabers, uniforms, and gallant cavalry charges. Lawton preferred the songs on the carousel like "Daisy," "My Wild Irish Rose," and "I'm Forever Blowing Bubbles" that he remembered from more innocent times. His mother liked everything she heard, and stared with childlike fascination at the families eating picnics, the children making sandcastles and riding donkeys, the young men in striped bathing suits and boaters lounging against the wooden windbreaks, while Lawton cast sneaking glances at the pretty young women splashing in the foamy sea with wet hair and their knee-length swimsuits.

All this seemed to revive his mother physically and mentally, so that it was almost possible to see traces of the beauty his father had brought back to Ireland and then to England like a rare tropical orchid more than thirty years ago. Age, madness, and poverty had twisted her face and hollowed out her eyes and cheekbones, but he could still remember the gentle woman who told him about the blood-drinking peuchen and the flesh-eating *cherufe* and the Mapuche warrior-hero Lautaro who had fought the Spanish. He and his sister had had her committed before the war. Even now she did not know that he had gone to South Africa or become a police officer, and there was no point in even telling her that he was going to Barcelona. By the time they returned to the asylum in the afternoon, she was beginning to look downcast and agitated once again.

"Everything will be alright, won't it hijo?" she said, gripping his arm tightly.

"Why wouldn't it be?" Lawton saw the taxi driver's raised eyebrows in the mirror and he glared back at him till he looked away. On reaching the hospital he took his mother back to the ward, where the nurse smiled at them benignly. "Did you have a nice day Estela?" she asked.

His mother stared down at the ground.

"We did," Lawton replied.

"I spoke to matron about Dr. Foulkes," the nurse said. "She does remember him, but she said she didn't know why his picture wasn't up there."

Lawton thanked her and handed his mother over. "Goodbye, Ma. I'll see you again soon."

His mother turned away without a word, and Lawton watched the nurse lead her out and wondered whether he ever would see her again. He walked back out toward the waiting taxi, past the men and women who were being led back into their wards. Once they had been out in the world, just like him, and one day he might find himself in a place like this. He would rather die first, and he wondered what his mother would have said if she had been presented with such a choice when they had had her committed. She had not been there when Foulkes was director, and now, as the taxi drove back toward Dover, he thought that it would not do any harm to call or send a telegram to Scotland Yard, and ask Maitland if he could find out why Randolph Foulkes had not received the honor that had been bestowed on his predecessors.

"Why do we kiss the hands of priests?"

Esperanza looked sternly around at the rows of children in their light blue smocks. All of them, including the girls, had had their heads shaven after the latest outbreak of lice. Some of them were dazed and drooping after the long day, but her favorite pupils still put their hands up as they always did whenever their favorite teacher asked them a question.

"Because priests are holy?" said Núria.

"Really?" Esperanza replied. "And what makes them holy?"

"God does!" Luis exclaimed.

"But who says God exists?" Esperanza asked. "The same men who ask us to kiss their hands!"

Luis looked crestfallen, and Esperanza immediately regretted her harsh tone. In a softer voice, she explained that priests were merely men, who deserved no more respect than anyone else. They told the poor to be content with their poverty, and promised them that they would be rewarded in heaven. But the Church was one of the richest landowners in Spain. Its convents and monasteries had grown rich at the people's expense. So of course its priests expected the poor to kiss their hands to show respect, but what they really showed was that were slaves.

It was a strong speech, and some of the children looked shocked at her vehemence. Esperanza knew that she sounded more emotional than usual, which was not surprising after another night lying awake worrying about whether Pau was dead or alive. This was not something she could explain to her class. If she even mentioned his name aloud she knew that she might cry, and then she would upset the children. But if Pau's disappearance had made her sad, it had also made her angry and even less inclined than usual to moderate her words in accordance with the director's instructions. The Élisée Reclus Institute was one of the few rationalist schools still functioning in Barcelona after the crackdown that followed Ferrer's trial. Most of the others had backed away from Ferrer's methods and ideas, and had begun to reaffirm their patriotism and their commitment to the Catholic curriculum. Esperanza knew it would not be long before her school did the same. Already Director Vargas had hung a picture of the king in the canteen and obliged staff and children to sing the national anthem at morning assembly. It was only a matter of time before they would be studying the catechism once again.

"My mother says if you don't kiss the priest's hand you don't go to heaven," Núria insisted.

"There is no heaven!" Esperanza sighed impatiently. "There's only this world and this life. And we are the ones who make it into heaven or hell—not the priests."

Once again she knew she had spoken too harshly. She looked beyond the rows of benches toward the photograph of the geographer Reclus with his long white hair and beard, and his gentle, intelligent eyes that seemed to twinkle approvingly. There had been a time when she had also believed the same things she was telling her class not to believe, when she had taken it for granted that the world was exactly what her elders said it was and that it would always remain the same. As a child she had assumed that she would always go on living with her parents and her two younger brothers in the Calle Provenza, with her dollhouse and toys, her teachers and her friends and the daily walks to the Ciutadella Park. All that had come to an end on the morning of June 29, 1896, less than a week after her seventh birthday, when the officers from the Social Brigade had come to take her father away, while he was eating breakfast and reading his newspaper in the gallery as he always did.

Even then, her father had been so calm and matter-of-fact as he put on his jacket and hat that she thought nothing of it. The next time she had seen him he had been lying in an open coffin. Now, more than a decade later, Spain was still a country where men could be taken away by police for no reason and with no explanation and there was nothing anyone could do to prevent it or get anyone to account for it. Mata had done all he could, and she was no longer sure what anyone else could do. Even now she thought of Pau, like her father, chained to a wall in the fortress, and she felt herself welling up.

Just then the bell rang out in the corridor and she turned away to compose herself, while the children queued up to hand in their slates, chalk, and smocks, which she stacked in the cupboard and hung on the rail. Afterward the children poured out of the classroom in a tumultuous flood, and Esperanza put on her hat and cloak, and gathered up her bag and her sheets of music. A part of her felt that it was frivolous to sing when Pau might be being tortured, but her mother had insisted, and she needed some distraction and consolation. She was about to leave when Director Vargas appeared in the doorway.

"Miss Claramunt," he said, with a smile. "I was hoping to hear singing from your classroom today."

"I've had too many other things to teach them, sir."

"I couldn't help noticing you didn't sing the 'Royal March' this morning." Vargas was not smiling now. "There's not much point in asking the children to sing the national anthem if their own teachers don't sing it, is there?"

"I'm sorry, sir," she said. "But I don't believe that national anthems of any kind are compatible with the rational education our schools were created to provide."

Vargas looked pained. "There's nothing reactionary about patriotism, Miss Claramunt. Times are changing and we have to change with them. I think you should reflect on that."

Esperanza was in no mood to do any such thing, but Vargas had clearly not intended to initiate a discussion, and he walked away without waiting for an answer. Esperanza waited till he had gone and then walked out through the little courtyard toward the entrance. No sooner had she stepped outside than she saw Ruben and Flor Montero standing under the plane tree on the other side of the street. There was no trace of mockery on Ruben's face now. Even from a distance, he looked wintry and somber as he stood holding his wife's arm. Pau's sister had the same stunned, devastated expression that Esperanza had once seen when her mother told her that her father would not be coming home.

Neither of them moved or said a word, but even as Esperanza walked across the street toward them, she felt as if the sun had just gone out and a cold freezing wind was blowing through the city, and she knew that Pau Tosets would not be coming back.

6

As the train moved south from Perpignan, Lawton remembered the last time he had seen the Mediterranean on the troopship returning from South Africa in the spring of 1902. The mood on board had been very different from the outward voyage. There were no racy music hall ditties, no boxing and wrestling matches, no drills or parades, only a sense of collective relief that it was over and amazement that they had survived. For some of the wounded survivors there had been no relief at all. One soldier's face had been completely covered in bandages except for his eyes and mouth.

From time to time someone gave the soldier a drag on a cigarette and he sucked on it with a hoarse rattling sound that still made Lawton stiffen with revulsion. It was during that voyage that Maitland told him that he was going to become a police inspector in Limehouse and suggested that he might also join the force. Had he not done so, he might have taken up boxing once again. Or he might have become a drunkard like his father and ended up in the workhouse, or worse. Now, thanks to Maitland, he was abroad once again, but this time he felt more like a tourist than a soldier. He had enjoyed the sight of the Eiffel Tower, the pleasure boats coming and going along the Seine, and the fashionable women in their open carriages with their wide-brimmed hats and parasols. It had been equally pleasant to sit on the train from Paris to Marseille and then to Perpignan, and look out at the whitewashed buildings with their pink tile roofs, the yellow fields and vineyards and palm trees, and the ocean stretching out like a great lake of silver toward the horizon.

Even before leaving Perpignan, he had spoken Spanish for the first time with Señor Camacho, the talkative merchant from Madrid who shared his carriage with him. Much of the time all he had to do was listen as Señor Camacho held forth about his native land, and told Lawton how to deal with beggars, the costs of meals, and hotels. Señor Camacho also had a great deal to say about Barcelona. Though he liked Catalonia, he had little regard for its inhabitants. Too many of them had been infected with the separatist virus, he said. Instead of speaking Spanish, they preferred Catalan—a language that sounded like barking dogs. Where even the poorest Spaniard was motivated by honor and patriotism, the Catalans thought only of making money and didn't care how they made it. Even the wealthiest of them had no respect for the fatherland or His Majesty King Alfonso. Those who were unable or unwilling to work for their bread had allowed their minds to be perverted by wild dreams of anarchy, separatism, and revolution, and most of these revolutionists were concentrated in Barcelona—a city with ten thousand prostitutes and just as many revolutionists.

Lawton had no idea how much of this was true, and he could not help thinking that Señor Camacho was laying it on thick. Immediately after crossing the border they stopped at the little coastal town of Portbou to change trains to the lighter gauge railway and he went in search of a moneychanger and some relief from the Spaniard's overbearing company. As he stood looking over the little bay, he wondered whether his father was still alive. He had no desire to see him or hear from him, and he assumed that he must have died from drinking or the clap. But it was also possible that the old bastard had hung on, with the same bullish strength that had once enabled him to hoist women above his head with one hand when he worked for the fairground as the Strongest Man on Earth.

An hour later the train pulled away once again, and the Mediterranean was constantly visible now as they made their way down the rocky coast past Tordera, Blanes, Arenys de Mar, and Mataró, and other towns that Lawton had never heard of. Most of these towns seemed modern and charming enough, but the countryside in between was like something from another century. They passed orange trees and wooden waterwheels, and stony fields where peasants in red caps and headscarves and sashes around their waists pulled plows by hand or toiled with mule- or ox-drawn plows, assisted by barefoot children and women in loose skirts, white scarves, and pinafores.

It was early afternoon when the sea disappeared behind rows of factories billowing smoke and tall chimneys that reminded Lawton of Manchester or Sheffield. Shortly afterward they pulled into a large cavernous station, and Señor Camacho announced that they had arrived in Barcelona.

No sooner had the train come to a halt than porters came onto the train, shouting out the names of hotels and offering to take their baggage. Lawton pushed his way through them without accepting their services. On the platform he shook hands with Señor Camacho and walked out to the main exit, where he asked one of the horse-drawn cabs to take him to the British Consulate. Within a few minutes they were riding alongside a port crowded with ships. Beyond them he saw a warship looming out of the water like a spiked metal wall, but he could not make out the flag. Despite Señor Camacho's warnings, Barcelona looked calm and reassuringly normal, as they turned right into a pedestrian thoroughfare lined by rows of plane trees, with streets running down either side.

Lawton knew immediately that this was the Ramblas, or "their Ramblas" as Camacho referred to them. Lawton thought that it was one of the prettiest streets he had ever seen. The tall trees formed a shaded canopy over the crowded thoroughfare and Lawton saw children eating ice cream and walking with their parents, and men and women of distinction looking down from the balconies of elegant brownstone buildings.

The driver stopped about halfway up the street, and Lawton read the words Consulado Britanico among the list of names outside the open doorway. He dropped a coin into the driver's hand and walked into a high vestibule with polished marble tiles on the floor and continued upstairs to the consulate. No sooner had he pressed the bell than he heard footsteps squeaking on the floor and the door was opened by a handsome young man wearing a white suit and polished leather brogues. His hair was combed back on his head and flattened with oil and he looked at Lawton's sweaty face, shabby coat, and suitcase with disdain and surprise.

"I'm Harry Lawton," Lawton said. "Mrs. Foulkes sent me."

"Ah, yes. Of course." The young man's face looked suitably somber and funereal, and he extended his hand. "Come in. I'm Gerald Smither. His Majesty's vice-consul. Mr. Pickering said you were on your way."

Lawton followed him into a high-ceilinged corridor, past portraits of the king and the late queen, and a range of illustrious figures including Wellington, Kitchener, and Lord Nelson, into a paneled room with another picture of the king looking down from the wall and a Union Jack in the corner. Smither sat down at a mahogany desk with a green leather top and looked at Lawton over the writing pad and a copy of *Wisden*.

"Cigarette?" He extended a leather cigarette case. "I would offer you a drink, but I've sent Catalina home."

"I'll be fine thank you." Lawton took a cigarette and Smither lit it for him.

"I'm glad you've come," Smither said. "The coroner has finished his report and the mortuary was asking me only yesterday what we're going to do with the body—what's left of it."

"I believe Mrs. Foulkes wants the remains cremated and the ashes returned to England," Lawton said. "But first I have to confirm his identity."

Smither nodded. "I assume you've brought the letter of authorization? You'll need it to carry out an examination."

"I have."

"You're going to have your work cut out, chap. That bomb was one of the biggest in years. Two dead. Ten injured. It made my teacup shake even from here."

"As long as there's something left, I'll be able to identify it," Lawton said.

"Well there isn't much doubt who it is. Dr. Foulkes was staying at the International Hotel. The bomb went off on the 14th. That morning Foulkes left his hotel and never came back. They even found a burned Baedeker at the café with his signature that matched the one at the hotel."

"Do they know who did it?"

"They do now. An anarchist named Cortéz. Someone tipped off the Social Brigade—the political police. They searched his apartment and found bomb-making materials, including the same bag the bomb was carried in. Covered in traces of nitroglycerin. Pamphlets by Kropotkin and Bakunin. Most's bomb-making manual. Copies of the *Soli*—exactly what you might expect."

"The *Soli*?"

"*Solidaridad Obrera*. Workers' Solidarity." Smither gave him an ironic look. "One of the anarchist papers."

"Was there a motive?"

Smither gave a snort. "These people don't need a *reason*, old boy. Anyway Cortéz is dead. Murdered by a lunatic. The tip off came after his death. Very bad luck for Foulkes to have wandered into this."

"Mrs. Foulkes says her husband had a female companion."

"Well there was a woman with him at the café. But she left before the bomb went off."

"Are the police looking for her?"

"Why would they? She's not suspected of anything. Perhaps she doesn't know what happened. And if there was anything . . . indiscreet about their relationship, I can't imagine she would want to come forward. Not if she was a woman with a reputation." Smither looked at his watch. "Look I don't want to be rude, but I have to be somewhere. Do you know where you'll be staying in Barcelona?"

"I was hoping you might advise me."

"The Hotel de Catalonia isn't bad. It's in the Plaza Reial. Turn left when you go out the building and head back down toward the harbor.

You can't miss it. It's not as quiet as some might like. But then nowhere is right now, with the Germans in town."

"Germans?"

"Yes, the *Helgoland* is docked just outside the port for a few days. The Germans are showing it off to the Spanish. We're all a little concerned it might be on its way to Morocco. By the way, we have Dr. Foulkes's things. I'll bring them to your hotel tomorrow."

Until that moment, Lawton had begun to feel confident and relaxed, and he had even begun to imagine that being in a different country might make him into a different person. Now he was suddenly conscious of the tingling sensation in his left hand and then his right, and he imagined himself twitching on the floor like a stranded fish in front of the vice-consul. He stubbed out his cigarette and hurriedly got to his feet.

"I'll be going then," he said, reaching for his suitcase.

"I'll come by at ten tomorrow morning. I'll take you to the medical school."

"Very good, thank you." Lawton was sweating now and he was conscious that Smither was looking at him oddly. By the time he returned to the street, the sweat was running down his neck and spine, and he felt the nausea rising in his stomach. As he hurried past the strolling crowds, coiling and uncoiling his hand, he prayed to the God he did not even believe in not to humiliate him once again in this foreign city, when he had only just arrived.

By the time he found the Hotel de Catalonia the tingling had begun to subside, but he still felt an urgent need to get off the street and be alone in a room again. The receptionist was a balding little man with a toothbrush moustache named Señor Martínez, who checked his passport and wrote down his details in the hotel registry and then on another form. Martínez performed his tasks with the laborious pleasure that Lawton had often observed in a certain breed of lowly official. He seemed to sense Lawton's impatience, but showed no willingness to respond to it as he ponderously announced that all hotels were obliged to pass on information about their guests to the Spanish police for security reasons.

"Are you here for business or tourism?" he asked.

"Business." Lawton coiled and uncoiled his left hand and tried to ignore the lightness in his stomach.

"What kind of business?"

Lawton had not expected a follow-up question. "International commerce," he said.

Señor Martínez seemed satisfied by this. "You speak excellent Spanish. It should be very easy for you to do business here."

Lawton was not in the mood for pleasantries. He shifted his feet as the hotelier wrote out his passport details. Finally he reached his room and closed the door behind him. By dusk his symptoms had disappeared completely and he had begun to feel hungry, but he was too rattled to risk going outside again. Instead he took his medicine and lay on the bed in his vest and underpants. Even with the window open the room was humid and sweltering, and the tepid brown water in the bathroom sink did little to cool him down. In the late evening he heard the sound of German sailors drunkenly singing "The March on the Rhine," which he had once heard some of their compatriots singing in Cape Town.

Even after closing the window he could still hear the sailors shouting and laughing as he lay staring up at the ceiling, while the same images from the war passed through his mind that he never seemed able to forget. Once again he saw the face of the young Boer he had bayoneted on the battlefield near the Tugela River, with the handsome face and the long black hair that made him look like an Apache Indian. He saw charred bodies in the ruins of burned farms, the desiccated corpses of horses lying near blocked wells with their eyes eaten away by maggots. He saw soldiers wasted by typhus; men without arms, eyes, and even faces screaming or bleeding to death from their wounds as the stretcher-bearers carried them away. He heard women wailing over the bodies of their dead children and the hymn that one Boer wife had played on her piano until he and his men dragged her away from it and smashed the instrument to pieces simply to spite her, because she would not tell them where their sons and husbands were hiding.

Wherever he went and however long he lived, he knew he would never be able to erase this procession of horrors from his mind. It was as if he was trapped alone inside a theater or one of the new moving picture houses, compelled to watch the same scenes over and over again. From time to time he was tempted to tell Dr. Morris about them and see if there was some medication for such things. But as far as he knew there was no medicine that could stop a person remembering what he did not want to remember, and there were some things that were better left unspoken. It was bad enough that the widow Friedman knew he was ill and that he woke in his sleep, but to admit to a doctor that he sometimes got the morbs would confirm in the eyes of the outside world what he already knew: that like his mother something inside him was broken and could not be fixed, and was very likely to get even worse.

7

He woke up in the early morning to the sound of a cockerel and the rattle of a streetcar, and lay there dozing for a long time while the cock continued to crow. Finally he got up and drew back the shutters. The sunlight made him blink as he surveyed the palm trees and sand-colored buildings and the shaded walkway lining the square. He took two drops of potassium bromide and performed his morning calisthenics before going out in search of breakfast. The square was only just coming to life, and he sat down at a terrace café outside the hotel and ordered scrambled eggs and toast.

The waiter looked blank when he asked for tea, and he ordered coffee instead and smoked his first cigarette of the day. He continued to sit in the shade smoking and watching the sunlight slowly moving across the square toward the little fountain at its center, until the vice-consul appeared, carrying Foulkes's bag and suitcase. Smither waited for him while Lawton took them up to his room and returned with the satchel Pickering had given him. The mortuary was only a few minutes away from the Ramblas, Smither said, and they walked out of the square and up between the rows of plane trees.

The central thoroughfare was already filling up with people from every social class, from gentlemen in straw boaters and top hats to workers in cloth caps and smocks, pushing wheelbarrows. Lawton was struck by the numbers of priests and nuns. There were more of them than he remembered even from Ireland. They seemed to be everywhere, in their soutanes and round black hats and habits of various orders. In Ireland men doffed their caps and women bowed their heads when a priest walked past. Here the clergy and the local population seemed to mingle without even recognizing each other's presence, as if they had made some mutual agreement not to look at each other.

In London there was only one police force and one uniform. Now he saw officers in gray uniforms and leather five-pointed hats, while others looked almost like cavalry officers in their braided uniforms of different colors. Unlike Britain, most of the police were armed, with pistols, sabers, and rifles. They had not gone far when Lawton was astonished to see two men in long coats and derby hats walking toward them with shotguns dangling from their shoulders, who did not look like police at all.

"Who are they?" Lawton asked.

"*Somaten*," replied Smither. "Militiamen. They support the police."

"Do the police need support?"

"They certainly do," said Smither sadly. "This isn't England, Harry. Here they have at least four different police forces and the only one that's any use are the Guardia Civil—the ones with the leather hats. So the Ministry of the Interior and local businessmen pay for the Somaten—just in case."

"In case of what?"

"In case of revolution, old boy. The government is nervous—and it has reason to be. This is a rebellious city in an unstable country."

Lawton remembered what Señor Camacho had told him on the train. "But Spain isn't Russia, is it? They have a parliament, don't they?"

Smither looked scornful. "They do. And political parties. They even have a Liberal and a Conservative party—just like ours. But they aren't like ours. Here the elections are bought by the *caciques*—local chiefs acting on behalf of themselves or their parties. They don't earn votes, they buy them. Both the main parties do it. The Liberals and the Conservatives think they own the country. They take turns in government while pretending to oppose each other. So the Conservative Party is in government now, led by Antonio Maura. But when the next election comes it will be the Liberals' turn to govern, and the political machine will make that happen. The whole system is rotten and no one seems able or willing to change it. Even rich Catalans have had enough of it now and they're turning to separatism. They think Spain's sucking them dry. Barcelona makes the money and Madrid takes the taxes. That's how they see it, and they're not entirely wrong. They want out, and when you see the way this country is run, you can't blame them. But Spain won't let them go."

"A bit like Ireland then," Lawton said with a grin.

"Some people might say that." Smither's disapproving expression made it clear that he was not one of them.

They turned left into a street called the Calle Hospital, and Lawton grimaced at the smell of raw sewage. The people around him were noticeably poorer now. Some of them had the same shrunken look as the inhabitants of East End rookeries, and there were numerous children wandering about like bony little ghosts, some of whom had no shoes and were bow-legged with rickets. Lawton noticed two women leaning against the wall with lipstick and rouged cheeks. One of them was smoking a cigarette, and she blew a stream of smoke at a passing priest, who walked on with an expression of haughty disgust that the two women clearly found hilarious.

Just beyond them, Smither turned into an enormous, ancient-looking building that dominated the narrow street like a fortress wall. Lawton was pleasantly surprised to find a large sunlit patio filled with rows of trees and benches, where sick-looking patients were being tended by nuns. This, Smither informed him, was the medieval Hospital of the Holy Cross, and the home of the Catalan School of Medicine, where the Nobel Prize winner Ramón y Cajal had once worked.

Lawton had never heard the name, and he followed Smither through a maze of corridors with high vaulted arches filled with doctors, nurses, and patients, until they reached the entrance to the mortuary. Smither asked for Dr. Quintana, and a few minutes later a mournful, cadaverous-looking man with a well-trimmed beard came out to see them, wearing a white coat splashed with blood.

"Good morning vice-consul," he said. "What can I do for you?"

Smither introduced Lawton and explained that he had come to identify the body from the Bar la Luna.

"Very good. You have the *permiso*?"

Smither handed him Mrs. Foulkes's letter, and Quintana looked it over briefly and returned it to him. "There are tables in the autopsy room that you can use," he said. "But it's not very private. There's a more secluded table in the medical school. I can have the corpse brought there."

"Fine with me," Lawton said.

"I'll leave you in Dr. Quintana's hands then," said Smither hastily. "I'll be at the consulate."

Lawton followed Quintana through the corridors till they reached two large doors with frosted windows. Quintana ushered him into a small auditorium with a marble autopsy table in the center, surrounded by circular rows of overlooking desks and benches.

"You'll need a smock," he said.

"I'd also like some methylated spirits," said Lawton. "And a sponge and towel."

Quintana nodded. "I'll have them brought to you. I'd like to watch, if you don't mind. I studied briefly under Lacassagne in France, and I'd be very interested to see an English detective at work. If it doesn't disturb you? I'm a great admirer of Scotland Yard."

Like most detectives, Lawton was familiar with Alexandre Lacassagne's work on bloodstain patterns and bullet identification, and even though he had not examined a body in more than three years, a part of him liked the idea of showing off his skills to a student of the French criminologist.

"Fine with me," he said. "But I'm an Irishman not an Englishman. And I hope you're not expecting Sherlock Holmes."

Quintana did not smile, and Lawton sensed that he was not someone who smiled very often. "I'll fetch the body then," he said.

Lawton took off his hat and jacket and rolled up his sleeves as Quintana walked away. Ten minutes later the pathologist returned with two orderlies who were pushing a metal gurney that contained a body covered in a white sheet. The orderlies lifted the stretcher onto the marble slab, and Quintana tapped the corpse on the chest with his fist. It gave off a hard, hollow sound, like a heavy cardboard box.

"Completely frozen!" He handed Lawton a white smock, sponge and bottle. "Ammonia works wonders. I assume you'll need these?" Quintana held out a syringe in one hand and a rectangular glass tray in the other.

"What's that for?" Lawton asked.

"Hombre, his blood type, of course."

"His type?"

Quintana looked at him in surprise. "Don't you use Dr. Landsteiner's categorizations in England?"

Lawton had no idea what Quintana was referring to. During his detective training he had learned that it was possible to determine whether blood traces were animal or human, and he had once had this test successfully carried out in a murder case some years ago. He had also found Lacassagne's work on blood splashes useful in determining the relative positions of a murder victim and the murderer in at least one investigation, but he had no idea who Dr. Landsteiner was, or what blood types Quintana was referring to. Whatever they were, they did not seem relevant to what he was about to do.

"We don't," he said. "We have . . . other methods."

The pathologist shrugged and sat down at one of the benches. He leaned forward and watched with interest, while the orderlies stood impassively beside him, and Lawton could not help feeling slightly self-conscious as he pulled back the sheet and looked down on the earthly remains of the man he had come so far to identify.

As a soldier and a policeman Lawton had seen many corpses, and the charred body lying on the autopsy table looked far more like a wartime casualty than any corpse he had ever encountered in peacetime. The face and the nose were almost completely black, much of the outer layer of flesh was missing, and the lips were no longer distinguishable from the horrid hole of a mouth through which a torn shred of tongue protruded from between its few remaining teeth. There was only one blue eye remaining in its right socket, the top of the skull had been shorn off, and tumescent traces of brain were visible through the tufts of stiff blackened hair that still remained like burned wheat stubble.

The rest of the body was similarly blackened and scorched. The explosion had sheared its left arm off at the shoulder. Its right leg was unattached to the thigh, from which a small stick of bone jutted out, and its groin and most of its backside were missing. Its right hand appeared to be intact, though blackened, and the left was missing three fingers, which now lay in a row where they should have been. The left foot had been blown off, though some of its pieces were lying neatly in an approximation of their correct position, as though the hospital staff had been trying to reassemble a jigsaw.

Lawton had seen men literally blown to pieces beside him in South Africa, and he was relieved to see that the first two toes of the corpse's right foot were missing, exactly as Mrs. Foulkes had said they would be. He was conscious that Quintana was following every movement as he opened the satchel and laid the tools he had brought with him next to the methylated spirits and sponge: first the magnifying glass and printers ink, the little roller and metal tray; then the writing pad, the tape measure and fingerprint copies, and finally the photographs of Foulkes that Pickering had given him. He was pleased to find that he had not forgotten the standard procedures, as he matched the descriptions and close-up pictures from Foulkes's Bertillonage "speaking portrait" to the body in front of him. He measured the skull first, both width and height; the length of the remaining arm from the fingertips to the neck; height, trunk width, and foot size.

Apart from some minor shrinkage, the measurements coincided exactly with the figures next to Foulkes's photographs, and he ticked them off one by one. The right hand was too burned to take prints, but the left was in better condition, particularly the three detached fingers. He cleaned them one by one and left them to dry while he poured a drop of ink into the tray and rolled it out. He held up the corpse's left hand and rolled the thumb into the tray before pressing it against the paper pad. He repeated the procedure with the forefinger and the remaining three fingers, and then leaned over the prints with the magnifying glass.

Quintana stood up now to get a closer look as he counted the numbers of arches, whorls, and loops and compared them to the prints Pickering had given him. In each case, Lawton explained to the pathologist, they were identical, from the number of whorls to the twinned loop on the little finger to the small scar on the thumb, and even though it was impossible to do the full count that the Henry System demanded, he had no doubt that the prints he had brought with him were the same as the ones on the corpse. He handed Quintana the magnifying glass and pointed out some of the similarities.

"Interesting," Quintana said. "Our police have only just begun to adopt Bertillonage, and in Madrid they are beginning to use fingerprinting, but the courts still don't accept them as evidence."

"Ours do," Lawton said.

For the first time in two years, he realized that he had spoken as if he were still a detective, but he was so pleased to discover that his knowledge and skills remained intact that it did not feel like a pretense.

"I can tell you," he said, "without any doubt. This is the body of Randolph William Foulkes."

"Bravo!" To his amazement Quintana clapped, and the two orderlies clapped too.

Lawton resisted the temptation to bow. In spite of himself he could not help feeling a certain pride, and now that he had successfully confirmed Foulkes's identity, he was ready to go and look for Mrs. Foulkes's trollop.

From the terrace of his in-laws' house, Bernat Mata watched his children chase the cat across the garden down below, and looked at the familiar view. Beyond the lawn and the flowerbeds, the pink roofs and white mansions protruded up through the trees all the way down through Sant Gervasi and Gràcia, and in the far distance he could see the point where the harbor merged with the dark blue sea. He had eaten well, as he always did at his mother-in-law's house, and now the trickle of running water and the humming of bees from the nearby roses lulled him into a postprandial torpor. He had just closed his eyes when he thought of Pau Tosets, lying in a heap of rubbish in an alleyway just behind the Nou de la Rambla.

It was three days since Bravo Portillo had summoned him to the Raval, and still the image of the bloodless naked body, lying in a heap of rubbish with flies buzzing around its bites and wounds, continued to sit in his mind like a trapped bone that he could not swallow. It was not only because the evidence of such violence was so shocking, disturbing, and inexplicable. Had Esperanza Claramunt not told him about Tosets's disappearance, he would have accepted Bravo Portillo's explanation that the murder was the work of a madman, because only a lunatic could have inflicted such cruelty on another human being.

Had he not already seen similar wounds on the body at the swimming club, he might have believed the Social Brigade when it said that Hermenigildo Cortéz was the perpetrator of the Bar la Luna bombing. But now that he had seen these things, he could not forget them, and he could not accept the fairy stories that were being told about them. Because if the Claramunt girl was correct, and the anarchist Tosets had indeed been snatched from the street by members of the Brigada, then it was even less likely that he had been murdered by a madman. The two murders had already attracted a great deal of morbid attention in the Barcelona newspapers and also in the national press. Much of this was fanned by the usual lurid artist's impressions of the supposed "Raval Monster" who looked variously like a vampire, an ape, or a wolflike man with claws and hair. The Catholic papers were blaming the murders on the anarchists, but the republican newspaper *El Diluvio* had published a cartoon showing a blood-drinking monster wearing a priest's robe and collar, abetted by a coven of nuns who looked like witches.

To its credit, *La Veu* had resisted such nonsense, but Rovira had refused to publish Esperanza Claramunt's declarations without further verification for fear of offending the military censors. Mata had persuaded Claramunt to accompany him to the Atarazanas district station, where she had told Bravo Portillo what she had seen. Bravo Portillo was unimpressed. It was possible, he conceded, that she had witnessed the kidnapping of Tosets by the man—or men—who had killed him, since even madmen did not always work alone, but he dismissed any suggestion that agents of the state were responsible for these events.

It was bad enough, he said, that the Radical Republican Party should now be accusing priests and nuns of these atrocious murders without any foundation, but anarchists were clearly no more to be trusted, especially when it came to the political police. It was obvious from the strange and barbarous nature of these murders, Bravo Portillo went on, that the two anarchists had been killed by a madman who hated anarchists. It was even possible that they were carried out *by* an anarchist, he said. Mata knew that Bravo Portillo hated anarchists, as most policemen did, but none of these explanations made any sense. He told himself that it was no longer any of his business, and yet even now he winced at the thought of Esperanza Claramunt's accusing, I-told-you-so expression when they left the station and he told her that he was not going to take it any further. He knew that he had confirmed his bourgeois inauthenticity and lack of integrity that she already suspected, and he felt offended by her condemnation. It was all very well for these young anarchists to pass judgment on everybody else—he had once done much the same when he was younger. But he was a married man now with children and responsibilities, and he had learned that not everything was black-and-white. Still he could not shake off a vague feeling of discomfort and unease as he stared down at his native city. He was still trying to suppress it when his father-in-law came out onto the terrace.

"You've heard the rumors?" the old man asked.

Mata suppressed a sigh and inwardly braced himself. Over the years he had learned to put up with Vicente del Bosch's bitter anti-Catalanism, his nostalgic reminiscences of the Cuban war and his tirades against the politicians who had betrayed the army and thrown away the empire. Such diplomacy was not just a concession to his wife; it was also necessary for his own good. It was Bosch's money that paid for his apartment in the Eixample, for the holidays in Puigcerdà, for the publication of his literary and artistic journal and his occasional books of poetry, and various other pleasures that were beyond the reach of an ordinary journalist. His father-in-law rarely let these fortnightly visits pass without taking the opportunity to remind him of his dependency, or provoke him politically.

"What rumors are those?" Mata asked warily.

"That we might be going to war."

Mata was not unaware of this possibility. It was little more than a year since the papers had hailed General Marina's less-than-heroic advance beyond Melilla into the Rif mountains as the beginning of a new African empire. The government claimed that Spain was only protecting the iron and lead mines that it had bought from the Rif tribesmen who were fighting the Moroccan sultan. But you did not need to be an anarchist to know that the escalation in military operations had more to do with the army's desire to do something great to make up for Cuba and the Philippines. Now the mining concessions at Monte Uixar and Monte Afra were being raided almost daily by Berber tribesmen, and the Spanish army was already bogged down in trying to protect its possessions.

All this was only to be expected, but these less-than-sterling achievements had done nothing to diminish the appetite for war in certain circles. On the contrary even Rovira—a staunch Catalanista and a fellow member of the Lliga—argued that Spain needed to acquire new colonies to compensate for the ones it had lost only a decade before. Even Belgium owned half of Africa now, Rovira said—the ultimate insult. The reactionary Spanish papers went even further. If Spain could not establish a permanent presence in Morocco, they argued, then France and Germany would swallow the country whole, and perfidious Albion was also lurking in the background as usual to see what it could bite off.

"The Ministry of War is considering levying new troops," Bosch went on. "And it may have to call on the Catalan reserves. Let's hope the Catalan press supports the army this time, eh?"

Mata knew he was referring to the ¡Cu-Cut! episode. His father-in-law had naturally taken the side of the army mob and regarded the offending cartoon as an insult to the honor of the armed forces. This was only to be expected from a retired general who looked as though he were on horseback even when sitting in a chair in baggy white trousers, espadrilles, and white shirt.

"It might be difficult to persuade anyone to support an adventure in Africa," he replied. "Not only the Catalans."

"Well you're the writer. Write a poem."

Mata was not sure whether this was intended as a taunt or an exhortation, but he had no intention of doing any such thing. Unlike his father-in-law, he worked in downtown Barcelona and he knew that its population was in no mood to fight another war. The anarchist papers were threatening to strike, and now the Radicals were attempting to compete with them, and warning that any attempts to call up the reserves would meet with resistance on the streets. There was no chance to explain any of this, and Mata knew that there was no point, as the old man launched into a familiar tirade about the regenerative qualities of war. Mata listened patiently to the tedious arguments that he had heard so often from his father-in-law and from the conservative papers: that a nation without colonies could never rejoin the great powers; that the country of Isabella and Ferdinand must show that it could honor its treaty obligations agreed with Britain and France and maintain order in Morocco; that a nation that was unable or unwilling to wage war was a nation that had lost its manhood and virility.

Had it not been his father-in-law, Mata might have replied that a country with Spain's record would do better not to fight another war that it could not win, and that a few Rif tribesmen were not the most challenging test of national mettle. Fortunately there was no need to say anything, as Sylvia and his mother-in-law came back onto the terrace with the maid, who was carrying a tray of coffee. With the arrival of the women the conversation turned from politics to Puigcerdà, where Sylvia, the children, and his in-laws were due to depart at the end of July. Mata managed to get through the rest of the afternoon without any further provocations from his father-in-law, and afterward he and Sylvia walked down the road to catch the funicular railway at Vallvidrera Superior.

Sylvia had arranged for the children to stay with their grandparents for two days, and as they sat down on the train, she moved closer to him and let her hand brush playfully across his thigh. Mata felt aroused and also anxious as the train crawled slowly down the hill. Because even though he loved his wife and took pride in the fact that a woman ten years younger had wanted to marry him, there were times when Sylvia was more passionate than he felt able to be, and he worried that she might look elsewhere.

These thoughts soon faded as she playfully sat on his lap and kissed him while they rode the taxi home from the Peu del Funicular, the way they used to during their courtship. As soon as they got home she took his hand and led him to the bedroom, and he untied her hair and unbuttoned her dress before slipping into bed in the dark so that she could not see his paunch. They made love slowly and luxuriantly in the cool dark room, and afterward she laid her head on his chest and he ran his fingers through her lustrous hair and told himself that he was luckier than any man had a right to be.

"You know that policeman you went to see last week," she said suddenly. "The one in Montjuïc?"

"Ugarte?"

"Yes."

"He's moving to a new apartment in the Calle Bailén."

"You're well-informed."

"Mother mentioned it. She knows his wife through the Catholic Women's Association. They're moving next week. One hundred square metres."

Mata got up to make himself some coffee, while his wife turned over to sleep. As he waited for the water to boil he went out into the gallery and stood in the shadows, looking over the interior courtyard, watching his neighbors come and go. Once again he thought of Esperanza Claramunt's accusatory expression. He knew the real reason why it bothered him: there were simply too many details about the murder of Pau Tosets and the Luna Bar terrorist that made no sense. How had Tosets's kidnappers known when and where to find him? How could a lowly police officer afford a one-hundred-square-meter apartment in the Calle Bailén? Why had the Social Brigade taken over the investigation of the body at the swimming club?

These were questions that Bravo Portillo should have been asking, and if he was not going to ask them, Mata realized gloomily that he might have to ask them himself.

"Hello Ignasi."

Ignasi looked up at the stranger standing over him in a white suit and fedora hat who seemed to know his name. He was sitting in his usual spot near the Hotel Oriente, with his wooden toy ship on wheels and the cardboard sign begging alms for the love of God. At first he was not sure whether the stranger was talking to him, as he stared up at the black moustache, the silver-handled cane, but then he saw the bag of sugarcoated jellies in his hand, and he took one and gobbled it down.

"Would you like an ice cream?" the stranger asked.

"Cram," Ignasi repeated.

"Ice cream, that's right." The stranger smiled indulgently. "Come with me. I'll buy you one."

Ignasi scrunched his face up now, because even though he really did want to eat ice cream, he knew that he was not supposed to leave his spot until his mother or one of his brothers and sisters came to fetch him.

"Don't worry," the stranger said soothingly. "You can bring your money with you. We'll give it to your mother when we come back."

Ignasi had not eaten since breakfast and he looked up at the stranger in the dazzling white suit and hat who knew his mother. He obediently gathered up his tin of coins, his cardboard sign and his ship, and hobbled down toward the port alongside his new friend. A few minutes later the two of them were walking alongside the port, and he was holding a cone with a scoop of chocolate ice cream, while the stranger held his ship for him.

"Shall we walk?" the stranger suggested.

Ignasi nuzzled the ice cream as they walked toward the customs house, past the sails, cranes, and ropes and the giant ship beyond the entrance to the harbor, with its guns and funnels. Soon the ice cream began to drip onto his trousers and wooden clogs.

"You need new clothes," the stranger said. "Do you know I have another suit, just like this one?"

Ignasi looked at the stranger's suit. It was as white as the Virgin of Mercy's skirts or the snow-topped mountains in the postcards and magazines along the Ramblas. He tried to imagine himself wearing a suit just like it, and smiled at the thought of his mother's face when she came to pick him up.

"Suit," he said.

"That's right," the stranger said. "You can have it. Come and try it on. It's in my palace. Have you ever been to a palace?"

Ignasi shook his head. He did not know what a palace was and he had never been away from the Ramblas without his mother or a member of his family. Somewhere in the distance he thought he heard a voice telling him to go back there, but it was so faint that he could hardly hear it or recognize whose voice it was. His new friend was still smiling at him expectantly, and now Ignasi was smiling too as he walked away to continue what was already turning out to be the very best day he had ever known in his life.

8

On leaving the medical school Lawton walked to the post office and sent a telegram to Mrs. Foulkes announcing that he had confirmed the identity of her husband. Afterward he ate lunch in a café on the Ramblas and withdrew to his hotel to look through the suitcase and the sealed bag the vice-consul had given him. Foulkes's case contained nothing that he would not expect to find among the possessions of a gentleman summering abroad. There was a three-piece evening suit, a starched high-collared shirt and black bow-tie, brown polished brogues, and a pair of opera glasses. Lawton also found socks, underwear, and pyjamas, a washbag, American Express traveler's checks, a large wallet filled with pesetas and francs, and a well-thumbed copy of *The Decline and Fall of the Roman Empire*. The sealed bag contained the remnants of the clothes Foulkes had been wearing on the day of his death, in addition to a smaller partly burned wallet and the charred Baedeker.

In his two years peering through the bedrooms of adulterers and bigamists, Lawton had learned to look for evidence of marital transgressions in everyday objects, and he carefully inspected each article of clothing and each object with a magnifying glass. There were no hairs, stains, lipstick traces, or aromas that might have indicated female company. In the early evening he went out to eat. He did not want to go far or stay out for long, and he found a table in the terrace at the Café Suizo, just on the corner of the Plaza Reial. Despite the grim tasks he had performed that day, he could not help feeling pleased with what he had achieved, as he watched the people walking up and down the Ramblas and ate another meal at Mrs. Foulkes's expense without having to worry how much he was spending.

Now that he felt like a detective again, he realized how much he had missed being one. He knew that the search for Foulkes's female companion was likely to be more complicated in a foreign country than it would have been in London, but even in Barcelona there were standard procedures that every detective was obliged to follow, and he looked forward to working his way through them the next morning. That night the square was quieter than it had been the previous day, but the image of Foulkes's blackened corpse continued to flit through his mind for some time before he finally fell asleep. At some point in the night he dreamed that a great bird had flown into the square. In his dream he heard the flutter of wings outside the half-open shutters, and then he looked up and saw a dark shadow in the window.

It was not until the figure came closer that he saw the dark-haired woman standing by the bed, looking down at him with a smile. She was completely naked and her gleaming wet hair smelled of seaweed and covered much of her face as she straddled him and pressed her hands against his chest. He made no attempt to resist her or question her presence, as her hair tickled his face and he felt the soft weight of her breasts against his chest. For a moment he thought she was going to kiss him, then he felt the sharp points of her teeth in his neck and her legs turned to coils that slithered underneath and around him.

It was only then, as his ribs began to crack and he felt his blood draining out of him, that he knew he had fallen into the fatal embrace of the peuchen. He tried to get out from under her, but he had no strength and no voice and he knew that his lifeblood was draining out of him. The dream was still fresh in his mind when he woke up the next morning. As he got dressed, he wondered why the strange and ridiculous superstitions that had once frightened him as a child should still find their way into his adult dreams.

Now, with the window open and daylight streaming into the room, the absurdity of these fantasies seemed obvious. Yet all he had to do was fall asleep and the old monsters from his childhood invaded his dreams. Perhaps it was the stories that adults told that kept them there. The peuchen was not that different from the vampire-women in *Dracula*, after all. And yet it seemed to him that some part of his mind had never changed at all, and that all the creatures that had once tormented him were still waiting somewhere beneath the surface. Perhaps someone cleverer than he understood why the mind behaved like that, but he had no explanation for these unwanted intrusions, any more than he understood why his memory continued to retain so many other things that it was more sensible to forget.

He put these thoughts behind him and went down to the square to eat breakfast. Afterward he asked Señor Martínez where he could find the Bank of Sabadell, and the receptionist directed him to an office on the Ramblas. Lawton walked around the corner and asked to speak to the branch manager. Shortly afterward a dour, neat little man came out from behind the counter and introduced himself as Señor Tressols. He ushered Lawton into his office, where Lawton explained that he was carrying out an investigation into a payment for £500 that had been withdrawn on the 18th of June. The manager listened politely as Lawton showed him a photograph of Foulkes and handed him the letter from Mrs. Foulkes asking for his cooperation.

"What kind of cooperation?" Tressols asked.

"Mrs. Foulkes would like to know the identity and the address of her husband's payee—a Marie Babineaux."

"May I ask why Mrs. Foulkes is making this request?"

"Mrs. Foulkes is not familiar with the payee," Lawton explained. "She's concerned that this payment may have been the result of deception."

"And why doesn't Dr. Foulkes make the inquiry himself?"

"Dr. Foulkes was killed in a terrorist bomb last month, right here in your city."

"At the Bar la Luna?" Señor Tressols looked genuinely pained. "Well, I'm very sorry to hear that, Mr. Lawton. But we don't reveal details about our clients. If Mrs. Foulkes has these concerns, she should refer them to the police—not to a private investigator."

"My employer doesn't want the police involved at this stage," Lawton persisted. "She hopes that the matter can be resolved by some discreet inquiries. If I could speak to your client, it would be easy to clear up the matter. I assume she must have an account here—to transfer such a large sum."

"As I've said, we aren't at liberty to reveal the details of our clients. Not without a formal request from the police."

"Mrs. Foulkes is willing to pay whatever fee may be required," Lawton said.

Tressols's sympathetic expression abruptly disappeared, and he looked embarrassed and faintly indignant now. "I'm not sure what you've heard about our Spanish bank practices, Señor Lawton, but here in Catalonia I can tell you there is no fee to pay, and you cannot have those details."

"Well could I at least see the check—to make sure the signature is genuine?"

"The check has gone to central office. But I can assure you it is genuine."

"What makes you so certain?"

The ghost of a smile flitted briefly across the bank manager's dour countenance. "Because Dr. Foulkes was with our client when she handed it in."

"Well may I ask what this client looked like?"

"No you may not."

Lesseps stood up to indicate that the conversation was over. The day had not begun well, Lawton thought. He had intended to go straight to Foulkes's hotel. On reaching the top of the Ramblas however, he was surprised to find that the Bar la Luna had reopened, and he took a seat at one of the outside tables. A chubby little waiter in a bow tie and white apron came over toward him, and he ordered a coffee.

"I'm surprised to find you open," he said. "After what happened last month."

The waiter shook his head sadly. "A terrible incident, Señor. Had I not gone inside to take an order I would not be here today. There are those who say we shouldn't have reopened so quickly. But a man must eat. And Barcelona does not surrender to terrorism."

"Good for you," Lawton said. "I understand a foreign gentleman was killed that day. Do you know where was he sitting?"

"Right over there!" The waiter pointed at an empty table just behind him. "And the spawn of the devil who killed him was sitting in the table next to him!"

"Was the señor sitting by himself?" Lawton asked.

The little waiter shook his head. "There was a woman with him. A very lucky woman—she left just before the bomb went off. I thought she must be his daughter—or something else. But she acted more like his mother."

"In what way?"

"He didn't speak. She did. When I asked the gentleman what he wanted, she was the one who replied. And she paid the bill, too."

"Maybe he didn't speak Spanish?"

"But he didn't speak at all. He just sat there reading his book. I thought if I was in his position I would be looking at the woman not the book. The señorita spoke Spanish. Not as good as yours. Her accent was stronger."

"Did you recognize it?"

The waiter looked blank. "No idea."

"What did she look like?"

"Very pretty. Blond hair. She was wearing a green dress and matching hat with flowers in it. And one of those little lace veils that French women like—the ones that come down just over their eyes. You're not from the international press, are you?"

"I'm a friend of the deceased."

"My condolences, Señor. And I hope that when you return to your country you will let people know there is more to Barcelona than bombs and madmen."

"Madmen?" Lawton stared back at the waiter and remembered his peculiar dream.

"The Raval Monster." The waiter crossed himself. "A murderer who drinks the blood of his victims. You haven't heard of him?"

Lawton shook his head, and he listened with some surprise as the waiter told him that a young man had been found murdered in the Raval and drained of every drop of blood. "What is the Raval?" he asked.

"Down there." The waiter nodded gloomily toward the port. "The lower part of the Ramblas. I would stay away from there if I were you, Señor. These are the *bajos fondos*—the lower depths. Not a place for tourists even in the best of times. But now . . ."

Lawton lit a cigarette as the waiter went to fetch his order. It was certainly a coincidence that the waiter should tell him about this vampire-murderer only the morning after he had dreamed about the peuchen, but it was not something worth dwelling on. He was more interested in why Randolph Foulkes had allowed a woman to pay for him when he had his wallet in his pocket. Even at a time when women were becoming more confident and forceful by the day, that was not how a gentleman was supposed to behave, or indeed any man. At first sight, the question of what Foulkes might have been doing with a woman less than half his age was not difficult to answer. But if Foulkes had come to Barcelona for an assignation then he did not appear to have been in a romantic or chivalrous mood that morning. Perhaps they had had an argument, or perhaps he was bored.

It was also possible that their relationship was an entirely business transaction. But men who paid for prostitutes did not usually parade them in public, even in foreign cities where they were not likely to be recognized. Was this companion the same woman who had cashed Foulkes's check? And why had she left him alone just before he was killed? Was she merely lucky, as the waiter suggested, or was something more than luck involved? Lawton smoked a cigarette and pondered these questions before setting off across the Plaza Catalunya toward Foulkes's hotel. From the grand façade it was obvious that the Hotel de Inglaterra catered to a better class of visitor than Señor Martínez's establishment, and the décor and the well-heeled clientele drifting through the lobby confirmed this impression. Lawton had already decided to take a different approach to the one he had used at the bank, and he told the receptionist he had been sent by Scotland Yard in London to investigate the disappearance of one of the hotel's guests.

"I assume you're referring to Señor Foulkes," the receptionist said. "A tragic and most unfortunate incident."

Once again Lawton was struck by the extent to which Foulkes's death was already more public than his widow wanted it to be, and he asked how long Foulkes had stayed at the hotel. The receptionist looked back through the register and found Foulkes's signature, which Lawton compared with the letter he had brought with him. The two were identical, and the date of his arrival was June 7, seven days before his death.

"Did he have visitors?" Lawton asked. "Female visitors?"

The receptionist looked aghast. "Señor, this is not that kind of establishment."

"Of course not," Lawton said. "I meant friends or relatives. Did anyone come here to meet him or take him anywhere?"

The receptionist shook his head. Apart from breakfast, Foulkes spent most of his time away from the hotel or in his room, he said, but he had had no visitors.

"I wonder if I could see his room?" Lawton asked.

"I'm afraid that's not possible, sir. The room is occupied. It has been ever since Señor Foulkes's things were removed. And there's nothing to see. Our cleaners are very thorough."

"I'll only be a minute." He looked pleadingly at the receptionist. "I have come rather a long way."

"I'm sorry, Señor. It's out of the question."

Lawton had encountered similar objections in far less salubrious establishments, and he had usually found a way around them. He thanked the receptionist and walked slowly away as a guest approached the counter in his stead. Lawton glanced over his shoulder as the receptionist reached for a key, and then he turned into the staircase. He went quickly up the stairs to the third floor and knocked on the room he had seen in the register. A moment later a middle-aged Spaniard with his tie half-undone appeared and looked at him suspiciously.

"Sorry to bother you sir," Lawton said. "But my wife and I were the last guests in your room. My wife has lost her wedding ring and she thinks she may have left it here. Do you mind if I have a quick look inside?"

The Spaniard was just about to reply when a female voice called, "What is it?" and a sweet-faced little woman in a long blue summer dress appeared behind him. The Spaniard repeated Lawton's request.

"Of course you can look," she said. "Your poor wife. She must be distraught."

"She is," Lawton murmured, as he came into the room. The Spaniard and his wife stood watching hopefully as he looked around the room, behind and under the furniture. It was soon obvious that the cleaners had indeed done their job well. Even under the bed the tiled floor looked spotless. He was beginning to think he had wasted his time when he noticed a little sliver of white paper beneath the dressing table. He bent down and pulled it out to reveal a torn ticket stub bearing the words: Wolfgang Amadeus Mozart. *The Magic Flute*. Gran Teatre del Liceu. He could not help smiling as he read the seat and row numbers, and the date June 13, the day before Foulkes's death, and put the ticket in his pocket.

"Do you know where the Gran Liceu is?" he asked.

"Of course. It's on the Ramblas." The Spaniard was looking at him with disapproval and suspicion now.

"And your ring?" His wife's stony expression made it clear that she no longer believed him either. Lawton smiled sheepishly and thanked them for their cooperation, and as he went back out in search of the theater where Randolph Foulkes had spent his last night on earth, he could not help feeling that the day was looking a little more promising.

At ten o'clock the funeral cortege accompanying the body of Pau Tosets came alongside the Montjuïc fortress. Esperanza had not been there since the day of her father's funeral. At that time she had not understood the political significance of the fortress, or the role it had played in her father's death, because her mother had not yet told her how he had died. Since then her family always avoided the fortress when they came to visit her father's grave on All Saints' Day, taking the longer way around to the necropolis from the sea. Now she walked alongside Flor Montero and Pau's mother Rosa, just behind the cart that carried Pau's coffin and his grandparents, and she remembered the black-clad mourners and the two black horses that pulled her father's coffin past the fortress, and the golden cross protruding from his curtained carriage.

Most of Pau's family and comrades had no black to change into, and the family had only been able to borrow a humble cart from the market, and they had rented two mules instead of horses. They had nevertheless draped the cart in black cloth and accompanied it with an impressive display of flowers that Ruben had collected money to pay for. As they passed the fortress Ruben raised a clenched fist, and Esperanza did the same. Flor was holding one of her children by the hand and carrying another wrapped in a shawl across her shoulder, and she also raised her fist, along with Arnau Busquets, the Ferrers, and her mother, who Esperanza had met for the first time that morning.

Esperanza knew of Rosa Tosets by reputation. According to Pau his mother had once been taken as a child to see Bakunin's Italian emissary Fanelli, when he had first brought the Idea to Barcelona in 1868. Fanelli's speech—delivered in Italian, which most of his listeners could not understand—had converted Pau's grandparents into anarchists. His mother had also gleaned something from Fanelli, and had grown up to be a tireless and fervent proponent of the Idea. In textile factories where she worked she had led women and even men out on strikes and walkouts. She visited anarchist prisoners in the Modelo prison. She distributed pamphlets and the *Soli*. She gave speeches, protested, and persuaded. Her husband had been shot in the castle during the repression of 1897. Now she had lost a son, and Esperanza felt a kind of kinship with her as the cortege descended the hill into the necropolis, moving slowly past the sculptures of griffins, skeletons, reptiles, and hooded angels that adorned the tombs and mausoleums of the wealthy.

Esperanza knew them all well, and as they passed the statue of the half-naked angel with wings and exposed breasts and her arms stretched across one of the tombs she remembered the unbearable piercing grief that she had felt on the day of her father's funeral, as though her heart had broken into little pieces that could never be put back. Now she felt strangely numb as the cortege made its way through the monuments and mausoleums to the walls where the poor were buried. Soon they reached Pau's niche, and Ruben and the other pallbearers lifted the coffin from the cart and slid it into the wall. Esperanza stood next to Flor and her mother listening to the speeches and eulogies, while the cemetery workers looked on. At her father's burial a priest had quoted from the Bible, even though her father was not religious. Pau's eulogists praised his passion for justice and his devotion to the Idea. Arnau Busquets quoted Kropotkin and hailed Pau as one of those "Men of courage, not satisfied with words . . . for whom prison, exile, and death are preferable to a life contrary to their principles."

Ferrer praised the man he had known as a writer and a dedicated revolutionist, and Ruben also made a short but emotional speech, in which he declared his love and admiration for his friend, comrade, and brother-in-law. Esperanza remembered what Pau had said to her about Ruben on the day he died, and it was clear that his death had already changed Ruben beyond recognition—or perhaps she had simply not seen what Pau had seen. It was not until the mourners began to sing "Sons of the People" that Esperanza's numbness melted and she cried hot tears at the thought of the man she had not had the chance to love as she sang: "*Son of the people/ chains oppress you/and that injustice cannot continue.*"

Afterward Señora Tosets put her arm around her and squeezed her tight as they watched the cemetery workers close the niche, leaving only Pau's name scratched into it with the date of his birth and the day of his disappearance. The mourners began to disperse now and Pau's mother invited Esperanza to ride back on the cart with the family. Arnau Busquets also rode with them. He sat directly opposite Esperanza, next to Señora Tosets, with his cap pulled down to shield his eyes from the sun. At one point he looked at Esperanza with a pained, sympathetic expression. Arnau often looked pained, and Esperanza was not sure whether this was due to his years in prison or the Cuban war, where he had contracted the malaria that still gave his lined face a slightly jaundiced pallor, or the burn marks on his chest and back that he had suffered during an accident at the foundry.

No one spoke as they passed the fortress and descended the hill into Poble Sec. As they rode back along the Parallelo, Esperanza remembered the Sunday afternoon when she and Pau had walked together past the cafés, theaters, and music halls, and paused to look at the shell gamers and card sharps, the fire-eaters, the fortune-telling birds, magicians, and acrobats.

Even then Pau had been unable to resist heckling one of Lerroux's speakers, until they had been forced to get away quickly to avoid a fight with some of his supporters. All this was little more than a month ago, and now Pau was gone forever, and it seemed both astonishing and intolerable that the city should go about its business as though nothing had happened. Arnau looked equally angry as he glared around at the busy avenue as if he wanted to shoot a passerby.

"We have to respond to this," he burst out suddenly. "They can't just kill us and get away with it."

"Respond how?" asked Ruben.

"You've heard Maura's planning to call up the Catalan reserves to fight in the Rif?" Arnau replied.

"He wouldn't be so stupid," said Señora Tosets.

"Well the newspapers think he is. And if he does the movement needs to oppose it—with a strike. That's what Pau would have wanted. That's how we avenge him."

Señora Tosets nodded. "You're right. It's the best way. The only way."

Arnau looked at Esperanza. "There's a meeting on Tuesday at the *Soli*—to discuss what to do if war breaks out. Can you come?"

"Of course."

"Good girl."

Señora Tosets, Flor, and Ruben looked at her approvingly, and Esperanza was pleased to think that they thought of her as one of them now, and she sensed that Pau would have approved of her, too. On reaching the Boqueria market she took the tram to Gràcia, and returned to her flat to find her mother with a pupil, sitting at the piano and playing Strauss's *Mein herz ist stumm*. The pupil was not singing it particularly well, but the melody immediately brought Esperanza's tears welling up again. She took off her hat and withdrew to her room to find Eduardo sitting on his bed drawing on a sketchpad pictures of flying machines that he had copied from an artist's illustration in a French journal. Already the wall was covered in them, and she knew that he would continue to draw them until his mind focused on something else.

She smiled at him and lay down on the bed to rest. She was still lying there when the lesson came to an end and her mother appeared in the doorway and looked at her with concern. Her mother was only fifty-two, but her graying hair and lined, careworn face made her look older.

"Señor Mata came around while you were out," she said. "I asked him to leave a message but he said you would know why. I told him you wouldn't want to see anyone today."

"Well of course I'll see him." Esperanza jumped up from the bed and reached for her hat.

"Is this about Pau?" her mother looked suddenly anxious. "There's nothing you can do. It's in the hands of the police now."

"That's supposed to reassure me?"

"So you just walk in and walk out?"

"If it's to do with Pau, yes."

"Go on then." Her mother sighed wearily. "Do what you want. You always do."

"Mama, please." Esperanza's voice was softer now. "The police have no interest in finding out what happened to Pau. If Mata wants to see me there must be a reason."

Her mother remained unmoved, and Esperanza knew there was nothing she could say to bring her around. She knew her mother was worried about her, but she also resented her attempts to make her feel guilty and she had no intention of succumbing. She went back out into the street again and walked quickly down into the Eixample till she reached Mata's house, where the concierge let her in. Mata's apartment was on the second floor, and she knocked loudly and waited. A moment later the door opened and Mata's great bearded body filled the doorway. He was wearing white trousers, espadrilles, and a loose white shirt that hung down over his protruding belly, and it struck her for the first time that he looked like Bakunin.

"Miss Claramunt," he said. "I owe you an apology."

"For what?"

"You were right. I don't believe that a lunatic killed Pau Tosets, and I want to help you find out who did."

9

On the morning of his third day in Barcelona, Lawton was sitting in the Plaza Reial when he heard the sound of drums coming from the direction of the Ramblas. Even from a distance the drums had an unmistakably martial beat, and as they came closer he heard the horns and trumpets accompanying them and he remembered the band that he had seen marching through Southwold in the summer of 1898 summoning the population to fight for the Queen, the Country, and the Empire. He had come into the town from the fair that day to look at the sea before his fights that afternoon when the recruiters and the musicians came marching along the sea front. They looked grand and smart in their starched new uniforms, and the main street was lined with holidaymakers and local people who had come to watch the soldiers march past on their way to fight the Boers.

The soldiers looked unbeatable, and that day he had felt unbeatable, too. He fought four times and won them all, and the next morning he went in search of the recruiting office and volunteered. Now he walked onto the Ramblas and watched the column of soldiers marching four abreast down the center of the promenade toward the port. Some were dressed in khaki and narrow forage caps, others wore striped gray uniforms and kepis with white covers over their necks, and gaiters over their unpolished boots. Despite the best efforts of their officers, they marched badly, with a noticeable absence of pride and zest. Some were armed with Remingtons and Mausers, but most of them had no weapons except for the bayonets in their belts. Others carried only wooden rifles.

Most of them looked as if they were being sent to their own execution, and the women and children who accompanied them looked equally gloomy. It was as unimpressive a demonstration of military might as he had ever seen, and unlike Southwold the spectators looked distinctly unmoved.

"Where are they going?" Lawton asked an old man who was standing nearby.

"To Melilla!" The old man exclaimed furiously. "To fight the Moors!"

"Why?"

"Why?" The old man threw up his hands as if he were trying to shake off something unclean. "Because the *ricos* think the Moors are going to take their mines! So of course they send the poor to fight for them! You see these sad soldiers? For some of them it's the only way to get a proper meal, Señor—if the Moors don't slit their throats or cut their balls off! But you know what I think?" The old man's eyes narrowed and he stuck his jaw out belligerently as if Lawton was personally responsible for all this. "I think the government can go to hell!"

Lawton did not know where Melilla was, and the old man seemed a little overheated and possibly unhinged. But as he walked on past the stream of soldiers toward the consulate, the sullen expressions on the faces of so many of the spectators made it clear that they were equally unenthused by the expedition. It was a very different crowd from the crowds that had once cheered his regiment onto their troopships.

Smither's secretary Catalina took him to the vice-consul's office, where he found Smither standing at the window, looking down at the soldiers. He looked as polished as his shoes and his glistening hair looked as though it were glued to his head.

"Good morning," he said. "You've seen this? President Maura is sending the reservists to Morocco."

"So I've heard. And people don't look very happy about it." Lawton sat down and lit a cigarette as Smither dispatched Catalina to make some tea.

"They aren't. The separatists don't want to fight another Spanish war. The anarchists and the unions are asking why the poor should fight when the rich can buy their way out of military service. The Radicals are saying that the Church is behind the call-up. They say the Jesuits own shares in mining concerns in the Rif. All these groups usually hate each other, but now Maura has finally given them something they can all agree on. Even the socialists are talking about a general strike now. Anyway, what can I do for you? You've not come for the ashes, have you? The cremation's not been done yet. It's not easy to arrange these things in a Catholic country."

"Do you know a man called Ferrer? Francesc Ferrer?"

The consul raised his eyebrows, as Catalina returned carrying a tray laden with tea, cups and saucers. "Everyone in Spain knows who Ferrer is, Harry. Why do you ask?"

Lawton helped himself to two sugars. "Foulkes went to the opera the night before his death," he said. "I visited the Liceu yesterday evening and showed his photograph to some of the staff. One of the waiters said he saw Foulkes with a man and woman during the intermission, talking to this man Ferrer. I assumed he was the same Ferrer who met Foulkes in London in April. Mrs. Foulkes told me he's an anarchist and a teacher."

"He's certainly a teacher," Smither said. "But whether you'd want your children to be taught by him is another matter. Last year there was a bomb attack on His Majesty Alfonso XIII and his wife in Madrid. Killed thirty people and wounded dozens more. The bomber was a Catalan—a librarian at Ferrer's school. The police shot him dead, but Ferrer was accused of financing and encouraging him."

"Accused or convicted?"

Smither shrugged. "A court found him not guilty last year."

"You don't agree?"

"Let's just say he's not the kind of person His Majesty's Government touches with a bargepole."

"Well I'd like to speak to him."

"That's your prerogative, of course." Smither sipped at his tea. "Ferrer lives on a farm in Montgat. It's a village about seven miles outside Barcelona. You can get there by train from the Estación de Francia."

"I'll go there now. Nothing else to do."

"Well it would be a turn-up for the books if Ferrer was connected to this." Smither looked faintly amused by this possibility. "Because I can tell you that a lot of people in this country would be very happy to see him hang."

By the time Lawton returned to the street the soldiers had gone, but he found them once again down at the docks, milling around in front of the waiting troopships. He walked around the edge of the port toward the Estación de Francia and bought a ticket on the next train to Montgat. An hour later the train crawled into a tiny village, which consisted of a few white buildings tumbling down the rocky hillside on one side, and a sandy beach to his right. The sun was at its fullest now, and Lawton took off his jacket and walked out of the station into a dusty little square, where a little man in a shabby suit and hat was sitting outside a bar with a sour, suspicious expression, watching the few passengers disperse. He looked even more suspicious when Lawton asked him for Francesc Ferrer's address.

"Walk up out of the village. Turn left at the first track."

Lawton walked along the dirt road through a landscape of mottled white rocks, olive and pine trees, and spiky tropical vegetation, with the sea down to his right. On reaching the track he walked up the hill to a large two-storey farmhouse overlooking the sea to find a long-faced man with a white beard kneeling in a garden plot outside the main entrance, picking weeds.

"Señor Ferrer?" Lawton asked.

"Which one?"

"Francesc."

"I'm José. Francesc is my brother." José Ferrer stood up and reached out a tanned arm. "He's around the corner. You're English?"

"Irish. I live in London."

"Good on yer mate!" Ferrer spoke in English now and laughed at Lawton's obvious surprise. "I spent ten years in Australia."

"Good to see that you learned Australian."

"Just a liddle mate!"

José laughed again. He had the dark, leathery skin of a man who had been working outside most of his life, Lawton thought, as he followed him around the side of the building. Immediately behind the house a short, stoutly built man was dozing in a deck chair under the shade of a plane tree. He was barefoot and wearing a floppy straw hat and there was a book lying on his lap.

"A visitor for you Francesc," José said. "All the way from London."

Ferrer lifted back the hat and stood up to shake Lawton's hand. If José Ferrer looked like a peasant, his brother looked more like a landowner or well-to-do farmer, Lawton thought. "London, eh? A fine city. I was there only a few months ago."

"I know. That's partly why I'm here. I want to ask you some questions about Randolph Foulkes."

"Oh?" Ferrer looked surprised and pointed toward the deck chair on the other side of the table. "José, bring out some lemonade for our visitor."

José nodded and walked away, while Lawton took his hat off and offered Ferrer a cigarette. Ferrer shook his head and looked at him curiously as Lawton lit one up for himself.

"Are you a policeman?" Ferrer asked. "Because if you are, you've come a long way to talk to me about someone I hardly know."

"I'm an investigator. I'm working for his wife."

"Really? And what are you investigating?"

"Dr. Foulkes has disappeared. He was last seen in Barcelona. His wife is concerned something may have happened to him."

Lawton had deliberately not mentioned Foulkes's death to see the reaction, and Ferrer looked genuinely shocked. "Good God. I saw him at the opera less than a month ago. It would have been—"

"June 13," Lawton said. *"The Magic Flute."*

"You have been busy," Ferrer said. "I hope they aren't trying to pin *this* on me."

"They?"

"You saw my little policeman at the station? He's there to see who visits me. He'd love nothing better than to see me taken up to the castle in chains."

"And what do you think they might be trying to pin on you?" Lawton asked.

"Please don't try to be clever, Mr. Lawton. I'm referring to Dr. Foulkes. Something bad must have happened to him or you wouldn't have come all this way."

"So you've no idea what happened to him?"

"None at all," Ferrer replied emphatically.

"I understand you met Dr. Foulkes when you were in England."

"Yes I met him. I went to his house to speak to Mrs. Foulkes about publishing one of her books, for use in my schools. Of course I knew of her husband by reputation, through his work on heredity. He's not someone I had any special interest in, but curiously, he was interested in me. He invited me into his study and asked me lots of questions."

Just then José came back out carrying a tray with a carafe of iced lemonade and two glasses. Ferrer filled them up and passed one to Lawton, as his brother returned to his garden.

"What kind of questions?" Lawton asked.

"Mostly about Spain and Barcelona. About my schools. He struck me as intellectually curious but thoroughly reactionary. He told me my work was pointless. There was no point in trying to improve society through political programs or education, he said. The problem with society was biological not political. The lower classes were poor because of the kind of people they were. All this sort of thing. He said education couldn't do anything about that. He said he wasn't a Catholic but he thought the Catholic Church was good for Spain because it taught the population good morals. We had very little in common, except for one thing—we both believed that physical exercise was good for children."

"Did you know he was coming to Barcelona?"

Ferrer shook his head. "He didn't say anything about that. He did mention that he was going to Vernet-les-Bains to write a book, but I was surprised to see him at the opera. I think he was surprised to see me, too. I don't think he believed anarchists went to the opera except to throw bombs at the audience."

"And he had company," Lawton said.

"He did. A Dr. Weygrand and his companion—a woman named Zorka. An unusual couple."

"In what way?"

"When I asked Weygrand what he was doing in Barcelona, he said he'd come to perform miracles. I asked him what kind of miracles. He invited me to come and see his show at the Edén Concert. He said he might surprise me."

"Did you go?"

"Christ, no. I don't have time to waste on nonsense like that."

"What did this woman look like?"

"Very attractive." Ferrer smiled at the thought. "The kind of woman you'd expect to find in the more tawdry romantic novels. Dewy green eyes. Dark hair. High cheekbones. A bit dreamy. I thought she might be a little crazy. To be honest with you, she was the only reason why I might have been tempted to see their show. You can see it too if you want."

"They're still here?" Lawton asked.

Ferrer nodded. "Every Thursday till the end of the month, according to the posters."

Just then they heard voices, and Lawton looked up to see four men coming toward them from the direction of the yard. Ferrer looked suddenly uncomfortable.

"Do you have any other questions?" he asked, as the four visitors took off their hats and stood at a respectful distance.

"No, that's all," Lawton said.

"Just a minute." Ferrer disappeared into the house, leaving Lawton and his four visitors staring at each other awkwardly. Finally Ferrer returned and showed Lawton a slim book. "Foulkes gave me this in London. It's the book he wrote for your Ministry of Education."

Lawton flicked through the drawings and photographs of children performing calisthenics and physical exercises.

"Every year a quarter of a million children die in Spain," Ferrer said. "Our schools have no air. No space to play. No freedom. So you see why this program could be useful. But look at this." He opened the book and Lawton read the handwritten message: "To Don Francesc

Ferrer—'Wake therefore, for ye know neither the day nor the hour.' Matthew 25:13. Best wishes, Randolph Foulkes."

"I think it was meant as a joke," Ferrer said. "A Biblical quotation for the anarchist who doesn't believe in God. But now it no longer seems so amusing. He was right, of course. None of us knows the day nor the hour. I hope his hasn't arrived yet."

Lawton thanked him, and walked back down the dirt track toward the sea. The news of Foulkes's companions was a potentially useful lead, and he should have felt excited by it, but whether it was his medication or the heat, he felt suddenly listless and sluggish. In South Africa he had sometimes marched for twenty miles a day. Now even this mild excursion had left him drained. He looked down toward the beach, where some adults and children were playing in the sparkling water.

A long time ago he had run through a rougher, colder sea in Donegal with the same careless pleasure. Until two years ago he had thought he might retire there one day after the long and illustrious career at the Yard that seemed to open up before him. Now that future was gone, along with every dream and ambition he had ever had, and nothing lay ahead of him but disintegration and decline. Like Mrs. Foulkes, he was wasting away and there was nothing he could do to prevent it. All he could do was slow it down and try to live with it. Once he would have relished the sight of the flawless blue sky, the sea and the sand, the palm trees, and the whitewashed buildings. Now they only reminded him of pleasures that were no longer available to him.

He tried to distract himself from these dismal reflections and thought back on what Ferrer had told him. The conversation had not revealed much, except that the woman in the opera house had dark hair, whereas Foulkes's companion was blond. Still there was something about Ferrer's description that chimed with the waiter's description, and as he walked back to the square past Ferrer's sour-faced copper, he resolved to do his exercises when he returned to his hotel room, and he promised himself that he would be attending Dr. Weygrand's next performance.

"The best crème brulée in Barcelona." Ferran Quintana laid down his dessert spoon and wiped his mouth with a napkin. "And now perhaps you could explain what I've done to deserve it?"

Mata looked hurt. "Can't old friends have lunch together?"

"They can. But they can do it more cheaply."

Mata laughed. The Maison Dorée was one of the most expensive restaurants in the city, and it was filled with men and women whose presence was evidence of its elevated status. A few tables away he could see the civil governor Ossorio y Gallardo chatting to some of his officials. Other customers included the Marquis of Comillas, the poet Joan Maragall, who was talking to Cambó and Prat de la Riba from the Lliga. In the far corner he saw Emiliano Iglesias, the editor of the Radical Party paper *El Progreso*. With Lerroux still in exile, Iglesias was acting as party leader, and Mata was not at all surprised to find him sharing his table with two high-ranking army officers.

Lerroux had often eaten at the Maison before his exile, in equally exalted company, and Mata had often wondered what his followers from the Raval slums would have said if they had seen the Emperor of the Parallel dining out with such men. No doubt Lerroux would have come up with some silver-tongued excuse, as he usually did for almost everything. Mata knew that most of La Maison's clientele was wealthier than he was, but he liked to come here at lunchtime when prices were cheaper. It was amusing to see the leaders of political factions that normally loathed each other united by a common taste for fine French cooking, and he knew how much Quintana liked it, too.

They had spent most of the lunch talking about politics and exchanging literary gossip. Quintana was an occasional contributor to his journal and wrote surprisingly good poems, which tended to revolve around the same themes of mortality, human frailty, and the decay of the flesh.

"I was hoping to pick your brains," Mata admitted. "So I thought I'd combine business with pleasure."

"What business?" Quintana asked.

"The Raval Monster."

"Thank you for waiting till dessert was over. Very well. But I don't want to be quoted or have my name mentioned in *La Veu*."

"It's an informal conversation," Mata reassured him as the waiter came over to take their plates. Mata ordered two coffees with brandy and cream and waited till he had gone. "Bravo Portillo thinks these murders were committed by a lunatic," he said. "Do you?"

"No sane person would murder people like that. It's not just the bites. It's the lack of blood. In the first case, the body might have bled out, lying in the water so long. But not the second. His blood was *taken*. I mean there was almost nothing left."

"Surely you don't think it was some kind of vampire or werewolf?" Mata asked incredulously.

"Hardly," Quintana replied. "Not in the supernatural sense, anyway. But there are human monsters, too. There was a case in France a few years ago at the end of the century—a vagabond named Vacher who killed people at random and mutilated their bodies. It was one of Lacassagne's early cases. Vacher mostly killed shepherds—girls and boys. He raped them and he also bit them and drank their blood."

"Charming."

"There was another maniac in France in the time of the revolution. A cannibal in the Pyrenees who also killed shepherds. He used to eat parts of his victims. But that isn't what's happened here. The teeth-marks on these bodies show large incisors. The kind you might find on a dog or a wolf. Except that dogs and wolves don't tie up their victims. And the second one—the anarchist Tosets—smelled of chloroform."

The waiter returned carrying their coffees and they fell silent as he laid them on the table. Mata remembered what Esperanza Claramunt had told him about Pau Tosets's lack of resistance during his kidnapping. "So he was subdued first?" he asked.

"Probably. And maybe the other one, too. But he'd been in the water too long to tell."

Mata skimmed off the cream with his teaspoon. "A beast that drinks the blood of anarchists and uses chloroform to subdue them? That's an unusual combination."

"It is," Quintana agreed. "And frankly, I don't think our police can deal with it."

"Who can?" Mata asked. "Mr. Arrow?"

Quintana shook his head. *"El Mister* just wants to pick up his final payment and go home. But there is someone who might be able to help. An Irish detective. I watched him examine one of the bodies from the Bar la Luna—the foreigner. Very thorough and professional."

"Why would an Irish detective be interested in a bombing in Barcelona?"

"The foreigner was an Englishman. His widow sent the Irishman to identify the body. I had the feeling he was here for some other reason, but he didn't say what it was. The question is why are *you* so interested in two murdered anarchists?"

Mata did not feel inclined to reveal his suspicions of state collusion in the two murders, and he was no longer sure how to reconcile this possibility with what Quintana had just told him. "It's a curious case. And the Monster does sell papers."

"Maybe so. But leave me out of it—at least for now."

Mata agreed. He was just about to pay the bill when Emiliano Iglesias came over to their table.

"Good afternoon Mata!" he said. "I couldn't help noticing Señor Quintana. Can I draw any conclusions from your presence?"

"None," Quintana said. "But that probably won't stop you from trying."

"It won't." Iglesias grinned. Mata wondered how long it took him to maintain his wavy black mane of hair and the points of his mustache that reached upward as though they were held up by invisible strings. "It's just that you wouldn't talk to my man last week and yet here you are having lunch with *La Veu.*"

"I'm having lunch with my friend—as you are with yours," Quintana nodded in the direction of the two army officers, who were standing near the door.

Iglesias's smile looked slightly frozen. "Two murders in a fortnight, Mata. And now a defenceless cretin has disappeared from the streets. I would have thought it's in the interests of the whole city to find out the truth about this Monster, wouldn't you?"

"You seem to have already made up your mind about him," Mata replied. "It was your newspaper that called him the Monster. And that cartoon—the vampire with the dog collar—is that 'the truth?'"

"There are rumors . . ."

"Rumors are not my concern," Mata said. "And they shouldn't be the concern of any serious journalist."

Iglesias was not smiling now, and he gave a little bow and returned to his army friends.

"I don't think he appreciated the lecture," Quintana said.

"And I don't appreciate him," Mata said. "He's as bad as Lerroux."

"Who may be returning from exile soon, from what I hear. Argentina didn't suit him."

"I didn't think it would," Mata said. "There aren't enough people to worship him in the Pampas. He must be lonely."

Mata paid the bill and the two of them walked out into the Plaza Catalunya. On the other side of the square Mata saw the line of soldiers from the Third Mixed Brigade streaming down the Calle Pelayo and onto the Ramblas. It was the third day since the mobilization for Morocco, and the latest contingent of soldiers was the largest yet. Already it seemed to stretch the entire length of the Ramblas, and once again the soldiers were accompanied by members of their own families, despite the efforts of their officers to shoo them away. Mata knew his father-in-law would be pleased, but he felt only desolation and foreboding at the sight of Catalans marching off to fight another Spanish war that Spain was bound to lose.

It was only eleven years since he had watched the Army of Cuba marching up the Ramblas in the opposite direction after the great disaster of 1898. They were as wretched a collection of soldiers as he had ever seen: dirty, malarial, dead on their feet, and marching out of step with their dusty uniforms hanging from their scrawny bodies. Nothing had changed since then to make it any more likely that the expedition to Morocco would not have a similar outcome. The army was stuffed with officers and generals like Iglesias's friends, who were more familiar with restaurants than battlefields. The rank and file consisted largely of men from the slums, who had no more interest in fighting than their officers. Yet men like his father-in-law and the gentlemen of the Hispano-Africa Society still continued to believe that Spain could carve

out a glorious African empire in the Rif from the crumbs that France
and England had left them.

"Well Mata," Quintana shook his hand as they reached the Calle
Hospital. "I hope the information I gave you was worth that lunch."

"Just your company was worth it, Ferran. As it always is."

Quintana laughed and turned away toward the hospital, and Mata
took the next turn right into the Calle Sant Pau. There had been a
time when he had known the Raval reasonably well, when he and
his friends had often roamed its brothels and absinthe bars in search
of pleasures that were easily available in the neighborhood. In those
youthful years the old city held an exotic fascination for students who
had read too much Huysmans and Baudelaire—coupled with a refusal
to acknowledge the risk of syphilis that some of them had paid dearly
for. At that time Pablo Picasso had been an occasional member of their
group. Mata remembered him hunched over his sketchpad in many a
downtown whorehouse, drawing whores and their clients. Now Picasso
was in Paris, his own bohemian days were long gone, and the streets
that had once seemed dangerous and alluring seemed sleazy, dirty, and
devoid of glamor.

In the daytime there was nothing romantic at all about the gaunt, fam-
ished men lurking in doorways with faintly predatory expressions or the
whores in their garish lipstick, their spots of rouge, and their lacy boots,
many of whom looked ready to lift their skirts right there in the street
at the drop of a ten-cent coin. Some of these women had clearly been
working in their profession for far too long, while others looked too young
to have ever embarked on it. Both kinds seemed to think he had come
there to seek their services, and Mata politely rejected their overtures as
he walked on resolutely through the narrow evil-smelling streets with
clothes hanging from balconies. He had to make some inquiries before
he found the address that Bravo Portillo had given him, and he walked
in through the main entrance and up the dank, greasy stairs, taking care
not to touch anything with his hands. He knocked tentatively on one of
the two doors, and a crone in a black dress opened the door and peered
out myopically into the gloom.

"What do you want?" she asked.

"Good day, Señora." Mata took off his hat. "I've come to see Hermenigildo's woman."

"For business?"

"Information. Which I'm willing to pay for."

"Angela!" The old woman called. "A gentleman to see you."

"What is it?" A younger woman appeared behind her, holding a baby with a dirty face. She might once have been pretty, Mata thought, but her bloom was already beginning to fade.

"I want to talk to you," he said. "About Hermenigildo."

Angela immediately looked wary. "Hombre, I've already spoken to the cops."

"I know. But *I* want to speak to you." Mata reached for his wallet and counted out some coins, which Angela immediately accepted. She stood back to let him in. The apartment was typical of many workers' flats in downtown Barcelona, consisting of two dark little rooms that gave off a pungent smell of olive oil, urine, paraffin, and fried fish. There were at least seven children and adults milling around the little kitchen. Through the open doorway at the opposite end of the flat he saw four mattresses on the floor, where Angela and her aunt had presumably expected him to have intercourse. Angela handed the baby to the old lady, and shooed the children away from the little table. She sat down and invited Mata to do the same.

"What d'you want to know?" she asked.

"Let's start with why your compañero blew up the Bar la Luna."

"I haven't the slightest idea."

"The police said they found bomb materials in your apartment. And other things."

"I knew about the pamphlets and newspapers. But not the other stuff they found on the roof. I never saw it."

"But you knew he was an anarchist?"

Angela shrugged. "Most of the time I knew him he was more interested in money. Then about a year ago he starts running with some of Rull's old crowd."

"The Sons of Whores? I thought they broke up ages ago."

"Not according to Hermenigildo. That's when he started talking about revolution. Oh capitalism is so terrible. Down with the church. Down with the state. Power to the workers. I thought it was just talk. Hermenigildo always talked a lot of shit, especially when he was drinking. And he drank a lot."

"So you never noticed anything unusual about his behavior before the bombing? Any nervousness or excitement?"

"The only thing he was excited about was the motorcar."

Mata looked at her. "What motorcar?"

"About two weeks before the bombing, he comes back looking all happy and pleased with himself. Says he's just been in a motorcar. A fancy car driven by a foreign gentleman. I said what gentlemen do you know? He says a mate introduced him—an anarchist mate. He says he's going to do something big—and make some money, too. I thought of course you are. On the day of the Luna bombing he never came back. I didn't think anything of it. I thought he'd left us. Next thing I know the Brigada is on my doorstep."

"Lieutenant Ugarte?"

"Him and some others. That's when I knew Hermenigildo did this crazy thing. And then they told me he was dead."

"This friend—the one who introduced him to the foreigner. Do you know his name?"

"Santamaría. Salvador Santamaría. Hermenigildo says he used to run with Rull. I told all this to the cop—he didn't seem interested. Didn't even write it down."

"This Santamaría, do you know where he can be found?"

Angela shook her head. "Hermenigildo never said. I didn't ask. I don't understand why this happened and I don't care. I'm going back to the village as soon as I can afford the fare. There's nothing there, but nothing is better than this shithole of a city right now."

Mata reached into his wallet once again and gave her a ten peseta note. "Maybe this will help you to get back there," he said.

Angela looked grateful, and Mata hoped that she really would use the money to get out of the filthy apartment. As he descended the dank stairwell once again he wondered why Ugarte appeared to have had so little interest in a possible foreign connection to a bombing that he was supposedly investigating. No sooner had he stepped out onto the street when he heard a sudden noise coming from an alleyway a few yards away on the other side of the street.

Mata generally considered himself to be a sensible and rational man, but now he thought of Pau Tosets lying in an alley and he felt the same fear that he had once felt as a child when his parents blew the candle out and left him alone in his bedroom. In the same moment he heard a low growl that made the hairs on the back of his neck stand on end. He turned and walked quickly away. Even as his footsteps echoed around the murky streets he continued to look over his shoulder, and it seemed to him that something he could not see was moving toward him in the shadows. Soon he came alongside the whorehouses once again, and he slowed down and wiped his forehead in an attempt to regain some dignity. Some of the women laughed at the large bearded man with the floppy hat who looked as though he were being chased by something.

It was not until he reached the Ramblas that he began to relax once again. And even as he smiled at his own ridiculousness, he promised himself that the next time he came into the Raval, it would be better to have company.

10

Ever since she had embraced the Idea, Esperanza had yearned for the great strike that Pau and the other comrades talked about—the strike that would turn the country upside down and usher in the possibility of a revolutionary transformation. She had been too young to participate in the February 1902 general strike in Catalonia for the nine-hour day. She remembered hearing the sound of shots for the first time, and seeing cavalry riding down the Mayor de Gràcia. But it was not until she joined the movement five years later that she learned of the lockouts and battles between the pickets and the forces of order in which dozens of workers had been killed. Most of the comrades who had participated in the strikes agreed that they had been a defeat for the trade unions and the movement as a whole. Pau used to say the same, even though his mother had been one of the organizers of the strike and had spent a year in jail as a result.

The strike had not been prepared properly, Pau said, and its defeat had allowed the Catalanistas and Lerroux's party to gain ground at the movement's expense. But Pau also believed that the Catalan unions were beginning to recover their confidence and strength. Now, as a result of the call-up and the fighting in Morocco, the possibility of another general strike seemed suddenly likely.

There was no doubt that Maura had made a mistake in calling up the Catalan reservists. Even in Gràcia, Esperanza heard women complain that their sons and husbands were being called up to fight the Moors and that there would be no one left to feed their children. In her lunchbreaks she went out into the Ramblas to join the protesters shouting at the troops heading for the harbor. In the evenings she attended meetings at the offices of the *Soli* or the Athenaeum, in preparation for the forthcoming annual meeting of the Catalan Workingmens Federation. On that day delegates from all over Catalonia would be gathering in Barcelona, and it was already clear that Morocco would be on the top of the agenda and that the conference would vote on a general strike.

Esperanza knew what Pau would have wanted, and she was conscious of his invisible presence as she went from one meeting to another. On Wednesday evening, one week before the federation conference, the Invincibles met at the Athenaeum once again, where Ruben and Arnau reported back from their meeting with Ferrer at Montgat.

Esperanza was disappointed to hear that Ferrer would not be attending the conference because he did not believe there was sufficient national support for a strike. Ferrer had become a kind of counselor as well as an inspiration to the group, and Esperanza could not understand why he would hold back, when even the socialists were discussing the possibility of a strike. The other members of the Invincibles seemed equally deflated, and Arnau tried to reassure them.

"Ferrer will come around," he said. "For now we're better off without him. He attracts too much attention. We don't want any coppers around here—not the ones we can see or the ones we can't."

The others nodded, and Esperanza remembered what Mata had told her: that someone from her affinity group must have told Pau's kidnappers where he was going to be on the night he was taken. She had not even known herself that he intended to walk her home, and she found it difficult to believe that any of the Invincibles had known—let alone that any of them could have turned such knowledge into betrayal. Arnau was out of the question. Pau had always told her that he was as unbreakable as steel, and he spoke with the same quiet authority and strength that Pau himself had once exuded.

Once, she might have suspected Ruben, but Ruben was no longer the man he had been a few weeks ago. She listened now, as he insisted that the Invincibles play their part in promoting the protest strike in factories, workplaces, and houses across the city. Arnau agreed that such action was necessary to ensure that the delegates at the conference made the right decision. Once again he turned toward the chair that they had all agreed to keep empty in memory of Pau. "You remember the words of Comrade Tosets," he said. "'The movement is recovering. The grass is dry and needs a spark to light it.' Comrades, Maura has lit that spark, and now it's up to us to set the city on fire."

Esperanza felt a knot in her throat as she looked around the table at the little man with the yellowed face who had endured so much and the earnest expressions on her comrades. In that moment she felt privileged to be in a movement that could produce such men, and she felt sure that Mata must be wrong, The meeting broke up shortly afterward, and Esperanza was about to go home when Ruben came over to speak to her.

"Do you have a minute?" he asked. "I need some advice."

"My mother's expecting me back."

"It won't take long. I've written something. I need someone to look it over for me—preferably a teacher."

Ruben seemed so earnest that Esperanza could not refuse. She followed him upstairs into the library, and out into the deserted gallery, where the two of them sat down on the little cane sofa.

"A pity about Ferrer," she said.

Ruben shrugged. "He's being watched all the time now. There was a copper at the station when we were there. And another one at his house—from London."

"From London? What did he want?"

"No idea." Ruben took a folded sheet of paper from his pocket and handed it to her. "Here it is. I thought it might go in the *Soli*."

Esperanza read the barely legible scrawl that looked as though it had been written by a child. Despite the numerous misspellings and crossed out words, it was essentially an extended version of the call to action that he had just made. On paper, it lacked the passion and conviction that had accompanied his surprising transformation into a persuasive orator.

"Can I be honest with you?" Esperanza asked.

"That bad, eh?"

"No. But in my opinion you should do what you do best. You're a good speaker. You speak from the heart. You win people over."

"Do I?"

"Yes, you do. And you should leave the writing to others."

For a moment she thought she had offended him, then Ruben nodded and gave a rueful smile. "You know what? You're right. Pau was always the writer, not me." He looked at her intently, and his hooded eyes looked suddenly guarded once again, as though he were trying to make up his mind about something. "Did you watch the procession last year? During the royal visit?"

Esperanza was surprised by the question. Like all the schools in the city, she had been obliged to take her class to watch the great parade on the Passeig de Gràcia. She had watched the soldiers kissing the Spanish flag, the Army of Africa marching in formation in their flat round caps, the cavalrymen with their sabers and horsetailed helmets, the young King Alfonso on his white horse with Maura riding beside him.

"I was at the parade, too." Ruben lowered his voice. "With a gun." He smiled grimly at Esperanza's shocked expression. "I hadn't been back from the penal colony for long. My head was a mess. I wanted to pay the bastards back for what they'd done. And to be honest with you I'd had enough of this world. So I got hold of a pistol from one of the comrades. Of course I expected to die. But I thought if I take down the king and maybe the president then at least I'll have achieved something. You know who stopped me? Pau. He heard what I was planning. He came to look for me."

Esperanza was too astounded to respond, and Ruben explained how Pau had guided him away from the crowd even as the king was approaching, and persuaded him to abandon the assassination attempt.

"A few more minutes and I would have taken a shot at the king," Ruben said. "And even if I hadn't killed him I would have got the rope or the garotte. So it's thanks to Pau that I'm still here. And now he isn't. And that's why I want to do this strike. Not just for the movement, but for him. But there's something else you need to know—I still have that gun."

Esperanza had the feeling that she had entered into a peculiar intimacy now that was not like anything she had experienced. "Do you?" She asked nervously. "What for?"

Ruben leaned closer. "Pau was often right. He was right about the king. He was right about assassinations—they don't achieve anything anymore. But not everything can be resolved through strikes and mass action. You and I know the coppers aren't going to find who killed Pau. They won't even look. But I can tell you this. If *I* find the son of a bitch, I will see that justice is done. So if your journalist friend finds out who he is, you'd do better to let me know, not the police."

Esperanza looked back into the dark intense eyes and remembered Michele Angiolillo, the Italian anarchist who had shot prime minister Cánovas in 1897, less than a year after her father's death. It was Cánovas who had ordered the repression that killed her father, and even then, at the age of eight, she remembered how the nuns had asked her class to pray for the prime minister's soul. Instead she had secretly offered her prayers to Angiolillo, the man who had traveled all the way from London to gun Cánovas down at a Basque spa town, and waited calmly with his wife for the arrest that he knew would lead him to the garotte.

Now she heard Pau's voice telling her, as he had told Ruben, that the age of assassinations and attentats was over and that revolutions were the result of the collective efforts of the masses, not guns and bombs. Then she thought of his bloodless body lying in an alley like a piece of meat, and her mouth tightened with anger. Ruben was still looking at her intently, as if he were gauging her reaction.

"Do you understand what I'm saying?" he asked.

Esperanza nodded and said that she understood very well.

At an early age, Lawton had understood that the surface of the world was subject to sudden unexpected fluctuations that threatened his well-being and survival. It was a lesson he had first acquired in childhood, watching out for the little shifts in his father's moods that preceded one of his rages. Sometimes these signs were obvious. It was generally preferable to stay out of the old man's way when he came home from the pub cursing instead of singing, or when he smelled of whiskey rather than beer. At other times such eruptions could come from nowhere. One minute the old man would be laughing or talking normally, and then there would be the sudden change of tone or the stone-cold stare into the distance, before he lashed out and hit someone or broke something.

Lawton had soon discovered that the world outside his family was equally unstable. Twice he had come home from school to find the bailiffs putting his family out on the street because the old man had drunk the rent away. In Belfast he had learned which route to take to avoid the Protestant boys who might overturn his barrow on his way back from the market. He had learned to read the mood of the Orangemen who passed through the neighborhood during the marching season, and take evasive action when the usual insults and shouts of "Taig bastard" gave way to physical attacks. He was the one who woke up first and smelled the kerosene-soaked rag pushed through their mailbox during the Home Rule Bill riots, because even at that age a part of him was already braced for disaster. The same anticipation that had saved him from the Prods had also served him well in other situations. In the ring, he had learned to look out for the wide punch that followed the feint, and keep his eye out for the kick to the shins or the crotch. During the war he had often been the first to spot the little glint or movement that signaled a Boer ambush.

After less than a week in Barcelona he had already begun to sense that something in the atmosphere was changing. It was not just the crowds he saw each day, remonstrating with the soldiers marching down to the port, or the speakers up and down the Ramblas angrily denouncing the king, the government, and the Jesuits, the Marquess of Comillas or the Count Güell and other names he had never heard of. Even the priests and nuns seemed to hurry up and down the Ramblas now, and the police and Civil Guard seemed more watchful and suspicious. On the Thursday evening before Dr. Weygrand's performance, he spent the afternoon in his hotel room, trying to shake off the headache that neither the nitroglycerin nor the amyl nitrate seemed able to relieve.

The headache was just beginning to recede when he heard the rattle of a drum and the shrill high-pitched squeak of a horn. Outside in the square a small crowd was watching a group of men, women, and children who were holding hands and dancing in a circle. It looked almost like a ceilidh, but the movements of these dancers were more measured and stately. At times they barely seemed to be moving at all as they raised their arms in unison and bobbed up and down. The dancing went on throughout the afternoon and the horns continued to shriek like a chorus of tortured parrots. In the late afternoon the music finally stopped, and he decided to go down to the square to see if some food might have some impact on his headache. On his way out he asked Señor Martínez if he knew where the Edén Concert was.

Martínez looked at him in alarm. "Señor, that is not a place for decent people."

"And why is that? It's just a music hall, isn't it?"

"Not only that sir. Upstairs there is a bor, a bord—" Señor Martínez's face reddened.

"A bordello?" Despite his headache Lawton could not help feeling amused at the receptionist's discomfort. "Oh don't worry about that. I'm not going for the whores. I'm only going to a magic show."

11

Outside the sun had disappeared behind the rooftops and the shadows were already spreading across the square. Lawton managed to force down an omelette, which made him feel less nauseous, but the pain continued to drill into his head as he followed the receptionist's directions to the Calle Conde del Asalto on the other side of the Ramblas. A queue was already forming outside the theater by the time he arrived, and as far as he could tell it was there for the performance not the bordello. Soon the line began to stretch out behind him, and he filed forward till he came alongside the poster of the man with the staring eyes, the slicked-down hair, toothbrush moustache, and outstretched palms, above the words, THE GREAT WEYGRAND: THE INFINITE JOURNEY.

The inside of the theater was illuminated by candles, and the stage was also lined with candles on two sides. Lawton immediately noticed a large painted image of what appeared to be a wheel or a black sun on the curtain at the rear of the stage. The design consisted of an outer wheel that was connected to a smaller wheel at the center by twelve jagged spokes that recalled the sig-runes in Foulkes's study. The stage itself was taken up by two chairs, a shelf unit containing a collection of books and colored bottles, and a table laid with an array of knives and other objects. Lawton took a seat ten rows back from the stage and waited for the performance to begin. Within half an hour the little auditorium was full, and the audience fell silent as the manager came out on stage from behind the curtain.

Lawton thought that he looked like a music hall impresario and he soon began to sound like one as he told the audience they should prepare to be amazed and astonished. For Dr. Franz Weygrand was no ordinary entertainer. He was a scientist who had gone beyond science; a psychologist and hypnotist who had studied the secrets of the ancients; a reader of minds and souls who had traveled to the furthest reaches of the earth from the Pyrenees to Timbuktu, from Samarkand to Mandalay, from the temples of Ceylon to the Gompas of Tibet, in search of the wisdom of the ancients. He had known Dr. Freud and Madame Blavatsky. He had studied with Hindu fakirs and the conjurers of Togo. He had been a guest of kings and queens, the Russian tsar, the shah of Persia, and the Chinese emperor.

The audience seemed impressed by this, but Lawton had heard too many overheated pitches at circuses and fairgrounds to take this melodramatic presentation seriously. During his own fairground days he had lost his virginity to Brenda the Snake Lady in the skimpy leopard-skin dress who once shared a glass cage with two drowsy pythons. To the credulous customers who came to stare at her in lust and wonder, she was Fatima Queen of Serpents, whose ancient kingdom had been discovered somewhere near Lake Victoria. People believed in such things because they wanted to believe in them, and Lawton suspected that the mysterious Dr. Weygrand's appeal was no different. As always, the manager concluded, Weygrand would be accompanied by the inscrutable, enigmatic and delectable Zorka, one of the world's true clairvoyants and a direct descendant of the ancient Cathars. Together they would take the audience on a journey that would challenge everything they believed.

Lawton doubted it, and as the manager left the stage, he wondered why a man who had performed for the tsar and the Chinese emperor should have ended up in a brothel-cum-music-hall. A moment later Weygrand stepped out from the curtain and walked slowly toward the audience. He looked much the same as he did on the poster, with his bulbous staring eyes and his curved moustache, except for his long white robes and a black turban that Lawton found faintly comical. He stood in silence for a long time, staring at the audience with a fierce and slightly mad expression, when a woman in a white dress stepped out from the curtain behind him.

There was a murmur of admiration from both male and female members of the audience, and Lawton forgot momentarily about his headache as he contemplated her high cheekbones and curved green eyes, her bare arms and ankles and the long dark hair that fell down her back. Her expression was serious, but also drugged and slightly dreamy, and her slow movements made Lawton think of a somnambulistic cat as she came alongside Weygrand, holding a long piece of cloth. Weygrand looked down at the rows in front of the stage and beckoned with his finger at a middle-aged little man who was sitting with his wife. The man obediently came up the stairs and stood waiting nervously while Zorka tied the cloth around Weygrand's eyes and turned him gently around so that he was standing with his back to the audience.

"What's your name, sir?" Weygrand asked, in Spanish.

"Martín," the man replied.

"Well Martín, I want you to kill someone for me. Will you do that?"

"I don't think so," Martín replied nervously.

The audience tittered, and Martín looked even more anxious as Zorka took one of the knives by the blade and placed the handle in his hand. Weygrand still had his back to the audience, and he told Martín to choose someone from the audience and give them the knife, and then return to the stage without saying a word. Martín was grinning now as he descended the stairs and handed the knife to a portly gentleman in the fourth row, before returning to the stage. The audience was absolutely silent, as Zorka turned Weygrand around so that the two men were facing each other and placed Weygrand's hand against Martín's forehead.

"Close your eyes," Weygrand ordered. "Think of the row and the seat number of your victim. Think of nothing else."

The two men stood facing each other in silent concentration, until Weygrand began to nod. "Your victim is in the fourth row," he said. "Seat number two."

There were gasps of amazement as the portly victim stood up brandishing the knife. Zorka accompanied the hapless murderer to his seat and came back with the knife while Weygrand remained standing in his blindfold and turban and reached out his arms as if in prayer.

"Señoras y señores, where can truth be found in this world? Where do we find mystery in a century where all mysteries have been explained? Where are our lost kingdoms and our buried treasures?" Weygrand tapped his temple with his forefinger. "In here, ladies and gentlemen, in the undiscovered spaces of the human mind, in the mysteries of consciousness. Here we can find virgin territory waiting to be revealed. Shadowlands darker than darkest Africa. Hidden depths that only reveal themselves in our dreams—and our nightmares. Here where even the most distant memories lie buried so deep most of us are not even aware of them. Here, where the known world ends and the borderland begins—this is where we find truth and beauty!"

In the fairgrounds and also as a detective Lawton had encountered his fair share of frauds and charlatans. He had known men who collected money for nonexistent missions in Africa or Patagonia; fake gypsies and fortune tellers; convenors of séances who moved tables and letters with magnets and hidden wires to convince grieving widows and parents that they could speak to their dead husbands or children; magicians who planted friends in the audience and pretended they could read their minds. As the evening wore on he had no doubt that Weygrand and his assistant belonged in their company. Some of their tricks were already familiar to him. Audience members were invited to choose cards or numbers and Weygrand told them what they had chosen. One man was given a bouquet of flowers and told to hand it to a beautiful woman in the audience, who Weygrand correctly identified through his blindfold.

All this was cleverly and expertly done. After half an hour Zorka removed Weygrand's blindfold, and he invited a young man from the audience onstage. Zorka guided him to one of the chairs, and Weygrand sat down directly opposite and passed his hands in front of the man's face and head. In a soft, soothing voice he told him his eyelids and arms were becoming heavy. Within a few minutes the man's eyes had begun to close, and Weygrand continued to repeat the same instructions until his subject was clearly in a trance. Weygrand told his subject that only his handclap would wake him, and handed the young man an onion. The audience laughed when Weygrand told him that it was a bouquet of roses and ordered him to sniff them. The subject breathed in the imaginary flowers, and Weygrand told him to get down on his knees and offer them to Zorka as a token of his love.

The audience was roaring with laughter now, as the hypnotized suitor offered the onion to Zorka, who accepted it with a coquettish smile. Finally Weygrand roused the subject with a clap, and the young man looked around him with embarrassment and confusion, as the audience laughed and applauded. Weygrand now summoned other members of the audience and put them in a trance. Some were told to dance, crawl around on all fours, or bark like dogs. One man was ordered to lie on the ground and Weygrand summoned two members of the audience, who hoisted his stiff body between the two chairs. Even when Weygrand sat on his stomach the body remained perfectly rigid.

Lawton could not help finding this foolishness mildly diverting, until Weygrand told one of his hypnotized subjects that he had the falling sickness and ordered him to fall to the ground whenever he clicked his fingers. Once again the audience laughed as Weygrand's subject fell and got up various times, but Lawton felt as though he were being personally mocked. Zorka continued to regard the proceedings with the same dreamy trancelike expression.

The performance now entered a new phase when Weygrand ordered Zorka to sit in one of the chairs. Once again he sat down and passed his hands over her body with a theatrical flourish and repeated the same soothing instructions. This time Weygrand held his assistant's hands and Lawton could not help thinking that he sounded more like a seducer than a hypnotist. Lawton sensed the vicarious excitement among the male members of the audience as she sat with her eyes closed and her lips slightly open, as if inviting a kiss. Finally Weygrand turned to the audience.

"Many years ago I met Zorka in Hungary," he said. "In a town called Kosice. I heard of a woman who could travel back in time. Who spoke the voices of the ancient dead. There were those who said this woman was a witch. But as soon as I heard her speak I knew what she was. A clairvoyant, ladies and gentlemen! A traveler through time and space. And not just hundreds of years! But millennia. To the very dawn of humanity. To the lands of the old Gods. Tell them, my dear. Tell them who your ancestors were."

"I come from Hyperborea," Zorka replied in heavily accented Spanish that sounded Russian or Polish.

"Please enlighten us, my dear. Many people won't be familiar with this place."

"In the continent of Plaksha. The kingdom beyond the North Winds," Zorka intoned. "In a temperate land where there is no age or illness or death. Where we spoke with our thoughts, not words."

"But if there's no death then why are these gods not here?"

Zorka looked mournful. "We mixed our blood with mortals. We mingled with the third root-race, with Lemurians from the land of Mu. Over time we lost our powers. We became weak."

"And what powers are those?"

Zorka turned her head and stared at the table, and there were gasps all around the auditorium as it began to wobble and shake. Lawton looked for ropes or wires, as the knives fell to the floor one by one, but there was no obvious sign of trickery. Finally the table stopped moving and Weygrand held up his hand to quiet the commotion.

"As you see ladies and gentlemen, some of us are only truly awake when we sleep. May I have a volunteer?" Weygrand walked to the front of the stage and picked out a young woman a few rows behind Lawton. "You, Señora. Will you come up please?"

The woman looked reluctant, and then came onto the stage, where Weygrand guided her to the empty chair and told her to take Zorka's hands. There was an entirely different mood in the theater now. The laughter and hilarity were absent, and the attention of the audience was entirely focused on the pale beauty who was sitting with her eyes closed as if she were straining to hear something in the distance. Suddenly Zorka jerked upright, as if she were in pain. Still holding the woman's hands, she shifted her body as though she were trying to shake off a heavy weight.

To Lawton's amazement she began to speak in a strange language that was not like anything he had ever heard. At first he was not even sure if it was a language or an incantation, as the tone of her voice became deeper, as though someone was speaking through her. The voice sounded like a complaint or a protest and then Lawton heard a more pleading tone, as though someone else was trying to speak, and she said, in a sweet, childlike voice, "Don't worry, mama, I'm here. I'm always here."

The woman stared at Zorka in dismay and let out a heartfelt sob, while Zorka repeated in the same plaintive voice, "Don't cry mama."

Weygrand raised his hand and Zorka fell silent. In the same moment one of the bottles on the shelf shattered and burst into flames. Some men from the audience were on their feet and shouting as Weygrand rushed over toward it and swatted at the flames with his turban to put them out. He returned to the woman and gave her a handkerchief and asked her in a gentle, sympathetic voice why she was crying. There was a collective gasp from the audience when the woman replied that she had lost a child in childbirth ten years before. Weygrand gave the audience a meaningful look, like a lawyer who had just proven a point to a jury, and laid a consoling hand on her shoulder. Zorka handed the woman a tissue and escorted her back to her seat, before Weygrand proceeded to summon other members of the audience. Each time Zorka spoke to them in the voices of dead or absent people that they seemed to recognize or that touched some chord in them.

With each intervention Zorka become more agitated, as if the effort of looking into their minds was taking its physical and mental toll. All this only added to the audience's fascination. Lawton did not know how these tricks had been achieved, but the more he observed this performance, the more he was convinced that he was looking at Marie Babineaux, and it seemed obvious to him how Foulkes had been induced to give away his money. Suddenly Zorka let out a gasp and her head slumped forward. Weygrand reached out to stop her from falling and roused her from her trance. Zorka sat limply in the chair, while Weygrand announced in an apologetic voice that the performance had placed too great a strain on her fragile health and that it was too dangerous to continue. The audience rose from their seats in one motion to applaud as Weygrand bowed, and escorted his ailing assistant to the rear of the stage.

Lawton was also on his feet, intending to go backstage, but even as he applauded he felt the tingling in his fingers and the tightening in his chest as he looked at the stagehands putting out the candles on stage and the burning red sun behind them. His head was screaming now, as though a long sliver of hot metal was being thrust into this brain as he pushed his way through the crowd, ignoring the protests and angry faces. By the time he reached the street he felt able to breathe again. He was still standing there when Weygrand and Zorka came out of a side entrance and climbed into a waiting carriage that already had a male passenger. Lawton was just about to walk toward it when he noticed a red-haired man in a black sailor's hat moving through the crowd on the other side of the street. Even as he watched the head bobbing up above the pedestrians moving toward the Ramblas, a part of him knew it could not be who he thought it was, and yet the sailor looked so much like his father that he could not dismiss the possibility, and when he turned into a side street, Lawton knew there was no choice but to follow him.

12

Until that evening Lawton had been out in Barcelona only during the day. Even when he went out for supper, he never went further than the Plaza Reial or the Café Suizo, and he was usually back in his hotel room before it was fully dark. Even then the gas lamps were usually on. Now he found himself in a maze of dark narrow streets without streetlamps, where the only light came from the apartments, taverns, and brothels on either side of him. It was difficult to make out the sailor as he followed him through the darkness. All around him men were chatting to the whores who stood outside open doorways or leaned over balconies in corsets, dressing gowns, and negligees.

If his father was in Barcelona then it was only natural to find him in a neighborhood like this. In his more vicious moments the old man liked to torment and humiliate his mother with tales of whorehouses from Port Suez, Mombasa, Buenos Aires, and other cities, and he had never cared whether his children heard him. Even if the red-haired sailor was the father he had not seen for fifteen years, Lawton was not sure what he would say to him. He might curse him or hit him. He might tell him all the things he had never had the chance to tell him when he was younger, but he needed to know whether the sailor was indeed his father or whether his brain was playing tricks on him again.

Already his head felt fit to burst and the faces of the people in the street seemed to drift past in the murky light like grotesque disembodied masks floating down a dirty stream. All around him he heard a babel of languages, some of which seemed to be calling to him. He heard lewd and raucous laughter and smelled the same combination of wine, cheap perfume, tobacco, and opium that he remembered from his Limehouse days. Finally he caught up with the sailor and laid his right hand on his shoulder. As soon as he turned around, Lawton saw that he had been mistaken. The sailor looked nothing like his father, and Lawton looked at the Kaiserliche Marine eagle and the red felt center on his black cap and wondered how he could have been such an idiot.

"*Was willst du?*" the sailor said angrily.

Lawton mumbled an apology and the sailor walked away, shaking his head and cursing under his breath. Lawton felt angry with himself as he watched him go, and he also felt afraid. In that moment he wished that he could take his head off his shoulders and shake out all the fancies and delusions that swarmed inside his overheated brain like spiders in a jar. Just then he heard the strumming of a guitar from a nearby tavern, and he caught the familiar sweet licorice smell. Even as he walked toward the open doorway he saw Dr. Morris shaking his head and telling him to go back to his hotel, and then he stepped into the crowded room and even as the smell of sweat, sawdust, smoke, and wine wafted over him, he knew it was too late.

The tavern reminded him of many similar holes-in-the-wall in the East End, with its rows of dusty bottles behind the bar, its domino and card players, and its general air of unrepentant vice. Some of the customers were sailors. Others had the slack, distorted features of men and women who had abandoned themselves to the night a long time ago. In one corner a seated guitarist was accompanying two couples who were performing a dance he had never seen before. The music was jerky, staccato, and compelling, and even though the dancers pressed their breasts and cheeks together they seemed to look past each other as they moved back and forth in the cramped space as if they had been forced together by accident.

Lawton walked over to the counter, where a gnomelike little man in a filthy apron was wiping glasses with an equally dirty cloth. He ordered a shot of absinthe and felt a sharp, physical craving that was almost like lust as the tavernkeeper poured the green syrupy liquid into a grimy glass. Lawton swallowed it down in a single gulp and shook his head like a dog shaking water as the hot bittersweet taste washed through his mouth and throat. Already the world seemed sweeter and more benign and the pain in his head gave way to a rush of giddy bonhomie.

"Now that is a fine drop!" he exclaimed. "And I'll take another, thank you. Even though my doctor says I mustn't drink. You know what I think? If a man can't have a drink or two then what in the name of sweet Jesus on the cross is the point, eh?"

The tavernkeeper seemed unperturbed by the profanity as he poured another glass and pushed it toward him. With his hanging jowls and baggy brown eyes he reminded Lawton of a weary bloodhound, and his face bore the look of resignation and disinterest of a man who had seen everything and cared about nothing. Whether it was the absinthe or the knowledge that nothing he said in this place would ever be noted or remembered, or simply the fact that he was speaking in Spanish, Lawton felt suddenly loquacious.

"I believe my father would've enjoyed your establishment, Señor," he said. "Though whiskey not absinthe was his tipple. Hopefully it will have killed the fucker by now. Either that or the clap. The strongest man in the world! Hah! I, on the other hand, have always drunk in moderation. And have no *transmitted* diseases." Lawton laughed and drank the glass down. "And yet now I am the one who must watch out for my health!" He spat the word out and reached for his cigarettes. "What kind of justice is that?"

Lawton held out the glass and once again the tavernkeeper filled it. "I used to box, you know. Working the fairs and doing well enough. So one day this gentleman comes up to me—fine clothes, waistcoat, and cane. You look good, he says, and I want to make you an offer. I want you to take part in a bareknuckle fight in London. A special fight. No

Queensbury Rules. No rules at all. I don't even have to win. All I have to do is fight Black Jack Owen—a coal miner from Merthyr Tydfil. You know where Wales is? Never mind. Take my word. He was a big man and a hard man, too. With a reputation. Just fight him, the gentleman says, and even if I lose, I get twenty percent of the takings. Naturally I accepted."

For the first time the tavernkeeper looked almost interested, and some of the other customers had gathered round to listen. Lawton felt himself warming to his tale now and he called for another drink, and proceeded to describe the epic fight that had taken place in the warehouse near Shadwell Docks in 1896. Fifty-two rounds spread over three hours, with no referee and no ring, only the circle of spectators yelling and howling and crowding around the two fighters as they battered each other till they were barely able to stand. It was not easy to find the words in Spanish to describe the intensity and ferocity of the encounter, and he took up his stance and demonstrated some of the moves and punches, right down to the final round when Owen caught him on the temple with a rabbit punch and followed up with a jab to the jaw. That punch should have finished it, he said, and he had felt himself going, and then the Welshman became overeager and dropped his guard, just long enough for him to deliver the right hook that finally knocked him down.

"The most beautiful punch I ever laid on anyone!" said Lawton nostalgically. He did not tell them how he had thought of his father in the moment that Black Jack Owen came toward him to finish him off with his fists by his sides; how the rage had enabled him to rally one last time. "The crowd couldn't believe it and nor could I," he said. "They carried me on their shoulders round and round the warehouse and gave me so much rum that I passed out. And when I wake up I find I've made a month's pay in one fight. Sixty percent of the takings. You see my gentleman friend had been betting against me! Never mind a broken nose, two broken ribs, and a headache that wouldn't go away for a week. Like a metal spike in my head. And sometimes I don't think it ever came out." Lawton felt suddenly deflated. He did not want to talk about his illness or even think about it. Nor did he want to tell them that he had never fought that well again. "Another glass please, Señor!" he turned to the guitarist. "Hombre, let's have a song! Do you know 'The Last Rose of Summer'?"

The guitarist shook his head.

"It's easy!" Lawton began to sing: "'*Tis the last rose of summeeeer/Left bloomiiing alooone/All her lovely compaaanions/Are faded and gooone.*"

The guitarist and the customers looked unimpressed by this rendition, and Lawton shrugged and turned back to the bar, as the guitarist began to strum a tune that sounded vaguely oriental. Already the euphoria was fading and he felt the morbs returning. Now he felt only terror and disgust at the thought that his mind had tricked him into believing that his father was in the city. That was how his mother had begun, seeing people no one else could see and even talking to them, and now he was condemned to follow the same downhill path. He did not know how many glasses he had drunk by the time he staggered back into the street to make his way back to the hotel. He had not gone far when he heard a smooching kiss, and he looked up to see a woman standing on the balcony in a dressing gown.

"You want to fuck me, Mister?"

She slipped the dressing gown over her shoulders and cupped one of her breasts in one hand and beckoned to him with the other. For a brief moment Lawton was tempted to go upstairs, then the nausea rose up inside him and he leaned forward and vomited. The woman cursed as he lurched off through the darkened street, holding the wall like a blind man. A few minutes later he saw Weygrand's bulging eyes staring from one of the posters outside the Edén Concert, and he stumbled on toward the Plaza Reial.

There was no traffic on the Ramblas now, and the pedestrian thoroughfare was deserted except for a few sailors and prostitutes moving around in the gas lights. The morbs held him fast now, and he felt only disappointment, disgust, and anger at the world that had taunted him with possibilities that a man from his background had no right to expect, only to snatch them away from him. Perhaps the old man had felt like that when he staggered or crawled back from the pub to terrorize his wife and family. But his father could never have dreamed of becoming a detective—or becoming anything at all.

And yet there had been a time—many years ago—when he really believed the old man was the strongest man in the world; when he listened to the stories of monsters, mermaids, and Indians that he brought back with him from the sea and imagined that he was just like Ulysses or Captain Cook—a hero, a navigator, and an explorer. But in the end his father had turned out to be a whoremongering drunk who drove his poor wife mad. How many times had the old man told him he would never amount to anything in this world? And now the world had proved him right; the man who had laid out Black Jack Owen was sliding down toward the workhouse or the asylum.

He was still trying to remember where his hotel was when he saw the three men walking slowly toward him. All of them were wearing bowler hats and overcoats, and as they came closer he saw that two of them had shotguns hanging from their shoulders. The other man was slightly shorter than his companions and he looked at Lawton with a disapproving, imperious expression that immediately annoyed him.

"Where you going, friend?" he asked. "Bit late for whoring."

Lawton straightened up. He was more than a foot taller than any of them, and even though a voice in his head told him to be respectful, he felt suddenly belligerent. "What's it to do with you?"

"That's not how you talk to the Somaten."

"I'll talk whatever shite I fancy, little man. So fuck off now."

"You need to wash your mouth out," the little man said.

"Do I now? And who will make me do that?"

"You're coming with us."

"The fuck I will. I shall be speaking to His Majesty King Edward about—"

The sentence went unfinished as one of the Somaten jabbed the butt of his shotgun into his stomach, winding him. Even as he bent over the other shotgun hit him hard in his lower back, pitching him face forward onto the cobblestones. He tried to roll away, but now the three militiamen were all kicking him and beating him with their guns as he tried to curl up and protect himself. High above the canopy of trees he could see the tiny glints of stars and he thought of all the good souls the priests had told him about, sitting at the right hand of the Lord and stretching back in their millions toward infinity. Millions and millions of souls, Father McGuire had told him, of all the good people who had ever been alive since Adam and Eve, burning like tiny candles for all eternity.

Lawton knew he was in hell, and there was no escape from it. Everything conspired to keep him there, from his poor, weak brain to the buildings and plane trees and the wrought iron balconies, and the three devils who seemed intent on kicking him to death. He thought he might be sick again, and then he felt the world slipping away from him, and the stars receded too, and he fell down into the pit of darkness that seemed to have been always waiting for him.

He woke up to find himself lying on a cold stone floor and stared up at the vaulted roof above his head. At first he thought he was in a church, then he smelled vomit and alcohol and saw the dusty stream of light descending at an angle from the high barred window. He sat up and looked around at the men sitting or lying all around him. Most of them were sleeping, and some appeared to be unconscious or dead. He felt for his wallet and pocket watch, and he was relieved to find that they were still there. He ached all over, and he knew that he had been beaten, but he could not remember anything beyond the point when he had set off in pursuit of the red-haired sailor. He stumbled over to the barred grille with a growing feeling of panic. On the other side of the room a uniformed policeman was sitting at a desk, doing some paperwork by the glow of a paraffin lamp.

"Excuse me officer. Can you tell me where I am?"

The policeman looked at him. "You're in Atarazanas District Police Station, Section 2," he said. "Awaiting deportation."

"Deportation?" Lawton rubbed the back of his head. "What for?"

"Drunk and disorderly behavior. Brawling with the Somaten."

"They attacked me!"

The policeman shrugged. "That's not what they said. And as soon as we find out where you came from, we're going to send you back there."

"I can tell you where I'm from, but I'd like to speak to the station chief."

"Inspector Bravo Portillo is too busy to deal with drunks."

Lawton tried to muster some semblance of dignity. "Look, my name is Harry Lawton. I'm a private investigator and I have a job to do in Barcelona."

"Is that what you were doing last night? Your job?"

Lawton was not in the mood to be mocked by jumped-up little policemen, but after last night's encounter there was not much he could do about it. He considered asking for Smither at the consulate, but there was no guarantee that His Majesty's Government would be any more sympathetic to a predicament that he had brought entirely on himself. The policeman was about to walk away when it occurred to Lawton that there was another possibility.

"Please ask the inspector to contact Charles Arrow at the Office of Criminal Investigation," he said. "Tell him Chief Inspector Maitland's Irish friend needs to see him."

The policeman seemed to know who Arrow was, and he agreed to give the inspector the message. Lawton wrote down Maitland's name for him, and the officer left the room and came back a few minutes later to say that he had passed on his request. He was followed shortly afterward by another officer, who began calling out some of the names in the cell. Over the next two hours the bodies began to thin out, until Lawton was able to sit on a bench. Finally the second officer called out his name. The desk officer opened the cell and Lawton followed his colleague up a flight of stairs and then up another floor, where the policeman ushered him into an office. Behind a desk a dapper little Spaniard with pointed, elf-like ears and a slick of black hair plastered to one side of his mostly bald head was sitting smoking a cigarette.

In front of the desk a tall, broad-shouldered foreigner in a smart two-piece suit was sitting with his hat on his lap. He looked in his late-forties, but his hair and moustache already showed streaks of gray, and he looked at Lawton with disapproval.

"Señor Lawton," said the man behind the desk. "I am Inspector Bravo Portillo. Inspector Arrow here has asked me to release you."

Lawton nodded gratefully. "I'm glad to hear it."

Arrow's stony expression did not change. "If Chief Inspector Maitland is prepared to vouch for you I assume there must be a reason," he said in English. "Though I suspect he might feel differently if he was aware of your behavior last night."

"Yes, sir. Thank you, sir."

"I will defer to the inspector in this instance," said Bravo Portillo. "But if you ever do anything like this again, you will be sent back to England on the first available ship."

Lawton thanked him once again and followed Arrow out into the corridor. He was surprised to find that the police station was in the same street as the Edén Concert theater, and as they walked back toward the Ramblas he saw Weygrand's face staring at him once again.

"Sorry about the bother," he said.

"'Bother' doesn't quite describe it, does it?" Arrow replied. "I don't normally pull drunken Micks out of the clink, believe me. Yet Chief Inspector Maitland said you used to be a detective."

"I was."

"Was this why you left the force? Drunkenness?"

"No sir. I left because of ill health."

"And yet James sent you here." Arrow looked at him curiously. "He says you're working for Randolph Foulkes's widow?"

"I am."

"And what's her interest in this?"

"She believes there's been deception, sir. As do I."

"Well there's a journalist here who's also interested in the Bar la Luna bombing. Name of Bernat Mata. He thinks there's some connection between the bombing and our local vampire—a madman the papers call the Raval Monster."

"I've heard of him," Lawton said.

"Mata says the man who blew up the Bar la Luna is one of the Monster's victims. He's got some crackpot theory the political police are involved. He's asked me to look into it. But I've had quite enough of Barcelona conspiracies, thank you. You never get to the bottom of them and no one even wants to. Oh they pretend they do! The city fathers invited me here to stop terrorist bombings—or at least to put on a public show that they wanted to stop them. They gave me a good salary and a lovely office but nothing else. Not enough police officers. No detectives. Even the police I did have I couldn't be trusted to keep a secret. Now most of them have gone, and the city wants me gone, too. The politicians and the other police hate me even more than they hate each other. Even Bravo

Portillo would stab me in the back if he could—the smarmy two-faced bastard. You can't get anything done in this city, Lawton. It's not like London. I see you speak Spanish though."

"Well enough."

"Well you might want to speak to Mata. He's a decent enough chap. A separatist, but he might know something that can help you. His offices are just across the road on Escudellers. Just ask for *La Veu de Catalunya*."

Lawton thanked him once again and returned to his hotel. He was relieved to find that Señor Martínez was not at his desk so that he would not have to explain his appearance and smell, and he got the key from the cleaner. The pain in his head had mostly gone now, but he was hurting almost everywhere else. There was a graze on his forehead and his lower lip was cut, and his back felt tender to the touch. He did not think he had broken anything, but this seemed little compensation for the humiliation and disgrace that he had brought on himself, and the thought of what Maitland would say when he found out only added to his mortification.

There was only one way to make amends, and that was to act like a detective once again. He splashed some water on his face and changed into another shirt and his second suit. He thought he still smelled of alcohol as he walked around the corner into the Calle Escudellers, until he reached the offices of *La Veu de Catalunya*. Through the glass window he could see a handful of journalists hunched over their typewriters, who stopped working when he came into the room.

"I'm looking for Bernat Mata," he said.

"He's not here," one of the journalists replied.

"Do you know where I can find him?"

"I do," the journalist said. "He's out looking at a corpse."

13

I n his childhood Mata and his family had gone regularly to Bare
Mountain for barbecues and picnics on Sundays and feast days. At
that time, in the 1870s, the mountain had been entirely undeveloped
and largely uninhabited, and he and his friends had run wild among the
trees and rocks, while the adults cooked chicken, *butifarra*, and smoked
pork in little fires.

The previous summer he had seen Gaudí's unfinished new park on
the mountain for the first time during the Floral Games. It was obvious
even then that the architect had achieved something remarkable even
by his standards. From the barren hump that he remembered from his
childhood, Gaudí had transformed Bare Mountain into an ornate semi-
tropical paradise, with mosaic walls crisscrossing the mountainside,
viaducts, and tree-lined terraces, chipped stone pillars that matched the
trunks of the palm trees above them, and shaded walkways and paths
curving up toward the Calvary Monument. The Floral Games had taken
place on the central esplanade, and Mata remembered how his eyes had

welled up as the sound of Catalan mingled with the crows and screeching parakeets. There were those who believed that Bare Mountain was the original site of the Garden of Eden, but that summer he preferred to see it as a Catalan Parnassus, to which the poets of the future Independent nation would return each year to celebrate their native tongue in exquisite verse.

That dream had not materialized, and the poets and the organizers of the games had balked at the idea of trekking all the way up to Bare Mountain each year and had opted to bring the competition back down to the city. Now he stepped down from the carriage and looked up at the two red gatehouses with their tiled eggs and curved Moorish towers. He trudged up the marble steps, past the crenelated walls, the fountain, and the mosaic dragon with the shield of Catalonia on its collar. By the time he reached the dusty esplanade he was sweating and breathing hard, and he continued to follow the shaded pathway up the hill toward the three crosses that protruded above the rows of palm trees like a hermitage. Finally he came around the side of the mountain to find Bravo Portillo standing at the foot of the Calvary Monument with a small group of onlookers. Mata saw Gaudí and Count Güell standing near the inspector. He knew Gaudí lived in one of the gatehouses and he had heard that his sponsor also had a house on the mountain now.

Gaudí looked as small and frail as ever in his gray suit and hat, and his beard seemed whiter than the last time he had seen him. He acknowledged Mata with a nod and Mata tipped his cap and looked up at the two Mossos d'Esquadra who were carrying a body down from the monument on a stretcher. Güell grimaced with revulsion as they laid the stretcher down on the ground, and made the sign of the cross. The architect looked distraught, and Mata could not blame him. Even as he stared bleakly down at the naked corpse he knew that he would never see Gaudí's park in the same way. Until then he had associated the mountain with leisure, childhood, and poetry. Now, less than a month after the murder of Pau Tosets, he found himself obliged to contemplate yet another insane and incomprehensible act of cruelty.

The victim appeared to be a boy of about fourteen, but one of his legs was bowed and slightly twisted and an oversized tongue protruded from his misshapen face. Like the other two bodies Mata had seen in the last three weeks, there were bites and gashes in his arms and throat, but this time there were a number of bluish patches and contusions that looked like internal bruises on his chest and a rash on his neck and arms.

"This will be the cretin who disappeared from the Raval a week ago," Bravo Portillo said. "Looks like our maniac has been at work again."

Mata suppressed his irritation. He had had about enough of Bravo Portillo's obstinate complacency, but he was also conscious of the reporters the inspector could call upon if he openly challenged him.

"But why bring the body all the way up here from the Raval?" he asked. "Whoever did this could have killed him there."

"Madmen don't have reasons, Mata."

"Satan does," said Gaudí sadly. "And this is his work. He mocks our city with this act of sacrilege."

"If it was Satan, then his instrument was certainly human." Count Güell's sunken watery eyes turned toward Bravo Portillo. "And I'm rather surprised—and disappointed—at the inability of the police to find him, Inspector."

"We will find him, Your Grace," Bravo Portillo replied. "My men are searching for him. We have extra people all over the Raval. We've alerted the watchmen."

"Why not just put the whole neighborhood under curfew?" Güell suggested. "It would stop this madman."

"We don't have authorization to do that, Your Grace. That would require the army."

"It would," Güell agreed. "And perhaps if we'd had the army on the streets when the terrorists were blowing us up these last few years we might have been able to stop them, too."

Gaudí was still staring at the body, and seemed to be mumbling a prayer as Bravo Portillo asked the two of them whether they had heard or seen anything unusual the previous night. Güell had spent the previous two nights at his palace in the Raval, but Gaudí said that he had heard a motorcar somewhere on the mountain at about two o'clock the previous night. The noise surprised him, he said, not only because of the lateness of the hour, but because motor cars rarely came to Bare Mountain even by day. He had not seen the vehicle, but he thought it had parked not far from the entrance, because the driver had turned its engine off, and then he had heard it start again about an hour later.

"Just long enough to carry the body up here and then get back down again," Bravo Portillo said.

"A lot of work for one lunatic," Mata suggested.

Bravo Portillo clucked his tongue and shook his head. "Look at him. Nothing but skin and bone. My wife could carry him."

Mata was tempted to tell him about Hermenigildo Cortéz's outing in the foreigner's motor car, but he remained silent as Bravo Portillo told the two policemen to take the body down to the mortuary wagon. Gaudí looked out across the city toward the unfinished walls of his Sagrada Familia cathedral that jutted up out of the empty plain. He looked so devastated that Mata felt an urge to console him. Just then he saw a big olive-skinned man in a derby hat trudging up the footpath toward them. As he came closer, Mata saw his unshaven face, grazed forehead, and bloodshot eyes. His features resembled a Toltec mask or the pictures of Red Indians from his childhood, and Mata caught a faint smell of alcohol on his clothing as he came closer.

"Mr. Lawton." Bravo Portillo made no attempt to conceal his distaste. "I didn't think I'd see you again so soon."

Lawton tipped his hat and glanced down at the corpse. "I've come to speak to Bernat Mata," he said. "Is he here?"

"He is," Mata replied. "And ready to return to the city."

Lawton stepped forward to take a closer look at the murdered boy, but Bravo Portillo's officers covered him and carried him away. Bravo Portillo stared coldly at Lawton and walked away with his men, as Lawton and Mata walked a short distance behind them.

"The Inspector doesn't seem to like you," Mata observed.

"We didn't get off to a good start." Lawton reached out his hand. "Harry Lawton, private investigator. I'm investigating the foreigner who was killed at the Luna Bar."

"I know who you are," Mata said. "Dr. Quintana thinks very highly of you."

"Glad someone does. Mr. Arrow said I should speak to you. He said you have a theory about the bombing."

"I do. And I understand from Dr. Quintana that you also have a theory about the victim—the Englishman."

"It's not a theory, sir. The victim's name is Randolph Foulkes. His widow sent me here to identify the body, and I've done that."

"Aha. So that's why Bravo Portillo doesn't want you here. He doesn't like Mr. Arrow. The Spanish don't like to be taught policing by foreigners. It offends their honor and national dignity—and it also shows how useless they are."

Lawton did not explain that Bravo Portillo had other reasons for his disapproval. "You don't feel the same?" he asked.

"I'm Catalan, Mr. Lawton, not Spanish. There is a difference, even if the rest of the world doesn't know it yet."

"I have heard that," Lawton replied. "Inspector Arrow says you believe there is some connection between the Luna Bar bombing and this . . . Monster?"

"There might be. But no one seems to want to look into it."

"Perhaps we can help each other."

"How so?"

"I believe Dr. Foulkes was the victim of a deception. I'm trying to trace his companion—a female companion."

"Ah yes. The missing lady."

"You're well-informed. May I ask what's your interest in this case?"

Mata told Lawton about the murder of Hermenigildo Cortéz, about Esperanza Claramunt, and the kidnapping and murder of the anarchist Pau Tosets. He told him his belief that the Social Brigade had been responsible for Tosets's disappearance and summarized the results of Quintana's autopsies. He was still talking when they reached the entrance, and Mata offered to take him back into the city in his taxi. Lawton was beginning to wonder what all this had to do with him, when Mata mentioned the foreign gentleman with the motorcar, and the motorcar that appeared to have brought the murdered cretin to Bare Mountain.

"Weygrand," Lawton said.

"Who?"

They had reached the esplanade now, and Lawton told him about Dr. Weygrand and his assistant, and his belief that the two of them had used hypnosis to bring Foulkes to Barcelona and defraud him of £500.

"Well, that's a novelty," Mata said. "I didn't know such things were possible."

"After what I saw last night I think it's very possible," replied Lawton. "I believe Foulkes was still in a trance when he died. And now I'm thinking something else. What if his death wasn't just bad luck? What if Weygrand got this Hermenigildo to bomb the Luna Bar in order to kill Foulkes? It's clever—he seems to be in the wrong place when a bomb goes off. No need for a police investigation. Case closed."

"Why would he kill Foulkes if he'd already gotten his money?"

Lawton shrugged. "Maybe he was worried hypnosis wouldn't be enough to keep him quiet forever. And then he had the bomber killed so that he couldn't talk about it either."

"Hombre, if you want to shut someone up a bullet will do perfectly well. I saw the body. It looked like a wild beast had attacked him. Same with Tosets and the boy up there. All of them killed in the same way—with their blood drained. Would this Weygrand be capable of something like that?"

"I don't know. What's Bravo Portillo saying?"

"The Luna Bar bombing is outside of his jurisdiction. It's gone to the Social Brigade as a political crime. He thought the first two murders were committed by a madman who hates anarchists. God knows how he'll explain the cretin. Look, where are you staying?"

"The Hotel de Catalonia."

Mata scrawled something on a notepad and tore out the page. "This is my home address," he said. "If you need anything, come to me or my newspaper. If I find anything of interest I'll let you know."

"Thanks." Lawton put the paper in his pocket. "And please don't mention Foulkes's name in connection with the Luna Bar in your paper. I need permission from his widow."

"As you wish."

They were approaching the Plaza Catalunya now, where a large crowd had gathered to listen to a man who was mounted on a podium holding his fists up at the sky. The speaker looked as though he were walking on a sea of hats and parasols, and his histrionic gestures reminded Lawton so much of Weygrand's performance that he half-expected him to hold up a pack of cards or a knife. Mata said it was a public meeting of the Young Barbarians, the youth wing of the Radical Republicans, whose leader Alejandro Lerroux was in exile in Buenos Aires for writing a seditious article. As the carriage pulled around the square the speaker yelled, "Burn the churches! Drive out the vampires who are sending your sons to die! Burn them all!"

"The authorities allow people to say such things?" Lawton asked incredulously, as the crowd roared back its approval.

Mata nodded wearily. "Lerroux likes to feed the masses raw meat. That's what he was famous for. I saw him speak various times. He was like a magician. He could make you believe anything—and make you believe he was anything, until you actually started to think about what he was saying. But the masses loved him, especially when he shouted at priests and nuns."

"Why do they hate the Church so much?"

Mata looked at him in surprise. "This is Spain, Mr. Lawton. Half the population believes in Jesus and the other half regards the Church as parasites. And no city is more hostile to the Church than Barcelona. Lerroux feeds that hatred. This is our age—the age of conjurers, illusionists, and fakirs, who brandish magic mirrors and perform political rope tricks to keep the masses distracted and entertained."

"I think Dr. Weygrand may be that kind of fraud," Lawton said.

"So is Lerroux. Even in his absence his disciples follow the same tradition. A useful tradition."

"Useful how?"

Mata looked out the window as the crowd roared once again. "The Radicals might hate the Church, but they hate the anarchists more. Most of all they hate my party—the Catalan Regionalist League. We want an independent Catalan state. The Radicals want a Spanish republic—or at least they say they do, and they want the army to deliver it. And the army and the government see the Radicals as a stick to beat us with—so they fund them—covertly, of course."

"The army funds a party that hates the Church and wants to bring down the monarchy?" Lawton asked.

Mata smiled. "The Radicals have offices and houses of the people all over the Raval. You don't pay for that with membership subs. You look confused. Well Barcelona is a confusing city. There are many different games being played here. Anyway Mr. Lawton, I must go back to the office and write another sad story. What will you do now?"

"I think I'll visit the Edén Concert," Lawton replied. "And find out where the Great Weygrand is staying."

Many years ago, in her village near Tarragona, Angela's grandmother had threatened her with the Sackman when she and her siblings misbehaved. The Sackman wore a hood, her abuela said, and he went out on the country roads at night in search of naughty children to fill the bag that he carried on his back. No one had ever seen his face or heard him speak, but the Sackman could find naughty children wherever they were. Even in their parents' house he would come in through the window and toss them into his sack like kittens or little puppies, and take them away to a place where they were never seen again. For most of her life, the Sackman had been the most terrifying thing she could think of. Now she half-expected to find him looking down at her as she opened her eyes and peered into the darkness, and wondered whether she was dreaming or awake.

She thought she was awake, but the room was so dark that she could not make out a single object. She could not even see her own body, and it was only when she tried to move her arms and legs that she felt the straps holding her tight to the chair. When she tried to lean forward she found that her chest was also strapped, and her head was held so tightly in some kind of container that she could only look straight ahead. In that moment she felt a terror that was not like anything she had ever felt before. It was something she could not even name, because she had no idea why she was in this room or who had brought her there. The only thing she remembered were the footsteps in the street behind her, the hand over her mouth and the hospital smell that was still on her clothes.

She wanted to call out to her abuela, because her grandmother was a kind woman who had only wanted her to be good and would never have wanted any harm to come to her. But it was impossible to make a sound because of the gag. All she could do was weep. Soon she had cried so much that her tears had soaked the gag. Still she could not stop crying, because she knew that she had been brought here to die and that her baby would grow up without her, and nothing in her life had prepared her to end her life like this, alone in the darkness in a place she did not know, and with no idea what she was even doing there.

Was it because she was a sinful woman who had strayed from the path of virtue? Or because she had told the journalist Mata about Hermenigildo and the foreign gentleman with the fancy motorcar? She knew that God must be able to see her, and that the Virgin could see her too, and she prayed to them to take pity on her, because surely they would understand that she had only sold herself because she was poor. Angela pictured the Virgin as she had seen her so many times, in the statues at the cathedral and the church of Santa Maria del Mar, in the festival of Raval and the procession of the Virgin of Mercy. She imagined her sweet, beneficent face looking down on her with a consoling expression and then she heard footsteps coming toward her and the sound of someone whistling a tune.

It was a pretty tune that sounded vaguely familiar, like something she might have heard from a marching band, and as it came closer she remembered another story from her childhood about a monster with a bull's head who lived in a maze underground and ate anyone who entered it. As a child she had pitied the monster that seemed as trapped as the victims it was forced to feed on. There had even been a time when she felt sorry for it. Now she strained at her bonds as the door opened behind her, because she knew that no one should be whistling in a place like this, and whoever it was, she knew that neither God nor the Virgin were listening to her prayers.

14

Lawton had been waiting for half an hour in the lobby of the Gran Hotel Colón when Weygrand and Zorka came down the stairs. They walked arm in arm, like a couple arriving for a ball. Without his robes and turban, Weygrand looked like a gentleman-tourist in his smart linen suit, monocle, and trilby hat. His moustache had been carefully waxed into two upturned points, and he was carrying a black cane with a silver handle shaped like a wolf's head. Zorka was wearing a large wide-brimmed hat with a bunch of artificial grapes and plums attached to it, and a powder-blue dress with a cream belt that accentuated the fine hourglass curve of her waist.

"Mr. Lawton, I apologize for keeping you waiting," said Weygrand, in excellent English. "And I'm sorry we weren't in when you came by yesterday." He smiled amiably, but his orb-like eyes were watchful. Lawton shook his manicured hand and tipped his hat at Zorka, who acknowledged him with the faintest of smiles.

"Not a problem," he said. "They told me at the theater you were staying here. I won't take up much of your time."

"As much as you need. Let's sit somewhere more comfortable, shall we?" Lawton followed them across the lobby to the café and bar, where Weygrand pulled out a seat for Zorka by the window.

"Can I order you a sherry, Mr. Lawton? Or would you prefer some other beverage? Unusually for Spain, they do afternoon tea here."

"Tea'll be fine." Lawton was conscious that Zorka was staring at his bruises and the bandage on his forehead, as Weygrand ordered two sherries and a pot of tea.

"I saw your performance on Thursday," Lawton said. "Very impressive."

"I'm glad you enjoyed it." Weygrand took a pack of Sobranie Black Russians from his jacket and slotted a cigarette into a silver holder. He offered the pack to Lawton, who accepted. "Your message said you're a private investigator. I assume you didn't come all the way from London to visit the Edén Concert."

"I'm working for Mrs. Randolph Foulkes," said Lawton. "Her husband's gone missing."

He had already decided not to mention Foulkes's death, but both Weygrand and Zorka looked alarmed.

"Missing?" said Weygrand. "Since when?"

"He was last seen here in Barcelona on June 13." Lawton looked up as the waiter returned with their drinks. "I understand you were at the opera with him the day before his disappearance was reported."

"May I ask how you know that?" Weygrand asked.

"A mutual acquaintance told me. Señor Ferrer."

"Of course," said Weygrand wearily. "Randolph didn't expect to find him there, and he wasn't pleased about it. But music knows no boundaries, does it? Especially when it comes to Mozart. I am surprised by what you say, though. Randolph came down with us from Vernet-les-Bains. He said he was going back there the next day."

"The police say he hasn't been seen there."

Weygrand looked unimpressed. "The Barcelona police aren't renowned for their thoroughness. Unlike Scotland Yard."

Lawton ignored the compliment. "May I ask how you met Dr. Foulkes?"

"In Vernet. At the Hotel du Portugal. That's where we usually stay."

"To take the waters?"

Weygrand laughed. "To earn my daily bread, Mr. Lawton. Vernet is a popular holiday destination for the better class of tourist. Some like to be entertained. Others require the services of a doctor and a psychiatrist—both of which I'm able to provide."

So far Zorka had not said a word. Now she suddenly raised her hand in front of Lawton's forehead. "Your aura is so white," she said sadly.

"My what?" Lawton instinctively pulled away from her.

"Your energy field," Weygrand explained. "All of us have one, but Zorka can actually see them. A white aura suggests illness and poor health. Do you have any health problems, Mr. Lawton?"

"None at all." Lawton reddened as Zorka passed her hand across his chest as though she were blessing him.

"You need healing," she said. "I see damage. And pain."

"You're mistaken." Lawton said.

"Oh, but I—"

Weygrand gave Zorka a warning look and she withdrew her hand. Lawton thought she looked slightly fearful now, and he wondered what the relationship was between them and he turned back to Weygrand.

"Is that how you met Dr. Foulkes? As a patient?"

"I did."

"What was his problem?"

Weygrand let out a stream of smoke. "I don't discuss my clients with strangers, Mr. Lawton. Just as I'm sure you wouldn't talk about your investigations to people who have no connection with them."

"Was the man in your carriage one of your clients? I saw you leaving with him after your performance."

Weygrand's expression did not change. "A friend. Nothing more."

"What was his name?"

"With respect, Mr. Lawton, I don't think my friends are any of your business. And I'm really sure why you're asking me these questions."

"Did you ever have occasion to hypnotize Dr. Foulkes?"

Still the black eyes showed no hint of emotion. "There was no need. We only had a few sessions together. We soon began to see each other socially.

Dr. Foulkes is a great music lover and so am I. Naturally we weren't going to miss a performance of *The Magic Flute*. We are committed to remain here till August, but Randolph intended to return to Vernet to continue working on his book. I had assumed that's where he was—till now."

"He seems to have spent some time here with a woman. You wouldn't happen to know who she might be?"

"I did see him with a woman in Vernet." Weygrand turned to Zorka. "Do you remember? A Frenchwoman. What was her name?"

"Marie," Zorka replied. "Marie Babineaux."

"That's it! Madame Babineaux. A widow. We met them in the Casino Park. But I didn't know she was in Barcelona. You're not suggesting there was something . . . untoward between them, are you? I find that difficult to imagine. Randolph is married. And he doesn't strike me as a passionate man. Wouldn't you agree, dear?"

Zorka nodded.

Lawton had met many liars and confidence tricksters in his time, and he had learned to look for telltale indications in their body language, facial expressions, and even in their breathing that might reveal signs of stress or tension, but Weygrand gave no indication of any discomfort.

"That may be so," he said. "But I would like to meet her."

"Well in that case you really should go to Vernet. No stone unturned. Isn't that the expression? I expect you'll find Dr. Foulkes in his hideaway. It's a bit out of the way, but that's why he goes there."

"I might do that." Lawton stubbed out his cigarette. "And maybe I'll come to your next performance. So I can see how you do those tricks of yours."

"You think they're tricks, Mr. Lawton?" Weygrand's eyes flashed. "Please do come. It's always a pleasure to disprove the sceptics. Perhaps I might hypnotize *you*."

"I doubt it. Thank you for your time." Lawton stood up and tipped his hat at Zorka. As he was leaving the hotel he saw Weygrand in the window, leaning forward to talk to her. He was talking urgently, as if he were criticizing her, and Lawton wondered why. Two days ago, watching her on stage, he had been convinced that she was the woman who had cashed Foulkes's check and accompanied him on the day of his death.

Now he felt just the tiniest chink of doubt, and even though he knew that Foulkes was dead, it did not seem like a bad idea at all to take up Weygrand's suggestion, and pay a little visit to Vernet-les-Bains.

In the winter of 1907, Esperanza went to a talk at the Athenaeum by a Russian comrade who had spoken about the great struggle that was unfolding in his native land. The Russian had been at the Winter Palace in 1905, when the Cossacks fired on Father Gapon's marchers on Bloody Sunday and set the country alight. That night she and the other members of the audience had felt some of that heat. Even in the very crude translation, the Russian's descriptions of strikes, marches, rebellions, and mutinies had thrilled his listeners, and afterward Pau said that it was only a matter of time before the workers and peasants of Spain followed their example.

Now she stood with Ruben, Arnau, and the other members of the Invincibles on the Via Laietana, watching the soldiers marching down toward the port past the lines of protesters, and she wondered if that time had come. Even old men and children were waving their fists and shouting insults at the army, the government, the Jesuits, the Count of Romanones, and the Marquess of Comillas. Esperanza knew that Comillas owned most of the troop ships, and that like Romanones and the Jesuits, he had shares in the Rif mines. Now she felt a common bond with the women who urged the soldiers not to fight for Jesuit gold and shouted insults at their officers. To her amazement, some soldiers dropped out of the line of march and slipped into the crowds, which opened up to let them through and then closed again to prevent their officers from following them. Esperanza had never seen anything like this, and her voice was soon hoarse as she and the comrades mingled with the crowd, whipping up chants against Maura and the ricos who sent their poor to fight their wars while they paid for their own sons to stay at home.

Arnau seemed physically transformed by the demonstration, and his normally somber face was a mask of passionate fury as he led the Invincibles in a chant of "No blood, no war!" which quickly spread through the crowd. At one point his eyes met Esperanza's, and he grinned as she joined in the chant. They continued to follow the soldiers down to the harbor, and mingled with the crowds, the melee of soldiers, mules, and horses, while the cranes loaded machine guns and boxes of supplies and ammunition onto the waiting ship. Esperanza saw the civil governor Ossorio standing next to a line of police, all of whom were holding their rifles at the ready. Behind them a deputation from the Catholic Women's Association stood near the gangway, handing out sacred heart medallions to the soldiers as they prepared to walk onto one of the ships.

Most of the women were wearing the well-cut dresses that she had seen on the wealthy Christian women who occasionally came to Gràcia to distribute alms to the poor. As usual, many of them were accompanied by their maids and servants, who held up parasols to protect their mistresses from the sun. Both the servants and their mistresses looked equally surprised and anxious as the crowd turned its anger on them. One woman was yelling at a well-heeled señora in an fashionable flowery hat and long white dress that she had no right to hand out medals unless her husband or sons were going to Morocco. The expression of embarrassment and hostility on the señora's face made it clear that she had no intention of doing any such thing. Some of the ladies of charity began to flutter their parasols and backed away in alarm as soldiers contemptuously threw their medals into the water. One woman ripped the medal from a young soldier who appeared to be her son, and led him away while the crowd cheered her on. The protesters were becoming so boisterous that the police raised their rifles so that the Catholic ladies could retreat to their waiting carriages.

Still the crowd pushed forward, and Esperanza saw Ossorio whisper something to one of his officers. To her horror, the police pointed their rifles at the crowd. For a moment Esperanza thought of Father Gapon's marchers, and she instinctively ducked as the police fired a volley just above their heads. The crowd fell back shouting insults and the same slogans—"Send the friars to the Rif!" and "No war!"—that Esperanza had heard all week. Others mocked Ossorio's vast bulk and said that the fat man should go and fight the Moors himself.

The crowd laughed, and then the police surged forward, grabbing whoever they could get hold of, and driving the demonstrators out of the port. The Invincibles eventually regrouped near the Columbus Monument. They were about to disperse when Arnau said that Ferrer was at the Café Espanyol and suggested that they go there to celebrate the demonstration and try to persuade him to get behind the strike.

"Good idea!" said Ruben. "Espe, you coming?"

Esperanza knew that her mother would be expecting her back, but she was also keen to see Ferrer, and it felt good to march up the Parallelo with the Invincibles, chanting slogans and calling on the people in the street to join the protest. They had nearly reached the café when they saw a small crowd listening to a Radical Party speaker with rapt attention. She had heard that Lerroux was coming back to Barcelona soon, and it was obvious that the Emperor of the Parallelo still dominated the neighborhood, as the young speaker called on his audience to protest the Church's war in Morocco.

"We want a revolution not a protest!" Arnau snarled. "Forget Lerroux. Workers' Solidarity!"

The speaker shouted back something that Esperanza could not hear, but which did not sound friendly as they walked on. The Gran Café Espanyol was one of the few cafés on the avenue that was still frequented by anarchists. The Invincibles went inside and threaded their way through the tables, past the pianist and violinist, the card and domino players, the couples exchanging intimate looks, and the tables filled mostly with men arguing loudly about politics beneath a pall of cigarette and cigar smoke. In the far corner Esperanza saw Ferrer sitting with Tomás Herreros, the director of the *Soli*, and some other men she had not seen before. Ferrer kissed her on the cheeks and moved over so that she could sit beside him, as Ruben and the others pulled up chairs around their table. Esperanza knew Ferrer's ailing young niece had died, but he seemed in good spirits as Ruben and Arnau described the scenes they had just witnessed.

"That sounds very promising," he said. "Let's see how the national situation develops."

Ruben pulled a face. "With respect Don Francesc, we shouldn't be waiting to see what others might do. We need to take action *here*. We ought to be preparing for an extended strike. In my opinion, we ought to be preparing to lead an insurrection."

Esperanza was taken aback by Ruben's outspokenness, but Ferrer showed no sign that he was offended by it. "I admire your enthusiasm," he said. "But history is filled with episodes in which ill-considered and precipitate action has resulted in disaster. You don't bait the tiger unless you can fight him."

"There are also times when people didn't take advantage of the opportunities that came their way," Ruben retorted, "even when the tiger was old and toothless."

Ferrer smiled tolerantly, as though he were rejecting an unreasonable request from a child. "That is also true," he said. "And we'll see what position the Socialists and the Radicals take."

"But we can still influence that position," Arnau said, speaking for the first time. "Especially if you make your own position known."

"Perhaps," Ferrer agreed. "But I insist—Barcelona cannot have an insurrection by itself."

Esperanza wanted to say something, but she was conscious that she was the only woman present and she felt suddenly shy. She knew her mother would be horrified to see her sitting in a café surrounded by men, let alone with a group of anarchists, as the waiter came over to their table, and Ferrer offered to buy her a drink. She asked for a glass of lemonade, and Ruben ordered a jug of beer for himself and the comrades. Esperanza was still trying to summon up the courage to contribute to the conversation when she felt the touch of Ferrer's thigh against hers. At first she thought the contact was accidental, but when she shifted her leg away from him, he moved his own leg outward, even though there was plenty of space between them. She tried to tell herself she must be imagining it, but then she felt his little finger brushing against her leg, as if he were stroking her.

All this was so unexpected and astonishing that she could not think how to respond to it. During their walk in Montseny, Ferrer had said that anarchist love should not be possessive, the way it was in bourgeois novels. Was this what free love meant? Was Ferrer's wife aware that he behaved like this? Was this how he would have behaved had Pau still been alive? Whatever anarchists were supposed to do, Esperanza felt angry and embarrassed by this unwanted contact, and powerless to do anything about it. She tried to concentrate on the conversation, but it was impossible to ignore the furtive movements of Ferrer's little finger brushing against her thigh as she sat rigid as a statue with her hands clasped primly on her lap. Just then she saw two men coming toward them in derby hats and gray suits. Even from a distance they had the shifty hostile arrogance of police or militia, as they headed towards their table.

"Lieutenant Ugarte," said Ferrer. "It's been a while."

The table immediately fell silent and Esperanza recognized the name of the officer Mata had visited in Montjuïc. Her embarrassment gave way to revulsion and anger as she looked back at Ugarte's scarred cheeks.

"I heard you were back in the city," Ugarte said. "I assume you know what happened at the harbor? Decent Catholic ladies," he glanced darkly around him to make it clear that none of the women in the café belonged to this category, "mocked and insulted by the mob. Rifles and medals thrown into the sea. A disgrace."

"I didn't know this," Ferrer replied. "But I haven't been anywhere near the harbor. You can ask my companions."

"And why would I ask them that? We all know you don't have to actually be present when these things are happening."

Ferrer's owl-like expression did not change. "I'm flattered that you think I have magical powers, Lieutenant. But I'm a free man in my own country. A subject of the king, in the company of my friends. And I've committed no offense."

Ugarte scowled. "You dare mention the king? Just because you weren't proven guilty doesn't mean you're innocent."

"The law says otherwise," Ferrer replied calmly.

The café had fallen silent now, and most of the customers were following this confrontation with obvious interest.

"You should go back to your farm, Ferrer," Ugarte said. "It would be better for you and better for all of us."

Ruben had been shaking his head throughout this exchange, and now he jumped to his feet as if he could no longer contain himself.

"Maybe you should go back to the castle, Lieutenant. Instead of threatening innocent men for no reason."

To Esperanza's amazement Arnau and the other members of the Invincibles got to their feet and gathered round Ruben in a protective cluster, and some of the men at the surrounding tables were also on their feet now. For a moment Esperanza thought she should stand up, too, as Ugarte's colleague reached for his pistol, but Ugarte shook his head and his companion immediately lowered his hand. The lieutenant looked past Ruben as if he had not seen him.

Ferrer had removed his hand from Esperanza's thigh now, and she took advantage of this distraction to establish some distance between them. Ugarte glanced at her with a faintly knowing smile. For a moment his black eyes looked into hers, and she had the disconcerting realization that he knew her, before he turned away. Ugarte's companion also seemed to recognize her, and it was only then, as he followed his boss out of the café, that she remembered the driver's hateful face looking at her from the carriage that had driven Pau to his death, and she realized with a shock that she might know him, too.

15

From the moment the train pulled out of the Estación de Francia, Lawton felt as if a weight was lifting from his shoulders. A few minutes later the factories and white buildings thinned out and the sea appeared once again. He already felt exhausted, and the medication and the rocking of the train added to his drowsiness. Finally he surrendered to it and closed his eyes. He woke up to see the mountains stretching out in the distance to his left and the sea on the other side of the railway line to his right. An hour later he arrived in Portbou for the second time in two weeks and waited for the change of gauge.

At three o'clock he arrived in Perpignan once again, and shortly afterward he caught the next train inland to Villefranche. The Raval seemed a long way away now as the two-carriage train puffed its way through a sun-drenched landscape of narrow valleys and steep hills, dotted with beige and white villages, churches, walled towns, and military forts, interspersed with forests, gorges, rivers, and fields of wheat and barley. Soon the mountains appeared once again on each side of the narrow river valley, looming up in a green wall, broken by patches of rock and gnarled rust-colored cliffs. Most of his fellow passengers were English tourists sitting among imposing piles of holiday luggage, whose plummy accents echoed around the carriage to the point when it was almost possible to imagine that he was in Richmond or the West End if he closed his eyes.

In the late afternoon the train arrived at Villefranche-de-Conflent station, where a line of porters was waiting to load their luggage onto the waiting carriages. Lawton carried his own suitcase to a coach, and sat waiting with an English couple and their two children while the driver lifted their trunk and suitcases onto the roof. As the carriage wound its way slowly up the paved road past an ancient-looking walled city with a military fortress of more recent construction overlooking it, the children talked excitedly about their holiday plans while their mother shot occasional wary glances at the bandage on Lawton's forehead and his scruffy appearance. They made no attempt to speak to him, and he had no desire to speak to anyone. Half an hour later the carriage reached the outskirts of Vernet-les-Bains, and the road followed the line of a river into the village. Lawton looked up at the whitewashed and terracotta houses and villas with red slate tiles that tumbled down the forested mountains. High above the church and castle, a fluted rock face curved upward and outward like a giant shell toward a curved ridge. The Englishman pointed toward one of the bumps along the ridge and said that this was Mount Canigou, the highest mountain in the Pyrenees, and that they might try to reach the summit.

As the coach came into the center of the village Lawton noticed the larger villas on the other side of the river; the ladies in long white dresses and parasols and gentlemen wearing top hats and carrying canes, and French and British army officers in dress uniforms. Apart from the occasional French peasants in clogs and berets it really did feel like Surrey-in-the-Pyrenees. Lawton followed the directions across the bridge to the Hotel du Portugal, and soon recognized the casino from the postcard Foulkes had sent to his wife. The Hotel du Portugal stood directly opposite, and he walked into the turret-like entrance and across the marble floor to the reception desk, where the receptionist greeted him in perfect English and took his details.

"Will you be visiting the baths, Monsieur?" he asked. "We can arrange that for you."

"I won't. But I'm looking for a friend of mine who sometimes stays here. Dr. Franz Weygrand. Do you know him?"

"Of course!" the receptionist said brightly. "Everyone knows Dr. Weygrand. But he's in Barcelona now."

"Would you believe I've just come from there?" Lawton shook his head ruefully. "Never mind. There are two other friends of mine you might know. Randolph Foulkes and Madame Babineaux?"

"I don't know any woman by that name. But Dr. Foulkes used to stay here with his wife. He has a little house outside the village when he comes to Vernet now. I haven't seen him since the meeting last month."

"What meeting is that?" Lawton asked.

"The Club des Explorateurs," the receptionist said. "It met at the Casino at the beginning of June, as it usually does. Dr. Weygrand is also a member."

"Is that so? You know I'm a bit of an explorer myself. I'd be interested to know a bit more about this club. I might like to join."

"You would have to ask Dr. Foulkes about that, Monsieur. But there's also a photographer in the village, Monsieur Béchard. He took pictures of their meetings. Perhaps he can tell you something about the club. You'll find his studio just off the main square."

Lawton thanked him and went up to his room. That night he ate supper in the hotel and afterward he ran a bath from a tap in his own room for the first time in his life. He doubted whether Mrs. Foulkes would have approved of a trip to Vernet, but already he sensed that the extra expense was worth it. As he luxuriated in the warm soap suds he thought of the photograph of the 1906 Greenland expedition from Foulkes's study. Unlike Foulkes, it was difficult to imagine Weygrand as a polar explorer, but then both he and Zorka had talked a great deal of nonsense during their performance about a kingdom somewhere in the Arctic, which suggested that they might have something in common with the Englishman apart from music.

Lawton had no doubt that Weygrand was more than he seemed to be. He already believed that the Austrian was responsible for Foulkes's death. But if what Mata had told him about the murdered anarchists was true, then Weygrand had not only had Foulkes killed; he had also murdered the bomber, and killed another man and an innocent cretin who did not seem to have any connection to Foulkes. Why would he do such things? Why were the Barcelona police so reluctant to follow up on what Mata and the anarchist girl had told them? What interest could the political police have in covering up such crimes? Lawton was still mulling over these questions as he lay in bed, listening to the hoot of a nearby owl and the sound of genteel laughter from the casino. Whether it was the fresh mountain air or the distance from the city, he had no difficulty falling asleep and he slept throughout the night, undisturbed by nightmares or strange dreams. He woke up feeling refreshed enough to perform his morning calisthenics, and afterward he shadowboxed on the carpeted floor, ducking and weaving in front of the mirror with some of his old lightness and grace.

His night of weakness in the Raval seemed like a freakish aberration now and he felt so alert that he decided not to take his medication. Instead he ate a hearty breakfast of bacon, croissants, and coffee, and crossed the bridge in search of Monsieur Béchard. He soon found the studio, with its rows of photographs displayed in the window. All of them seemed to have been taken in Vernet, and most of them were portraits of men and women of obvious wealth and distinction. Lawton was surprised to find Lord Roberts, his former commander in the Transvaal, standing in full uniform with his drooping white moustache alongside a uniformed French general and various men and women in civilian clothes. Other pictures showed groups of ladies in walking boots with their skirts tied up just below their knees; family portraits taken against a canvas painting of the mountain overlooking the town, and men and women sitting on benches by a lake filled with swans that looked like a miniature version of Hyde Park. He went inside and found a youngish-looking man in his early thirties sitting behind a counter.

"Monsieur Béchard?"

"I am." Béchard replied in English. "How can I help you, Monsieur?"

"I was wondering, do you keep copies of the photographs you've taken?"

"Some of them." Béchard looked at him curiously. "Why do you ask?"

"I understand you photographed a meeting of the Club des Explorateurs this year."

"I did. And the year before. The club has met here in Vernet for the last two years."

Lawton looked pleased. "Well that is good news. You see I'm working for the *London Illustrated News*. We're writing a story about Vernet—what makes it so special?"

"It is special," Monsieur Béchard agreed. "They don't call it the Paradise of the Pyrenees for nothing. We get all kind of people here. Generals, counts, bankers . . ."

"So I've heard. But I don't think many people realize that some of the world's great explorers also come here. We'd really appreciate a picture of the club to go with my piece. You would be credited, of course."

Béchard said he would take a look. He disappeared into a back room and returned with some negatives and two photographs. Both portraits showed the same group of eight men sitting around a long table, with a banner bearing the name of the Club des Explorateurs and the same sig-rune symbol that Lawton had seen in Foulkes's Greenland expedition. At the far end of the table Foulkes sat stiffly upright in a dark suit and high collar, looking back at the photographer with a slight frown. He was sitting next to Weygrand and a man who looked about the same age, with a thin, hatchet face and a mane of silvery hair that was combed back behind his ears. To Weygrand's right, Lawton recognized one of the men from Foulkes's Greenland photograph. Unlike the others, he was smiling faintly, and without his parka, Lawton could see what looked like a dueling scar on his right cheek above a well-trimmed beard.

"Do you know this man?" he asked.

Béchard shook his head. "I only know Dr. Foulkes. And Dr. Weygrand and his lovely assistant, of course. But I believe he was German. I heard him speak to Dr. Foulkes in German. It was a very international gathering. I heard French spoken also. And Spanish."

"Do you know what they talked about?"

"I didn't attend the meetings, Monsieur. But I believe they discussed geography, archaeology, and travel. They brought slides and photographs with them, which I saw when I was taking my own photographs of the group. Very interesting pictures, Monsieur. Tibet. South America. The Arctic. Negroes and Eskimos. It was obvious to me that they were well-traveled men. I told Dr. Foulkes he and his friends should give lectures here in Vernet. We have such distinguished visitors here, who would certainly be most interested in such things. I told him I could arrange some public lectures with the mayor."

"What did he say?"

"He was not very keen." Béchard replied. "I'm not sure if he thought my suggestion a little vulgar. He said these meetings were intended for scholars and men of science—not for entertainment. Of course I never mentioned it again. Would you like me to make copies of these pictures for you? I can have them ready this evening."

Lawton thanked him and asked for directions to Foulkes's house. Any residual guilt about spending Mrs. Foulkes's money had vanished now, as he walked up through the winding streets and white houses overlooking the main square and asked at the town's hotels for Marie Babineaux. No one knew the name. Some receptionists remembered Foulkes's wife, but no one had seen him in any other female company. In the afternoon Lawton decided to go to Foulkes's house. He walked out of the town and up the main road through the forest. Apart from South Africa, he had never been in real mountains, and he had spent most of his time there being shot at, marching, or looking out for ambushes. Now the woods on either side of the road exuded peace and serenity, as he listened to the chirruping birds, the trickle of running water, and the faint rustle of leaves.

After about twenty minutes he followed a narrower track that led up through the forest to his left behind a group of houses overlooking the road, as receptionist at his hotel had told him to do. Even after a few minutes it was obvious why Foulkes's widow had stopped coming to Vernet. The path was too narrow for a carriage and it was not an easy track for neurasthenic ladies. He had been walking for about ten minutes when he heard the whine of a motorcar coming up from the direction of the town. He continued walking as the engine died away, till the path began to open up and he saw a small two-storey white house in the middle of a wide clearing up ahead. The house looked as though it might once have been a farm, but its window shutters were all closed. He walked around behind it, to a large dirt yard that reached back toward the looming wall of trees. At the center of the yard a round firepit surrounded by stones had been dug into the ground, and a pile of chopped wood was stacked in a wooden log store in the far corner.

Beyond the yard the forest was so dense that he could barely see through the trees at all. He wondered why Foulkes had chosen such an isolated house when there were so many more well-appointed villas in the town itself. The back door was locked and the windows were also shuttered up, but as he walked back and forth he noticed that one pair of shutters was slightly ajar. He slipped the fingers of both hands under one of the shutters and pushed them deeper into the space before wrenching the shutter back. The wooden flap flew open, and he bent down over the firepit and picked up a stone. As he did so he noticed the remains of Russian cigarettes lying in the ashes, and what appeared to be some white chicken's feathers scattered near the stones.

Even as he approached the window he knew he had no right to do what he was about to do, but he had not come this far to look at an empty house. He turned his face away and smashed the stone against the glass just above the window latch. There was a sudden flutter of wings from the forest before the silence returned and he slipped his hand in through the hole to open the window.

He climbed over the window sill and found himself in a small, low-ceilinged living room furnished with a sofa and armchair, a chair and a table with a pile of notebooks where Foulkes had obviously been working. There was also a well-stocked bookshelf near the table with three skulls on the top shelf. Through an open doorway he heard the buzzing of flies and he saw the remains of a stale baguette on a kitchen sideboard, and another door that led off to a little hallway and a flight of stairs.

As far as he could see the house had no lighting, except for the kerosene lamp on the table. He looked through the notebooks on the table and recognized Foulkes's tiny crablike handwriting. Some of the books were unused, but others were crammed with drawings and notes. One book contained sketches of skulls, noses, foreheads, eyes, and ears, with some of the same incomprehensible classifications that Lawton had seen in Foulkes's study.

In London Lawton had found Foulkes's interest in such things incomprehensible and vaguely distasteful. Now he felt unsettled by them as he went out into the little corridor to see what other artifacts the house contained. At the top of the stairs he saw a marble bust of a male head on a window ledge that looked like an ancient Roman or Greek, and had clearly been placed in front of the window to catch the sun's light. Lawton was about to go upstairs when he noticed the doorway leading off the stairwell. He slipped the latch and opened it, and peered down the steep flight of wooden steps into a dark basement that smelled of dust, rotting vegetables, and something curiously sweet.

He gripped the wooden banister with one hand and held up his lighter as a flashlight with the other, before backing his way down the stairs. Even as he descended, the cold air seemed to move up his legs, and he tried to dispel the thoughts of skulls, madmen, and things that slithered in the dark. As soon as he reached the dirt floor he saw the hooded white robes hanging on hooks from the wall by the stairs. There were five of them altogether, all emblazoned with the same wide-pointed red cross.

Lawton thought of all the photographs he had seen of Foulkes, and tried to imagine why the stern Victorian scholar with the white sideburns would want to keep such garments in his basement. He was even more surprised to see the same black sun that he had seen at the Edén Concert theater painted on the far wall. As he came closer he saw a row of candles and sticks of incense on a table just beneath it, and a little silver chalice that appeared to be stained with wine or dried blood. The incense sticks explained the sweet smell, but nothing else made any sense at all, and he was conscious of a chill in the air that was only partly due to the basement itself.

All this was unsettling and disturbing, and he hurriedly climbed the stairs and shut the door behind him with a little sigh of relief. In the same moment he thought he heard a movement outside the house. He paused in the doorway of the living room, but there was no other sound except for the birds outside and the flies buzzing in the kitchen. Even as he stepped back into the living room, he saw the raised arm in the open window and the fizzing black ball came rolling across the floor toward him. He jumped back into the hallway and slammed the door behind him as the bomb hit the tiles and skittered across the floor.

The explosion blew the door to pieces, and chunks of plaster dropped from the wall and ceiling onto his head as he lay stretched out in the hallway. As he picked himself up the dust and smoke were pouring into the hallway and his ears were humming as though an engine had become stuck inside his head. Even through the shock he knew he could not stay where he was. He gripped the banister and pulled himself to his feet. Everything in the living room was broken or burning, and the room was so full of smoke and flames that he could barely make out the window. He could smell paraffin and burning paper, and the smoke made him cough as he stumbled toward the window.

He was about halfway across the floor when he tripped over one of Foulkes's skulls and fell flat on his face. He writhed away from it in disgust and lurched to his feet once again. The smoke was so thick now that it was difficult to breathe as he pressed himself against the wall and looked out into the yard. During the war he had been bombed and shot at many times, but he had never been attacked in an enclosed space without a weapon and he had never felt so exposed and helpless. He was wondering if his attacker was out there waiting, when he heard a shot from the direction of the road. His lungs were burning now, as he skirted round the rising flames and hurled himself through the open window. He fell out into the yard and scrambled to his feet, crouching and zigzagging to avoid any waiting shooter.

He continued running, crouching and zigzagging to avoid any waiting shooter, and continued running back down toward the road. He was about halfway down the track when he heard the baaing up ahead and he saw a flock of sheep swirling around in front of him. As he drew nearer the animals scattered into the forest, to reveal the body of a man lying on his back, with his cap by his head and a shepherd's staff lying by his outstretched hand. Lawton looked down at the bloody stain on his chest, and then he heard the engine splutter into life. By the time he reached the road the motorcar had vanished, but even as he continued to follow the fading motor back down into Vernet-les-Bains, he knew that it was on its way back to Barcelona.

16

G entlemen, it cannot be denied that there are forces intent on reducing our city to chaos and ruin." Civil Governor Ángel Ossorio y Gallardo looked at the assembled journalists, who were sitting in front of him with their pens and notebooks poised. "They are using these disturbances to further their aims, but you can rest assured that they will not succeed. Those who break the law will feel the full weight of the law."

Ossorio was a big man in his late thirties, whose balding head and dark sober suit made him look older. His size and his girth had made him an object of mockery among both anarchists and republicans, but Mata knew him as an intelligent and thoughtful conservative, who had struggled during his two years in office to reform the Barcelona police and bring the rule of law to a city that was too often indifferent to it. Mata had met him on a number of occasions, both socially and professionally, and it was partly because of these personal contacts that the *Veu* was the only Catalan newspaper invited to a select gathering of the usual conservative journalists who could be relied upon to disseminate the government's views. Despite his attempts to project confidence, Mata thought the civil governor looked under pressure, and he asked him whether he would declare martial law in the event of a general strike.

"That won't be necessary," Ossorio replied firmly, "because there will be no strike."

Mata pointed out that the socialists in Madrid had called for a national strike, and the workers' organizations in Barcelona seemed likely to follow suit.

"Madrid is not my concern," Ossorio said. "But there will be no strike in this city. Law, order, and common sense will prevail. That is all gentlemen."

Ossorio ignored the barrage of questions that followed, and his secretary ushered the journalists from his office. Despite the civil governor's serenity, Mata did not feel reassured. In the last few days he had seen the Fat Man openly mocked in the street when he went out with his officials. On two occasions he had observed the police firing warning shots at crowds protesting against the war. It was only a matter of time before someone was wounded or killed. Even though Ossorio had banned public meetings in an attempt to defuse the situation, Radicals, anarchists, and socialists continued to address smaller gatherings on street corners and public squares, where they denounced the war and talked of strikes, revolution, and setting fire to convents and churches.

All this was alarming enough, and the mood in the workers' districts had become more belligerent and more openly seditious as a result of the stream of rumors and bad news coming from Morocco. It was said that the soldiers lacked food and ammunition; that the reservists had been attacked by Rif tribesmen almost as soon as they had landed at Melilla; that Maura was about to announce a full mobilization of the army and issue a declaration of war. In this febrile atmosphere Hermenegildo Cortéz's woman Angela Romeu—the same woman he had spoken to little more than a week ago—had been found floating in the harbor, next to one of the troop ships.

Once again the newspapers were inflaming the population with wild and fantastic rumors that had no basis in fact. One newspaper claimed that the Raval Monster had been seen prowling the docks dressed as a priest in search of prostitutes; another described him climbing buildings in the Raval like a giant ape. Such pernicious drivel might sell newspapers, but Mata had no doubt that Romeu had been killed because she had spoken to him, and that knowledge felt far more alarming than any of the fantasies circulating in the press. He left Ossorio's offices and walked down the Ramblas, past the police, Civil Guards, and Somaten, who had been deployed up and down the thoroughfare in even larger numbers than usual. Mata knew they were intended to reinforce Ossorio's message of order and control, but he could not help finding the presence of so many armed men intimidating and depressing, as he walked on to keep his appointment with Quintana. Cities that worked well did not need to be protected in this way, and the murder of Angela Romeu was further proof that his city was not working well at all.

It was less than twenty-four hours since he had watched the long-shoremen fish the prostitute's naked body out of the harbor, and he was not looking forward to seeing her again as he turned into the Calle Hospital and continued into the medical school. He had arranged with Quintana to take photographs of the murdered woman, and he went directly to the autopsy room, where one of the orderlies went to fetch Quintana. A moment later he emerged wearing his bloody surgical clothes and holding a knife in his hand, like an Aztec priest returning from a sacrifice.

"Bernat," he said. "I'm glad you came. I've got something interesting to show you."

Mata followed him gloomily to one of the slabs, where Quintana drew back the sheet covering the body of Angela Romeu.

Mata took the usual photographs of her head and shoulders, and then Quintana pulled the sheet down further. Mata lowered the camera and stared with pity and disgust at the cavity that reached down from her neck to her ribs where Quintana or one of his colleagues had opened her up, and the bites and wounds that he had already seen.

"Have a look at this." Quintana held up the dead woman's left arm with one hand. Mata leaned forward, as the pathologist prised apart a small cut in the vein just below her elbow.

"I don't understand," Mata said.

"It's not a bite or a wound!" Quintana looked as excited as Mata had ever seen him. "It's an incision. Made with a surgical instrument. Exactly where you would expect to find a tube for a phlebotomy."

"A what?"

"A blood transfusion. This is where the blood would go in. Or out."

"You mean her blood was drained through a tube?"

"That's what it looks like. And she's not the only one." Quintana walked along the row of corpses and drew back another sheet to reveal Ignasi the cretin. Once again Mata photographed his face, before Quintana drew back the sheet and showed him the same incision on his left arm.

"You see?" he said. "The same thing. And that made me think about these blue marks and the rash. That suggests a haemolytic reaction. When you mix two incompatible blood types."

"You mean he had someone else's blood put into him?" Mata stared at him in confusion.

"Exactly. But it was the wrong kind. We found traces of blood type A and AB—according to Landsteiner's classification. That would have caused agglutination. It may even be that that's what killed him."

"Before these wounds were made, you mean?"

"Possibly."

"And the other victims?" Mata asked. "Hermenigildo and Tosets? Did they have these incisions?"

Quintana shrugged. "I didn't see them. The bodies were too badly mauled. Anyway they're both buried now."

"You've told Bravo Portillo about this?"

"I did," Quintana said. "He didn't seem to think it was significant. He still thinks a madman did this. And maybe he's right. Only it's not the kind of madman we thought it was."

"But what about these other wounds? You said yourself they were bites or claw marks."

"They are." Quintana frowned. "And I don't understand it. It's as if these victims were attacked by two different people—assuming that whatever made these marks is human."

"What else could it be?"

Quintana shrugged. "It's clearly some kind of animal. But a phlebotomy requires science. I don't know why anyone would perform such procedures, but I can tell you this: Bravo Portillo is completely out of his depth here. And who can blame him? These aren't the kind of murders we're used to. This is something for your Irishman."

"I don't know where he is. I went to his hotel. The receptionist says he's out of the city."

"He's not gone back to London?"

"I don't see why he would. But I hope he comes back soon."

Mata left his friend still poring over the murdered woman's body and went back out onto the street and returned to his office to write up Ossorio's conference. It was nearly dark by the time he set off home, and as he walked back to his house he had the feeling that the city of his childhood and youth was changing into something darker and more sinister than he had imagined possible. He thought fondly of the Barcelona of his youth and childhood: the city of the World Exposition, of Verdaguer's ode, of dragons, devils, and human towers; the city of painters, poets, and builders of dream palaces; the Paris of the Mediterranean and the capital of the future independent republic of Catalonia.

Now he imagined Barcelona as Sodom and Gomorrah or Pompei; as a patient on its deathbed, slowly rotting away from a disease that had not yet been named, that could be seen only in its external symptoms. He arrived back at his flat and shut the great wooden door behind him with a feeling of gratitude and relief. The children were being put to bed, and Sylvia asked him to read Carles a story. Mata sat by his son's bed and told him from memory the tale of the wolf who tried to eat the seven children. His father had once read him the same story, and Carles listened with the same fearful satisfaction that he had once felt as he described how the wolf was cut open and filled with stones.

"Do they have wolves in Barcelona, papa?" he asked.

"Definitely not." Mata leaned forward and kissed his son on the forehead, as an image flitted through his mind of Angela Romeu lying on the autopsy table. In the same moment he thought of Lieutenant Ugarte sitting down for supper with his wife and children in his new flat, and wondered once again why Ugarte had not followed up on the information the murdered woman had given him.

"Is everything alright?" His wife's voice broke into his thoughts and he looked up to see her smiling at him sympathetically.

"Yes, fine," he said.

"I don't believe you."

"I'm tired, that's all."

He gave her a wan smile, and tried to concentrate as his wife talked about the preparations for their forthcoming exodus to Puigcerdà. Like his son, there were things that it was better for her not to know about, and the way things were going the sooner they were out of the city the better. But for the time being he had other things on his mind. After supper he withdrew into his study. He had thought he might write a poem to lift his mind to a better place, but even as he stared at the blank paper with his favorite fountain pen, the fine verses refused to come. Instead he found himself thinking of the hairy anarchist beast depicted by the cartoonist from *El Universo*, leaping across the rooftops of the Raval with an unconscious woman under his arm. The woman had a sash around her with the word ORDER written on it, and the ape-like creature had a copy of *Solidaridad Obrera* protruding from a trouser pocket. Such caricatures were only to be expected from a Catholic newspaper, but the Radical Party papers had their own variants. *El Progreso*'s latest showed a young woman strapped to a bed frame surrounded by vampiric nuns, while a Jesuit with bloodstained hands stood watching approvingly.

The newspapers seemed only too willing to pander to the prejudices of their readers, and present them with monsters of their own invention. Meanwhile poor women died like dogs and their murderers sat down to eat supper with their families on a government salary and no one even cared enough about the victims to uncover the truth. The more he stared at the blank paper, the more intolerable it seemed that such a situation could be allowed to continue. Because poetry was all very well, but poetry without justice was like burning incense in a sewer. For much of his adult life the verses of Baudelaire, Verlaine, Verdaguer, and Maragall had moved and inspired him, but none of them could help him now. It was less than a year since Joan Rull had been garrotted, taking his secrets with him, and once again his city was being manipulated by puppeteers pulling invisible strings.

Mata did not know who or what the Raval Monster was, but he was certain it was not what the papers or the police said it was. Someone was lying, and their lies needed to be exposed. What Barcelona needed right now was not poetry, but a voice like Zola's—an angry, passionate voice that denounced lies and corruption and upheld the cause of truth, just as Zola had once denounced the false charges against Dreyfus and the men who had manufactured the evidence against him. Unlike Zola, he could not name names, because he did not have enough evidence against Ugarte or anyone else. But he could point out the flaws and inconsistencies in the official investigation, and try to generate enough of a scandal to force the public and the authorities to do something about it. The more he contemplated this possibility, the more he felt his desolation recede.

In the end, no matter how bad or how hopeless things seemed, writers could do nothing else but write, even if they told people things they did not want to hear. That was what the Frenchman had done, and even though he might not be Zola, he had his own accusations to make. By the time he sat down at his desk and picked up his pen, the sentences were already beginning to form in his mind, and the more his hand moved across the white page, the more he felt hopeful that his prose might shake his city out of its delirium, just as it was sometimes necessary to shake or even slap someone who had become hysterical.

On Friday morning, Esperanza Claramunt was walking past the School of the Sacred Heart of Jesus on her way to work, when she found the caretaker trying to erase the word *monsters* from the school's main entrance, while some of the nuns stood watching gloomily. She had seen similar slogans scrawled on convents and churches in Gràcia and other parts of the city throughout the week. She had heard the stories circulating in the newspapers and on the street that priests and nuns were kidnapping children and young women and torturing them in underground torture chambers, and she had heard some of her own pupils repeat these stories.

Even if she had never known Pau or witnessed his kidnapping, she would not have taken such stories seriously. Now their stupidity and absurdity made her angry, and she could not help feeling that these rumors were being deliberately manufactured for purposes that were not yet clear, as she continued on toward her own school for what she knew might be her last day of work before the general strike. The following day delegates from all over Catalonia were coming to the city to attend the meeting of the workingmen's federation, where they would vote on whether to call a strike in response to Maura's war.

Esperanza had done everything possible to make sure they made the right decision. In the evenings she went out with the Gràcia comrades in her own neighborhood, distributing leaflets and making speeches calling for a general protest strike. On other days she and the Invincibles visited the workers districts in Clot, Pobleneu, and Sant Andreu. In the last week she had visited factories and workplaces, libraries, public squares, anarchist meeting places, and cafés to hand out leaflets or listen to speeches by Ruben, Arnau, or Pau's mother. As she went about these preparations she often wondered how Director Vargas would react if he found out what she was doing, and she had taken pains to avoid the subject of the strike while she was at school.

That morning, however, Vargas informed the staff and children that the school would remain open in the event of a strike. Vargas also referred for the first time to certain rumors that had been circulating through the neighborhood. Although the Elisée Reclus school was not a church school, he told the children, they should not believe that nuns and priests were murderers. Such stories were nonsensical and they were also lies, and just because some adults were foolish enough to believe such things, there was no reason for them to do the same.

Vargas did not need to describe these rumors, and even though Esperanza agreed that they were nonsensical, it also annoyed her that he should declare so emphatically against a strike. Her mother often asked her what would happen to her and Eduardo if she lost her job, and Esperanza had hoped that Vargas would resolve this dilemma by closing the school. Now she would have to choose whether to work or strike after all, which might also mean that she would have to decide whether to come in to work or disobey Vargas's instructions. The director's appeal failed to have its desired effect on the children. No sooner had she entered the classroom than she was showered with questions. What was a strike? What was the difference between a strike and a revolution? Was it true that the churches were going to be burned? Did she know that the Monster was a priest who moved through the Raval in secret tunnels?

Esperanza knew her answers might reach the director's ears, and she chose her answers carefully. A strike, she said, was what happened when workers stopped working. The last time this had happened in Barcelona was in 1902, before most of the children were born. People went on strike, she said, to protest against things that were wrong or unfair. Sometimes they did this in order to change their working conditions and sometimes they united with other workers for political reasons that went beyond the workplace. The war in Morocco was one of those reasons. Many people across the country did not agree with the war, she said, and did not want to fight it. But that was not the same thing as a revolution. A revolution was what happened when the people overthrew their king or government, as the people of France had done in 1789.

Could the strike become a revolution? one of the children asked. Once again Esperanza chose her words with caution. It was possible, she said, but as far as she knew nothing of that sort was being planned in Barcelona. She did not think that any churches would be burned, and she agreed with Director Vargas that the so-called Monster was not a priest. These answers only produced more questions. If the Monster was not a priest or a vampire then what was it? Why was the war in Morocco wrong? Two of her children raised their hands and said that their fathers had been sent to Morocco, and another girl said her brother had also been called up. Would they be all right? Was it true that the Moorish women beat prisoners to death with clubs?

Esperanza answered these questions as best she could. For the rest of the morning she struggled to get her pupils' attention. Some of the children were still discussing the Monster at lunchtime, and Vargas announced that the next child to bring up the subject would be given detention. They were about halfway through the meal when the care-taker came in and said that Miss Claramunt had a visitor. Esperanza was surprised by this. She had already arranged to go out into the Raval with Ruben and the Invincibles after choir practice and she was not expecting a visitor now. She was even more surprised to find Bernat Mata waiting for her by the entrance. They walked away from the school to a nearby plane tree, where Mata leaned on his stick and began fanning himself with his hat.

"I'm sorry to bother you," he said. "But I wanted to warn you about a piece I'm writing in the paper—about the murders. It should appear tomorrow."

"Why do you need to warn me?"

"Because I will be saying some hard things. And some people— powerful people—may not like them. I wanted to alert you in case there are any . . . negative repercussions."

"Such as?"

"You've heard about the woman who was killed two days ago? The one in the harbor?"

"The prostitute? I read about her. Poor thing."

"That was the woman I spoke to. Hermenigildo Cortéz's woman."

Esperanza had not known this, and Mata's concerned expression made her feel suddenly anxious. "Do you know who killed her?" she asked.

"No. But I'm certain she was killed because she spoke to me. I thought you should know that."

"You're not suggesting I'm at risk?"

"No, not at all." Mata gave a reassuring smile. "Just keep your eyes open, that's all. Probably better not to go out alone. Oh, and I have a question, you don't happen to know an old terrorist named Salvador Santamaría?"

Esperanza raised her eyebrows. "I'm not sure why you think I consort with terrorists." she said.

"I just thought you might have heard of him," Mata said impatiently.

"Well, I haven't. Sorry."

"Maybe you could ask your 'comrades'?" suggested Mata.

Esperanza ignored the condescension. "We're rather busy right now."

"I don't doubt it," said Mata. "Chaos takes a lot of organization."

"A protest against an unjust war is not chaos, Señor Mata."

"We'll see. In any case the police are too busy dealing with you and your friends to investigate these murders. Let's hope there aren't any more of them, eh?"

For the rest of the school day, Esperanza tried not to think too deeply about the warning Mata had given her. That day school ended two hours early for the weekend. Despite her mother's pleading, she had arranged to go out with Ruben and the Invincibles into the Raval in the early evening to prepare the population for the strike. There were rumors that the Civil Governor intended to stop the federation from meeting the next day, and all the comrades agreed that crowds were needed in the streets to make sure it did.

Most of the Invincibles were still at work, and there was no point in going to the Athenaeum so early. Instead she walked over to the conservatory for choir practice, which she had missed for the last two weeks. As a child she had loved the sound of church choirs, and there had been a time when she had imagined that these were the sounds she would hear in Heaven. Long after she had stopped believing in God she had continued to sing in her local choir, not for the words but for the melodies and beauty of it and the pleasure of harmonizing her voice with others. Her mother wanted her to sing in the Orfeó, the most prestigious of Catalonia's choral societies, but Esperanza preferred the New Catalan Choral Society, because the Nova Catalunya was more of a workers choir than the Orfeó, and she enjoyed the pieces that Enric Morera selected for them.

That afternoon she was pleased to find that Morera had chosen the Hebrew slaves chorus from *Nabucco*. Morera's frown as she came into the hall made it clear that he was not pleased by her absence. He told her that her voice was sounding hoarse, and she saw no need to mention that she had been shouting and giving speeches all week. By the time she left the conservatory her voice was even more strained, but she felt stirred by Verdi's music as she hummed the melody to herself.

The Invincibles were already waiting for her outside the Athenaeum, and Arnau said that they would go out into the Atarazanas district near the harbor. Esperanza walked next to him down the Ramblas, with Ruben on the other side of her.

"I hear things are going well in Gràcia," Arnau said.

"They are," she replied. "The people are absolutely behind the strike. Even if the vote goes badly tomorrow."

Arnau looked pleased. "It won't go badly. If the masses come out to support it, the delegates will have to listen. And when it passes we should come up and give you a hand."

"It's all organization now," Esperanza said. "Maura's done most of the work for us. Even my neighbors are talking about a republic. And some of them even talk of bringing Maura down."

"Good for them," Ruben said. "But revolutions need leadership."

Arnau agreed. The more comrades there were in Gràcia, he said, the more chance they had of shutting the Radicals out. The Radicals were not true revolutionists, he said, and a republic with soldiers, police, and priests was no different from a monarchy with soldiers, police, and priests. Esperanza knew he was right. But the Radical Party was very strong in Gràcia, and she doubted whether the Invincibles could do much about it. Soon they reached the bottom of the Ramblas and turned right into the lower part of the Raval. Esperanza knew the neighborhood behind the old Atarazanas shipyards was one of the poorest in the city, and even though some of her pupils came from there, she had never been to this part of the Raval herself. Now she looked indignantly at the moldering tenements and wooden shacks, and she felt the same outrage and astonishment that human beings could live in such places. Once again she heard the choir singing "*Oh mia Patria sì bella e perduta! O membranza sì cara e fatal!*" But there was no slave chorus to redeem these stinking, unpaved streets, only the men and women standing outside their shacks and hovels like prisoners of war, while their spindly barefoot children played in pools of dirty water.

As in Gràcia, almost everyone they spoke to was in favor of a general strike. Even the prostitutes denounced the war and said that they would be joining the protest. Esperanza was disappointed once again to find that much of their anger was directed at the Church rather than the government or the army. Many buildings were already daubed with Radical Party slogans blaming the war on the monks, Jesuits, and convents, and many of the people they spoke to were Lerroux's supporters. Their loathing of priests and nuns was visceral and profound, and Esperanza sensed that it was not simply due to the war or even to the Radical Party's propaganda. Arnau and Ruben both agreed that such hatred could be useful, and they made no attempt to challenge the Radicals as they continued to work their way through the streets and rows of shacks.

After two hours the sky began to darken and the smell of fried meat and fish began wafting through the neighborhood. Esperanza was beginning to feel hungry herself, when she heard the sound of gunshots coming from the direction of the port. The shots were immediately followed by a louder and more coordinated volley. Esperanza heard angry shouts and another ragged burst of pistol shots. A few moments later a group of young men came running up the street toward her from the direction of the Ramblas. They looked as if they were running from bulls, but some of them were armed with pistols, and they ducked into doorways as other members of the crowd ran past shouting "Long live the Republic!" and "Long live Lerroux!"

Within minutes the narrow street was swarming with running men and women, and she could see helmeted police running toward them. Some of the youths at the rear of the crowd began to fire at the police, and the police took shelter and fired back. Esperanza had never seen anything like this, and she felt the same hysterical claustrophobia that she had once felt as a child when she witnessed the Mercè procession for the first time, as the crowd stampeded past her. She remembered how she had screamed for her father when the dragons came charging toward her with fireworks exploding and flaring from their nostrils, and he had reached down and plucked her to safety.

She was still looking around in panic and confusion when Ruben came up behind her and pulled her toward a nearby doorway. He stood with his back to the crowd and his arms outstretched to protect her. Esperanza was glad Ruben could not see the terror on her face, as she stared down at the street and tried not to scream. She was still standing there when she saw something fall from his jacket pocket. He bent down to scoop it up, and she was surprised to see a thick roll of peseta bills in his hand. She had no time to see how much it was, but she could not help thinking that it was a lot of money for a humble factory worker from Poblenou. Soon the pressure of the crowd began to ease, and Ruben stepped away and looked at her with concern.

"You alright? Lerroux's young barbarians eh? Always too early or too late."

Esperanza smiled tensely. As far as she could see no one had been killed, but Arnau said they should get out of the neighborhood in case the police came back. Esperanza had no objections. It was only now, as the group made its way back onto the Ramblas, that it occurred to her that she had just been in her first gunfight and she realized that her hands were trembling. Ruben offered to walk her to the tram, but she politely refused. She had intended to ask if he had heard of Salvador Santamaría, but now she had no desire to speak to him about anything at all. As she walked back up the gloomy thoroughfare, she thought of Mata's warning not to be out by herself, but she felt more angry than frightened now. Because the more she thought about the money that had fallen from Ruben Montero's jacket pocket, the more it seemed to her that this was something that Mata would want to know about.

Once again Lawton saw the factory towers up ahead and he knew that they were nearly in Barcelona. To his left he could see patches of ocean, beyond a field splashed with red poppies that gave onto a citrus orchard. Three days ago these same views had pleased him, now he was anxious to get back to the city. Even with the upper window open, the heat was suffocating, to the point when he almost envied the passengers sitting on the roof. He had not felt inclined to join them. His right knee still felt stiff and painful from where he had fallen at Foulkes's house, and there was a faint whining in his left ear, as though an insect was trapped inside his head.

As he willed the train to move once again, he remembered Dr. Morris's advice. He was not doing very well at avoiding difficult or stressful situations, but it was not his fault that militia thugs had beaten him with rifle butts, or that someone had tried to kill him for the first time since the war. He had no doubt Weygrand had sent the would-be assassin, and he had been ready to return to Barcelona even as he walked back to Vernet from Foulkes's house the previous day. It was clear to him then that he could not talk about his investigation to any officials who might ask him about it. Instead he brushed himself down and washed his face and hands in the stream as best he could and then limped back to the hotel, where he told the receptionist at the Hotel du Portugal that there had been an explosion at Dr. Foulkes' house, and that he had found a dead man in the forest.

He did not mention that he had broken into the house himself, but the horrified receptionist immediately called the police in Villefranche and sent a messenger to summon the fire wagon and a doctor. By the time the fire wagon went racing up the road, Lawton had already begun to make his own discreet inquiries about the motor car. He soon established that a red Delaunay-Belleville with a passenger and driver had passed through Vernet and returned by the Villefranche road. He knew they had come from Barcelona, and he hurried to Monsieur Béchard's studio to pick up his photographs. On returning to the hotel, he found two French policemen waiting in the lobby, who ordered him to accompany them to the gendarmerie at Villefranche.

There he was interrogated by a police officer who proved to be more zealous than most provincial policeman he had known. The officer took his statement, but seemed reluctant to accept that he had nothing to do with the explosion or the murder of the shepherd. Eventually Lawton managed to convince him, but not before the officer had telegraphed Paris, for reasons he did not explain. As a result he had missed the last train to Perpignan and spent the previous night in an inn just inside the medieval walls of Villefranche. Now he had wasted much of the day waiting for trains that stopped for no reason or moved at the same glacial pace.

Finally the train resumed its snail-like progress through the Barcelona suburbs, and an hour later it pulled into the Estación de Francia once again. Despite his pains and bruises, Lawton rushed out of the station to catch a taxi. Once again he rounded the harbor, and he was pleased to see that the Helgoland had disappeared. Even before the cab pulled up alongside the Hotel Colón he had his coins ready, and he dropped them into the driver's hand and rushed toward the entrance. Some of the guests looked askance at his sweaty, disheveled appearance and his breathless urgency as he strode across the marble floor and asked the receptionist for Dr. Weygrand. The receptionist replied that the doctor and his companion had checked out of the hotel that morning, without saying where they had gone.

17

L awton was not surprised to hear this, but it did nothing to lift his spirits. As he crossed the Plaza Catalunya, he was conscious once again of the limited resources available to him in a foreign city where he knew almost no one. In London he might have persuaded Maitland to get the police to look out for Weygrand and even place the ports on alert. In Barcelona he had no influence and no strings to pull. He had no idea whether Weygrand and Zorka were even in the country, and there was no one he could ask. The heat added to his grim mood, and he tried to think what he could do next. Compared with the mountains the city felt sticky and airless even in the late afternoon, and the sunlight was so glaring that it was an effort to look around him.

If Weygrand was not at his hotel, it was at least possible that the theater might have another address for him. As he turned into the Ramblas he was surprised to find that the top part of the central thoroughfare was covered in sand, and he saw two wagons filled with sand moving slowly down the promenade. On both sides of the wagons, workmen in blue smocks were shoveling and spreading the sand all around them, in accordance with instructions from an army officer on horseback.

Lawton knew enough about policing crowds to know that these preparations were intended to stop horses from slipping on the cobblestones, and he wondered what had happened to make them necessary. The plane trees provided some relief from the sun, till he reached the Conde del Asalto, and walked past a group of armed police standing on the corner to the Edén Concert. Outside the theater a workman was taking down Weygrand's poster, and the box office attendant said that Weygrand had canceled his remaining concert due to illness and returned to Vienna.

Once again Lawton was not surprised to hear this. He was just walking away when it occurred to him that there was still one more thing he could do. He crossed the Ramblas and walked down to Escudellers, where he followed the curve around to the *Veu de Catalunya* offices. He was relieved to find Mata sitting in front of his typewriter in a half-empty room, with his sleeves rolled up, and Mata looked equally relieved to see him.

"Harry!" he said. "I thought you might have given up on us. I wouldn't blame you."

"I've been to Vernet-les-Bains," Lawton replied. "Looking for Madame Babineaux."

"Did you find her?"

"No. But someone found me." Lawton lowered his voice as a typesetter hurried past in an ink-stained apron. "Can we go somewhere?"

"Of course."

Mata picked up his jacket and put on his wide floppy hat. With his long beard and broad shoulders, he looked not unlike a Boer, Lawton thought, except that it was very difficult to imagine a man of his bulk and girth riding a horse. Mata picked up a newspaper from his desk and they went out to a café on the other side of the street, where Lawton told him about his visit to Vernet-les-Bains. He spoke angrily and quickly, and Mata looked increasingly incredulous when he described his visit to Foulkes's house.

"You didn't see who threw the grenade?"

"No. But whoever it was, Weygrand sent him. He's the only one who knew I was going there. Do you have a pen and paper?"

Mata handed him his notepad and pen, and Lawton drew the cross with the wide points that he had seen in Foulkes's basement. "Do you know what this is?" he asked.

"Of course," Mata said. "It's a Templar Cross."

Lawton looked blank, and Mata explained that the Knights Templar was a crusading order from the Middle Ages. "I found it in Foulkes's basement—on some robes," Lawton said.

"What kind of robes?"

"Hooded robes. The kind monks wear."

Mata looked confused. "So the basement was some kind of chapel?"

"Not any kind of chapel I've ever seen." Lawton drew the black sun and told Mata about the bloodstained cup and the other objects and images he had found in Foulkes's basement. "That's the same sun I saw during Weygrand's performance, and you see these spokes? The ones that look like lightning flashes? They're called sig-runes. It's some kind of Viking letter. I saw it in Foulkes's laboratory in London."

"You're sure it was blood in this . . . chalice?" Mata asked.

"Definitely. Probably chicken's blood. And look at these."

Lawton showed him the photographs of the Explorers Club, and pointed to the sig-rune banner. "Here it is again. It was the stamp of Foulkes's Greenland expedition in 1906. And this man—the one sitting next to Weygrand and Foulkes—he was on that expedition, too. I don't know the others."

"Well I can help you there," Mata pointed to the thin-faced man with the silvery hair. "That's the Count of Arenales."

Mata explained that the Count of Arenales was the son of a well-known Catalan *Indiano*—an emigrant to the Indies, who had returned to Cuba in the middle of the previous century after selling his estates there. Arenales's father had invested his money in armaments and textiles, and bought himself a title, but his famously eccentric son had not shown the same entrepreneurial instincts. In his youth Arenales had spent much of his time traveling abroad, and he had variously been an amateur scientist, an art critic, and a poet, who had published mediocre books with his father's money that no one could remember. For some years he had lived a reclusive life, Mata said, dividing his time between his estate in the Collserola hills outside the city and a palace in the old city.

"Arenales is a crank," he said. "And he's also a terrible reactionary. He used to write occasionally for the Catholic papers. All strikes should be banned. No trade unions. Anarchism should be declared illegal, that kind of thing. He once wrote a piece saying women shouldn't be allowed to ride bicycles because the seats might arouse them. I haven't heard from him in years, and I heard he'd become a recluse. But if this Weygrand is the kind of man you say he is, he will know that Arenales has a lot of money. And Arenales would certainly be drawn to this kind of mystical quackery. But what kind of club is this Explorers Club?"

"I don't know, but Weygrand does. And I need to find him. Foulkes's bank has the address of this Babineaux woman. If I find that address I might be able to find Weygrand, but they won't give it to me. Not without a police request."

"From Inspector Arrow?"

"Exactly."

"I'll take you to him. But first I have something to show you."

Mata unfolded the copy of *La Veu de Catalunya* and showed him the two-page article with the headline, Qui es el monstre? The article had been modeled on the maestro Émile Zola, Mata said proudly, and he had written it in the same spirit of indictment. Lawton had no idea who Émile Zola was, but Mata proceeded to summarize the contents of his own article. In it he had rejected the idea that the Raval Monster was a beast, a vampire, or a member of the Church. Without naming names, he had accused certain police departments and individuals of failing to follow up lines of investigation and overlooking or ignoring autopsy results that made it clear that the victims had been killed by someone with a basic knowledge of medical science.

The article continued onto the next page, and Mata opened the broadsheet to reveal three close-up photographs of corpses lying on a mortuary slab. "The motive for these crimes remains unclear," Mata read out aloud. "But the authorities appear to have little interest in investigating the murders of men and women who had little value to society when they were alive."

Some of the other customers were staring at them now, and Mata lowered his voice and looked at Lawton expectantly. "Well?" he asked. "What do you think?"

"Very good." Lawton was not entirely sure what Mata wanted him to comment on. "So you're saying this Monster is some kind of doctor?"

"That's what Quintana says. Someone who knows how to perform blood transfusions."

"Has there been any reaction to this?"

Mata shrugged. "Not yet. But right now the city has other priorities. Tomorrow the workingmen's federation is supposed to vote on a general strike against the war. The civil governor has banned the meeting, but this is Spain not England. Over there you allow things and they don't happen. Here you ban something and it always becomes more likely. Let's go and look for Mr. Arrow. You can keep this as a souvenir."

Mata handed him the newspaper, and they walked back up the Ramblas once again and across the Plaza Catalunya and up the wide avenue of the Passeig de Gràcia till they reached the Novedades restaurant. Lawton followed Mata into an enormous hall filled with billiard tables and lined with cubicles where groups of mostly men were eating and drinking. They found Arrow at the far end of the hall, bent over one of the tables in a shirt and waistcoat, lining up his cue while his opponent and a small group of spectators looked on. Lawton noticed the little pile of money on a nearby table, and he and Mata watched as Arrow expertly racked up a break of forty. Lawton could see that Arrow was winning and it was not until the game was over and he had actually won that he came over toward them.

"Mr. Lawton," he said. "Didn't take you for a sporting man. Nor you Bernat, for that matter."

"Could we have a word, Charles?" Mata asked.

Arrow made no attempt to conceal his displeasure. He pocketed his winnings and asked his friends to save the table for him, before following Lawton and Mata out onto the street.

"So what can I do for you gentlemen?" he asked.

"I need some information, sir," Lawton said. "In connection with Randolph Foulkes."

Arrow sighed. "I thought I'd made it clear that I have neither the time nor the desire to get involved in a private investigation."

"I know that sir. But I believe Dr. Foulkes was defrauded and murdered. I believe the man who blew up the Bar la Luna may also be connected to the Raval Monster. In London this combination would normally attract the attention of the police."

Arrow looked slightly more interested as Lawton told him what he knew about Weygrand and described the attempt on his life in Vernet-les-Bains.

"So you're saying that this—mesmerist hypnotized Foulkes in order to take his money?" Arrow asked. "And then sent him to his death by putting him in a trance? That's quite a story, Mr. Lawton. I've never heard of anything like it."

"Nor have I," Lawton admitted. "But Foulkes's bank has the address of his female beneficiary. If I find her I'll also find Weygrand. But they won't give me her details. Surely there's enough circumstantial evidence to justify a request from the Office of Criminal Investigation?"

"Such a grand title." Arrow said sadly. "If only I'd been able to justify it. Very well, I'll see what I can do. But you know the bank doesn't have to accept such a request. If it refuses that's as far as I'm prepared to take it."

Lawton and Mata thanked him, and the two of them walked back down the avenue as Arrow returned to his billiards.

"So you got what you wanted," Mata said.

"Like pulling teeth."

"Would you like some supper Harry? Sylvia and the children are going to Puigcerdà tomorrow morning, but I'm sure we can find room for you."

Lawton was hungry, but he felt wrung-out and dirty and his body seemed to hurt almost everywhere. Even above the noise of the city he could hear the whining in his head and he noticed that Mata's face was beginning to blur. He tried to blink it away, but the Catalan's face seemed to be cracking in front of him, like a jigsaw or a piece of shattered glass, and he felt suddenly unsteady on his feet. "Thanks," he said. "But I could use an early night after what's gone on the last two days."

"Of course. But I have a proposal for you. Why don't we go and visit Arenales tomorrow? He might be in the city. And perhaps we can try and find the anarchist Santamaría—the one who introduced our bomber to the foreign gentleman. Unless you have other plans?"

"No that's fine."

Mata looked pleased. "I'll come by your hotel at one o'clock then."

Lawton's shirt was damp with sweat now and his collar felt tight as Mata's blurred, bearded face continued to fragment in front of his eyes.

"Are you all right Harry?" Mata looked at him with concern. "You don't look well."

"Just the heat." Lawton smiled weakly. "We're not used to it in London."

"Would you like a cab?"

"No need for that." Lawton would not have minded a cab, but to accept Mata's offer seemed like an admission of weakness, if only to himself. If he was to have a fit, he would rather have one surrounded by strangers than in the presence of someone he knew. But what he wanted most of all was to be alone in a room with four walls around him and no one to see whatever might be about to happen, and Mata's concerned expression only made him more anxious to get away.

The gas lights were only just coming on as he hurried back down the Ramblas, past the carriages, bicycles, and trams moving past him in the dusk. Apart from the police and militia there were not many people on the thoroughfare, but now, for the first time since coming to Barcelona, he had the feeling that someone was following him. He stopped and pretended to peruse a kiosk that was still open, but no one stood out among the shadowy pedestrians moving back and forth. In London there was no reason for anyone to follow him, and he was more likely to be following other people. Yet even there he sometimes felt the same sensation, as if invisible eyes were pressing against the back of his skull. Now he was in Spain, and it was little more than twenty-four hours since Weygrand had sent someone to kill him, and only a few days since the police had nearly deported him. Even though the doctor was supposedly in Vienna, Lawton sensed the bulbous eyes staring fiercely down at him from some place he could not see. He cursed the illness that produced such foolish delusions, even as he quickened his pace to put them behind him.

By the time he reached the hotel the faces and objects around him had begun to regain their solidity. Even the sight of Señor Martínez's smooth bald head and scowling visage seemed like a comforting barometer of normality. Señor Martínez did not ask where he had been, and Lawton did not tell him, but he was pleased to find that his old room was still empty. He took some of the potassium and broke open a vial of amyl nitrate before undressing for bed. That night he kept the wooden bit on the bedside table beside him as he lay on top of the sheets in his underclothes. Despite the heat and his aches and pains, he quickly fell asleep. In the mountains he had had no dreams at all. Now he dreamed of Boers in their bush hats, of horses surging through bloody rivers, and trenches filled with bodies. He was woken up by a gunshot. At first he thought he was still dreaming, then he sat up as the shots continued in a short ragged exchange before the night fell silent once again. His watch gave nearly four o'clock, and he lit a cigarette and listened to the streetcar rattling northward from the direction of the Ramblas.

He was just about to lay down again when he found himself thinking of the skulls and Bertillonage mugshots in Foulkes's house and his museum-laboratory in London. In the same moment he thought of the pictures in Mata's newspaper, and he felt suddenly awake. He lit the lantern and opened up the newspaper. Years ago he had attended a lecture at Scotland Yard, where a visiting professor of criminology had explained Cesare Lombroso's theory of atavism. According to the professor, Lombroso believed that certain categories of crime were carried out by men and women who had slipped down the ladder of evolution and civilization to an earlier phase of human development. This reversion included not only ordinary forms of criminality and moral insanity but political crimes such as anarchism.

Lawton had never taken these theories seriously, but Foulkes clearly did, and the skulls of the murdered cretin and the anarchist Tosets would have fit easily into his collection. Tosets bore all the physical hallmarks of the Lombrosian throwback, with his wide brachycephalic skull, his close-set eyes, and large ears, while the cretin-boy Ignasi looked much like the other lunatics and idiots on the walls of Foulkes's museum. The more Lawton considered these similarities, the more it seemed to him that he might have found an explanation for the Raval Monster.

18

Even before the first rays of sunlight lit up the square, he was already dressed and shaved. After breakfast he went to the post office to see if there were any telegrams or letters for him. There was only a telegram from Mrs. Foulkes acknowledging his identification of her husband's body, and informing him that he was free to make this information public. Lawton sent a telegram to Maitland, reminding him of his earlier request about Foulkes and the Everdale Asylum, and returned to the hotel to wait for Arrow or Mata.

Mata arrived just after one o'clock. He looked more relaxed than the previous night, and said that his wife and children had left for Puigcerdà with his in-laws. He was relieved they were out of the city, he said, the way things were, and he looked forward to joining them at the beginning of August. Lawton also hoped that he would be gone by then. Perhaps it was the aches and bruises, but he felt a sudden yearning for murky English light and summer drizzle, for a cup of tea and a Cornish pasty, for his gramophone records and his street full of Jews. To his surprise he even felt fondly toward the widow Friedman, and thought that he might send her a postcard. As they walked across the square, Lawton told Mata that he had received permission from Foulkes's widow to make her husband's identity public.

"I don't think there's much interest in the Luna Bar bombing now," Mata said. "The Moroccan expedition is already coming apart. While you were away our reservists were attacked in Melilla. They'd only just got off the boat. I'm sure the workingmen's federation will be thinking about that when—if—they vote today."

"What if I told you the Explorers Club was murdering people in the streets of Barcelona? Would your readers be interested in that story?"

Mata stared at him. "Well I certainly would."

"Have you ever heard of Cesare Lombroso?"

"Of course."

"What's the word for *eugenics* in Spanish?"

"*Eugenesia*. Hombre, I'm impressed. All Arrow thinks about is billiards and his pension. And some of our detectives here can't even read, and here you are talking about Lombroso and eugenics. But what does this have to do with the Explorers Club?"

"A lot—I think. Last night I was looking at the photographs in your newspaper and I thought of the pictures and skulls in Foulkes's study and the ones I saw in Vernet. Three victims: An anarchist, an idiot, and a prostitute. As you said yourself, people who had no value to society when they were alive."

"I don't see—"

"What is eugenics?" Lawton asked.

"The science of improving the population by controlled breeding," Mata replied.

"Yes, but that's not all there is to it, is it?" Lawton said. "In one of Foulkes's books he talked about removing or separating certain groups of people from society. What he called unwanted or inferior stock."

"You're not suggesting that's what this Explorers Club has been doing?"

"That's exactly what I'm suggesting."

They had reached the Ramblas now, and Mata stood tapping his stick as they waited for a break in the traffic. "Well I know quite a few people who would like to eliminate the anarchists—my father-in-law for example. And some think we have too many feebleminded people in Spain. But nobody recommends killing them."

"My father was a sailor," Lawton said. "He traveled a lot. One time he told me about a tribe of savages in South America who killed their sick and old people. They just put them in a canoe and pushed them off a waterfall. Everyone accepted it. That was how the tribe survived."

"Spain is a nation, not a tribe, Harry. And what about the bites and wounds? If all you want to do is eliminate unwanted people, you don't have to do it like that. And why drain their blood?"

"Weygrand and Zorka talked about ancient gods during their show," Lawton replied. "Some kind of kingdom where people could talk to each other with their thoughts. At the time I thought it was just gibberish. But the robes in Foulkes's house? That symbol on the wall? What if this Explorers Club was some kind of cult or sect?"

"Like the Freemasons?"

"As far as I know the masons don't go around murdering people. Not the ones I knew in London, anyway."

"And you think your Dr. Foulkes was involved in this?"

Lawton shook his head. "Foulkes is dead. All these murders have taken place since he died. But maybe he knew what was going to happen and he didn't want it."

"And that's why they killed him," Mata said.

"After taking his money."

"Well that does sound plausible," Mata agreed. "But it does raise another question."

"What's that?"

"What in the name of all the devils has Barcelona done to deserve this?"

It soon became clear why Mata wanted a companion as they walked through the Raval. Even by day its evil-smelling streets made the East End look almost prosperous, but here the misery and wretchedness seemed even more glaring and pitiful beneath the cloudless blue sky. It did not seem the kind of neighborhood in which to find a palace, but

Mata said many members of the old aristocracy had lived in the Raval before the extensions of the last century, and some still did, because their palaces were too large to sell or rent.

After about ten minutes they came to a cracked and slightly crumbling tenement building overlooking a narrow square. It looked no different from all the others, except for the large curved wooden doors that were wide enough to take a carriage. Mata said that this was the Arenales palace, and he knocked loudly on the great metal door knocker. There was no response, and the shuttered windows gave no sign of life. Mata knocked again, and once again there was no answer.

Lawton glanced up at the shuttered windows. For a moment he thought that someone was looking down at him through the slats. He could not be sure, and after what had happened after Weygrand's performance he did not trust himself enough to voice it. After Mata knocked one more time without an answer he suggested that they look for the anarchist Santamaría.

As a policeman, Lawton had never had much to do with anarchists, who generally came under the jurisdiction of the Special Branch. His knowledge of anarchists and anarchism consisted mostly of what he had gleaned from Lombroso and the occasional stories that appeared in the press, which were almost always associated with attempted bombings and the discovery of bomb parts, or the occasional gunfight between foreigners and police. In Britain the Special Branch had the anarchists mostly under control, and that was partly because there were so few of them. From time to time he read of anarchist outrages on the Continent that reminded him of why such vigilance was necessary, whether it was bombings and assassinations or desperate suicidal shootouts with police that invariably seemed to involve Russians.

Now they walked back and forth through the streets on either side of the Ramblas, and visited anarchist cafés and taverns, printing presses and workingmen's clubs. He was surprised to find that most of the men and women they met were not raving fanatics, but polite, mild-mannered, and ordinary working men and women who were mostly devoid of any obvious Lombrosian features.

"Very domesticated anarchists you have here," Lawton observed.

"Not all of them," said Mata. "We still have some wild men left. Bombers and crazies who dream of killing kings and heads of state and frying the bourgeoisie. But the propagandists of the deed are a minority now. The Barcelona anarchists are mostly syndicalist. Workers' solidarity and the general revolutionary strike—that's the strategy. Still the same utopian nonsense, of course. The same belief in human perfectibility. In this sense the anarchists are even more bourgeois than the bourgeoisie they want to overthrow."

"They seem to like you, though."

"They like me because I supported Ferrer," Mata replied. "And anarchists are fond of poets. But Lerroux and the Radicals are the ones who control the Raval now. The anarchists are falling behind."

As they walked through the neighborhood, Mata pointed out some of the Radical Party cafés, clubs, and neighborhood associations. Even in Lerroux's absence, he said, his party remained the dominant political force in most of the workers' districts, with an infrastructure that the anarchists could not match.

For the rest of the morning they continued to walk back and forth across the Ramblas, and each time they came to the thoroughfare there seemed to be more people running back and forth or conferring in huddled groups on street corners, and there also seemed to be more police. In the early afternoon they heard cheers coming from the Ramblas, and a group of workers came running toward them shouting "Strike! Strike on Monday!" at passersby and the people looking down from the balconies above them.

"Looks like the federation has made its decision," said Mata.

They ate lunch at a café on the Ramblas as crowds of workers marched triumphantly past the police and Civil Guard, as if the strike had already begun. A group of workers were sitting at a nearby table talking excitedly about the strike, and Mata asked them what had happened. One of the men said that the federation had not been allowed to enter the meeting hall. Instead the delegates had taken the vote in small groups in cafés and even in the streets.

"That's that, then," Mata said to Lawton under his breath. "Expect all hell to break loose."

After lunch they continued their search. A few anarchists had heard of Salvador Santamaría, but no one knew where he was. Finally Mata spoke to an anarchist he knew, who directed them to a bodega near the port where Santamaría was often found drinking. Once again they threaded their way through the Raval, until they came to a little tavern with a low vaulted ceiling and stained barrels of wine stacked up against the walls. At the back of the room a bearded man with a mane of white hair and the red cheeks of a long-term drinker was sitting hunched over a glass of sherry.

"Señor Santamaría?" asked Mata.

"Who wants to know?" the old man replied in a slurred, rasping voice.

"I'm Bernat Mata from *La Veu de Catalunya*."

Santamaría looked unimpressed. "I don't like separatists. Or newspapermen." He looked at Lawton. "I'm not partial to coppers either."

"I'm not a policeman." Lawton said. "I'm a private investigator. From London."

"From London! Not one of Mr. Arrow's little helpers?"

"He isn't." Mata sat down at the table. "We just wanted to ask you some questions—about your friend Hermenigildo Cortéz."

"Never heard of him."

"Well that's strange." Mata pulled up a stool and Lawton did the same. "Because I understand that Hermenigildo used to be in the Sons of Whores—and that you were too."

"Dunno who told you that."

"The same person who told me he was visited by a foreign gentleman before his death. And that you were the one who introduced them."

Santamaría's face was blank. "I've no idea what you're talking about."

"That's not what Hermenigildo's woman told me." Mata reached into his wallet. "Now she's dead, too."

"That's too bad," Santamaría said. "But it's nothing to do with me."

Mata laid some coins on the table. "Perhaps this will refresh your memory?"

Santamaría glanced at them disdainfully. "I think the Catalan bourgeoisie can pay a little more than that for my memories."

Lawton pulled a silver twenty-peseta coin from his pocket and added it to the pile. Santamaría swept up the coins and slipped them into his pocket. "I don't know who this foreigner was," he said. "He just came in here last month. Said he'd got my name from an Italian comrade and he wanted someone to carry out an action in the city."

"What kind of action?"

"He didn't say. Just that it was going to be something big and he needed someone special to carry it out. Of course I thought it was a setup. And not a very good one. Anarchists don't walk around in white suits—not the kind I respect, anyway. And they don't walk around offering to pay people they don't know to carry out 'special actions.' It was obvious he was some kind of provocateur."

"So what did you tell him?" Mata asked.

"I sent him to Hermenigildo. As a joke! Hermenigildo was always talking about doing something big. He was going to shoot the king. Assassinate the captain-general. Throw a bomb at the opera house. We all thought he was a police agent, too. Or a fool." Santamaría grinned and Lawton saw that most of his front teeth were missing. "Turns out Hermenigildo had a pair of cojones after all."

"What was this foreigner's name?" Lawton asked.

"He didn't say. But I know he was German."

"How do you know?" Mata asked.

"His accent. The Kaiser's men are always whoring around the neighborhood. Believe me I know a German when I hear one."

Lawton showed him the photograph of the Explorers Club and pointed out Weygrand. "Was this the man you spoke to?"

Santamaría peered at the picture, and Lawton saw that he had a cataract in one eye. "Not that one!" He jabbed a yellow forefinger at the bearded man with the duelling scar. "This is the man."

"Are you sure?" asked Lawton.

"'Course I'm sure. I'm not blind."

"Did you tell this to Lieutenant Ugarte?"

"Ugarte?" Santamaría held up his hands, and Lawton saw that his fingernails were missing. "The Brigada did this to me back in '97, after Corpus Christi. The lieutenant was just a humble little torturer back then." Santamaría's face was stiff with hatred. "I haven't seen him in at least two years. But I can tell you this. If I was ever still tempted to believe in hell it would only be in the hope that Ugarte might end up there. So no, señores, I have not spoken to him about anything."

Neither Mata nor Lawton had any more questions, and they left Santamaría brooding at his table.

"As I told you, not all our anarchists have been tamed," Mata said, as they stepped outside. "That bodega was one of Rull's hangouts. The Ramblas bomber. He also used to be a member of the same group."

"I've heard that name—from Inspector Arrow."

"Arrow knew a lot about him. And he suspected even more."

As they walked back through the backstreets Mata explained that Joan Rull I Queraltó was both an anarchist and police informer who had carried out dozens of bombings around the Ramblas, before his arrest and execution the previous summer. At his trial, Mata said, it was revealed that many of Rull's bombings had been carried out in order to convince the police that his services were required.

"You mean he was blowing things up to get the police to pay him?" Lawton asked in amazement.

"That's what the prosecutor claimed. And it wasn't just Rull. His mother and his brother were helping him. They were pardoned, but Rull got the death penalty. Rull always insisted he was innocent, right up to the end. He was still saying it even with the garotte around his neck."

"Did you believe him?"

"No. And nor did Arrow. And a lot of people agreed with him that there was more to it."

"Such as?"

"So many possibilities! Some people said Rull was working for the Spanish state—planting bombs to discredit the nationalists and justify a state of emergency. Some said Catalan businessmen were paying Rull to discredit the Spanish government and prove that the state had lost control over the city—another justification for independence. Then were those who said Rull was working for both sides at the same time. There were even rumors that he was working for the last civil governor!"

"And what did you believe?"

"Like I told you, this is a complicated city, Harry. But I don't believe Catalans would pay a man like that to blow up our people. Catalonia doesn't need men like Rull. Spain does."

Just then Lawton heard a murmur of voices and the sound of someone coughing behind him. He glanced around and saw a gang of about ten young men coming toward them. All of them were wearing loose-fitting trousers, clogs, and floppy caps, and some were carrying wooden clubs and knives.

"I think we have trouble," he said, as five more youths came sauntering toward them from the opposite end of the street. Mata looked around at the oncoming groups with a fearful expression. One of the hooligans was beating a club against the palm of his hand with a slack grin, and Lawton thought that he must be the leader. It was not a promising situation, and he was still trying to think how to get out of it when he noticed that one of the nearby doors was open.

"Run!" He pushed Mata toward the doorway. He had just managed to reach it himself when the leader came running toward them. Lawton swung around and ducked to avoid the circular swing of the club, which smacked into the wall. Before the hooligan could raise it again Lawton delivered a sharp jab to his abdomen, and then brought his knee up to his face as he doubled over. The leader let out a howl and fell back, holding his bleeding nose, as Lawton jumped back into the open doorway and slammed the door behind him.

The hooligans surged in a pack toward the doorway, and one of them forced his club in through the gap as Lawton tried to push the door shut. Lawton wrenched it from his hand and ran back into the hallway. Mata had already reached the next landing and was staring helplessly down at him. Lawton had forgotten all his pains and bruises now as the hooligans came pouring into the building. Outside in the street he knew he would have had no chance against them, but the narrow hallway and the stairway gave him a temporary advantage as he backed up the stairs, lashing out with the club and taking care to keep his distance so that they could not drag him down.

Mata was clearly not intending to make any contribution to this, and Lawton was wondering how long he could keep the gang at bay by himself, when he heard the leader calling them back out into the street. The gang immediately withdrew, and Lawton heard their footsteps trail away as he stood panting in the gloom. He waited until the noises had receded before going back downstairs. The street was deserted now, and it was only then that Mata emerged from the building behind him, looking relieved and also slightly awed.

"I'm sorry I couldn't be more helpful," he said. "I'm a man of the pen not the sword. But you—"

"We all have our talents," Lawton said. "Any idea who they were?"

"A TB gang," Mata replied. "They've all got tuberculosis. There are lots of these gangs in the slums. They'll be lucky to make it past twenty-five. They don't care what they do. Mostly they just rob people."

"Well they weren't trying to rob us." Lawton's shoulder was aching now and he stretched his arm to relieve it. "Someone sent them to do more than that. And that means Weygrand is still in Barcelona."

From the back seat of the Delaunay-Belleville, the man in the top hat and fur-collared coat stroked the leather seat with a gloved hand as the automobile throbbed beneath him. Below him he could see the spiked cathedral spire and the factory towers, and the chain of streetlamps that stretched from the mountains to the sea. Beyond the port the lights of fishing boats sparkled like fireflies as they headed out toward the dark horizon. Most of the inhabitants of Barcelona would be settling down for the night now, ready to begin another day that would be no different from all the others. There were millions of people like them all over Europe, sleepwalkers living lives without purpose in their teeming anthill cities. They copulated and gave birth. They scrabbled for their daily bread in the slums or wallowed in wealth that they had not earned or fought for. Incapable of nobility or grandeur, they lived out their insect lives without having done a single thing to deserve the gift of life.

The man in the Delaunay-Belleville knew that this was not his role. He was fully awake and fully conscious. Unlike the insectoid swarm down below, his life had meaning, greatness, and beauty. Even now, as he looked up at the fortress and saw the two men coming toward him, dragging a third man between them, he had no doubt that his name would be remembered. The prisoner's hands were bound behind him and his head was lolling on his chest as the driver got down from the front seat.

The driver opened the side door without a word, and the two men brought their prisoner to the side of the car. The man in the top hat reached out and held the captive's head upright in the palm of his hand. He turned it briefly from side to side, and then gave a nod of approval. The two men hauled the prisoner up into the back seat, where he sat with his head slumped forward and turned slightly to one side, like a drunken reveller returning from a party. The driver handed an envelope to one of the two escorts, and they walked back to the castle. Behind them the driver returned to the wheel and drove the Delaunay-Belleville slowly back down the hill.

19

S o you're not going to work on Monday?" Señora Claramunt tried
to keep her voice calm, because Eduardo could not cope with any
agitation. He was staring at his breakfast with a frown, and Esperanza knew that the voices in his head had become stuck. She placed a
piece of muffin in his hand to remind him to eat and pointed toward the
cup of hot chocolate.

"I can't not go on a strike that I helped organise, mama," she replied.

"And what will happen to us if you lose your job!" Eduardo gave his
mother a startled look and she reached out and patted his hand.

"The school can hardly remain open when the whole city is on strike,"
Esperanza said.

"There could be riots," her mother insisted.

"I doubt it. The strike is too well organized."

"And martial law."

"Ossorio has promised not to do that."

"These things can't be controlled! You didn't see what happened in 1902."

Esperanza did not reply. On the other side of the room, her father's sepia portrait stared at her from the wall. The picture had been taken shortly before his death, and it depicted the father she always remembered: a serious, principled, and thoughtful man who would have been a gift to any other country but Spain. Had he been alive she would have told him how the police had tried to prevent the workingmen's federation meeting the previous day by blocking the entrance to the conference hall. She would have told him how the workers held their own impromptu meetings in cafés and street corners; how they voted unanimously to go on strike and created a three-man committee to prepare for it.

That, she would have told her father, was true democracy, and whatever happened in the next few days, she would never forget the courage and defiance of these humble workingmen. And now that she had seen these things, she could not walk away from them. She would have liked to explain all this to her mother, but Esperanza knew she would only make her more anxious. Esperanza knew that her single overriding aim was to protect her children. As a daughter, she respected these motives and aspirations; as an anarchist there was only one option open to her.

"It's just a protest strike, mother," she said. "Twenty-four hours and it will be over."

"But why can't you just . . ."

Esperanza gave her mother a warning look before she could say "find a husband," because such advice was an insult to her, and it was also an insult to Pau. She knew her mother understood this, and she did not want another quarrel with her now. Instead she put on her hat and cloak, and Eduardo hugged her tightly, just as he had done almost every day since he learned to walk. Her mother remained cold and disapproving, and Esperanza knew she was trying to make her feel guilty. Despite her irritation, it succeeded, and the twinge of guilt persisted as she left the apartment. It was not until she opened the front door and saw the two men standing on the other side of the street that her guilt gave way to a shiver of fear as she recognized Lieutenant Ugarte.

For a moment Esperanza was tempted to go back inside, but even the thought that Ugarte might enter her mother's apartment seemed suddenly unbearable. She turned and walked up the street as though she had not seen them. Even without looking she knew that they were following her. Surely they were not going to take her away in broad daylight? She quickened her pace, but Ugarte and his companion were so close behind that she could hear their breathing. She was wondering whether she should run or shout for help when Ugarte said, "Señorita Claramunt."

Esperanza turned around to face him and touched her glasses, as she always did when she was frightened or nervous. "What do you want?" she asked.

Ugarte screwed up his pineapple face. "I'm sure Director Vargas wouldn't be pleased to hear that one of his teachers is helping to prepare a general strike. And that would be a pity for your mother and that brother of yours. I mean, *he's* never going to get a job, is he? And your mother is working so hard. She'd be very disappointed if you lost yours."

"And I can't imagine your mother would be pleased if she knew you were threatening women in the street," Esperanza retorted. "To say nothing of the other things you do."

Ugarte shrugged. "My mother passed away some years ago, God rest her soul. But she would understand that the Social Brigade must do whatever is necessary to protect society from its enemies. Sometimes it's necessary to take people in for questioning. And that can be rather frightening for those who . . . lack the mental aptitude."

For a moment Esperanza thought he was talking about her, then she realized to her horror that he was talking about Eduardo.

"What do you want?" she asked.

"Just a little warning," Ugarte said. "Stay at home tomorrow. It would be better for you and your family. And Poblenou really doesn't need your help, does it?"

Esperanza could not think of anything to say to this, and she turned away in disgust. She half-expected them to follow, but there were no footsteps behind her. She took the streetcar all the way down to the bottom of the Ramblas, and then rode another into Poblenou. It was not until she saw Ruben, standing with Flor, Arnau, and some of the other members of the Invincibles outside the anarchist club on the Calle Llacuna that she wondered how Ugarte had known where she was going. She had agreed to come to Poblenou with the Invincibles to help spread the word about the strike, but it soon became obvious that these efforts were not really required.

As in Gràcia, the workers of Poblenou had already heard about the general strike and they fully supported it. The Invincibles were invited to a meeting at the local workingmen's association as a show of solidarity, and Ruben gave one of the fiery speeches that Esperanza had come to expect from him. Arnau looked on approvingly, and turned to Esperanza with a smile. "Not the same man is he?" he said.

Esperanza agreed that he was not.

"The struggle changes men very quickly," Arnau said. "Just as it's changed you. Pau would be proud of both of you."

Esperanza did not want to be praised, but she could not help feeling moved that a man like Arnau was able to appreciate her. For a moment she was tempted to tell him about Ugarte, but there was so much else that she would have to tell him that she thought better of it. In the late evening Ruben walked down into Poblenou with Arnau and the other comrades to continue with the agitation, while she and Flor rode back to the Plaza Catalunya in a street car.

"Have you noticed anything unusual about Ruben?" Flor asked suddenly.

Esperanza looked at her in surprise. "He certainly seems different," she replied cautiously.

"I know. He's quite the revolutionist, isn't he? Quite the big man." Flor smiled bitterly. "No, I don't mean that. The other day he didn't come home. He said he was at some meeting and he had to stay the night somewhere. But I'm not an idiot. His jacket smelled of perfume. A whore's perfume."

Esperanza could not think how to reply to this, and Flor looked angry and sad as she stared out at the street. "I shouldn't have told you," she said. "Now isn't the time to talk about my broken heart."

"No, no it's fine," Esperanza said. "I'm sorry to hear it."

"My mother says I'm just being stupid and bourgeois," Flor went on. "Getting jealous at a time like this. But I know Ruben doesn't love me. I don't think he ever has. Not the way Pau loved you."

"What do you mean?" Esperanza was conscious that her voice sounded shrill.

"He didn't tell you?"

"Tell me what?"

"He wanted to marry you. The day before we went to Montseny with the Ferrers, he told me all about it. He told me all about it. He'd walk you home—and then he'd tell you. He was always saying he was going to do it. I said do it! " Flor looked remorseful now. "So he didn't?"

Esperanza shook her head. Her throat felt suddenly tight as she remembered how awkward Pau had been that evening.

"That's a shame," Flor said. "I told Ruben what Pau was going to do that same night. I was so excited. I said ' Looks like I'll have a sister-in-law soon.' He was pleased too."

In that moment Esperanza felt as if she been punched, and she remembered Mata's warning that someone in her group must have known where Pau was going to be on the night of his death. She had never really believed him. Now it was clear that two people had known. Flor would never have betrayed her own brother, but Ruben was another matter. Ruben was the anarchist with a pocketful of pesetas. It was Ruben who had offered to be Pau's avenger and asked to be kept informed about what Mata was doing. Ruben had known she was going to be in Poblenou that evening, and Ugarte had known it, too. And according to Flor, Ruben had also known that Pau was going to walk her home on the night of his death.

"Are you all right?" Flor looked at her with concern. "Maybe I shouldn't have told you. I just thought you knew."

For a moment Esperanza considered telling Flor that her husband was an informer who had colluded in the murder of her brother, but this possibility still seemed so unbelievable and incomprehensible that she could not bring herself to say it.

"It's all right." She patted Flor's hand. "I'm glad you told me."

Flor looked relieved. But as they rode back home through the gathering dusk Esperanza could barely contain her anger, sadness, and revulsion. It was not until she lay in her bed with the light out that she finally allowed herself to cry for the man who had never had the chance to tell her that he loved her. She tried to cry in silence, but Eduardo heard her and came to comfort her as he always did, curling up on top of the bed beside her. Finally she took him back to his own bed, and even as she held his hand to help him sleep, Esperanza knew that it was time to speak to Mata again.

That Sunday Lawton was woken up by cathedral bells. He had slept well, despite his aches and pains. His right shoulder was stiff from the brawl with the TB gang, but he felt the same sense of pride and indestructibility that he once felt after a victorious bout, or an ambush or battle that had not killed him. His illness never made him feel like that. After each seizure he only ever felt weak, humiliated, and disgusted with himself.

Now he lay in bed listening to the bells summoning the population to mass, and he felt ready to fight whatever enemies Barcelona could throw at him. But today was Sunday and there was nothing he could do but rest and wait for the week to begin. He was just getting dressed and thinking what to do to pass the time when there was a knock on the door. He opened it to find Señor Martínez looking at him suspiciously, holding an envelope that a policeman had just delivered. Lawton took the message and shut the door behind him. He felt initially pleased to read the handwritten message from Charles Arrow announcing that the Bank of Sabadell had released the address of Randolph Foulkes's beneficiary.

His satisfaction immediately faded when he read the lines informing him that the Office of Criminal Investigation intended to carry out a search of the beneficiary's house at midday and make any necessary arrests. Lawton stared at the message in disbelief. Until now, Arrow had shown no interest in his investigation. It had been difficult enough to persuade him to issue a formal police request. Now he was preparing to arrest Foulkes's client himself, presumably so that he could claim credit for it. This prospect filled Lawton with sudden fury. He grabbed his hat and jacket and hurried out into the corridor. Martínez was still looking at him expectantly, but Lawton strode past him without a word. His serenity and confidence were completely gone now as he walked up the sandy thoroughfare through the strolling crowds. At the top of the Ramblas, a group of armed police were looking warily at the passing pedestrians and he saw that some of the men were being stopped and searched. He arrived at the OCI's office to find Arrow sitting at his desk, surrounded by four uniformed policemen.

"Mr. Lawton," he said. "You got my message."

"I did." Lawton glanced down at the Browning semiautomatic on Arrow's desk. "May I ask what's happening, sir?"

"As I said. We're going to arrest this Weygrand and his companion."

"With respect sir, I only asked for the address."

"You did." Arrow slotted the pistol into a waist holster. "But I've been thinking about what you said. If this Weygrand was responsible for the Bar la Luna bombing then this is a matter for my department. Especially as the Brigada doesn't seem interested."

"But I am." Lawton tried not to raise his voice. "As you know. I'm carrying out a private investigation, and I would have preferred to watch the house and see who comes and goes from it before any arrests were made. There are other people involved in this."

"Any relevant information will be obtained in an interrogation," Arrow said, with a shrug. "Which I will conduct. You're welcome to accompany my men. That's why I told you what we're doing."

Lawton was tempted to tell Arrow that he had no idea what was relevant or not, but he had no desire to share any more information with a man who was clearly only out to win glory for himself and his department. Arrow stood up and his officers accompanied him down to the street. Lawton followed them and waited as they clambered into the waiting cab with their sabers and shotguns. He squeezed in beside them and stared morosely out the window as the cab trotted northward up the Calle Muntaner, into a hillier part of the city that Lawton had not seen. Soon the carriage turned left, past a velodrome where a stream of cyclists was riding around a raised dirt track while young men played football in a sports park at the center.

The tension in downtown Barcelona was distinctly absent in this part of the city. From these heights Barcelona looked as tranquil and sedate as Regents Park on a Sunday afternoon, and its population seemed entirely dedicated to innocent pleasures that were difficult to associate with murder cults, bombs, and strikes. After rounding some apartment blocks of recent construction they entered a neighborhood of broad streets lined with trees and opulent-looking mansions and villas that made Lawton think of a Mediterranean Kensington. This, Arrow explained, was Sarrià, one of the wealthiest areas of Barcelona, where Foulkes's client had given her address. Most of the streets were unpaved, but a steady stream of cyclists, carriages, and expensive-looking automobiles drifted past the beige villas, monasteries, well-kept gardens, and strolling families.

Some of the pedestrians stopped and stared as the cab came to a halt and Arrow and his men got out with their weapons. Arrow walked just ahead of Lawton and his men. Despite his annoyance, Lawton could not help feeling a certain excitement and anticipation as they turned into another elegant street lined with palm trees. They were about halfway along it when Arrow paused in front of a brown three-storey villa. As soon as Lawton saw the cracked façade, the shuttered windows, and overgrown yard, he sensed that something was wrong. Arrow was also frowning as he pushed open the little iron gate and marched up the dirt path. Lawton glanced warily at the cracked balcony overlooking the door, as a white cat hissed at them and retreated to a nearby bush, while the four policemen stood facing the door like a firing squad with their shotguns raised.

Arrow banged the rusty doorknocker. There was no response, and he knocked again. He was just about to look around the back, when Lawton heard the sound of a bolt being drawn back from inside the house. Finally the door opened and an elderly lady in a long black dress stood blinking like a mole in the sunlight as Arrow's men lowered their weapons.

"Señora, I am Inspector Arrow from the Office of Special Investigations," said Arrow in his clumsy Spanish. "We're looking for Marie Babineaux and Dr. Franz Weygrand."

The old lady stared at him with a look of total incomprehension. Even when Arrow repeated himself, her stupefied expression did not change. It was not until Lawton explained what Arrow was looking for that she seemed to understand him.

"But I don't know these people, Señor!" she exclaimed. "My name is Nuria Solana. I've lived alone here since my husband died. There are only my cats here."

"Well we need to search the house," Arrow said brusquely.

Señora Solana seemed to understand him this time, and she stood back anxiously as Lawton and the policemen followed Arrow into a wide hallway that smelled of dust and cat urine. The house did not look as if it had had many visitors in a long time, Lawton thought, as he stood with Arrow and the old lady in the vestibule, while Arrow's men spread out through the house.

"These people you're looking for, are they friends of yours?" Señora Solana asked.

Lawton said they were not, and asked her if she ever received any other visitors.

"Who would visit me, Señor?" she exclaimed. "My eldest daughter comes once a week to bring food for me and the cats. She says I should move in with her. But my whole life is in this house. And who would look after my animals?"

Lawton nodded sympathetically. "The name Marie Babineaux doesn't mean anything to you?" he asked.

"Never heard of her."

After a few minutes, the policemen returned and said that no one else was living in the house. Arrow apologized for the disruption and withdrew his men. Lawton followed them back along the pathway, past the small crowd of bystanders who had gathered by the front gate, and back down the street to the waiting cab. Arrow did not even look at him now. He stared out the window as the cab made its way down into the city. It was not until they arrived at his offices that Arrow sent his men inside and turned back toward Lawton.

"Please don't bother me with any more pointless requests, Mr. Lawton," he said. "I really don't have time for wild goose chases."

Lawton was tempted to reply that he had plenty of time for playing billiards and that he had only himself to blame for such a pointless expedition, but he thought better of it, and Arrow turned on his heel and walked back into his offices in obvious high dudgeon. Lawton did not particularly care if he never saw him again, but it was also clear that his last hope of finding Weygrand had faded. There was nothing else he could do that day, and he decided to go and tell Mata. Lawton knew that he would not be in his offices, and he walked into the Eixample and asked for the address Mata had given him.

It did not take him long to find Mata's building, where the concierge let him in. He found Mata standing in the doorway of his apartment in a white shirt and trousers and a pair of rope-soled shoes.

"Good morning Harry!" he said cheerfully. "You have news?"

"Nothing good."

"Well I'm glad to see you. And I have a visitor. I think you'll be interested to hear what she has to say."

Lawton wondered who the visitor was as he followed Mata down the corridor and glanced at the paintings on the high walls, and the study filled with books. At the far end of the apartment, he saw a young woman sitting in front of a large open window. She was sitting in profile, framed by the window and sipping at a glass of water. She was not wearing a hat, and her hair was tied up behind her head to reveal a long neck that made Lawton think of flamingos he had seen in South Africa, as he realized that he had finally met the anarchist Esperanza Claramunt.

20

Lawton's first thought as she stood up to greet him was that yet another anarchist had failed to bear out Cesare Lombroso's expectations. Her skull was long and distinctly dolichocephalic and her high cheekbones and rosebud mouth showed no signs of atavism. Her wide brown eyes were earnest and slightly sad, and no closer than they ought to have been, and her glasses made her look studious rather than fanatical. Mata introduced them and Lawton shook her soft hand.

"Mr. Lawton," she said. "Señor Mata has been telling me about you."

"The three of us have certain things in common," Mata said, as Lawton sat down. "And we are probably the only people in Barcelona who have any idea what they are."

Lawton lit a cigarette and sensed that the Claramunt girl was giving him the same kind of appraisal that he had given her. Through the open window he heard the laughter of children echoing from the interior courtyard, and he could see Mata's neighbors sitting out on their balconies reading newspapers, hanging clothes on washing lines, or dozing in cane chairs like passengers on an ocean liner.

"Nice view," he said.

"Light, space, and community," Mata replied. "As Cerdà intended."

Mata explained that the Eixample—the Extension—had been designed the previous century by the architect Ildefons Cerdà, following the demolition of the old city walls. The new neighborhood had been built in accordance with its designer's socialist principles, he said, with wide streets and large courtyards to provide the sunlight and ventilation that was missing from the Raval and the Gothic Quarter.

"A fine socialist idea," Esperanza said scornfully, "which curiously enough only ended up producing expensive apartments for speculators and the bourgeoisie."

"Please don't include me in those categories," Mata protested. "I don't speculate and I'm not rich. But it is true that the experiment didn't live up to expectations, sadly."

"Sad but not surprising," Esperanza said. "When capitalism tries to reform itself it rarely does live up to expectations."

Mata rolled his eyes. "So Harry, what news? You can speak openly in front of Miss Claramunt. She will certainly speak openly in front of you."

Lawton told them about the botched raid in Sarrià, and Arrow's reaction to it.

"Well, well," Mata said "So our Sherlock Holmes thought he'd get his name in the papers. And now he's sulking, and you have nothing once again."

"So it seems. Weygrand must have just picked that address at random. Or maybe he thought the house was empty. Either way I have no idea how to find him now."

"Well we do have another potential line of inquiry. You remember the anarchist Tosets—the one who was kidnapped in Gràcia?"

"Of course." Lawton looked at Esperanza. "I'm sorry about your friend."

"Thank you," she said. "But I want justice, not sympathy."

"Miss Claramunt believes that a member of her affinity group may have colluded with Tosets's murderers," explained Mata.

"What's an affinity group?" Lawton asked.

"Like-minded anarchist comrades," Mata replied. "They meet and agitate together. They even go hiking in the mountains."

"Ours is called the Invincibles," Esperanza said.

"Of course you are," said Mata.

Esperanza ignored this, and proceeded to explain her reasons for suspecting her comrade Ruben Montero of acting as a police informer. When she had finished, she and Mata looked at Lawton expectantly.

"Well?" Mata asked.

"It's not the most conclusive case I've ever heard," Lawton replied.

Esperanza's face hardened. "And your theory that Pau was murdered by a eugenic religious sect? How conclusive is that?"

Mata was smiling now, but Lawton was beginning to think that Esperanza Claramunt might be a little too outspoken for her own good. "The money this Montero was carrying could have come from something else you don't know about," he said. "It's certainly not something any policeman could arrest him or question him for—not in London, anyway."

"We're not in London, Mr. Lawton," Esperanza said. "And I'm not talking about the police."

"Surely this man is worth investigating," Mata said, "in the absence of anything else?"

Lawton stubbed the remains of his cigarette. "Are you a good liar, Señorita?" he asked finally.

"If I need to be," Esperanza replied.

"When are you seeing this man again?"

"Tomorrow."

"You said this Ruben wants to know who killed his brother-in-law. So tell him you've met me. Tell him I've got evidence that Ugarte is involved in these murders and I know the man who's been helping him. If he's what you say he is, then Ugarte will have to react—and perhaps Weygrand, too. And if that happens then we'll know that your suspicions are correct. And I can take further action against this Montero and also against the lieutenant."

Mata stroked his beard nervously. "Haven't you made enough enemies already, Harry?"

"One more won't make much difference. As things stand I have no other way of finding out if Weygrand or this German are even in the city. If they are here, and Montero is the informer you say he is, then they will have to come for me, and I'll be waiting for them. Are you able to do that, Señorita? Because I don't want to place you in danger."

"It's a little late for that." Esperanza described her encounter with Ugarte and his veiled threat against her brother. She was visibly angry as she spoke. Beneath the swanlike neck, the neat clothes, the glasses, and the well-coiffed hair, Lawton sensed the same steely quality that he found in the suffragette women. Some of them looked equally delicate, until they bit your hands and kicked your shins, and it was not difficult to imagine Esperanza Claramunt in their company.

"So he's already trying to intimidate you," he said. "Be careful."

"I'm not afraid of Ugarte," Esperanza replied. "Anyone who threatens my brother is to be despised, not feared. But tomorrow it will be Ugarte's turn to feel afraid."

"Why's that?" Lawton asked.

"Tomorrow Barcelona goes on strike."

"Oh yes, I'd forgotten," said Lawton.

"I wish I could," said Mata with a sigh.

"Señor Mata doesn't approve of the war, Mr. Lawton," Esperanza said. "But he also doesn't like it when the masses protest against it. It's the bourgeois paradox."

Mata looked cross. "You know this strike is going to be more than a protest."

"Do I?"

"You only have to listen to what Lerroux's barbarians are saying."

"Sometimes in politics you can't choose your allies. Don't you agree, Mr. Lawton?"

"I don't get involved in politics," Lawton said.

Esperanza looked at him with an expression of disdain and surprise. "What a thing to say! Suppose your government wanted to send you to die in a war to make the rich richer? Wouldn't you want to oppose that? War is a terrible thing, Mr. Lawton."

"So I've heard. But sometimes they're unavoidable, don't you think?"

"All wars are avoidable, Mr Lawton. Poor working men fighting poor working men. It's only the state that benefits from them. This one is no exception."

To Lawton's relief, Esperanza picked up her handbag and stood up to leave. Mata suggested that she and Lawton exchange addresses, and he gave her the name of his hotel while she wrote down her address in Gràcia for him.

"Good day Mr. Lawton," she said. "I'll do what you suggest. And I hope you enjoy tomorrow. It's an opportunity to see our city the way few visitors have ever seen it. And maybe you'll change your view of 'politics.'"

Mata escorted her to the door. On his way back Lawton heard him walking into another room, and he returned shortly afterward carrying a revolver and a box of ammunition.

"I think you should have this," he said. "My father used it during the last Carlist War. It's no use to me. I don't fire guns. But I have a feeling you might have a better idea what to do with it."

Lawton looked at the revolver. It was a Model 1 Smith & Wesson, a gun that he had not seen since South Africa, and Mata said it had not been fired since 1878. Lawton broke open the chamber and saw that it was already fully loaded. "You might be right," he said.

"So what do you think of Miss Claramunt?" Mata asked.

"She certainly has some strong opinions. As many women do nowadays."

"So did her father. He was a liberal and a republican. He was tortured in the Montjuïc fortress in 1896 after the Corpus Christi bombings."

"Rull?"

Mata shook his head. "Before his time. Someone threw two bombs at the Corpus Christi procession outside the church of Santa Maria del Mar down the harbor. Killed five people and wounded forty-five. My parents were in the procession, standing further back, thank God. Afterward the Brigada and the police rounded up hundreds of people. Anarchists, trade unionists, liberals—anyone the state didn't like. All of them tortured in the castle. Claramunt was one of them. He died of a heart attack under interrogation. In the end five anarchists were executed the following year, but none of them did it. They never found out who did. Hombre, I'm

surprised you never heard about this. Lerroux made his name writing
about the Montjuïc trials—he seemed like a proper journalist back then.
And there were protests about trials all over Europe. Inquisitorial Spain
they called it, and with good reason."

"I didn't read the papers much back then."

"Well, if his daughter seems a little fierce, that's definitely one of the
reasons. And Ugarte was one of the interrogators."

Lawton felt a little more well disposed toward Esperanza Claramunt
now. He had not handled a gun since the war, and he had not expected
to hold one again, but the curved wooden handle felt comforting in his
hand now, and he tucked the revolver into his trouser belt before emptying the spare ammunition into his pockets.

"Are you going to work tomorrow?" he asked.

Mata shook his head. "I won't be in the office. The Barcelona newspapers have all agreed not to publish tomorrow. But I'll be out on the street
at least some of the time, so I can write something later."

"Well, be careful."

"I think you're the one who needs to be careful, Harry," Mata
warned.

Lawton decided not to risk walking down the Ramblas in case he was
searched. Instead he took the longer route down the Passeig de Sant Joan
toward the Estación de Francia, where he turned back along the port toward
the Columbus Monument. As he walked back along the harbor, past the
rows of boats, ships, and white sails, he wondered what Maitland would say
if he knew that he was walking the streets of Barcelona with a revolver tucked
into his belt, looking for the men who had twice tried to kill him. Even in
the midafternoon, the city felt airless and muggy, and the sun seemed to
burn right through the hat Mata had given him.

In Africa it had been just as hot, but that was before the sickness had
ruined him. Now he could not be sure whether it was the heat or his own
brain that made the objects around him seem so hazy and insubstantial,
from the bobbing ships and the shining sea to the palm trees and tall
buildings on his right. Even as he scrunched up his eyes the city seemed to
be dissolving in front of him. Only the statue of Columbus seemed solid,

pointing toward the sea and beyond it, high on the hill, he could make out the castle where Esperanza Claramunt's father had died.

Once again, Lawton asked himself what he was doing in this beautiful but incomprehensible city that seethed with threats and dangers unlike anything he had experienced before. The trains still seemed to be running at the Estación de Francia, and he knew they might not be running the next day. It would be easy enough to check out of his hotel and catch the next train northward, and leave Barcelona behind before it killed him. He could tell Maitland and Mrs. Foulkes what he had found out and leave the rest to them. He would not get his full payment, but he could at least save his own skin, and write the whole thing off as a strange adventure that had cost him nothing. Yet even as he considered this option, he had no desire to take it. Whether it was curiosity, stubbornness, or some lingering copper's instinct to see an investigation through, he was not prepared to walk away until he had found Weygrand and whoever was working with him.

Despite Mata's article, he doubted that they could get much help from Arrow or Bravo Portillo, and it did not seem right to leave Mata or Esperanza Claramunt to deal with this by themselves. Whatever conspiracy Weygrand and his companions were involved in, it would take more than a poet-journalist and a naïve young anarchist to get to the bottom of it. The three of them might not be the most obvious material for an investigating team, but right now it was the only team there was. He had intended to go back to his hotel to rest, but as he came alongside the entrance to the Plaza Reial he thought of Arenales's palace and it occurred to him that there was still one more thing he could do that day.

He hurried across the Ramblas, past a small group of Somaten, and threaded his way back into the Raval, until he found the little square that he and Mata had visited two days before. Some children were playing hopscotch in the center of the square, and Lawton saw that one of the shutters in Arenales's palace was now open, and the French windows behind it were slightly ajar. His lassitude immediately faded. He considered walking up to the building and knocking on the door. Instead he took up a position in a shaded doorway in the narrow street on the far side of the square, and lit a cigarette.

He continued to work his way through the pack, listening to the children chanting and the warble of pigeons from the square. He had been waiting for about an hour when a man appeared in the window. It was not Weygrand or Arenales, but a tall black man wearing eighteenth century livery who appeared to be a servant. The servant looked out across the square, and Lawton pulled away as he grasped the shutters. By the time he looked back the shutters were closed.

Once again Lawton considered knocking on the door. Instead he decided to wait and see what would happen. It was not until the great wooden doors began to open, and the two black horses appeared, pulling a carriage behind them, that he broke away from his hiding place. The children paused in their games and stared at him as the servant locked the doors behind him. Lawton saw immediately that it was the same carriage and the same horses he had seen on the night of Weygrand's performance, as he came alongside it and shouted "Hola?" at the curtained window.

The curtain opened and he saw the hatchet-faced man he had seen in the photographs of the Explorers Club, with the wispy silver hair combed back over his ears beneath histop hat. Now his gaunt cadaverous features were fixed in a hunted, frightened expression as he looked down at Lawton.

"Count, I want to talk to you!" Lawton said. "About the Explorers Club! About Dr. Randolph Foulkes!"

Arenales continued to stare at him like a mesmerised rabbit as the servant came between them and jumped onto the running board. Arenales banged his stick twice, and the driver flicked his reins and urged the horses forward. Lawton drew the Smith & Wesson from his belt and began to chase after the carriage, and the children backed away from him in alarm. Even before the carriage turned into the street he realized that the revolver was pointless. He had no justification for firing it that anyone would accept, and it would not do him any good to be caught in the Raval waving a gun at an aristocrat who had committed no known crime. He sheepishly tucked the revolver back in his belt.

He arrived back at the hotel to find Señor Martínez sitting behind the receptionist's desk, looking even more disapproving than usual.

"A woman was asking for you," he said sourly. "A young woman."

"Did she say who she was?"

Martínez shook his head. "No. But she left a note." He handed him an envelope and Lawton read the message: Passeig de Gràcia, 6.1. Ten o'clock tonight. Will tell everything. Please come, Zorka.

For the second time that day, Lawton found himself summoned to a meeting that he had not expected, and whatever was behind this unlikely invitation, he knew that he had no choice but to accept it.

Ruben Montero sat on the roof and waited for his children to go to bed. During the first year after his return from the Rio de Oro, the roof had provided his only escape from a city that seemed as oppressive as the prison he had left. In the penal colony it had at least been possible to look out at the desert from the window of his cell and feel that the world was somewhere out there waiting for him. In Barcelona there were only the same dark rooms where he had spent most of his life that were too cold in winter and two hot in the summer; the same old man coughing his guts out from the opposite building each morning; the same smell of olive oil and fried cod; the same room that he shared with his two children, Pau, Flor, and her mother.

That was the freedom they had sent him back to, and it was made even worse by the knowledge that there were rich men only a few streets away who lived in palaces with silver cutlery; who ate in fine restaurants whenever they felt like it; whose women slept on scented sheets and whose children had playrooms as big as his family's apartment. Less than a year ago the city had seemed so unbearable that he had been prepared to get himself killed in order to escape it. Now the city seemed suddenly full of promise and possibilities. They were not the possibilities that Pau had dreamed about when he sat up reading one of his books or pamphlets by candlelight stub, or holding forth about Kropotkin or Proudhon.

Pau was clever, but he was a dreamer, and the world he dreamed about was as unobtainable as Heaven—a world of perfect justice where everyone shared everything, because people were naturally good and it was only the system that made them bad. Had his brother-in-law spent time in prison, he would have learned the lessons he had learned: that people were divided not into the good or bad, but the weak or strong; that survival depended on making friends with those who had power; that there was no such thing as the collective good, but only those who took from others and those who allowed themselves to be taken.

Ruben would have liked to explain all this to Pau, but even if his brother-in-law were still alive, he knew he would have had to deceive him, the same way he deceived everyone else. He himself was surprised how easy and simple it was, once he had set his mind to it. All you had to do was tell people what they wanted to hear and most of them were willing to believe you. That was what he had done ever since his return, and he could not help feeling pleased at his success as he looked out toward the reddening sky. He quickly checked himself, because overconfidence was weakness, and weak people made mistakes that could ruin them. He continued to sit on the roof until the sun had gone down, and then went back downstairs. He found Flor still sitting at the kitchen table with her mother, his other sister-in-law, and her husband. To his annoyance, there were still children running in and out of the three rooms, shouting and screaming. If there was a hell, it could not be much worse than this, he thought, as Flor looked at him with the sorrowful and resentful expression that made him want to slap her.

"I'm going to Poblenou," he said. "I'll take the bike."

"Of course," Flor said. "Can't keep the comrades waiting, can we?"

Señora Tosets gave her daughter an exasperated look. Ruben knew that Flor wanted a confrontation, and he had no intention of giving her the satisfaction.

"No, I can't," he replied testily. "Because there's going to be a strike tomorrow. And I've got people to see and leaflets to give out."

Flor continued to look at him with cold hostility as he put on his cap and jacket, and picked up the canvas bag filled with leaflets. The bicycle was out in the hallway and he carried it downstairs. He no longer thought of Flor now as he cycled down the Ramblas, past the carriages lined up outside the opera house, where men in top hats and ladies in evening dress hurried past the beggars who were trying to opportune them despite the presence of police. He turned into the Calle de Fernando and cycled past the closed-up shops and through the Plaza Sant Jaume, past the

City Hall and the Generalitat building, where a circle of soldiers had gathered around a brazier.

There was a pleasant breeze on his face now as he cycled around the Ciutadella Park, past the Eastern Cemetery, and into Poblenou. From time to time he saw the ocean sparkling in the moonlight as the bicycle whirred softly through the dimly lit and mostly empty streets, past monasteries, churches, and factories, past the Lebon gasworks, before turning northward into the Calle Lope de Vega. He continued cycling beyond the Jupiter Club football ground, and then turned east once again till he reached a solitary apartment block. Even as he turned the key in the door he felt as if he were passing from one life into another. He hoisted the bicycle over his shoulder and carried it up to the third floor. The door was unlocked, and he opened it to find Matilde lying on the narrow bed painting her nails. He was pleased to see that she was wearing the negligée he had bought her, but his smile immediately faded when she held up the Beretta and pointed it directly at him.

"What the fuck are you doing?" he said.

"You promised to take me to the beach," she replied, in a petulant little girlish voice that sometimes excited him. "Now I might have to shoot you."

Ruben glanced at the little chest of drawers on the other side of the room, and took the pistol from her hand. "You've been going through my things." He sat on the edge of the bed and laid the leaflets down beside her. "Didn't I tell you not to do that?" Matilde heard the menace in his voice and she looked cowed now, as she reached under the pillow and handed him a small pile of notes and coins. Ruben counted them and reached for the little metal box under the bed. He laid the notes inside it and lifted out an ammunition clip. "You shouldn't play with guns," he said, slotting the clip into the pistol. "Even when they're unloaded."

"I won't do it again, papi," she said, in the same childish voice.

"I know." Ruben reached out with his free hand and yanked her head toward him by the hair, so that she was lying across his thigh. She let out a muffled yelp as he forced the barrel into her mouth.

"If I tell you not to do something, you don't do it! And if you ever disobey me again I swear I will blow your fucking brains out, do you understand me?"

Matilde's eyes were bulging wildly, but she managed to nod as Ruben withdrew the gun. She was only seventeen, and he knew from her terrified expression that she would not repeat the same mistake. This was the only way to talk to whores, and it would not have done his nagging wife any harm to be treated in the same way. The sight of her wet cheeks and the soft weight of her hair excited him, and he laid the gun on the floor and turned her over onto her stomach. She lay there rigid with fear as he unbuttoned his fly and forced himself into her with a grunt. As he moved back and forth inside her he remembered the punishment cell in the Rio de Oro where he had lain beneath the boards for three days half-crazed from lack of food and water. At one point he had been so delirious that he hallucinated naked women. They came to him in an endless procession of delight, like the temptations of Saint Anthony, pouting and touching themselves obscenely before they writhed away from his outstretched hands. In the desert, these phantom-women had driven him mad, but Matilde was real. She belonged to him, and she could not escape him. Through his half-closed eyes he saw the scattered leaflets calling on the workers of Poblenou to come out on strike. In a few hours he would distribute them to the early morning shift, but now he wanted only to take his pleasure, and even as he brought himself closer to the point of no return, he imagined that it was not Matilde lying underneath him, but Esperanza Claramunt.

21

At seven o'clock Lawton was already sitting in a café on the Passeig de Gràcia. On the other side of the avenue, beyond the rows of trees and lampposts and the trickle of carriages, trams, and motorcars that moved dreamily back and forth between them, he saw the glass entrance to the address he had been given. From time to time some of the residents came and went, but there was no sign of life from the shuttered window on the sixth floor. Lawton was tempted to walk across the street and enter the building, but he continued to wait until the appointed time approached, smoking one cigarette after another and ordering the occasional coffee to justify his presence.

All around him men and women in smart clothes and stylish hats sat talking animatedly as the sky grew darker. It was not until the sun dropped below the skyline and the electric lights came on that the tables began to thin out. Lawton ordered a small plate of squid and fried potatoes and continued to watch the building through the bright glow of the arc lamps. Even now the new electric lamps amazed him. In Limehouse, in his first year on the force, he had spent whole nights on the beat in streets without any lights at all, apart from his police bull's-eye lamp. Even then he didn't always use it, because the metal got too hot to hold and sometimes it was better to have no light until he really needed it. His first few months on the night beat had been terrifying—more terrifying even than the war. In Africa he usually had people around him. From the moment he left the Limehouse station till he returned at dawn smelling of oil and covered in soot, he was on his own in streets that were badly lit or not lit at all, armed only with a truncheon and a pair of cuffs, and a whistle that his colleagues might not even hear.

Now the new lamps extended the day into the night, and it was only a matter of time before they were found in every city and every street, even in the slums. He waited until the café was nearly empty, and then took up a less conspicuous position in a sheltered doorway a few buildings away. At half past nine the glass door opened once again, and he ducked back into the shadows as Weygrand stepped out onto the street, wearing a cape and top hat and holding his silver-handled cane. Lawton felt quietly triumphant and considered following him as he walked off briskly in the direction of the Plaza Catalunya, then he looked up at the sixth floor and saw the red glow through the open shutters.

He waited till Weygrand had disappeared before crossing the avenue. There was no concierge, and he pressed the bell to 6.1. The door immediately buzzed open and he stepped into the hallway. He heard the whirring of a generator and the sound of someone playing a waltz on the piano as he walked up the stairs. As he approached the fifth floor he untucked the revolver from his belt and held it by his side with his finger resting on the trigger. The door to the apartment was slightly ajar, and he pushed it open with his free hand, holding the gun in the other, to find Zorka standing at the end of the hallway.

She was holding a lantern and wearing a blue silk dressing gown emblazoned with peacocks, and her dark hair fell back across her shoulders as she stared anxiously at the revolver.

"You don't need that, Harry," she said softly. "He's not here."

"I know." Despite his wariness he could not help noticing that the dressing gown only reached down to her knees and that she was not wearing shoes. He took the lantern from her hand and looked around at the table and two chairs before inspecting the bedroom, the kitchen, and the little sitting room leading out onto the balcony. He quickly satisfied himself that there was no one there. Zorka had already sat down at the table, where he noticed the pack of Black Russians and an ashtray with a half-smoked cigarette butt.

"Where's he gone?" He sat down on the other side of the table and laid the pistol on his lap.

"Gambling with his friends. He won't be back till the morning."

"Does one of his friends drive a red Delaunay-Belleville?"

She stared back at him blankly.

"You don't happen to have a blond wig lying around, do you?"

"I don't understand you," she said.

"Don't play the innocent with me girl. We're not in the theatre now. Your man Weygrand tried to have me killed and I'm not happy about it."

"I don't know anything about that, Harry! *I* don't murder people."

"But you helped kill Foulkes. After you'd fleeced him. And you tricked me into the bargain. Tell me something, Marie Babineaux—was she a Hyperborean too?"

"You're angry, Harry. But before you judge me, maybe you should hear what I have to say."

She looked sad and plaintive now, the way she had looked toward the end of her performance. Despite himself, Lawton could not help finding her husky voice alluring. In the light of the lantern, with the darkness all around them, her face had the luminous purity of an old religious painting.

"I'm listening."

"So is Franz." She put her fingers to her temples. "Even when he's not here. I've learned how to keep him out. I can put a wall around my mind, but only for a short time. If he knows it's there he might wonder why."

"Christ almighty," Lawton said. "Will you stop with the mumbo jumbo now? I may be Irish but I wasn't born in a fucking peat bog."

"You don't believe me, Harry. Or perhaps you only believe in things you can see—and touch?" There was the trace of a smile on her lips. "But Franz understands the world we don't see. That's what makes him dangerous. He's not what you think he is. And I'm not who you think I am."

"So what are you then?"

"A prisoner! The young girl who Franz stole from her family when she was only fifteen years old. Who he promised to take to Vienna and write a book about because he wanted to study my mind. My mind! Hah! So he paid my parents money and then he took the one thing a young girl should only lose with the man she loves."

"Well isn't that a heartrending tale," Lawton said. "If I only had a violin. And if it wasn't coming from a liar and a fraudster I might even shed a tear."

"You're too harsh, Harry! Franz made me do things. Dirty things that made me ashamed! He can always make people do what he wants. Franz has too much power, and he uses it—for himself." Her shoulders were trembling now, and she bit her lip fetchingly. If she was acting, Lawton thought, it was a performance to impress the Divine Miss Sarah herself.

"Most of the time we didn't do anything that bad." Zorka went on. "Just the tricks and illusions like the ones you saw. And what's wrong with that that? People believe what they want to believe. So we gave it to them—for a price."

"What about Foulkes?" Lawton asked impatiently.

"We met him in Vernet," she said. "He was a scientist—like Franz. Franz saw that he liked me. He liked me a lot. More than you would expect a man like that to like a woman. So he got me to persuade Foulkes to come to Barcelona. The plan was simple. Franz would put him in a trance. He would get him to make a payment. A large payment."

"To Marie Babineaux."

She nodded. "By the time the trick was discovered we would be out of the city. Foulkes wouldn't remember anything and no one would ever know what had happened to his money. I didn't know Franz was going to kill him!"

"You expect me to believe that?"

"I'm telling you the truth!" she pleaded. "Franz just said send him to the toilet and then leave. I didn't know there was a bomb in there!" She reached for the cigarettes, and took one before she offered him the pack. Lawton accepted and lit them both.

"I feel so bad, Harry!" She drew on the cigarette and let out a stream of smoke. "And so alone. Don't you feel alone? Haven't you been waiting for someone like me?" Her pink lips were parted and her eyes were shining as she reached out a pale hand and laid it on his wrist. Lawton did not move his arm away. He felt suddenly light-headed and a little giddy.

"What about the Explorers Club?" he asked.

"What would you like to explore Harry?" Her voice was soft and purring now and she lifted one of his hands to her breast as he sucked nervously on the cigarette again. In the same moment he noticed that her features had become vague and slightly blurry, and he sniffed at the cigarette.

"Bitch!" The cigarette fell from his hand he reached groggily for the revolver, but he seemed to have no control over his movements. He was still groping for the weapon when he felt a sharp prick in his neck and he looked up to see Zorka looming over him. There was a triumphant and faintly tigerish smile on her face as she pushed the syringe down into his neck and stepped away from him. Even as he reached toward her, he felt his strength failing, and as he fell face down toward the floor he heard the click of the door in the hallway, and he knew that he was going to die and that it was his own stupid fault.

It was still dark when Esperanza woke up and reached for the rattling clock. On the other side of the room Eduardo gave a snuffle and turned over in his bed as she walked barefoot across the tiled floor in her night-dress. She had spent much of the night worrying about Ruben, and the strike and what Ugarte might do to her or her brother, and she still felt anxious as she got dressed by candlelight. She pinned her hair up and put on the same blouse, skirt, cloak, and hat that she normally wore to work, in case her mother woke up.

Finally she let herself out, and held her boots in one hand as she quietly closed the door to the apartment with the other. She put her boots on in the hallway and went downstairs. There was no sign of Ugarte or his companion, and she walked quickly up to the Plaza de Lesseps, where the Gràcia strike committee had established its headquarters. Already there were men and women milling around the square talking in low voices, while women and children carried trays of hot chocolate, brandy, and cakes. Esperanza stopped just long enough to check with the strike committee that everything was in place, and let them know that she had to go downtown. She wished them luck and promised to be back by midday, and then headed off down toward the Diagonal. As she walked along the Passeig de Gràcia she was pleased to see that there were no trams or streetcars or any traffic at all. She was about halfway down the avenue when she saw the stationary tram.

Esperanza was not entirely surprised that one of the Marquess de Foronda's drivers should have broken the strike, because Foronda had pledged to keep all his trams working. But as she came closer she saw some thirty men and women standing around the vehicle shouting at the few passengers to get out. Neither the driver nor his passengers needed much persuasion. No sooner had they moved out of the way than the crowd moved to the pavement side of the tram and began to rock it back and forth. It took barely a few minutes before the street car fell over with a crash.

The crowd cheered, but Esperanza felt both amazement and trepidation as she stared at the stricken vehicle lying on its side like a wounded mammoth. Further down the avenue an even larger crowd was beginning to form at the Plaza Catalunya, and a mounted detachment of Civil Guards was lined up in front of the Sarrià station, watching the people coming into the square. The *guardia* sat impassively in the saddles in their green capes, four-cornered hats, and leather boots, with their sabers and carbines protruding from scabbards and holsters.

Esperanza hurried past them onto the Ramblas, where groups of men and women were moving back and forth between the Raval and the Gothic Quarter. None of them seemed to be on their way to work. Esperanza saw women carrying extra bread and baskets of food back from the market, and groups of protesters listening carefully to instructions from their respective anarchist, socialist, and Radical Party organizers. The Athenaeum was packed with unionists and strike organizers who were shouting the names of streets and rendezvous places to each other, and

Esperanza immediately began looking around for Ruben, when Arnau Busquets came up to her with a wide grin.

"Espe!" he said. "Have you seen? It's working! I thought you'd be in Gràcia all day."

"I'm looking for Ruben," she replied.

"He's in Poblenou but he's going to meet us at the docks later. Why don't you come with us?"

Esperanza was about to reply when she noticed some comrades comforting a woman who looked about her same age, who was sobbing quietly on the other side of the room. Arnau said she was the compañera of a Russian comrade named Klimov, who had disappeared three nights ago, coming back from the night shift.

"She thinks the Monster got him," he said.

Esperanza felt as if an icy finger had run down her spine. "Has she told the police?"

"She did. Fat lot of good it did her. The coppers only have one thing on their minds now—and so should we. For today at least."

Esperanza knew he was right. In a city where even her own comrades could not be trusted, it was comforting to know that there were men like Arnau Busquets around, who still burned with the pure flame that had first attracted her to the Idea. Arnau was like tempered steel, hardened in oppression and adversity, but the same could not be said of Ruben, and now it was obvious that he had done his filthy work once again.

Arnau would know what to do with Ruben. For a moment she was tempted to abandon Lawton's plan and tell him everything she knew, but there was no time to talk as the Invincibles and the other strikers headed out toward the Ramblas. Soon they were back on the sand-covered thoroughfare, and she no longer cared if Director Vargas or Ugarte saw her as the crowd marched past the policemen and Somaten, with children running alongside them. It soon became obvious that what she had seen on the Passeig de Gràcia was not an exception. At the Calle Hospital she saw a crowd pelting a tram with stones and a group of women haranguing a shopkeeper outside his shop, one of whom was waving a revolver. Even though the woman wore the red Radical Party bow on her dress, the comrades cheered and raised clenched fists as they continued marching toward the harbor.

Despite the presence of Civil Guards, militiamen, and police at various points along the Ramblas, none of them made any attempt to intervene as the crowds grew larger and angrier. At the bottom of the Ramblas a group of protesters were setting fire to the guard house where the customs taxes were collected, while a contingent of soldiers stood watching passively from the barracks.

They reached the harbor just as the sun was coming up to find the dockworkers standing calmly next to the unloaded crates and the cranes that loomed over the water's edge. Only the pier at the far end of the harbor beneath Montjuïc still remained operational, and two ships were still being loaded with ammunition and soldiers. Elsewhere the dockers, stevedores, and warehousemen were in complete control and they appeared to have accepted these exceptions. Just then Esperanza heard shots coming from the direction of the Plaza Catalunya, and as she looked past the burning excise house she saw a cyclist coming toward them, and even before she could see his face she recognized Ruben Montero.

The sight of him filled her with an almost physical disgust, as he came toward them and dismounted. Arnau and some of the other comrades gathered around as Ruben reported that all the factories in Poblenou were now on strike or closed for the day. The Lebon gasworks and the electricity plant were also closing, he said, and it would not be long before Poblenou, Sant Martí, and Clot were completely shut down.

"Excellent!" Arnau gave him a pat on the back. "And Raval is with us, too. And Gràcia. And as you see the docks are ours. Except for two troop ships. Too many soldiers guarding them. But it doesn't matter. There won't be any others."

Ruben nodded with satisfaction. "That's good. I saw people breaking into gun shops on my way over. And they say the comrades in Clot are getting ready to attack the police station. Ferrer was wrong. This is more than a protest now."

Arnau and the comrades looked thrilled at the prospect, and Esperanza wanted to shout out at them that the great revolutionary was a liar and a traitor and an agent of the state. Once again she resisted the temptation. There was no reason to remain at the docks now, and Arnau suggested that they go back to the Athenaeum. Esperanza was not sure whether Ruben had detected her hostility, but he looked slightly wary as he pushed his bicycle alongside her, and described how he and the comrades from Poblenou had stood outside one of the Marquess of Comillas's textile factories that morning and persuaded the entire early morning shift to turn back at the gates.

Esperanza tried to look pleased. "I have news too," she said, lowering her voice. "About our other matter."

"Oh?"

"Mata introduced me to a foreign detective yesterday. He knows who betrayed Pau. He says it's one of us. An Invincible."

"What?" Esperanza thought she saw a flicker of alarm in Ruben's black eyes, and then his face hardened. "Did he tell you who it is?"

"No. But he's going to give the name to Mr. Arrow."

"Well we need to get to him first. You need to get that name. The police can't do anything today. When the strike is over we'll deal with this. I'm meeting Ferrer this afternoon. I'll ask him what he thinks we should do about this murderer."

"Ferrer's in Barcelona?" Esperanza looked at him in surprise. "So he's supporting the strike after all?"

Ruben shrugged. "He's here on some other business. But he wants to be kept informed. I'm meeting him at his office. I'm going to try and bring him around. When he sees what's happening . . ."

Once again Esperanza felt incredulous that anyone could be as depraved as Ruben and yet lie so convincingly, to the point when even Ferrer had been taken in.

"I can't," she replied. "I need to be in Gràcia."

Ruben nodded. "Well, I'll tell you what Francesc says."

All along the Ramblas strikers were ordering shopkeepers to close their shops, and some shops had had their windows smashed. Just beyond the Plaza Reial, an angry crowd was pelting an empty streetcar with bricks and bottles while its driver sat hunched over the wheel with his hands over his head. An even larger crowd was gathering on the corner of the

Conde del Asalto, and Rosa saw that some of its members were armed with pistols and shotguns.

As they came closer to the Plaza Catalunya she heard the sound of shouts and broken glass coming from the adjoining streets, and she saw people running toward them from the top of the Ramblas, yelling and screaming. Some of them had blood on their clothes and faces. Behind them she saw the black hats and capes of the Guardia Civil and the glint of sabers as they came charging down the central thoroughfare. Even as she and the comrades ran into the side streets to take cover, she imagined Ruben lying to Francesc Ferrer, as he had lied to everyone else, and she told herself that she could not allow this to happen, and that the teacher she still regarded as an inspiration needed to know exactly what kind of man he was dealing with.

22

Lawton woke up to hear the crackle of gunfire breaking in the distance like a summer storm. At first he thought he was back in Africa, moving up with his regiment toward the front line. He could smell blood, and he could see the lines of stretcher bearers and wagons bringing back the dead and wounded. But there were no cannons, and the shooting was feeble and intermittent. He knew he was not dreaming, and even though he was conscious he did not seem able to move. It was not until be blinked and saw the ceiling and the light above his head that he remembered that he was still in Barcelona.

In the same moment he caught the smell of sweat and cheap perfume. He felt the unmistakable softness of a woman's skin against his shoulder, but it was colder than any living woman should be. For a moment he thought it must be Zorka, but it was difficult to keep his eyes open and focus. After several attempts, he managed to sit up. Beside him a woman he had never seen before was lying with her head turned to one side and her thick black hair spread out across her bare shoulders. There were dark patches on the sheet that covered the rest of her body, and it was not until he turned her over that he saw the bruises and teeth marks on her chest and throat. Apart from the few splashes on the sheets and bedclothes, there was very little blood around her, and yet it was obvious from her pallor that she did not have much blood left in her body.

Lawton felt a mixture of pity, panic, and revulsion at the sight of her dead fishlike eyes. From her jet-black hair he thought she must be Spanish, and the smudged lipstick and the smell of perfume made it clear what her occupation had been. He tried to stand and immediately fell back against the wall. As he picked himself up he tried to remember what she was doing there and why he had been lying naked in the bed beside her. He saw his clothes draped across a chair at the foot of the bed, and his revolver was lying on the chest of drawers nearby, but he could not remember taking his clothes off or what had happened afterward. He was still looking around him when he spotted the wolflike creature in the little mirror on the wall with the blood on its face. On moving closer, he realized that he was looking at his own reflection, and when he raised his hands he saw that they were stained red, too.

In that moment he remembered the stories and legends his grandparents had told him, of Airetech and his three werewolf daughters, of the priest who encountered a talking wolf on the road from Ulster to Meath. He thought of dogmen and apemen and the Raval Monster. Now the face in the mirror seemed to tell him that he had finally become the monstrous thing that had always feared himself to be. And yet another part of him refused to accept it, and as he felt the bump on his forehead he remembered the cigarette that Zorka had given him, the strange taste in his mouth, and the needle in his neck before he fainted. He turned away and went out into the little sitting room, but there were no cigarettes or even an ashtray on the table. Had he made them up? Had Zorka even been there at all? Why could he not remember anything?

He was still trying to answer these questions as he stumbled into the kitchen and washed the blood from his face and hands. Afterward he returned to the bedroom and put his clothes back on. The murdered woman continued to stare at him accusingly, and he leaned over her to shut her eyes. In the same moment he noticed that he was treading in water, but there was no sign of a bottle or a glass.

He peered down through the shutters, and looked out at the flawless blue sky and the deserted boulevard. The café where he had spent the previous evening was empty and a black touring car with its top up was parked in front of it. Further back, a charred streetcar was lying on its side, and he heard another exchange of shots coming from the direction of the Ramblas. It was only then that he remembered the strike. He looked at his watch and saw that it was two o'clock in the afternoon. He sat down at the table now, in the same chair where he had sat talking to Zorka the night before, and lit one of his own cigarettes. As far as he could see there were only two explanations for the corpse in the next room. Either Weygrand or whoever had come into the apartment had brought her with them and killed her. Or else Weygrand had put him in a trance and got him to kill her with his own hands, and perhaps his teeth as well.

Could Weygrand have gotten him to drink her blood? The possibility was too revolting to contemplate. Just then he heard the sound of horses' hooves coming from the street below. Once again he went into the bedroom and looked down through the shutters. He watched as the black police wagon pulled up below the building and Inspector Bravo Portillo and three police officers jumped down and came running toward the main entrance. It was only then that he roused himself from his stupor and ran back into the bedroom.

He grabbed the Smith & Wesson and his jacket and stumbled out into the corridor. Even as he climbed the short flight of stairs to the rooftop, he heard the footsteps coming up from down below. The door was closed with a bolt, and he drew it back and ran outside. The sunlight was so bright and so intense that he had to stop to accustom his eyes to the glare before he looked around him for a way out. To his left a low wall separated him from the next building. He ran toward and climbed over, and continued running toward the next entranceway.

The door was locked from the inside, and he stepped back and gave it a kick. He heard shouting from behind him as the door flew open, and then he was running down the darkened stairway with the revolver in his hand. By the time he reached the ground he could hear the police coming down the stairs behind him, and he slipped the door open and ran out into the street. On the other side of the avenue the touring car's engine was throbbing gently, and he thought the driver was looking in his direction. To his right a uniformed police officer was standing by Bravo Portillo's carriage, holding a shotgun by his side.

Lawton was still trying to decide what to do when the driver of the police carriage yelled and pointed toward him. Even as he sprinted up the boulevard he saw the policeman with the shotgun running toward him. There had been a time when he had been able to outrun most of the villains he pursued, but now he felt drained and weakened by whatever poison Zorka had given him. He had just turned the corner when he heard the engine starting up behind him. He knew without even looking back that the tourer was coming toward him. There was a stitch in his side and he was still wondering whether he would have to use his revolver when the car pulled up alongside him.

"Get in." The driver spoke in English, with a French accent. Lawton looked hesitantly at the craggy face, the curly gray hair beneath the driving cap, the leather driving coat, gloves, and goggles, and the cigarette stub protruded from his lips.

"You don't have a lot of choice, *mon ami.*"

Lawton looked back. The policeman was aiming his shotgun now. Even as he jumped into the passenger seat, he heard the metal pinging off the back of the car, and it was not until the officer was out of sight that he realized that he had left his hat in Zorka's apartment.

Lawton did not ask where he was going, and the driver did not speak to him. They drove northward through streets that seemed devoid of traffic and pedestrians, as if the population had retreated from a plague. As they drove up through Gràcia, he noticed that some side streets had been barricaded and he saw men, women, and even children carrying cobblestones, pieces of furniture, and bed frames to make the barricades higher. Soon the streets disappeared, and the tourer slowed to a crawl as they made their way up a winding mountain road, past occasional villas, shacks, and cultivated plots.

They continued to drive at the same pace until they reached the top of a mountain overlooking the city. Lawton knew this was the mountain he had often seen from the Ramblas, as the car pulled into an open esplanade next to a pavilion-like building bearing the words GRAN HOTEL TIBIDABO. The hotel appeared to be open. Some customers were sitting at the terrace tables and a few cars were parked outside the main entrance. Some of their passengers were standing by the edge of the esplanade looking over the city, while others were making their way to what seemed to be an amusement park. The driver parked away from the restaurant, and switched off the engine before drawing back the googles. He pulled a pack of Pall Malls from his jacket pocket and offered it to Lawton.

"So, Monsieur Lawton." The Frenchman held up a lighter and lit their cigarettes. "I'm sorry to find you in trouble with the police again."

"Again?" Lawton sucked on the cigarette and released a long stream of smoke.

"*Alors*," the Frenchman replied. "Let me introduce myself. My name is Captain Georges Bonnecarrère. I work for the French government."

" In what capacity?"

"Let's just say I'm not a tax collector. And you, my friend, are definitely not a tourist, even though you said in your statement in Villefranche that you were."

"Sweet Jesus, you've been following me! And I never even saw you."

Bonnecarrère looked pleased. "I am good at my job, monsieur. And grenade attacks are not common in Vernet. My department's responsibilities include the protection of our frontiers. We had reason to believe that you were connected to men who are already of interest to us. Enemies of my country. It seems our instincts were correct, seeing as you have led me to both of them."

"Weygrand and Zorka?"

"Weygrand, yes. And Herr Klarsfeld."

"Never heard of him."

"Well, he has certainly heard of you. I saw you enter Weygrand's building last night. Twenty minutes later Weygrand and Klarsfeld arrived in a red Delaunay-Belleville, carrying two large wooden boxes, and accompanied by a woman. It wasn't until 0600 hours that he and

Weygrand came downstairs with the boxes, accompanied by Weygrand's female companion, but there is no sign of you or the woman. I thought maybe I should follow them, but it's too obvious—one car following another through an empty city. So I waited for you instead. When you do finally appear, you come running out of another building with the police after you. And where is the woman, I ask myself?"

Lawton felt vaguely nauseous now, as Bonnecarrère looked at him expectantly. "I assume you know Dr. Randolph Foulkes?" he said.

"Indeed. We know a great deal about him."

"So you know he's dead?"

Bonnecarrère frowned. "No, we didn't know that. We knew he came here with Weygrand."

"Well, he got blown up by a terrorist bomb. And I was sent here by his widow to find out what happened to him. And I think Weygrand did it."

Bonnecarrère looked increasingly mystified as Lawton summarized his investigation and told him what he suspected about Weygrand. He told him about the Luna Bar bombing, his meeting with Weygrand and Zorka, his visit to Vernet and his suspicions about the Explorers Club, right up to the point when he had woken up to find himself lying next to a corpse in Zorka's apartment. He could not bring himself to tell the Frenchman that he had been naked and covered in blood himself, but Bonnecarrère still looked disgusted.

"You mean this woman was drained of all her blood, and you didn't see any of this?" he asked.

"I told you. I was drugged. Weygrand must have done it—to frame me."

"So what happened to the blood?"

Bonnecarrère was looking at him suspiciously now, Lawton thought.

"I'm not sure," he replied. "By those marks in her throat she should have been bleeding like a stuck pig, yet there was hardly a drop spilled. That means whatever blood she had was in those boxes. They took it from her and they took it away."

"Took it? How?"

"Those boxes must have had bottles inside them. And I can tell you this—if that's what they did with her, then Weygrand and this Klarsfeld will have done the same to all the other victims of this so-called Monster."

"But why would anyone do such a thing?"

"I don't know. I might be able to make more sense of it if you told me who this Klarsfeld is."

Bonnecarrère looked momentarily doubtful. "Very well. His name is Manfred Klarsfeld. Or Baron von Klarsfeld, as he calls himself. Though he's no more of a baron than I am. And that may not be his real name. Klarsfeld has been many things."

Lawton continued to stare down at the city as Bonnecarrère described the many lives of the Baron von Klarsfeld. According to the Frenchman, Klarsfeld had been an adventurer, a scholar, a polar explorer, a smuggler, and a soldier. He had spent time in Africa, including some years as a member of King Leopold's militia, the Force Publique, in the Congo Free State, before it became the Belgian Congo. He had fought with the Boers as a volunteer and he had also taken part in Germany's campaigns against the Herero and Nama peoples in South West Africa. For the last four years, the French secret service believed that he was working as a spy for the German government in Vernet, Bonnecarrère said, and also in Barcelona.

"Obviously this is of interest to us," Bonnecarrère said, "but it should also be of some concern to your own government. Klarsfeld and Foulkes were both members of the Institute for Racial Hygiene. They both took part in the 1906 Greenland expedition. Klarsfeld, as I told you, used to be a smuggler when he was in Africa. He specialized in an unusual and distasteful form of contraband. He supplied scientists and collectors with human skulls. Specific types and sizes. In most cases these items were taken from corpses or cemeteries, but we have reason to believe that Klarsfeld may have used other methods."

"What methods?"

"I mean he may have killed natives in order to collect these artifacts."

Lawton reached into his pocket and showed Bonnecarrère the photograph of the Explorers Club meeting in Vernets. "Is this Klarsfeld?" he pointed to the man with the duelling scar.

"That's him, yes. And that is the Count of Arenales. Well that makes sense."

"What kind of sense?"

Bonnecarrère shrugged. "At the moment Spain is not a member of any of the great alliances. It's in Germany's interest to change that. Germany also has ambitions in Morocco. It's possible that Klarsfeld is seeking to shift the Spanish position. When the war comes, it would not be helpful to France to have a hostile Spain. Especially with a Spanish army in Morocco. Arenales might be useful in facilitating these contacts."

"And Weygrand? What do you know about him? Apart from the fact that he's a fraud and a murderer."

"Weygrand may be those things, but he isn't a complete charlatan. He is a genuine doctor. Or used to be. We believe that he may also be connected to German intelligence. Until now, we thought that he and Klarsfeld may have infiltrated this Explorers Club in order to obtain intelligence information. Vernet is a good place to do this. There are members of the British general staff who go there for their holidays, as well as some high-ranking officers from my country. Klarsfeld may have been using Foulkes for this purpose. But now these murders. Hypnotists. Monsters. Draining people of their blood. It's *très pertubant*—very confusing."

"It is," Lawton agreed. "And I would very much like to speak to Klarsfeld and Weygrand and see what they have to say about it."

"I don't know where they are. But we have intercepted a telegram that was sent to Klarsfeld from Berlin on Saturday." Bonnecarrère took a piece of paper from his wallet, and Lawton stared at the message: Excelsior. M. S Bertran. 28. 24.

"What does this mean?" he asked.

"Well, Wednesday is the 28th. The second number could be a time."

"So twelve o'clock on the 28th?"

Bonnecarrère nodded. "Perhaps. But I don't know what the rest of it refers to."

"Excelsior was the name of the 1906 Greenland expedition."

"What does Greenland have to do with Barcelona?" Bonnecarrère asked.

"I don't know. But there is someone who might be able to help us."

"Your journalist friend?"

"You really have been following me, haven't you?"

Bonnecarrère grinned. "My superiors would not be happy if I revealed my identity to a newspaperman. I'll let you ask Señor Mata. And then you can tell me if he's been helpful. I'm at the Hotel Internacional. It's very near where you're staying."

"I know where it is."

"*Bien*. But I advise you to be careful, Monsieur. A lot of things have happened while you were sleeping. The city is under martial law. There are mobs in the streets. It's not a good time for a manhunt. And if what you say is true, the people we are looking for may also be hunting *you*."

"Well, next time I'll be ready for them."

Bonnecarrère reached for the crank, and got down to start up the car. "I very much hope so," he said. "Because next time I may not be around to help you."

23

By the middle of the morning it was clear to Esperanza that the strike had exceeded all its expectations. In downtown Barcelona, public transport had ceased to function, and there were no trains coming in or out of the city. So many trams had been attacked, blocked, or destroyed that the Marquess of Foronda called all the remaining vehicles back to their barns. The post and telegraph offices were also closed, along with the shops, offices, hotels, barbers shops, businesses, and warehouses in and around the Ramblas. Some shopkeepers closed because they supported the strike, others did so in order to avoid the Radical Party women who roamed the streets, smashing the windows of any shops that dared to stay open.

At ten o'clock the Invincibles joined the metalworkers from the Hispano-Suiza factory in the Calle Floridablanca in a mass walkout. Shortly afterward she heard shooting coming from the direction of the Ramblas, and it was not until an hour later that she learned of the armed assault on the Atarazanas police station. All morning news continued to circulate through the neighborhood of assaults, gun battles, and cavalry charges from different parts of the city. There were rumors that the whole country was now on strike; that the Maura government had fallen and the king was about to announce his abdication; that the civil governor of Barcelona had resigned; that soldiers were refusing to obey orders to suppress the strike. In the backstreets of the Raval, she saw crowds enthusiastically building barricades from cobblestones and furniture, while men and even women armed with rifles and pistols took up defensive positions around them.

Esperanza did not know whether troops were really refusing to obey orders, but it was clear that they were making no obvious attempt to prevent these activities. Apart from a few police and Civil Guards protecting some of the offices on the Ramblas, the security forces seemed to have abandoned the streets to the roving crowds who moved back and forth chanting slogans denouncing the war and celebrating the Republic. All this was thrilling and exhilarating, as if the city had become an entirely different place to the one she had known. As Esperanza roamed the streets with her comrades she had the feeling that they were riding an irresistible wave that might take them anywhere.

At half past one, news reached the Athenaeum that the civil governor Ossorio had resigned, and the captain-general Luis de Santiago had taken command of the city and declared martial law. As she listened to the wild cheers that greeted this announcement, Esperanza felt that she was about to witness something no less momentous than the fall of the Bastille and the Paris Commune. It was at that point that she decided to go to Ferrer's offices to warn him about Ruben. She was surprised to find Ferrer's secretary calmly editing a manuscript by Kropotkin, and she was even more astonished when the secretary told her that Ferrer was having lunch at the Maison Doreé.

She arrived at the restaurant to find the Great Teacher sitting by a window overlooking the Plaza Catalunya, where the Civil Guard and protesters had clashed only a few hours before. Esperanza had never been to the Maison Doreé, but she knew of its reputation and she felt disconcerted by the sound of clinking cutlery and glasses and the polite murmur of genteel conversation all around her. Ferrer looked equally surprised to see her and not at all displeased.

"Miss Claramunt." He smiled graciously and kissed her on the cheeks. "To what do I owe this unexpected pleasure?"

Esperanza could smell the wine on his breath, and as she sat down she wondered why the country's most famous anarchist was having lunch in the city's most celebrated restaurant in the midst of a general strike. "I need to speak to you, Señor," she said.

"Of course. Can I get you something?"

Esperanza glanced at his bowl of onion soup. She had not eaten since the early morning, but it seemed wrong to eat in any restaurant on a day like this, and she could not understand how Ferrer was able to do it. She asked for some water, and Ferrer filled her glass. He asked how the strike was going, and listened attentively as she told him some of the things she had seen and heard that morning.

"This does sound promising." Ferrer sipped his wine. "And I've heard that soldiers have refused to fire on the strikers at the port. And that Santiago has withdrawn the army to barracks because he's afraid they might mutiny. So are we looking at a revolutionary strike? Or is this just a protest? What do you think, Esperanza—you don't mind if I call you that, do you?"

Esperanza felt Ferrer's foot against her boot, and she hastily moved her leg away. "Well, the strike committee is meeting this evening to decide whether to extend it for another day," she said.

"And if they do?"

"Then anything is possible."

Ferrer looked pleased. "I appreciate your insights. And your caution. I'll be interested to see what your comrade Ruben has to say. Something tells me he won't be quite as circumspect."

"No, he won't," Esperanza said. "And that's why I wanted to talk to you. Señor, you cannot trust this man."

Ferrer's face fell. "Why on earth not?"

"Because," Esperanza leaned forward and lowered her voice, "he is a liar and a traitor!"

Esperanza had spoken quietly, but her vehemence seemed to reverberate around the nearest tables, as if a stone had been dropped into a pond, so that some of the nearby customers directed curious glances in their direction. She waited until the waiter had replaced Ferrer's soup bowl with a plate of boeuf bourguignon, and then proceeded to explain her suspicions about Ruben. Ferrer's face darkened as she went on, and he made no further attempt to touch her foot.

"These are serious allegations, Miss Claramunt," he said. "In fact they couldn't be more serious."

"I know. But when I heard that Ruben was coming to speak to you, I felt I had to warn you."

"That's very sweet of you. Well it's true that Ugarte would like to see me dead. And he isn't the only one. But these allegations need further investigation—and not by the police."

"I know."

Ferrer looked thoughtfully out the window. "It's not really a good time to carry out such an investigation, and I have to return to Montgat tonight. But there is someone I can speak to before I leave. I'll see if he can make some discreet inquiries—without alerting Ruben obviously. In the meantime I think it's best that you stay away from him. Go back to your barrio, and leave this with me."

"I will. Thank you."

"On the contrary my dear, I'm the one who should thank you." Ferrer smiled once again and laid his hand on hers. "I promise you we will get to the truth of this. And when it's over, I do hope you can come to Montgat. I know Soledad would like to see you again. And so would I."

Despite the reference to his wife, Ferrer's hand remained there for just a little too long. Esperanza felt that she had done her duty, but she was relieved to get away from his discomforting presence, and equally relieved to step out of that incongruous outpost of bourgeois comfort. Even as she hurried back across the square, she caught a whiff of gunpowder and she heard what might have been gunshots or fireworks coming from the direction of Poblenou. In that moment it occurred to her that she had set in motion a chain of events that might lead to Ruben's execution, and she thought of Marta Tosets and Pau's mother and wondered if she had done the right thing. The Passeig de Gràcia was still largely devoid of traffic, and the streetcar she had seen earlier that morning was still lying on its side, but it soon became obvious that her own neighborhood had changed dramatically in her absence.

At the corner of the Mayor de Gràcia and the Diagonal, men, women, and children were cheerfully assembling a barricade out of cobblestones, old bed frames and pieces of furniture. Similar barricades were being built in some of the backstreets, and as in the Raval some of the strikers were armed. As she passed the Travessera de Gràcia, she saw another barricade under construction and she heard what sounded like a gun battle unfolding from the direction of the market. At the Plaza Lesseps, she found a contingent of infantry and cavalry camped out in the north side of the square, armed with Mauser rifles and two pieces of artillery, while a large crowd of strikers occupied the south side, where the local strike committee had its headquarters. Despite the presence of the army, the atmosphere in the square was relaxed and even convivial, as some members of the crowd took food to the soldiers and tried to persuade them to hand over their weapons.

Esperanza was glad to be reunited with the Gràcia comrades, and she finally ate a sandwich as she described the situation downtown. As in the Raval, it soon became clear that her comrades were being carried along by events that they had little control over. No one had given orders to build barricades, yet they were going up everywhere. Some of the workers had broken into armories and had laid siege to the Guardia Civil Electricity Factory near the Travessera. Others had declared Gràcia an independent republic and were preparing to defend it at the barricades, and there were rumors that the churches and monasteries were going to be set on fire.

The strike committee seemed at a loss to know what to do next. It was not until seven o'clock that a messenger arrived by bicycle from the Raval. The messenger announced that the central committee had decided to extend the strike for another twenty-four hours, and instructed all local committees to destroy train and telegraph lines leading into the city in order to prevent the authorities from bringing in troop reinforcements. As night fell groups of volunteers dispersed through the darkened streets, armed with pickaxes, wire cutters, and dynamite to cut the train and telegraph lines that passed through the neighborhood.

Esperanza spent the evening walking around the neighborhood with her comrades, making sure that bakeries and the market opened the next morning for long enough to buy food, and that food would be distributed to those who needed it most. It was nearly midnight when she finally returned home. Even though she took her boots off in the hallway, her mother immediately emerged from her bedroom in her nightdress, holding a candle. Esperanza knew she had been up waiting for her, and she braced herself for recriminations, but her mother looked more relieved than angry. She said that she had left some supper out for her, and that Eduardo had been frightened by the shooting, and was sleeping in her bed, and then she withdrew to her room.

Esperanza was glad she did not have to tell her mother that she had not been to work, and she did not feel any need to justify herself. Because a part of her no longer belonged to her family now, but to the masses, who were out there on the barricades and reclaiming the city for themselves. She had no idea whether they would succeed, but even as she sat eating the food her mother left her, she already had the feeling that 1909 would take its place in the list of momentous years 1789, 1848, 1870, and 1905 as a year that had transformed the world and set her country on a new path. And it was only afterward, when she lay in bed, listening to the sporadic shots and explosions that had frightened her brother, that she felt alone again, and she felt suddenly afraid of what the next day might bring.

"In England you use butter on your bread. We Catalans do things differently." Mata held up half a tomato in one hand and a grater in the other. "And this is more or less the only thing I know how to do in the kitchen. I usually eat in restaurants when Sylvia's not here."

Lawton lit a cigarette and watched Mata grate the tomato pulp into a bowl. He had spent the last two hours sitting outside Mata's house, after Bonnecarrère had been turned back by soldiers at the top of the Ramblas, who informed them that the city was now under martial law. Further down the thoroughfare Lawton saw a line of soldiers with fixed bayonets marching in formation toward a large and angry crowd. It was not the ideal moment to walk to his hotel, and even if he managed to reach it there was every possibility that he might not be able to get out of it. Bonnecarrère also decided against trying to get to his own. Instead he had dropped him off outside Mata's house before going off to stay the night with one of his contacts at the French consulate.

Lawton had begun to think he might have to sleep in the street, when Mata finally returned. Now he told him about Bonnecarrère and the events of the last twenty-four hours, while the Catalan made supper. Once again, Lawton could not bring himself to admit that he had found himself in bed with a murdered woman, but Mata looked aghast as he cut a head of garlic in two and rubbed the heads along the large slices of white bread.

"So Weygrand and this Klarsfeld murdered a prostitute in order to blame it on you?" he said. "And Bravo Portillo was part of this?"

"Not necessarily. Weygrand may just have told him where to look for me."

"Well you can thank the strike he didn't come earlier." Mata drizzled some olive oil across the bread slices and spooned some of the tomato mixture onto them. "The Atarazanas station was attacked by a mob this morning. Bravo Portillo was trapped there for hours. It was a real battle. There were people killed. I've never seen anything like it, not even in 1902. And tomorrow there could be more of this. But now another woman is dead—simply in order to make it look as if you were the Monster?"

"That's not the whole reason," Lawton said.

"What, then?"

"They could have just killed her." Lawton stared through Mata as though he were not there. "They could have just left her bleeding for the police to find. The police charge me with all these murders, and that's the end of it. But they drained her blood and took it away with them. You asked me before why they would do that?"

"You have an answer?"

"Maybe. When I was at school, the priest told us the Aztecs offered blood to the Sun, otherwise it wouldn't rise and the world would end."

"That's what you think is happening here?" Mata looked at him incredulously. "Blood sacrifice?"

"I know it sounds mad. But think about it. The Templar robes. The black sun. But we have five bodies all drained of blood. What if they're using it for some kind of magic?"

"But what about this Klarsfeld? You said he might be a German spy. You're not suggesting that the Kaiser's government is involved in this? This is Germany, Harry. The most advanced industrial nation in the world. It's not some magic blood cult."

"Perhaps not," Lawton said. "But the more I think about it, the more I think the blood is the whole point of this."

"Well, right now all this talk of blood is ruining my appetite." Mata laid some strips of ham on the bread and handed it to Lawton. "There you are, my friend. *Pan amb tomaquet*. Bread with tomato. The authentic taste of Catalunya."

Lawton looked dubiously at the reddened bread. It was not like any sandwich he had ever seen, but he was too hungry to care. He took a large bite and nodded appreciatively.

"This is good." he said.

"Of course it's good! It's Catalan!" Mata held out a bottle of red wine. "Have a glass to wash it down."

"I'm a teetotaller," Lawton said. "Generally speaking."

"Well I'm definitely not." Mata poured himself a glass. "Sylvia thinks I drink too much and smoke too much. But I need a drink after a day like this. It's no joke out there, Harry. I've seen two people shot dead in front of me, and there'll be more if this madness continues. No one is in charge. The strikers can't control the strike and the government can't impose order. If things don't go back to normal quickly, anything could happen."

"Such as?"

Mata shrugged and poured Lawton a glass of water. "The king might dissolve the government. There could be an anarchist revolution or a Republic. There might be civil war. No one can tell. And now we can't even speculate, at least not in public, because the military censors won't allow the newspapers to report on what's happening. I tell you, you're lucky to live in England, Harry. A sensible, stable country where people don't do stupid things and the army stays in the barracks."

Lawton pointed toward the loaf of bread. "Is there any more of that?"

"There is. But now you must try it with *escalivada*."

"I have something to show you." Lawton reached for his jacket as Mata cut another slice of bread and spread it with tomato and layers of burned peppers and aubergines. "Do you know what this means? Bonnecarrère thinks it's a date and time."

Mata looked at Bonnecarrère's telegram. "Excelsior—the Latin word for *higher*."

"Even I knew that. It's the 'M.S Bertran' I don't understand."

"That's because you're not a *Barcelones*, Harry. It means 'Muelle de San Bertran'—the San Bertran wharf. It's in the Port of Barcelona."

"So *Excelsior* is a ship?"

"Most probably. And it's arriving at midnight on Wednesday. In theory. The dock was on strike today. Two ships went out only because the army was protecting them. By Wednesday, who knows?"

"Well Bonnecarrère will want to be there. And so do I."

"And what about me?" Mata looked at him indignantly. "I still have a story to write—even if the censors won't let me write it yet."

Lawton had spent many hours of his life watching people, and from what he had seen of Mata during the attack by the TB gang, he did not see the corpulent poet-journalist as the ideal companion in a mission of this kind. He doubted that Bonnecarrère would approve either, and he was still wondering how to say no when there was a loud knock on the door. Mata went out into the corridor, and Lawton's eyes flickered toward the window on hearing Inspector Bravo Portillo's voice. A moment later the inspector appeared in the doorway, accompanied by two policemen. Lawton looked back at his mournful undertaker's eyes and upturned moustache. Bravo Portillo did not take off his hat, but Lawton saw that the inspector was carrying his own.

"Señor Lawton," he said. "I've been looking for you."

"Is that so?" Lawton tried to sound surprised. "Any particular reason?"

"A woman was murdered in the Passeig de Gràcia. The killer ran away from us. The last we saw of him he was being driven away in a car."

"I'm sorry to hear that."

Bravo Portillo continued to stare at him with a cold, dismal expression, and held up the hat. "The killer left this behind him at the scene. Where's your hat, Señor Lawton?"

"It's in the hallway," Mata said suddenly. "I'll get it for you."

Lawton was as surprised as Bravo Portillo seemed to be. Mata went out into the corridor, and Bravo Portillo stared gloomily at the doorway until he came back holding a derby hat that looked almost identical to the one Bravo Portillo held in his hand. "Here it is," Mata said cheerfully. "Where you left it last night."

"Oh, yes." Lawton took the hat and tried it on, while Bravo Portillo continued to stare at him suspiciously.

"Señor Lawton was here last night?" he asked.

"He was," said Mata. "We sat up for a long time talking and drinking. As men do when their wives are away. No wonder you couldn't remember where you put your hat, Harry."

"No wonder," Lawton shook his head ruefully. "I do like a drink."

Bravo Portillo was clearly struggling to comprehend this unexpected revelation. "I've been misinformed," he said finally.

"May I ask by whom?" Lawton asked innocently.

"That's none of your business."

"Well I'm pleased you've found time to investigate a murder after everything that has happened today," Mata said. "I'm sure our readers will be impressed by your zeal."

If Bravo Portillo had noticed the irony he showed no sign of it, and he bowed and left the room with his men. Mata showed them out, and came back looking pleased with himself.

"Lucky for you my father had the same taste in hats and the same size head," he said. "Now what were we talking about? The docks on Wednesday, wasn't it?"

"It was," Lawton said. "And I was just about to say that of course you should come."

Klarsfeld rolled a fifty-peseta note into a tube and snorted two lines of white powder from the glass table. He rolled out two more lines for Zorka, who was perched on the edge of the bed, unpinning her hair.

Klarsfeld closed his eyes as the drug erupted in his head and then opened them again to see Zorka running her fingers through her long hair. He had only slept for a few of the last twenty-four hours, but he felt fully awake now as Zorka stood up and let her dress fall slowly to the floor, till she was standing in her corset and garters.

In the candlelight, with the shadows flitting across her skin and her lustrous brown hair, it was easy to believe that she really was the reincarnation of some Hyperborean queen. She sat on his lap and took the rolled peseta note, and he ran his hands down the hourglass curve of her hips and buried his bearded face in her hair. She turned and kissed him, and he could taste the cocaine on her tongue as she licked the inside of his mouth. He was just about to carry her to the bed when there was a knock on the front door. Klarsfeld knew it could not be Weygrand, who had his own key and was not due back that night. He took the little Schwarzlose semiautomatic from the drawer, shut the bedroom doors behind him, and padded barefoot toward the entrance to the apartment.

His face immediately fell at the sight of Ugarte's pockmarked face peering at him from the hallway. He was even more surprised to find Arenales standing next to him, looking even more like a startled fox than usual.

"We need to speak to you, Baron," Arenales said.

Klarsfeld stood back to let them in. "What is it gentlemen? I'm rather tired."

"Our man got away," Ugarte replied.

"Is that so?" Klarsfeld let out a sigh. "And how did that happen?"

"Bravo Portillo was caught in a gun battle at the station. He couldn't get to the apartment till the afternoon. The Irishman escaped over the roof. Someone drove him away in a motorcar."

"Mata?" Klarsfeld glanced at the open window, as a flame rose up out of the night sky like a giant candle.

Ugarte shook his head. "Mata doesn't drive. I don't know who this person is."

"This is not good," said Arenales in a panicky voice. "Not good at all."

Klarsfeld suppressed his irritation. With his olive skin, his black eyes and eyebrows, and his little black moustache, and the faint smell of garlic, Ugarte was a typical example of the Mediterranean type, and the smallpox scars only made him more distasteful. Arenales might be an aristocrat with the blood of El Cid and Don Quixote in his veins, but absinthe, and—so Klarsfeld had heard—a youthful predilection for kif had obscured his noble lineage and drained his mental strength. What he did have was money—a great deal of it, and that was useful. But even though Klarsfeld was obliged to rely on such men, they rarely failed to disappoint him.

Now Arenales complained about Mata's article in the paper, and said that the Irishman had come to his house and tried to stop his carriage on Sunday, as if all that were his fault. It was clear that the two of them were unnerved by these unexpected events and lacked the initiative to respond to them effectively, and they had even been stupid enough to come to see him together, when they might well have been followed.

"Where is Lawton now?" Klarsfeld asked.

"With Mata."

"Well you know what needs to be done then," Klarsfeld said.

Arenales looked pained. "Mata's not just some piece of rubbish from the street. He's a poet and a journalist with a reputation."

"I don't care about his reputation. He's spent too much time with the Irishman. God knows what he knows, or thinks he knows. No point in getting rid of one without the other. And what about the puppy?"

"She's been talking to Ferrer," Ugarte said. "Our man says the Irishman knows who he is."

"In which case he'll know your name, too. And so will she. The puppy needs to be put down."

"Hombre, she's just a girl."

"A puppy that will grow into a dog."

Ugarte's pockmarked face creased into a scowl. "This is dirty work. If I'd known it was going to be like this . . . What was done with that whore last night—it wasn't necessary."

Klarsfeld had neither the energy nor the desire to debate what was necessary with a mere hireling. Nor was he disposed to explain to a man who only understood the value of money that even the noblest historical tasks sometimes required a willingness to get one's hands dirty.

"See to the puppy," he said. "I'll see to the other two."

"I'll try. But the city's like a madhouse right now. The mob has started burning churches. Even the army has given up the streets."

"All of which should make our work easier. And you can consider this as overtime—a special payment when it's done. Now if you'll permit me, I need to speak to the count alone for a moment."

Ugarte looked as if he wanted to say something else, but he shrugged and left the room. Klarsfeld closed the door behind and smiled calmly at Arenales.

"Are you all right, Count?"

Arenales nodded, but Klarsfeld noticed a film of sweat on his brow and his sharp, pointed face looked paler than usual. Arenales generally had the corpselike pallor of a man who lived mostly at night, and not for pleasure, but for the dusty volumes that he pored over like a medieval monk. Now he looked as if he had died and come back to life.

"I don't care about *him*." Klarsfeld gestured toward the door. "But I need to know that you still have faith in the project."

"Of course." Arenales nervously touched his long neck. "I just wasn't expecting this kind of . . . difficulty."

"Every great enterprise encounters the occasional obstacle. It's nothing we can't deal with." Klarsfeld's voice was soft and soothing now. He nodded toward the open window, where the candle-like flame in the distance seemed bigger now. "It's working. Everything is working. We're achieving miracles and you are part of that."

Arenales looked out the window and his thin lips twitched. In profile he looked like a crow, Klarsfeld thought, and it was difficult to believe that he was not a Jew.

"You have my word, I'll take care of this," Klarsfeld laid one hand on his hunched bony shoulders and wondered whether Arenales had ever slept with a woman he had not paid for. "Now go home. And don't come to see me again unless I ask you to. Is that clear?"

Arenales looked anxious once again as Klarsfeld escorted him out and shut the door behind him. He silently cursed this degenerate, backward country that still seemed sunk in its ancient oriental torpor. Spain really was closer to Africa than Europe, he thought, and men like Arenales and Ugarte reflected that. No wonder its soldiers were floundering in the Rif. He would not be sorry to leave such a country, and unless Arenales pulled himself together it might be necessary to take action against him. But now he opened the doors to the bedroom and saw Zorka lying naked and glistening in the summer heat, and he put these thoughts aside and prepared to enter the garden of earthly delights.

24

Lawton looked around at the rows of dolls, the neatly arranged collection of little cowboys and American Indians on the shelves, and the pictures of animals and faraway places on the walls. Every object in the room seemed to have been chosen with an eye for what pleased children that had been entirely missing from the brutal desolation of his own childhood. Most of the houses he had shared with his siblings had been small, rented, and temporary, with bare walls and sparse furnishings that rarely included more than straw mattresses and a table. His parents owned almost nothing, and his mother had sewed and resewed his clothes so that they lasted for years.

Now he envied the little boy he had seen in the painting with Mata, his wife, and his sister, who slept in clean sheets in a soft bed, with the friendly face of a clown watching him from the clock on the other side of the room. It was not until he smelled coffee that he got dressed and went out into the kitchen to find Mata in an apron, boiling eggs as he laid out ham, cheese, escalivada, and fresh bread.

"Good morning, Harry!" he said. "You slept well?"

"Has anyone ever told you you'd make a good wife?"

Mata laughed and said that he had gone out early to the bakery to find himself the only man among the women who were already queuing up to buy bread as the strike entered its second day.

"Help yourself to anything," he said. "I even have Robertson's jam. Sylvia and the children are very fond of it."

Lawton looked at the black golliwog on the label. "Home sweet home," he said.

"Where is home for you Harry?"

"I live in the East End. Jewtown they call it."

"With your family?"

Lawton shook his head. "My father's from Donegal. But he moved around a lot doing different jobs. Farm laborer. Fairs and railways. And a sailor, of course. That's how he met my mother. In Valparaiso."

"So that's how you learned Spanish."

Lawton nodded. "And some Mapuche. The old girl never really learned English. My father taught me nothing—except how to use my fists."

"You learned well."

"Had to, where I come from. I used to fight on the fairground circuit. You got paid a percentage of the takings if you won. Just food and a place to sleep if you lost."

"Are your parents alive now?"

"My father disappeared years ago. Went off to sea and never came back. My mother—" Lawton hesitated. "Well, she's no longer with us."

"I'm sorry."

"Ah, it's a long time ago. The rest of us live all over. Manchester. America. I don't see 'em."

"You don't have a wife?"

Lawton thought of the widow Friedman, and spread the jam on the bare bread. "No," he said.

"You don't want one? Or you just haven't found the right woman?"

"I'm not for marrying."

Lawton was beginning to wish that they could change the subject when he noticed a framed photograph on the wall that he had not seen the previous evening. The picture had been taken in a street packed with people, and at the center of it a group of men wearing headscarves were standing on each other's shoulders in a pyramid-like formation. All of them were wearing the same identical sashes and white shirts, and the point of the tower was occupied by a little boy, who was standing almost level with the third floor of the buildings on either side of him, and raising his arm toward the sky.

"What is that?" he asked.

"That, my friend, is a *castell*—a human tower. And that boy on top—that's me."

Lawton stood up to examine the picture more closely while Mata described the tradition that he had first seen as a child during visits to his grandfather's house in the town of Vilanova. He explained how the *castellers*—the castle makers—were chosen according to their build, strength, and size, with the strongest on the ground, all the way up to the child known as the *enxaneta*, who climbed to the highest level and waved his arm in the air to show that he had reached it. All this was done with the help of the crowd, who provided additional support to the men in the tower to the sound of drums and horns.

"But why would you do such a thing?" Lawton asked.

"Why? To see how high we can reach! That picture was taken in the summer of 1865, and my grandfather arranged for me to be the *enxaneta*. I was so terrified I thought I'd wet myself. Then I realized that if I fell the people would catch me and I climbed up the tower like a monkey. That is something you never forget. Standing at the top of the castle, with my arm raised up to the sky, and all those hundreds of people looking up as if I was a little prince." Mata patted his belly with his two large hands. "Look at me now. I would most definitely be in the *pinya*—the base—except I don't have the strength. But next year I intend to take Carles to Vilanova so that he can be an *enxaneta*, too. Every boy should have memories like that, don't you think?"

Lawton nodded. In that moment he remembered the first time he had knocked a man out, at the age of sixteen, how the referee had held up his arm while the spectators had cheered. It was the first time in his life he had found he could do something well, and he still liked to think about it whenever he needed to cheer himself up.

"Harry I have a question for you," Mata said suddenly.

"What's that?"

"Why did you leave the police force? You'd make a better inspector than Bravo Portillo."

Lawton was silent for a moment, and then he said, "I have epilepsy."

As soon as he pronounced the despised word he immediately regretted it. He never called his illness by its name to anyone except Dr. Morris, and now he felt as if he had stepped out from a hiding place with his hands up.

"I'm sorry to hear that," Mata said.

Sympathy always made Lawton feel uncomfortable, and he tried to deflect it with a shrug. "I'm not too pleased about it either. My doctor says it might have been the boxing—though I didn't have any symptoms back then. Or it might have been the war. I was nearly killed by a Boer shell once. Blew everyone in my trench to pieces. I was the only one left standing. Three months in the hospital. Still got a piece of metal in my head somewhere. Doctors said it was too dangerous to take it out. Another quarter inch it would have killed me. Lucky me—I thought. Of course you can't be a copper in that condition."

If Mata had noticed the anger he showed no sign of it. "But you are lucky. You're still here aren't you?" he said. "And if you hadn't told me, I never would have suspected."

"Well I hope you won't go telling the world about it."

"Of course not."

Lawton could not think of the last time he had ever revealed anything of significance about himself to anyone, and he was surprised to find that it did not make him feel that bad. "The woman who was killed yesterday," he said. "Where will they have taken her?"

"To the medical school, I presume. Why?"

"I'd like to speak to the pathologist who was with me when I identified Foulkes," Lawton said. "He won't be on strike, will he?"

"Quintana? Definitely not. We can go there after breakfast, if you like."

"You have time?"

"There's no newspaper today and I doubt there'll be one tomorrow. I only have to go to the offices in the afternoon."

"Good. Because I also want to see this Montero—the informer, if that's what he is. Maybe Miss Claramunt can arrange it."

"They'll be harder to find today. They may not want to be found."

"Also." Lawton looked embarrassed now. "I was wondering if I could borrow some money. I need to pay my hotel and I'm assuming the banks will be closed."

"Hombre, of course. But why don't you stay here till the strike is over? The Ramblas is a battleground right now."

In ordinary circumstances Lawton would have rejected this invitation, but Mata was so amiable and hospitable that it seemed churlish to refuse.

"I accept," he said. "Thank you."

"Don't thank me, Harry. I'd like to see London one day. Maybe you can take me to Baker Street. To see the house of Mr. Holmes."

"It'll be a pleasure," Lawton said. "But Sherlock Holmes doesn't exist."

"I know that," Mata replied, with a grin. "But I'd still like to see where he lives."

Half an hour later they left the building. Mata was wearing his fedora hat, light gray cloak and carrying a cane. Lawton wore the hat Mata had given him, with the revolver tucked into his trousers beneath his waistcoat. They passed a few women carrying baskets filled with loaves of bread, and the city seemed calm enough. No sooner had they turned the corner however, than he thought he could smell burning. There was no sign of a fire, and even though he felt no other symptoms he began to feel anxious as they walked along the Calle de las Cortes toward the Ramblas. On reaching the Plaza Catalunya he was almost relieved to see the column of black smoke rising up from the direction of the port. Further back to the west, another black trail rose up in the distance beyond the cathedral spire.

"What is that?" Lawton asked.

"Whatever it is, it can't be good," said Mata. "Something must have happened during the night."

It soon became obvious that Mata was right. The Plaza Catalunya had become an army camp, and hundreds of soldiers and police were sitting or lying round the square, with their rifles beside them. At the top of the Ramblas, they passed a dozen Civil Guards in gray uniforms who looked equally exhausted and disheveled. Unlike the previous afternoon, the security forces made no attempt to turn them back, and a trickle of bicycles and carriages were moving up and down the roads on either side of the thoroughfare. The shops and kiosks were still closed, and Lawton saw crowds of people milling about, some of whom were clearly drunk and holding bottles in their hands. Others exuded a more purposeful defiance and Lawton was amazed to see men and even women openly carrying shotguns, rifles, and revolvers. There were no soldiers on the Ramblas now, and the few police and Civil Guards who remained looked nervous and unconfident. Whoever was in control of downtown Barcelona, it was not the government, and as Lawton looked beyond the crowds and the lines of plane trees toward the smoke-stained sky, he wondered if anyone was in control at all.

Mata kept shaking his head and sighing like a teacher observing unruly behavior in the playground as they made their way into the backstreets. A few minutes later they arrived at the Athenaeum where the strike committee had established its headquarters. Outside the main entrance groups of workers were engaged in agitated conversation and the atmosphere inside the building was equally febrile. As they pushed their way into the crowded reading room, Mata pointed out the socialist leader Fabras Riva and the other two members of the strike committee, who were sitting at one of the tables, looking at a map of the city. All around them men and women in white armbands were listening expectantly or shouting instructions to each other.

They had barely entered the room when an older man with a lined malarial face and a cloth cap came toward them, accompanied by two younger men, with pistols in their belts.

"Aren't you Mata from *La Veu*?" the older man asked.

"I am," Mata replied. "I'm looking for Ruben Montero."

"He's not here," the old man said coldly.

"Are you from the Invincibles?" Mata asked.

"The bourgeois journalist comes looking for his story," the anarchist said mockingly. "Would you like a quote, Mata? 'The city belongs to us now. And we will never accept Maura's war.' How's that?"

"Excellent," Mata replied. "But I'm not here to write a story. I'm looking for Esperanza Claramunt."

"Never heard of her," the old man replied. "And you should leave. And take the copper with you."

Mata looked as though he were about to say something, and then he let out a sigh of irritation and walked away shaking his head. "You see what these lunatics are like?" he said. "Now they think they're in control? Can you imagine what the country would be like in their hands?"

"It doesn't seem to be in anyone's hands right now," Lawton said.

By the time they returned to the Ramblas the smoke had begun to form a swirling black cloud above the trees, and Lawton thought another fire was in progress further east beyond the Edén Concert. One stout middle-aged lady was standing in the middle of the Ramblas looking toward the port with a Browning pistol in her hand and a red Radical Party bow on her dress. Mata stopped to ask her what was happening.

"The youth are burning the churches and convents!" she replied. "To drive the rats away!"

Mata gave Lawton a long-suffering look and shook his head wearily as they walked down to the Calle Hospital. Lawton found it difficult not to cough as the light ash swirled and billowed through the street and settled on his jacket. Once again they walked through the vaulted corridors of the medical school to the mortuary, where Mata asked for Quintana. He came out to meet them in a bloody white coat, looking even more tired and cadaverous than the last time Lawton had seen him.

"Good morning Bernat," he said. "Mr. Lawton. You've heard what's been going on?"

"You mean the fires?" Mata asked.

"That—and the gun battles that took place during the night. And the railways and telegraph lines that were blown up or cut. Now there are no more soldiers and no more orders from Madrid. As of this morning Barcelona is entirely isolated from the rest of the country and the world. We had dozens of people here yesterday, mostly with bullet and saber wounds. I haven't been home or slept. You're not planning to write about this, are you Bernat?" Quintana looked at him warily. "Santiago has prohibited any mention of casualties."

"We aren't publishing," Mata said. "But Mr. Lawton has some questions about our Monster."

Quintana stifled a yawn. "We had a woman brought in yesterday afternoon. It looks like his handiwork. I've only just had a chance to examine her. Come." They followed him into the autopsy room, where two orderlies were laying the corpse of a young girl on the last empty table.

"They say she was shot by the Civil Guard yesterday," Quintana said. "On the Ramblas. I took a Remington bullet from her chest this morning."

Lawton was more interested in the woman lying on the table next to the little girl. She looked much the same as she had when he had first seen her less than twenty-four hours before, except for the cavity running down through the center of her chest.

"Here she is," Quintana said. "I don't know who she was and no one has asked for her."

"Bernat told me that you found traces of different blood in one of the victims," Lawton said.

"In the cretin, yes. There were signs of red blood cell agglutination. It may even be what killed him. But not in this case."

Lawton did not have a very good ear for scientific or medical detail, and he was soon struggling to concentrate as Quintana explained the classification system developed by Dr. Karl Landsteiner of the Institute of Pathological Anatomy in Vienna, that Quintana had mentioned to him when they had first met. In 1900 Landsteiner identified three distinct human blood types, A, B, and O, and his colleagues subsequently discovered a fourth, which they called AB. Not many scientists were aware of Landsteiner's findings, Quintana said, but he had studied hematology at medical school and he had had his paper translated from German into Spanish. The Barcelona police had no interest in such matters, but he had begun to take blood samples from some of the corpses that were brought to him, to see whether the different types matched Landsteiner's conclusions.

"So you've tested this one?"

"I have." Quintana held up a small rectangular glass slide, with a little funnel of red running through the middle. "She's blood type AB. No mixing. But she was completely drained."

"And how long would it take to do that?"

Quintana clicked his tongue. "Difficult to say. The average human body contains five liters of blood—five pints as you say in England. An ordinary blood transfusion from a living person, taking one pint say, can take anywhere from two to four hours. But that's because you need to take care of the donor and the recipient. There are questions of hygiene to take into account, the speed with which different recipients can absorb the fresh blood, and the effect that giving it has on the donor. Some people may give blood with no ill effects. Others may suffer complications. In which case—"

"I'm not talking about a transfusion to save a life or make sick people healthy," Lawton broke in. "I want to know how long it would take to remove all the blood from a human body."

Quintana blinked. "That depends on how it was extracted. Most trans-fusions are carried out by anastomosis—suturing or fixing the vein of the donor to the recipient. You cut the donor's vein and clip it shut, and when the suture is complete you release the clip to allow the blood to flow. You see these wounds?" Quintana pointed to the gash in the dead woman's throat. "You would expect a wound like this to bleed a lot. But the police said there was hardly any blood. And this is the reason." Quintana held up the murdered woman's left forearm and pointed out a small hole with a bruise above the elbow. "This has been made by a needle. That's how the blood was removed from her. But it wouldn't have been just by filling and emptying each needle. I'm assuming it was attached to some kind of catheter, connected to a container. And that's not something I've ever seen before. I didn't even know it was possible."

"What kind of container?" Lawton asked.

Quintana shrugged. "Bottles or tubes, I imagine. There's no other way to have removed it."

Lawton stared at the bruise and grimaced with disgust at the thought of Weygrand, Klarsfeld, and Zorka standing over him while these pro-cedures were performed. "So she was dead before these wounds were made?" he asked.

"Most certainly."

Lawton gave a little sigh of relief now, because it was now clear that whatever Weygrand had done to him, he was not responsible for the woman's death. "What can you do with a dead person's blood?" he asked.

"Do with it?" Quintana looked confused. "There's not much you can do with blood from a corpse except put it into someone else's—a sick or wounded person who needed blood, say. But the recipient has to be present in order to do that. You can't take blood from one place to another."

"Why not?"

"Because blood clots very quickly. And if you put clotted blood into someone else's veins the recipient is likely to get ill or die. That's not even taking into consideration the effects of mixing blood types. So there's not much you can do with a dead person's blood except study it."

"What would you want to study?"

"So many things! How to perform transfusions effectively and save millions of lives. How to use healthy blood to restore the sick and wounded or help us to resist disease and infection. One day we will be able to store blood the way we now keep money in banks. Police will be able to use blood types to connect murderers to their victims. There are those who believe that blood may carry the secret of human origins and heredity—the cells that Mr. Darwin called gemmules. Some believe that culture, intelligence, racial characteristics, even religious beliefs, are passed on through the blood. Here in Spain we had the concept of *limpieza de sangre*—purity of blood. We—they—used to believe that Christians could be corrupted if they had Jews or Moors in their ancestry."

Mata gave a snort. "Spanish superstition, Harry."

"Not just Spain, Bernat," Quintana corrected him. "Look at Santo Domingo. Or the American South. Look at your British Empire. Don't you have octoroons and mulattoes and all the other categories? All defined by their percentage of white and black blood—and we don't even know for sure if such things even exist! So you see Mr. Lawton, blood is a very interesting subject, and not only for doctors. Do you have any more questions? If not I have work to do. Because I fear there will be a lot more blood flowing in our streets in the next few days."

Lawton thanked him, and he walked back with Mata out into the cloister.

"Well?" Mata asked. "You seem pleased."

Lawton did not want to tell Mata how happy he was to know that he was not a maniac or a murderer, and he was not sure yet what conclusions to draw from what Quintana had told him.

"It confirms what I said yesterday," he replied. "These people were killed for their blood. Now all we have to do is find out why."

"Well I can't help you now, Harry. I need to go to the office and find out what Rovira wants us to do."

Just then they saw a large, turbulent crowd walking past the main entrance in the direction of the Parallelo. As they came closer to the street, Lawton saw that some members of the crowd were carrying bottles and cans of kerosene. Mata asked one man where they were going and he replied that they were on their way to burn the Church of San Pau and liberate the tortured.

"What tortured?" Mata asked.

"The young virgins!" the man replied. "The ones the priests and nuns keep in their dungeons!"

Once again Mata looked wearily at Lawton and rolled his eyes, while the crowd continued down the street. "If they carry on like this we'll be lucky if there's any of Barcelona left standing by the end of the day," he said.

"Why doesn't the army stop it?"

"I have no idea."

They separated at the entrance to the Plaza Reial, where Mata gave him a set of keys and promised to return in the afternoon. At the hotel Señor Martínez was sitting at the counter in exactly the same position that Lawton had last seen him in.

"Señor Lawton," he said resentfully. "Once again you go away and don't tell us when you're coming back."

Lawton apologized and paid him for the previous two nights with the money Mata had lent him. The hotelier looked slightly less morose now, and he seemed almost disappointed when Lawton announced that he was checking out of the hotel.

"Your vice-consul came to see you yesterday," he said. "Señor Smeether." He said he has a message for you."

"He didn't say what it was?"

Martínez shook his head. Lawton wondered what had prompted this visit, and he went to his room and packed his bags. On his way up the Ramblas he stopped at the Hotel Internacional, and told Bonnecarrère what Mata had said about the docks. Bonnecarrère agreed that they should be at the harbor at the appointed time. He did not look pleased that Mata was also coming, but he did not object. Lawton agreed to pass by the hotel with Mata at eleven o'clock the next evening, and he continued up the Ramblas toward the consulate. He was not surprised to find it closed. He could hear shots coming from the streets to his left, and a few minutes later the crowds on the Ramblas scattered as a group of mounted soldiers came charging toward them, slashing at them with clubs and the flat of their sabers.

Lawton thought it best to return to Mata's house and wait to see if things calmed down. By the time he reached the Plaza Catalunya, streams of smoke were rising up out of the city in all directions. More soldiers were streaming into the square on foot and on horseback now, and Lawton saw officers shouting instructions to the artillerymen who were lining up small field guns at the tram station. It would not be good to be out on the streets when they started using those weapons, he thought, and he quickened his pace and walked along the Calle de Las Cortes toward Mata's street. He had nearly reached it when the sound of a pistol shot made him jump, and he reached instinctively for his own weapon. On the other side of the Passeig de Gràcia he saw tiny dark shapes moving about on the roof of one of the buildings, who seemed to be firing down at something that he could not see. The shooting unnerved him, and he continued to glance warily up at the rooftops as he walked back into Mata's neighborhood.

Soon he reached Mata's cool, empty apartment and shut the door behind him. Once again he heard the sounds of ordinary domestic life emanating from the balconies and apartments all around the sunlit courtyard beneath him, as if the residents were unaware of the smoke that stung his nostrils or the dark trails that he could see above the rooftops. There was nothing else to do that day as far as the investigation was concerned, and he took his boots off and stretched out on the sofa.

He had nearly fallen asleep when he heard a loud banging on the door. As he walked back to the front door his first thought was that the police had come again, but when he looked through the peephole he saw Esperanza Claramunt, standing in the hallway, looking agitated and distraught.

"Señorita Claramunt," he said, opening the door. "Is something wrong?"

Esperanza took off her glasses. Her lips were moving and she seemed to be struggling to form words, before she finally said in a thin, defeated voice, "They've got my brother."

25

L awton never cried, and he was not comfortable when other people did. As a child he had seen his mother cry so often that he had ended up recoiling from her, rather than trying to soothe her. During the war, he had watched Boer women weep when he and his men burned and ransacked their farms. He had learned to harden himself when he watched them weeping as they buried their children in the internment camps, not only because too many soldiers had died at the hands of their men, but because he had seen the native women wailing at the destruction of their families by the Boers. After a while he had felt no pity at all, to the point when it seemed perfectly natural to follow the orders they were given, and leave Boer women alone in the veld for the Boers to come to their rescue—knowing that such an outcome could not be guaranteed.

It was not until afterward that he looked back and wondered how he could have listened to them weeping and not done anything about it. As a policeman he had come to regard women's tears as an occasional ordeal, to which he responded with stony indifference or sympathetic detachment, depending on whether he regarded the tears as faked or genuinely heartfelt.

There was no doubt which category Esperanza Claramunt's tears belonged to. As soon as he shut the door behind her, she let out a choked sob, and Lawton nudged her toward the kitchen and pulled up a chair. Even then she buried her face in her hands and continued to cry while he looked around for a hand towel and waited for her to cry herself out. Finally she wiped her face and told him that her brother had left the house while her mother was sleeping that morning and had not been seen since. Her brother was two years older than she, she said, but he was like a six-year-old child and he never went out in the street without her or her mother.

That morning Esperanza had been out of the house helping with the strike in Gràcia, when her mother woke up to find Eduardo gone. Her mother had spent the morning looking for him, Esperanza said, and she had only just found out what had happened.

"She's still out looking for him," she said. "She thinks he's got lost. Or he might have been shot in the fighting."

"What fighting?"

"This morning the army attacked the strikers outside the Electricity Factory with a cannon. There were casualties."

"Have you asked there?"

Esperanza shook her head. "Ugarte warned me that something could happen to Eduardo. I couldn't tell my mother so I came here to find you and Bernat. I know they've taken him and he's going to end up like the others. And it's all my fault!"

"Maybe he just wandered off?" Lawton suggested hopefully.

"We would have found him by now. He never goes far, and everybody knows him in the neighborhood."

"So there's nothing that could have attracted him?"

Esperanza thought for a moment. "He does love fire," she said.

"Are there any fires in Gràcia?"

"There are. And there may be more to come."

"Well then, "Lawton said. "We better go and look for them."

Esperanza still seemed dazed as Lawton picked up the pistol and put on his hat and jacket. He wrote a quick note to Mata explaining what had happened and the two of them went back downstairs. By the time they reached the street Esperanza seemed to have recovered some of her composure and her determination, and they walked quickly up through the largely deserted streets. The smoke was even more pervasive in Gràcia than it was on the Ramblas, and Esperanza said that a number of monasteries and convents in the neighborhood had been set on fire that afternoon.

"I thought the strike was about the war," Lawton said.

"It's not us," Esperanza replied. "It's the Radicals—Lerroux's people. They've been telling their cadres to burn church buildings, and now the masses are doing it themselves and we can't stop them."

Within a few minutes of entering Gràcia, they reached the first barricade. Lawton counted five men armed with a motley assortment of pistols, hunting rifles, and a Remington carbine defending the pile of cobblestones and furniture. Behind them stones had been heaped up for obvious use as weapons. Lawton found it difficult to believe that artillery had been required to overcome these barriers, and it was obvious that anyone who tried to defend them against a serious military assault would be killed.

He walked on beside Esperanza through the narrow streets with his face screwed up against the billowing smoke, until they reached the Electricity Factory. Outside the main entrance some two dozen soldiers were standing in a line with their rifles at the ready, and another contingent of soldiers was standing next to a small piece of field artillery nearby. Esperanza could not bring herself to speak to the soldiers, but Lawton asked one of their officers if there had been any casualties that morning.

"Of course there were casualties," the officer snapped. "They were holding Civil Guards hostage! Are you from the foreign newspapers?"

"I'm not," Lawton said. "I'm looking for a young man who has nothing to do with this. He has Down syndrome and his mother is worried about him. He has Mongol eyes and a large head."

"I haven't seen anyone like that," the officer replied.

For the rest of the afternoon Lawton and Esperanza continued to walk back and forth across Gràcia, asking the same questions over and over again. But there was no sign of Eduardo and no one had heard of him. Esperanza looked increasingly demoralized as they made their way through the barricaded streets and followed the trail of burning convents and monasteries. Whenever they came to a burning building they carefully scanned the crowds of onlookers who stood gazing at the flames with the dreamy fascination of spectators on Bonfire Night.

Lawton was appalled by the destruction, and he was pleased to see that the priests, monks, and nuns who lived in these buildings were not being harmed. In most cases they stood watching helplessly or made half-hearted attempts to remonstrate with the mobs roaming through their buildings carrying cans of paraffin and gasoline. Despite the presence of the soldiers he had seen earlier, the authorities appeared to have abandoned any attempt to prevent the destruction, leaving the arsonists all the time they needed.

By the early evening there was still no sign of Eduardo, and the sky above them was lit up by a lurid red glow that reminded Lawton of the Great Unexplained Event the previous year. Esperanza continued to ask desperately for her brother, but Lawton was beginning to sense that the search was futile. It was nearly ten o'clock when Esperanza said that they should stop looking. She looked utterly crushed now, and Lawton knew there was nothing he could say to make her feel any better. They had not been walking long when an animated group of men and women came toward them.

"Espe!" One young man exclaimed. "Aren't you going to the Sagrada Familia?"

"Why should I go there?" Esperanza asked wearily.

"For the public meeting! Fabra Rivas is speaking. Patricia saw your brother there earlier."

"Eduardo was at the Sagrada Familia?" Esperanza stared at him. "She's sure it was him?"

"That's what she said."

A smile of pure delight spread across Esperanza's face now, and she and Lawton hurried back in the direction they had just come from, through the barricades and faceless crowds that roamed the darkened streets. After about fifteen minutes they came to what looked like an open field, and Lawton heard goats bleating in the darkness as they made their way toward an enormous building whose windowless walls and half-finished towers loomed out of the darkness like the remnants of a breached fortress. On the outskirts of the building thousands of people were listening to a speaker surrounded by men holding lanterns, and Lawton recognized the socialist Fabra Rivas, whom he had seen at the Athenaeum earlier.

Fabra Rivas was talking about the strike, and appeared to be appealing for calm, but Lawton paid no attention to the speech. He followed Esperanza through the crowd, and then suddenly she let out a cry and ran away from him. Lawton was surprised to find the little monk-like man he had last seen in the park overlooking the city sitting on a pillar of stone next to a young man with a large head, who was staring at downtown Barcelona with an expression of rapture and wonder. Even in the darkness Lawton could see tears in Esperanza's eyes as Eduardo wrapped his arms around her and she covered his head with kisses.

"Thank you for looking after Eduardo, Señor Gaudí," she said finally. "I'll take him home now."

"And you are?" The little man peered up at her myopically.

"Esperanza Claramunt. You knew my father, Rafael Claramunt."

"Ah, yes." Gaudí nodded sadly. "I didn't know this young man was your brother, my child. But he is an innocent in this city of sinners." He looked out over the burning red sky with a pained expression. "This is truly Satan's night. He has come to Barcelona and brought his demons with him."

"Shouldn't you be home, too, maestro?" Esperanza asked.

"I need to make sure they don't burn my cathedral," Gaudí replied. "Go home, child. I'll be fine here."

Esperanza thanked him once again. She beamed at Lawton and took her brother's hand, and the three of them walked happily together back toward Gràcia. From time to time Eduardo stopped and pointed at the sky or a burning building, and let out a roar that reminded Lawton of the sea lions he had seen in London Zoo, but each time Esperanza steered him resolutely home. Finally they reached her mother's building, and she invited him in for something to eat.

"Bernat will be expecting me," he said. "But I would like Montero's address. I'll take care of him from now on. You look after your brother."

Esperanza gave him the address. "Thank you," she said.

"No need to thank me," he replied. "Glad it turned out all right."

Esperanza leaned forward and pecked him on the cheek, and Lawton was smiling to himself as he walked through the burning city to Mata's house. If he achieved nothing else in Barcelona, he thought, at least he had done this, and he hoped that Mata would have some of that strange tomato-stained bread waiting for him.

At six o'clock Mata left *La Veu de Catalunya*'s offices. He decided not to take his usual route home up the Ramblas to avoid the mob. Instead he walked east along Escudellers and then turned up the Calle d'Avinyo toward the Plaza Sant Jaume and the city hall. His route was only partly intended to bypass the ongoing mayhem. Even if he could not write about it, he was still curious to confirm the rumors that a revolutionary government had been formed at the city hall, that the cathedral had been set on fire, and that General Santiago was preparing to bring his troops back onto the streets.

Compared with the Raval, the backstreets behind the city hall were quiet and almost tranquil. Mata had not expected to spend so much time downtown, but Rovira had sent his staff out into the streets to take notes on whatever they saw so that they would be ready to write about it when the time came. That afternoon Mata had witnessed the burning of the Church of Santa Maria del Mar, and the convents and monasteries of Sant Frances de Paula, Sant Pau de les Puells, the Caputxins, the Agonizants, and the Church of San Pau de Camp.

It was clear that the protests had unleashed a rage and hatred that went beyond the opposition to the war in Morocco. Even Fabra Rivas had all but admitted to him that the strike committee had lost control of the strike. Without any clear political goals, the masses had given themselves over to purposeless destruction, superstition, and outrage. At the convent of the Caputxins the mob had disinterred the bodies of long-dead nuns to see if they had been tortured and murdered. At the Dominican monastery he had watched a crowd search in vain for a tunnel where the monks supposedly walked beneath the city to engage in orgies with the Conceptionist sisters.

Isolated from the rest of the country and devoid of government, Barcelona had become a city where nothing could be proven and anything could be believed, where the security forces had abandoned the streets to the mob. Now the Radical Party young barbarians roused their audiences to new outrages; the anarchists put up barricades to seal off their neighborhoods, and even prostitutes and madams now terrorized the nuns who had once humiliated them. There was a kind of mad gaiety about it all, as if the looting and burning had become an extension of the feast of San Juan.

But people were dying and more would die, unless sanity and order could be reimposed. This possibility seemed suddenly more remote, when he arrived in the Plaza Sant Jaume and found another crowd gathered outside the city hall. As Mata came closer he saw a row of open coffins containing the corroded bodies of nuns leaning up against the wall. All of them had the same freakish contortions and distortions of the long-dead, and their hands and feet were tied according to the Hieronymite tradition. In front of them a young man with a cloth cap was haranguing the crowd with the histrionic gestures and absence of logic that Mata had come to expect from the Radicals.

"You see!" he yelled. "This is the eternal life they promised you! The same eternal life they promised these poor young women they murdered and tortured in their dungeons!"

The crowd listened with horrified attention, but Mata felt suddenly weary. There was no point in trying to convince the spectators that nuns would not have done any such thing. His city had gone mad, and he had seen enough for one day. He walked across the square with a heavy heart and turned into the narrow street that led up toward the cathedral. He was about halfway up the street when he heard footsteps behind him. He glanced over his shoulder and saw the dark outline of a man silhouetted against the light from the square. Mata immediately sensed that he was walking with a different purpose to the other people in the streets, and he stopped and turned around, as the man came toward him at the same leisurely pace. Mata was still trying to make out his face when heard the loud pop, like a bottle of champagne, and he felt a hot pain in his chest.

He touched his waistcoat and realized to his astonishment that he was bleeding. The man was only a few yards away from him now, and Mata could see the pistol in his hand with the tube attached to it. He tried to raise the cane to protect himself, but another shot hit him in the stomach and his legs gave way beneath him. He fell hard onto his knees and remained there, like one of the beggars on the Ramblas pleading for alms, as the cane slipped from his hand. For a moment he saw himself as the *enxaneta* once again, looking down on the sea of hopeful, smiling faces that all wanted him to succeed. Once again he reached his hand toward the fiery sky, and thought of Sylvia and the children. Another shot hit him in the chest and he rolled over onto his side. As he looked up into the dark eye of the silencer he felt as if he was also rushing like a train into a tunnel, and then he saw the flash of light and he was no longer conscious of anything at all.

26

As soon as Lawton returned to Mata's apartment and found it empty, he knew something was wrong. Mata should have been back hours before, and he could not think of any reason why he would not be there. It was possible that he had come back and gone out again while he had been in Gràcia, but his note was still there on the table and Mata had not left any of his own. Even if he had gone to his office, he should have been back by now. Wherever he was, Lawton had no idea where to look for him, and it was not safe to go into the city at night the way things were. He turned on the gas light in the kitchen and ate some bread and ham before going out into the gallery to wait.

From the courtyard down below he heard the sound of laughter, a piano playing a waltz, and to his amazement he looked down to see a group of Mata's neighbors dancing on one of the terraces beneath the flaming sky. Lawton wondered if the entire city had lost its senses as he watched the dancers elegantly spinning around while the flames licked at the sky above the rooftops behind them, and the gunshots continued to pop from all directions. He lay on the sofa with the light out, smoking his way through the rest of the pack until the music stopped, and even though there was still no sign of Mata he felt himself drifting off to sleep.

At some point he woke up to find the sky illuminated by the same fiery red glow. The building was silent now, and looking at his watch he saw that it was three o'clock. His first hopeful thought was that Mata might have come back without waking him, but when he went into his bedroom his bed was empty. It was impossible to shake off the oppressive sense of dread now, as he walked back to the gallery, past the paintings and books and the portrait of Mata's pretty wife and children. Even as he sat in front of the window and waited impatiently for the day to begin he was conscious of Mata's wife and children staring down at him from the wall, and urging him to go outside and look for him. By five o'clock he had had enough of waiting. Once again he picked up Mata's gun and his father's hat and went out into the burning city.

He walked quickly, with his shoulders hunched and his hat pulled down, glancing warily around him at the trees and darkened doorways that might conceal a potential attacker. On reaching the Plaza Catalunya it was clear that the city was very far from returning to normal. Even though it was not yet fully light, lines of cavalrymen and infantry were already filtering into the square from the direction of the university, and he saw at least two pieces of field artillery and a machine gun among the horses and wagons bringing fodder, food, and supplies. In every direction he could see black columns of smoke and little tongues of flame rising up from different points of the city, and there was smoke in his eyes and the taste of ashes on his tongue as he walked back down the Ramblas.

Apart from the women hurrying back and forth from the market near the top of the thoroughfare, the crowds had dispersed, and a cluster of police and Civil Guards were gathered among the trees with their rifles at the ready. Some of the backstreets leading off the Ramblas were still barricaded, and a few pale and fearful faces stared at him out of the gloom as the fires continued to burn behind them. Lawton had seen enough war to know when a battle was about to begin, and he walked hurriedly down to the Calle Escudellers to get away from it

As he had expected, Mata's offices were closed. There was only one other place he could look for him now, and even the thought of it filled him with gloomy trepidation. Once again he walked back into the Calle Hospital and into the medical school, past the fountain and the palm trees, and up the ancient stone steps. He headed down the corridor toward the autopsy room, past the corpse of a woman lying on a wooden stretcher who appeared to have been shot in the chest, and a worker in a bloodstained white smock who was sitting on a bench with a bandage around his head. Even as he pushed the two doors open he saw Quintana standing over one of the tables, and then the pathologist turned to look round and Lawton recognised the body of Bernat Mata stretched out beneath him.

In death Mata looked even more like a Boer, or some great bearded warrior from a more distant era waiting to be laid on a funeral pyre with his sword beside him. But Mata was not a man of the sword, and Lawton knew that he was not supposed to die like this, with the hole in his forehead and the dark stains on his chest and stomach.

"They brought him in during the night," Quintana said. "The night watchman found him near the city hall. This is terrible. I can't even tell his family because the telegraph isn't working. He must have walked into some kind of fight."

"I don't think so," Lawton said.

"You know who did this?"

"I have an idea. Do you know where the Calle del Carmen is?"

"It's just around the corner behind the market. Turn right when you go out of the school and then turn right again. Shouldn't you tell the police about this?"

"I don't think they're likely to be very interested today, do you?"

Quintana nodded and said nothing, and Lawton turned away and threw the doors open once again, nearly knocking over a startled orderly. In his career as a policeman and detective he had encountered some revolting acts of brutality and cruelty, but none of them had ever filled him with the fury that he felt now, as he made his way out of the medical school beneath the swirling canopy of smoke. Even as he crossed the courtyard it occurred to him that he would be lucky to get out of Barcelona alive, but he no longer cared. In that moment the only thing he wanted to do was find Mata's killers, and there was only one person left in the city who could lead him to them.

Ten minutes later he reached the dingy apartment building in the Calle del Carmen that matched the address Esperanza Claramunt had given him. He glanced up at the rows of mean little balconies and slipped the revolver from his waistband, and then stepped past the boxes filled with uncollected rubbish and pushed open the unlocked door. He had nearly reached the third floor when he heard a door open just above him. He held the Smith & Wesson up in front of his chest, and waited on the dark stairwell as a young woman emerged from Ruben Montero's apartment. She was carrying a wicker basket and wearing a shawl over her shoulders. She turned yawning toward the stairway and immediately recoiled at the sight of Lawton and the revolver.

"*Ay dios mío.*" She put her hand up to her mouth and stared at Lawton as he came onto the landing, with one finger to his lips and the revolver pointed at her head.

"I'm looking for Ruben Montero," he said.

"Ruben? He's not here. What do you want him for?"

"Who are you?"

"His wife. Flor."

"Where's your husband, Señora?"

"He's in Poblenou. I don't know where. I never know. And now with the strike on . . . Are you a policeman?"

Lawton lowered the revolver. "You're Pau Tosets's sister, aren't you? Miss Claramunt told me about you."

"Espe?" Flor looked more confused than afraid now. "What does she have to do with this?"

"She knows that your husband is a murderer. And now another man has been killed because of him."

"What?" She stared at him uncomprehendingly.

"You heard. When you see him, tell him Harry Lawton's looking for him. He'll know why."

Flor continued to stare at him with the same stupefied expression as he turned and walked back down the murky stairway. By the time he reached the Ramblas his fury had begun to subside, and he realized how foolish he had been. This was not the way to conduct an investigation anywhere, let alone in a city like this. He promised himself that he would not allow his emotions to control him again, but it was difficult to think what to do next as he walked the short distance to the Hotel Internacional, where he found Bonnecarrère calmly eating breakfast in the hotel restaurant.

"Monsieur Lawton," he said. "Would you like some coffee?"

"I would. And a cigarette if you have one." Lawton sat down, and Bonnecarrère poured him a coffee and gave him his pack of Pall Malls.

"Has something happened?" he asked.

Lawton lit a cigarette and let out a stream of smoke. "Mata's dead," he said. "They killed him last night."

Bonnecarrère clicked his tongue and continued to eat his breakfast while Lawton told him what he had found in the morgue.

"Merde, these people are serious, aren't they?" Bonnecarrère said, when he had finished.

"They are. But so am I."

Lawton told him about his conversation with Ruben Montero's wife, and it was obvious that the Frenchman did not approve. "This isn't the way for a policeman to behave," he said. "Like a cowboy in the Wild West. We need to use our heads, mon ami."

"I know that."

"I assume you're intending to go to Poblenou to look for this Montero?"

Lawton looked at him in surprise. "Of course."

"If I were you I would keep off the streets till our appointment this evening. The city is a battlefield right now. You don't even know where to find him. If you go looking you may also find yourself in the mortuary."

"So what do you suggest I do? Nothing?"

"I suggest you stay off the streets. Tonight we'll go down to the docks and see what this Excelsior is bringing. Until then, rest."

Lawton knew that he was right. He finished his coffee and walked back up the Ramblas toward the Plaza Catalunya. He had nearly reached the British consulate when he saw a column of dragoons coming slowly down the central thoroughfare. They looked imposing and incongruous in the midst of so much mayhem, in their blue uniforms and yellow braiding, their pointed helmets and knee-length leather boots. Lawton was surprised to see Smither standing on the pavement outside the consulate, watching the soldiers with an enraptured expression, as though he were watching a Horse Guard parade on the Mall. He looked around as Lawton came toward him.

"Harry," he said. "I see you've got my message?"

"I came by yesterday, but you weren't open."

"Not much point, old boy. But I thought I'd have a peek at the office. It seems General Santiago is going to take back the Raval today. And not soon enough. Come on up."

Lawton followed Smither up the stairs and into his empty offices. He hung his hat on a rack and sat behind his desk as Lawton sat down opposite him. The urn containing Foulkes's ashes was still on the shelf, and Lawton looked at the Union Jack in the corner and the king's portrait on the wall, and thought of the England that Smither belonged to: a country where police carried no weapons, and wise men of high estate looked down on the world from a great height. As a representative of His Majesty's Government, he knew that Smither would be interested to know that two people in his investigation were connected to German military intelligence. But that would involve telling him that he had nearly been charged with murder, that he had shot at a Spanish policeman, and that he had been saved by a member of the French secret service.

"Any closer to taking these away?" Smither nodded toward the ashes. "Charlie Arrow says you've had some . . . complications?"

The vice-consul gave him a faintly pitying look, and Lawton wondered what else Arrow had told him. "The investigation has been a little more difficult than I anticipated," he said. "But I'm making progress."

"Glad to hear it." Smither reached into his desk and handed him the letter. "This came to you from Scotland Yard. Sent through the diplomatic post for some reason."

Lawton opened the letter, and immediately recognized Maitland's neat, precise handwriting:

Scotland Yard.
June 19

Harry.

I apologize for not replying sooner, but it took a little more time than I expected to find the information you wanted. It seems your instincts were correct as usual: there was a reason why Dr. Foulkes was not honored at the Everdale Asylum. In 1900 three of Foulkes's patients died, in circumstances that were not made clear, but there was a suggestion that inappropriate medication may have been used. Foulkes also acquired skulls from some deceased inmates of the asylum, again without any permission or authorization. These improprieties were not made public, but Foulkes was relieved of his duties prematurely.

As you can imagine, it was not easy to obtain this information. Neither the staff nor the current director were very forthcoming, but I managed to find a former member of the Board of Trustees at Everdale, a Reverend Fraser from Folkestone, who said that Foulkes may have carried out unwarranted medical procedures in which some patients may have died. The reverend did not know what these procedures were, and there was no formal investigation into them, but it was not seen fit to honor Foulkes's directorship with the traditional portrait.

I hope this information is useful to you. I spoke to Mrs. Foulkes and she does not appear to have been aware that anything untoward took place at Everdale. She tells me you've confirmed her husband's body.

I assume that means you've completed your investigation?

Yours.
Maitland.

Lawton had just put the letter in his pocket when the boom of a cannon sounded from the street. The vice-consul stood up and stared down excitedly at the Ramblas as the dragoons surged forward into one of the backstreets.

"There they go. There aren't many cities where you can watch a real saber charge from your own office!"

Lawton nodded vaguely, and looked at the urn containing Foulkes's earthly remains. Even though he had not met Foulkes, he had never liked him. Now he stared bleakly at the ashes on the vice-consul's bookshelf and wondered what other secrets had died with him, and how many more people would have to die before he completed an investigation that was unlike anything he or Maitland had foreseen.

Esperanza knew that most of her relatives and neighbors admired her and her mother for looking after Eduardo, while others pitied them for the burden they had to carry. But she had never thought of her brother as a burden. No one, not even her mother, understood the happiness and pleasure that he brought her. Even now, as she sat on the edge of her bed and watched him sleeping on the other side of the room, she felt a great wave of love and affection toward the strange but magical creature who had been her constant companion ever since she was born. She could still remember how Eduardo had laid his head on her shoulder when he found her crying on the day of their father's death. Even now, as a young man, he still laid his head on her shoulder in exactly the same way, and even though he could not speak he always seemed to know when she felt sad or when she was happy.

It was impossible to even consider putting him in the madhouse, as her grandparents still recommended. Even now, as she prepared to go out into the burning city once again, she wanted to protect him. Had she believed in God she would have thanked him for bringing him back to her the night before, but she knew that God would not have accepted her prayers. He would have told her not to go back onto the streets if she really wanted to protect her brother, that it was reckless and irresponsible of her to risk her life when her mother and her brother needed her at home. But even as she looked down on Eduardo, she knew that she could not hide away in her mother's apartment when her friends and neighbors were preparing to defend the Republic of Gràcia.

Still she flinched, as she tied up her boots, at the thought of a saber cut or a bullet or a cannon ball tearing into her flesh, because there was no doubt that the army would assault the barricades sooner or later, and it was obvious that Gràcia was no more able to resist riflemen, artillery, and cavalry than the workers at the Electricity Factory. Had the Communards known they were going to lose when they went out to face Thiers's troops? Or had they actually believed they could win? Perhaps there were moments in history when it was necessary to fight even when you knew you would lose the battle and might even be killed yourself, she thought gloomily, so that others could remember what had happened and take inspiration from your sacrifice.

She went out into the little room and looked at the table and four chairs. In spite of everything, she found herself making the sign of the cross like a kind of blessing, and she quietly pleaded to be allowed to sit there again at the end of the day, and not for her sake, but for the sake of Eduardo and her mother. In the same moment her mother emerged from the bedroom and stared at her with an anguished expression.

"Don't go," she begged. "Please."

"I have to go!" Esperanza snapped. "I'll be back."

Her mother bowed her head in resignation, and Esperanza kissed her on the forehead and embraced her. "It's alright, mama," she whispered. "Everything will be alright."

The words sounded hollow even to herself, and she pulled away and put on her shawl but not her hat, because there was no need for a hat on a day like this. Her mother was still looking at her as Esperanza went into the hallway. Outside the sky was still dark and tinged with the red glow of the fires. She was just about to set off to the Plaza Lesseps, when a shadow detached itself from the opposite doorway. She instinctively backed away, and prepared to run, and then she recognized the familiar jaundiced face of Arnau Busquets beneath the flat cap.

"Arnau? What are you doing here?"

"Waiting for you," he said. "We have Ruben."

"You have him?"

Arnau nodded grimly. "Thanks to Ferrer. You should have told us about this before."

"I didn't know who to tell," she replied. "I wasn't even sure."

"Well, he's confessed. He's a stool pigeon. He gave Pau up to the Brigada. You know what has to happen now?"

Esperanza knew what Arnau was referring to, and now it seemed obvious that there was no other possible outcome. "I do," she said.

"Good, because we've brought him up here."

"To Gràcia?"

"With Flor and her mother. They thought you should be there, too—because of Pau."

Esperanza bit her lip. Already the day was turning into something very different from what she had expected. Even though she had braced herself for the possibility that she might also be killed, the prospect of attending Ruben's execution seemed suddenly more frightening than facing the army on the barricades.

Arnau seemed to sense her hesitation. "Sometimes these things are necessary Esperanza," he said. "Ruben needs to face justice—our justice."

Esperanza knew he was right. They could hardly hand over a police informer to the police, and there was no possibility of redemption or forgiveness for a man who had allowed one of his own comrades to be murdered. In a city without justice it was entirely logical that Ruben should be killed, and even though she told herself that such a punishment was an execution, not murder, she thought of her father's opposition to the death penalty and she heard his voice telling her to back away from this.

"The carriage is waiting, we need to go."

Despite his determination, Esperanza sensed that the old anarchist was nervous, too, as he walked beside her along the Travessera and up toward Sarrià. She had expected the carriage to be nearer, and she was surprised when Arnau turned toward the convent of the Capuchins, but she supposed they had taken this route to avoid the army or the police. Esperanza had not known the convent had been set on fire, and she stared at the flames that were reaching up through the roof and windows.

The building took up much of the street, and the side facing north was windowless, and the light from the flames was less intense, so that she did not immediately see the little carriage sitting on a dirt road at the edge of a darkened field. It was a good spot for an execution, but there was no sign of Flor or her mother. She could not even see the driver. It was not until she came alongside the carriage that one of the doors opened and she saw Lieutenant Ugarte smiling back at her. For a moment she was too shocked to move or cry out, and then she turned to run, to find Arnau standing with a pistol pointed at her stomach.

"Sorry about this, Espe," he said sadly. "This wasn't my choice."

Esperanza was still staring dumbly back at him when Ugarte grabbed her around her shoulders and pressed a cloth over her mouth. Even as the fumes came flooding into her nostrils and throat, and her legs gave way beneath her, she felt something like grief at the thought of her mother standing in her bedroom doorway, because it was now obvious that she would not be going home again after all.

27

During the war, Lawton had learned to read the sounds of battle long before he reached the battleground itself. Even in open country, without even seeing the front lines, he could tell whose cannons were firing and from which direction, and whether the rifle fire that followed came from the Boer commandos or his own side. From Mata's apartment, he could hear shots and explosions emanating from different parts of the city, and by midday it was obvious that the security forces were winning. Most of the exchanges were short, consisting of undisciplined and ragged bursts of small arms fire followed by coordinated volleys and artillery barrages.

From time to time he was tempted to go out and see what was happening, because it was a mournful thing to while away the hours in a murdered man's apartment, listening to the sounds of war and knowing that his wife and children were expecting him to come on holiday with them. But he knew that he needed to remain alive if he was to have any chance of bringing Mata's murderers to justice, and he would be foolish to do anything that might prevent him from meeting the Frenchman that night. He spent the day pacing the apartment or sitting in the gallery, and tried to distract himself by reading some of the old magazines and newspapers in Mata's study. One of them was a Catalan magazine called ¡*Cu-Cut!* that contained a number of articles by Mata, and there were also clippings of his articles from other publications spanning more than twenty years.

Most of them were written in Catalan, and even though he could not understand them in detail, the language seemed close enough to Spanish to glean something of their subject matter. In addition to crimes, bombings, and murders, Mata had written about art, poetry, music, and restaurants. He had commented on the Spanish-American war; on Spanish and Catalan politics; on Arthur Conan Doyle, and a poetry festival called the Floral Games. Some of the clippings and journals contained his own poems celebrating mountains, Barcelona, and the Mediterranean, and one poem was dedicated to his wife.

Bernat Mata was a big man, Lawton thought, who lived in a world that was much bigger than his own. A man like that should have grown old to see his grandchildren playing around him. Instead he had been shot down like a dog because of an investigation that Lawton had brought with him to the city. Even now his family would be waiting for him to join them, and soon they would return to an apartment that already echoed with his absence. Whatever happened that evening, Lawton promised himself that he would not leave Barcelona until justice was done. And if the law could not deliver justice then he would administer his own.

It was half past nine when he stepped once again into the darkening street and walked back toward the Ramblas. The gas and electricity had still not been restored, but the fires still cast enough light to see by. As he drew alongside the Plaza Catalunya, he heard another brief exchange of shots from the other side of the Ramblas, and he saw lines of soldiers queuing up for food or standing around braziers and lanterns while their horses fed on piles of fodder.

Lawton was conscious of the revolver in his belt and the bullets weighing down his pockets as he walked on through the dusk, past the few pedestrians and the police, Civil Guards, and soldiers who had taken up positions up and down the promenade. He found Bonnecarrère waiting outside his hotel, smoking a cigarette as though he had just stepped outside to take the evening air.

"Good evening Harry," he said. "So you managed to keep out of trouble?"

"I took your advice."

"Very sensible. The army went into the Raval today. I saw some of the fighting from my hotel room. Snipers on the rooftops shooting at the soldiers. Soldiers shooting back while their comrades entered the buildings—it reminded me of the Commune! But this was a little more crazy. I even saw a young man dancing with the corpse of a nun. While someone played the violin! A very strange city, Harry. Thank God the army has taken down the barricades, and the strike is coming to an end."

"What about the docks?"

"They were calm enough when I went out this morning."

"So you didn't take your own advice?"

Bonnecarrère grinned. "I'm luckier than you are Harry. My guardian angel keeps a close eye on me. And unlike you, I actually listen to her."

There seemed little risk of being shot now, as they strolled down the central thoroughfare toward the port. The forces of law and order had clearly regained the upper hand, and the police, Civil Guards, and soldiers exuded a confidence that Lawton had not seen for the last few days. At the bottom of the Ramblas detachments of cavalry and infantrymen were standing guard outside the barracks and another building overlooking the sea. On the other side of the Columbus Monument, just behind the burned-out skeleton of a customs shed, a small group of soldiers guarded the entrance to the port. None of them seemed interested in Lawton and Bonnecarrère as they walked away to their right until they were out of sight of the soldiers, and then turned in toward the railway sidings.

There was no sign of any activity either on the railway line or at the docks themselves as they made their way past the stationary railway cars and the piles of crates, sacks, and boxes that lined the loading bays and the wharves. As far as Lawton could see, nothing was being loaded or unloaded anywhere in the harbor. Beyond the line of boats and ships at the water's edge, a thicket of masts bobbed gently in the darkness and Lawton could see the moonlight reflected in the ocean beyond the seawall.

Bonnecarrère had already located the San Bertran wharf during his visit to the port, and Lawton followed him through the rows of sheds, wagons, and railcars till they reached a stack of crates that gave them a vantage point over the pier. For the next hour and a half they stood in silence, smoking Bonnecarrère's cigarettes and listening to the creaking ships and the water lapping against the wharf. From time to time Lawton heard shots coming from the city, but the docks themselves appeared deserted. It was nearly midnight, when Bonnecarrère pointed out to sea, and Lawton saw the white sails curving toward them. From a distance it looked like a large fishing boat, but as it came closer he saw that it was a two-masted cutter, about thirty feet long, of the type that the Royal Navy used for harbor defense. Even as the ship drifted in toward the wharf, Lawton saw a group of men coming toward the pier from the main entrance to the docks, one of whom was carrying a lantern.

Bonnecarrère drew his FN automatic and moved toward another pile of crates nearer to the edge. Lawton followed close behind him with the Smith & Wesson in his hand, and the two of them peered at the ship as a voice shouted something from the deck. Lawton could see the crew members moving around on deck now, and the man with the lantern shouted at them to throw down ropes in a voice that sounded vaguely familiar. Lawton was still trying to think where he had heard it as his companions attached the ropes to the cleats. The crew had just lowered a gangway when Lawton heard the sound of a motorcar, and he looked back to see a pair of headlights driving slowly along the water's edge toward them, followed by a team of four mules pulling a canvas wagon.

Bonnecarrère pointed toward a small fishing boat lying on the pier about fifteen yards away from the ship, and crouched down and ran toward it. Once again Lawton followed close behind. He dropped down behind the Frenchman and watched the Delaunay-Belleville approach the man with the lantern. It was not until the motorcar came alongside them that he recognized the malarial anarchist who had thrown Mata out of the

Athenaeum on the first day of the strike. There was no time to think what this could mean, as the man in the photograph of Foulkes's Greenland expedition got down from the Delaunay-Belleville and shouted at the crew members in German.

Lawton could see lights moving around on deck now, as the crew began to carry boxes and crates down the gangway, which they loaded into the wagon. His driver remained in the front seat with the motor running and the headlights on while Klarsfeld stood in the headlights next to the anarchist from the Athenaeum. The loading continued for about half an hour before Klarsfeld returned to his car, and his driver began to wheel the vehicle around. The car was about halfway through its turn when the headlights fell on the place where he and Bonnecarrère were concealed and a voice from the cutter yelled, "*Dar is jemand! Hinter dem boot!*"

The driver abruptly stopped, leaving the headlights pointing directly toward their hiding place. Even as Lawton crouched down a shot smashed into the top of the boat above his head. He heard voices shouting in Spanish and German as Klarsfeld and his men began to spread out. Shots were coming at them from different directions now, and Lawton knew that they could not remain where they were. He was just about to fire back when Bonnecarrère laid his hand on his arm and shook his head.

"We need to separate," he said. "Try to find out where they go."

Before Lawton could reply the Frenchman leaned around the boat and fired. Lawton heard the pop of broken glass, and another round of shots followed as the Frenchman ran back toward the row of crates they had come from earlier, firing as he did so. In the same moment Lawton wriggled away on his stomach in the opposite direction toward a pile of nets and ropes. Behind him Bonnecarrère had reached the crates safely, and Lawton saw that he had shattered the car windshield. The crew members and Klarsfeld's men were still firing at the Frenchman when Klarsfeld's driver wheeled the car around, training the headlights at the crates where Bonnecarrère was hiding.

"*Da drüben!*" shouted a voice from the ship.

Lawton could see the Frenchman illuminated in the headlights now as he fired back at the car. He continued to wriggle away, till he reached a smaller pile of boxes that was almost in line with the canvas wagon. Once again no one had seen him, but he could see Klarsfeld resting on an open door firing at Bonnecarrère through the shattered windshield. Lawton was thinking how easy it would be to shoot him when the Frenchman broke his cover and ran out onto the pier. Once again the driver spun the Delaunay-Belleville around to face him. Bonnecarrère raised one hand to shield his eyes from the headlights as he stood at the edge of the wharf and fired back at the motorcar. In the same moment Lawton heard the crack of a rifle and the Frenchman dropped his pistol and stepped back as if he were about to fall over.

He looked up just in time to see the silhouette kneeling on deck aiming the rifle, and then another shot sounded and Bonnecarrère toppled sideways into the water. Lawton cursed under his breath and ran the last few yards to the back of the wagon. He climbed over the wooden rim, crawled into the space between crates and boxes, and lay on his back holding Mata's revolver in both hands, ready to shoot the first head that came through the canvas flap. A few moments later the wagon creaked and swayed as the driver and his companion climbed on board. Lawton heard the driver click his tongue and flick the reins, and even as the wagon followed the Delaunay-Belleville out of the harbor, he knew that Monsieur Bonnecarrère's luck had finally run out.

They had not gone far when the wagon came to a halt once again. Lawton knew they had been stopped by the soldiers, and he heard Klarsfeld explain that the wagon was carrying a special shipment for His Excellency the Count of Arenales.

"What was that shooting?" one of the soldiers asked.

"Nothing to do with us, Sergeant," Klarsfeld replied. "Just some anarchists fighting each other. You know what they're like."

"Don't I just!" The soldier laughed. "Well on you go then. Can't keep His Excellency waiting."

Klarsfeld thanked him, and Lawton wondered if money had just changed hands as he heard the motorcar pull away. He thought they were going toward the Estación de Francia, but a few minutes later the car accelerated and the engine faded away. Soon it disappeared altogether and he lowered the revolver. He continued to lie still, as the smell of tobacco came wafting in from the front of the wagon and mingled with the smell of dung. After about twenty minutes the wagon swung left and began to climb. Soon the road became steeper, and the driver cracked his whip to urge his animals forward. Lawton sat up and drew the flap back just long enough to see the dark outline of trees and the sprinkling of stars, and then he lay back again. They had been traveling for about an hour when the road flattened out, and shortly afterward it descended down a rutted track that made their progress even more laborious.

Lawton could feel all his accumulated aches and bruises now as the wagon bumped and careened down the road and the boxes pressed against him. Finally the track began to level out again and he heard the driver call out a greeting and the sound of dogs barking in the distance. He sat up once again and peered out through the canvas flap. Behind him he could see a high wall and gate with two armed sentries sitting beside it, and he knew that they had arrived at their destination. He waited until the sentries were almost out of sight before lowering himself over the wooden flap. Even as he dropped to the ground he half expected someone to shout, but there was no sound except for the barking dogs. He ran toward a clump of trees and crouched down in the darkness to catch his breath. Once again he heard the dogs barking and he hoped they were chained up. Yet even as he gripped the wooden handle of the Smith & Wesson in his sweating hand, he felt more curious than fearful, and he sensed that he was close to answering the questions that had brought him here.

Ruben left the Franciscan monastery in Poblenou through the kitchen door, carrying a sack on his back. The building was still burning, and even though the crowds were long gone, the flames lit up the surrounding streets, and Ruben held the Beretta in his free hand, because he had no intention of getting shot for looting. Nor did he want to arouse the suspicions of his Poblenou comrades and set off any rumors that might get back to the Invincibles. Because the strike committee had given specific orders not to burn churches and religious institutions, and he himself had passed on those same orders, he had even visited some of the buildings that were being burned and told the crowds not to burn them.

At the same time he had also helped himself to any cash, silver, and articles of value he was able to get his hands on. Already he had a substantial collection of silver chalices, plates, and candlesticks in Matilde's room, ready to sell when the moment presented itself. Now he could add the cutlery, glasses, and a silver tray that the Franciscans had tried to hide. All in all it had been a profitable three days, in which he had managed to add to his wealth whilst simultaneously enhancing his reputation. Not many people were clever enough to do both things at once, but not many people were as clever as he was.

In Poblenou he had helped bring the workers out on strike, and encouraged them to build barricades and defend the Republic. At the same time he took care not to be on the barricades himself when the army came into the streets. While his comrades in Poblenou believed that he was fighting in the Raval, the Invincibles believed that he was fighting on the barricades in Poblenou. In this way he had been able to live two equally heroic lives in two different places, while avoiding any situation that might have put his life at risk.

As a result the strike had been almost entirely pleasurable. By day he was Ruben the revolutionary. At night, he and Matilde lay in bed while the churches and monasteries burned and the army and the workers fought each other. The previous night he had amused Matilde by making silhouettes with his hands in the shape of monsters, animals, and reptiles, while the flames danced across the walls. Later he took her to the beach in the middle of the night. They walked together past the barricades and gasworks, and she took her shoes off and walked in the sea while he watched the Church of Sant Pere Pescador burning in the distance.

Even now, as he unlocked the main entrance to her building, he felt a thrill at the thought of her straddling him in the sand, lifting her skirt and easing him into her while the sea lapped against the beach behind them. He put the Beretta away now as he walked up the stairs. He hoped she was still awake, because his balls were beginning to ache once again, but there was no sound from her room. As soon as he opened the door, he saw her lying on the bed in the darkness. At first he thought she was sleeping and he wondered why she had the shutters closed. Suddenly she began to moan and he saw the gag over her mouth and the bonds on her hands and feet. In the same moment he felt the barrel of a gun against the back of his neck and a voice behind him growled hoarsely, "One move and I'll blow your head off."

Ruben caught a smell of absinthe as the gunman took the sack and drew the Beretta from his jacket.

"Take these." The gunman handed him a candle and a box of matches. "Light it."

Ruben did as he was told. It was only then that he recognized the bearded face of Salvador Santamaría, the old terrorist from the Sons of Whores. Santamaría reached into his sack with the pistol trained at his stomach and held up a silver cross.

"Found God have you?"

"Comrade, these aren't for me!" said Ruben indignantly. "This is for the cause."

Santamaría let out a rasping cackle that sounded as though he were being choked. "Of course it is. Let's go up on the roof, shall we?"

"The roof?" Ruben said nervously." What do we need to go up there for?"

"Someone wants to see you." Santamaría gestured with the gun toward the door, as Matilde continued to writhe on the bed.

"You're going to leave her like that?" said Ruben.

"She'll be alright." Santamaría opened the door. "But you won't be if you don't do what I say. Keep your hands where I can see them."

Ruben was beginning to feel seriously afraid for the first time now, as he walked slowly upstairs to the roof. The door was already open, and his fear turned to incredulity at the sight of his mother-in-law, sitting on the edge of the roof, calmly smoking a cheroot. Ruben saw to his alarm that she was holding a noose at the end of a piece of rope that was tied around the chimney stack. Behind her he could see the flames from Sant Pere Pescador, but now they no longer seemed as beautiful as they had the night before.

"Rosa? What's going on?"

Señora Tosets said nothing, as Santamaría prodded Ruben toward the balustrade. "Sit down," he ordered.

Ruben sat down next to Rosa Tosets with his back to the street as Santamaría slipped the noose over his ankles and pulled it taut.

"What are you doing?" he asked.

"You need to answer some questions, *cabron*," his mother-in-law replied as Santamaría began to wrap the slack rope around his own wrist. "And answer them honestly."

The sweat was pouring down Ruben's back now and his bowels felt suddenly loose. "I'm married to your daughter!" he protested.

"And yet you allowed my son to be killed like a dog."

"That's a lie!"

"Where is Esperanza?" Señora Tosets asked.

"How the fuck should I know?"

Señora Tosets tied a cloth around Ruben's mouth now, and Santamaría turned Ruben around so that he was kneeling over the balustrade and facing down over the street. Ruben was still howling into the gag when the old terrorist gripped his ankles and tipped him up so that he was hanging over the edge. Below him he could see the streets of Poblenou laid out in their neat blocks, and the lights from the burning buildings, and even as he writhed on the end of the rope with his hands outstretched like a diver, he was ready to tell them whatever they wanted to know.

28

There had been many times in Africa when Lawton had expected to die. Now as he sat kneeling in the copse of trees, he knew that his prospects of survival were not promising, and he calculated what he might do to improve them. He assumed that he was in the Count of Arenales's estate in Collserola and he briefly considered going back to Barcelona to get help. But Bonnecarrère and Mata were dead and there was no one else in the city who could help him. As things stood, he was completely alone and surrounded by people who had shown again and again that they would kill him in an instant. So far, none of them knew he was there, but that advantage was only likely to last till daylight.

From his hiding place, Lawton could see Klarsfeld talking to three men, one of whom was carrying a lantern, in front of a long two-storey building. To the left of the wagon and the Delaunay-Belleville, he could see what looked like outbuildings, and beyond them a number of smaller structures were scattered around the grounds whose functions were unclear. The estate also contained plenty of bushes and trees, and a low hedge that ran the length of the driveway in front of the house. The wagon pulled around in front of the automobile now and moved slowly down the drive, followed by Klarsfeld and his companions.

The wagon pulled up outside one of the outbuildings, and Klarsfeld's companions began unloading the boxes. Lawton looked back toward the gate, and then ran across the path toward the hedge. He paused behind a tree, and then crawled across a stretch of open ground that sloped down behind him to a small lake or ornamental pond. Still holding the Smith & Wesson, he wriggled across the grass. Once again he heard the dogs barking, before he reached the hedge and lay on his stomach, directly opposite the wagon.

Lawton saw Weygrand standing next to Klarsfeld in the lighted doorway, before the two of them went inside. For the next twenty minutes he lay behind the hedge while the unloading continued. Even out of the city the night was humid and breezeless, and the moon seemed much too bright, and yet he was surprised how cold he felt. He tried not to think about what it might mean, and tried to ignore the numbness in the tips of his fingers. He could hear the sound of boxes being opened now, and a few minutes later the wagon driver and his co-driver mounted the wagon and turned the mules around. They had nearly reached the main gate when Klarsfeld and Weygrand emerged from the building with their companions and shut the door behind them.

For a moment Weygrand seemed to look toward him, and Lawton coiled his finger around the trigger, before he walked away with the others toward the main building. Lawton waited till the lights in the building began to go out, and then walked stiffly toward the outbuilding, standing on his toes to lessen the scrunching of his feet on the gravel. He opened the door and stepped inside. No sooner had he closed the door behind him than he felt the numbness spreading through his fingers and a voice in his head told him to get back outside. But the curiosity was too strong to resist and he lit his cigarette lighter and walked toward the pile of boxes.

Some of the boxes had their lids lying loosely open. One of them was filled with Browning revolvers. Another contained rows of bottles filled with white powder, lying on a bed of straw and muslin. Lawton just had time to read the label "Natriumcitrat" on one of the bottles when he smelled burning. In the same moment his hands began to tingle and his head began to pulsate, as though his brain was opening and closing like a flower. He dropped to his knees and gripped the edge of the crate, like the gunwale of a storm-tossed ship, and then a great wave seemed to crash over him, pulling him away to a place where no one could save him.

"Mr. Lawton. We meet again."

Lawton opened his eyes and stared at the painting of a swordsman on horseback slashing at a sea of turbaned heads on the opposite wall. At first he thought it was a scene from the Indian Mutiny, but as his vision cleared he saw that the swordsmen were wearing knightly armor and had red crosses on their chests, and their enemies looked more like Arabs. He tried to wipe his eyes, but the handcuffs were holding his arms tightly behind a chair, and now he lowered his gaze and saw Dr. Franz Weygrand sitting directly opposite him with his arms folded on the table. Lawton stared blearily back at the pop eyes and waxed moustache and the sig-rune flash on his ringed index finger.

He looked around the room and saw the Count of Arenales sitting to Weygrand's left, with his silver hair combed back across his forehead and a long thin pipe protruding from his lips like a bee's proboscis. Arenales still had the pale sallow texture of a man who did not see much sunlight, and his watery eyes were slightly bloodshot, but he no longer looked frightened. At the far end of the table, Klarsfeld sat sipping a small glass of brandy or liqueur while his other hand rested lightly on the handle of a 1900 Parabellum. There was no sign of Mata's revolver, and Lawton realized that the bullets were missing from his jacket pockets.

"So Zorka was right," Weygrand said. "You are in need of healing. Did you know the Greeks believed the falling sickness was sacred? A gift from the Gods that enabled men to see visions. Do you see visions, Mr. Lawton?"

"Right now I only see a filthy gang of murderers."

"And I see a man whose time is up," said Klarsfeld. "Who was with you at the docks?"

From Klarsfeld's photographs, Lawton had assumed that he was in his mid-fifties, but his face was smooth and surprisingly unlined. His dueling scar was just visible above the well-trimmed beard, and his pale blue eyes were cold and pitiless. Lawton's head was throbbing now and he felt as if his skull had been scooped out by a hot spoon, as he silently cursed the disease that had placed him in the hands of such men.

"Was there someone with me?" Lawton said.

Klarsfeld smiled faintly. "Believe me, I don't have to ask politely."

"And I don't have to tell you anything. But I might make an exception if you answer my questions."

"Such as?" said Weygrand.

"Such as why you and your crazy band of monks have been murdering innocent people and draining their blood."

Weygrand looked at him pityingly. "Murder is such an emotive and judgmental term. Isn't war murder? Yet who condemns that? And innocence is in the end a matter of perspective. An ant is innocent. But how many of us step on them without a second thought? We merely terminated the lives of people whose existence had no more significance or importance than any insect. In death, we gave them more value than they ever had in life."

"Value to who?"

"War is coming, Mr. Lawton," Weygrand replied. "It will be a war like no other. Millions of young men will die. Some will be killed on the battlefield. But many more will bleed to death when the battles are over, because we have not known how to perform blood transfusions effectively—until now." Weygrand paused as Arenales looked at him in alarm. "It's alright, Count. It's not as if Mr. Lawton is going anywhere. Here in Barcelona, we have successfully performed blood transfusions using glucose and sodium citrate as anticoagulants to prevent clotting. We have succeeded in storing blood, for up to five days in a refrigerated unit. We have even managed to transport blood from one place to another, using ice as a refrigerant. We—"

"So that explains the water in the apartment."

"Very good, Mr. Lawton. Do you understand how significant this is? Our discoveries will change medical history. And they will also change the course of the war. Countless wounded soldiers will now survive. Our soldiers obviously—this is not a humanitarian enterprise. This is the great scientific work that we have been engaged in! All carried out in this little corner of Europe—entirely in secret."

"Scientists don't normally bite people and rip their throats out," Lawton said.

Weygrand shrugged. "In studying battlefield trauma and shock, it was necessary to inflict some trauma on our subjects. The count's dogs were very effective in this regard."

"Then why leave the bodies in public? Why draw attention to yourselves?"

"Good question." Weygrand turned to Klarsfeld. "Perhaps the baron can explain it?"

"We did keep them secret," Klarsfeld said. "Till Cortéz was washed ashore."

"You mean there were others?" Lawton asked.

"Of course there were others," replied Weygrand. "And there will be more. Until our work is complete."

"They were nothing people," Klarsfeld went on. "Beggars, whores, and idiots. Anarchists. Vagabonds who no one knew nor cared out. Obviously the count didn't want such people buried in his estate, and who can blame him? So we took them out to sea and weighed them down. It worked very well, until the little anarchist floated back up, all the way to the swimming club. When we saw the hysteria in the local press—all this talk of vampires and monsters—the count came up with a very clever idea."

Arenales chuckled and sucked on his pipe. "Based on my reading of Poe and Stevenson," he said. "The newspapers—and the rabble—wanted monsters. So we gave them one."

"The count also has friends in the Spanish officer corps," Klarsfeld explained. "They think the king's household is too eager to please the English. They would like to have a larger piece of Morocco, and so do we."

"They are patriots," Arenales said. "They've had enough of the Reds and the separatist swine. They are tired of seeing the Church and army insulted, and our children corrupted by degenerates like Ferrer. They believe—as I do—that this country needs to be guided by a strong hand."

"I don't follow."

"Have you seen what's happened in Barcelona these last few days?" Arenales asked. "The attacks on our soldiers? The mobs burning churches and committing sacrilege? Our monster is partly responsible. He helped turn the masses against the church. Vampire. Ape-man. Werewolf. Everyone sees the monster they want to see, and they always hold someone else responsible. It works the same way in politics as it does in life."

"So you wanted churches to be burned in order to defend the Church?" asked Lawton incredulously.

Arenales shrugged. "Churches can always be rebuilt. The important thing is the long-term result: a patriotic dictatorship that is willing and able to finally cleanse the nation of its enemies. A Spain that takes its place among the Great Powers once again—on the side of Germany. This is what God intends."

"We haven't quite reached that point yet," Klarsfeld said. "But we're getting there. The Brownings will help, once we distribute them to the right people today."

"Ugarte?" Lawton asked.

Weygrand shook his head. "Ugarte merely provides us with subjects. According to our specifications and requirements. We have other channels—in the army, the Church, even in the Radical Party. All of them will be able to find uses for these weapons."

Lawton was still struggling to take this in. "And the German government sanctions these . . . abominations?"

"I wouldn't say that," Weygrand replied. "These aren't experiments that any government can support officially—not yet, anyway. But we have received discreet assistance from sympathetic individuals in the military, some of whom are aware in broad terms of what we're doing. Such as tonight's shipment."

"Which brings me to my original question," said Klarsfeld. "Who was with you on the docks?"

"Ah, now that would be Captain Georges Bonnecarrère from the French secret service Your operation isn't as secret as you thought. And when Bonnecarrère's colleagues get here, it'll be even less so."

Arenales looked anxious once again, but Weygrand shook his head. "I don't think so," he said. "If they knew where you were, they'd already be here."

"We'll see," Lawton replied. "But I have another question. What did Foulkes have to do with this? Why did you have him killed?"

"An excellent question," Weygrand said. "And I think the answer will surprise you."

Klarsfeld got up to open the door, and a moment later his driver came into the room accompanied by two hard-faced young men in white shirts, cloth caps, and black trousers, and the black servant Lawton had seen outside Arenales's palace, who still looked as though he had stepped out of an old eighteenth-century print. One of them had a pistol in his belt and the other had a shotgun hanging over his shoulder. Klarsfeld nodded at Lawton, and the two of them hoisted him upright and marched him out into the hallway.

Arenales went upstairs, while Klarsfeld, Weygrand, the driver, and the two guards led Lawton outside. The sun was just coming up now, and the first hints of pink and purple were beginning to appear above the wall of pine trees that surrounded the estate as they stepped out onto the gravel drive. Lawton heard a cock crowing, and various birds were hooting, cooing, and chirruping all around the grounds that reminded him of the birds he had heard in Africa. He looked around at the tall palms and exotic trees, the bushes with their red flowers and pink cones, the pink flamingos standing in the lake amid the low layer of mist that hovered over the water, and the black servants carrying water from a well to the main house.

"Pretty isn't it?" Weygrand said. "Arenales had the estate modeled on his family's estates in Cuba. He even has negroes, and the same breed of dogs they used to catch the slaves."

He chuckled as they walked around behind the outbuildings. The barking immediately began again, as they came alongside a large cage, where two red-eyed Dobermans hurled themselves against the bars.

"Behold the Raval Monsters!" said Weygrand.

Even with the bars between them, Lawton flinched at the sight of the drooling red-eyed hounds. Arenales made some sucking noises and the dogs immediately fell silent and the dogs immediately fell silent and began to pace restlessly up and down the cage. They continued to walk around the back of the house, until Lawton saw what looked like a chapel or sanctuary some thirty yards behind it. Another armed guard was standing outside the doorway, and the two guards remained with him while Klarsfeld and his driver led Lawton into the building. At first sight the chapel looked like any other place of worship, with its altar, dusty pews, and mouldering hymn books. But now Lawton's escort led him down a flight of stone stairs near the choir, and waited while Weygrand unlocked two large doors that looked as though they had been recently installed.

The driver pushed Lawton forward into a vaulted tunnel that might once have been a tomb or catacombs. The tunnel was longer than the chapel itself, and Lawton was surprised to see that it was dimly lit with electric lighting. He heard the humming of a generator and he also thought he heard the sound of voices crying out in fear or pain. The voices grew louder as they walked toward the end of the corridor, and seemed to be emanating from the floor itself. They were about halfway along the tunnel when he noticed the metal grill just ahead of him and the ladder lying next to it. As they came closer he stared down at the faces peering up at him through the gloom.

"Señores!" cried a male voice. "Help us! Por favor, señores!"

Lawton thought there were at least five people down there, but he had no time to look as Klarsfeld's man pulled him roughly away toward a doorway at the end of the corridor. Weygrand opened the door and stepped inside. Lawton followed him into a large laboratory-like room of recent installation, with a linoleum floor and crisp white walls that had clearly been recently plastered. One wall was lined with cabinets, a sink, and a long counter, and directly opposite there was another counter containing measuring instruments of the type that Lawton had seen in Foulkes's study, a shelf containing a small collection of skulls, and a display of Bertillonage photographs of frightened-looking men and women.

At the far end of the room he saw the same black sun-wheel painted on the wall, and immediately in front of it, two men in bloodstained white coats were bent over a man who was lying naked on an autopsy table, with a bloody bandage wrapped around his right thigh. The man looked as if he was dead or dying, and a bottle was hanging upside down from a tall frame containing a thick orange liquid, that was connected to his right arm by a rubber tube.

Lawton was so shocked by this that he did not immediately notice the two wooden restraint chairs, of the type that he had once seen in his mother's asylum, standing alongside each other about two feet part, facing the far wall like seats in a theater. One of the chairs was empty, but as he came alongside the other he saw Esperanza Claramunt was sitting with her eyes closed and her head fixed in the wooden box, with straps tied around her feet, arms, and chest.

Lawton rounded on Weygrand. "What the hell have you done to her?"

"Nothing—yet. She was hysterical when she woke up so we gave her a sedative."

"So she's another of your ants? Like him?" Lawton looked at the wounded man in the chair.

"His name is Klimov. A Russian Ugarte brought us from the Raval. Now you can't tell me that Bolsheviks are innocent. And Miss Claramunt has been troublesome—like you."

"And those poor bastards out there?"

"The detritus of humanity, Mr. Lawton. Worthless mouths. All of whom are about to serve a useful purpose for the first and only time in their lives. So that something greater than they will ever be can exist and thrive." Weygrand turned to the two men standing over Klimov. "Well?"

"Pulse stopped fifteen minutes ago, sir. Subject did not respond to plasma transfusion."

"Well get him out of here then." Weygrand opened a metal door onto a refrigerated room that gave off a strong smell of ammonia. At first Lawton thought it was a mortuary, then he saw the rows of bottles on the shelves. Most of them were empty, but some were filled with powder or transparent liquid. Weygrand opened a metal cupboard that looked like a large safe to reveal rows of bottles of blood.

"This is the future, Mr. Lawton," Weygrand said proudly. "Imagine entire rooms like this. Filled with blood, donated in advance. All categorized according to type and ready to be distributed to whoever needs it. Imagine portable refrigeration units that can transport blood directly to our field hospitals."

Weygrand was standing so close that Lawton could smell his eau de cologne and the tobacco on his moustache. Suddenly he jerked his head back and drove his forehead hard between the bulbous eyes. Weygrand let out a curse in German and put his hand up to his bleeding nose, as Klarsfeld's driver yanked Lawton's arms up behind his back, forcing his head downward.

"No!" Weygrand tilted his head back and dabbed at his nose with a handkerchief as Klarsfeld gripped his pistol by the barrel and prepared to bring the handle down on Lawton's head. "Put him in the chair."

Klarsfeld expertly flipped over the pistol and held it against his forehead. "One more trick like that and I'll put one between your eyes. Just like I did with the fat man."

Lawton stared back at him. "I think you should. Because if you don't I swear I'm going to kill you."

Klarsfeld gave a vicious jab to Lawton's solar plexus that made him double over once again. His driver pushed Lawton back into the room and unlocked his handcuffs while Klarsfeld stood with the Parabellum pointed at Lawton's head. By the time Weygrand came back into the room, Lawton's hands, feet, and chest were securely strapped into the chair. The box only allowed him to see straight ahead and slightly to the side, and he watched the two orderlies carry Klimov's body out on a stretcher.

"I hope you enjoyed that little moment," Weygrand said. "Because I can assure you that you are not going to enjoy the rest of your day. And the next time blood flows in this room, it won't be mine."

The three of them walked away with the two orderlies and Lawton heard the door shut behind him. Once again he heard the moaning prisoners and then the voices and the footsteps died away, and the only sound he could hear was Esperanza Claramunt's breathing.

"Miss Claramunt," he said. "Wake up!"

There was no answer. Lawton pushed against the straps with his arms and legs, but he could barely move them. After a few minutes he gave up the effort and the fear spread through him, as he looked at the blood-stained dentist's chair and the strange black cross. He had been sitting there for about half an hour when he heard footsteps coming down the corridor and the sound of someone whistling a tune he did not recognize.

Once again the voices in the corridor began shouting and pleading, and then the door opened and he heard the footsteps squeaking on the linoleum floor, but it was not until they came alongside and in front of him that he looked up and found himself face-to-face with Randolph William Foulkes.

29

For a few delirious seconds Lawton thought his brain was playing tricks on him again, but the man standing in front of him in the blood-speckled coat looked exactly like the man in all the photographs he had seen. He had the same white Victorian sideburns, the same bushy eyebrows, and domelike forehead, the same remote expression in his eyes, as if he was gazing at some point beyond the present. But the Foulkes in the photographs exuded wiry strength and ageless resilience. The man in front of him looked gaunt and slightly ill, and as frail as he would expect any man in his late sixties to be.

"Mr. Lawton," he said. "So we meet at last."

Foulkes's voice was soft and almost sorrowful, and there was a gentleness in his smile that Lawton found disconcerting, as he tried to reconcile the face that he remembered from so many photographs with the burned and almost faceless body that he had identified in Quintana's autopsy room less than a fortnight ago.

"You seem surprised," Foulkes said. "Can't say I blame you. It's not every day you find yourself speaking to a dead man."

"But everything matched!" Lawton exclaimed. "The prints. The missing toes. Even the measurements."

"I'm sure you were very thorough. More than anyone here would have been. But we were very thorough, too. The prints weren't mine. And the toes were removed—under anaesthetic. And the measurements, well we were very careful in our choice."

"Your choice?"

"The corpse you examined was a tramp by the name of Biggins. I knew him from my work. He looked a lot like me. Close enough not to be able to tell the difference after a bomb explosion at any rate. Dr. Weygrand brought him here under hypnosis. Poor chap never knew what was happening, not even when he died. We expected a coroner's report and perhaps a visit from London, so we substituted his prints before I left London."

"So there was no Marie Babineaux?"

Foulkes shook his head. "Afraid not. The money was mine and it went to me—to the work to be precise. There had to be some explanation for my presence in Barcelona. We knew the French secret service had taken an interest in the Explorers Club. It was only a matter of time before my government did the same. So Klarsfeld arranged the little incident at the Bar la Luna to ensure that I disappeared. So completely that no one would ever find me. Ah, I see the sleeping beauty awakes."

Lawton looked over at Esperanza, who stared back at him like a frightened rabbit. "Harry?" she said. "What's happening?"

"I don't speak much Spanish, Mr. Lawton," Foulkes said. "But tell this creature that she will have to be quiet or I shall have to give her another sedative. I have no patience for bleating women."

"Her name's Esperanza," Lawton said.

"I know who she is. And I know what she is. One of Ferrer's disciples. Polluting the children of the slums with nihilist ideas. Well not anymore. Her career is over—and so is yours."

"What's he saying?" Esperanza asked weakly.

"He says you have to be quiet," Lawton replied, as Foulkes walked over to the counter and began to take out various objects from the cupboard.

"But what's he going to do with us?" she insisted.

"I told her not to speak," Foulkes said. "I won't ask again."

Lawton repeated the warning. Foulkes inspected a large cone-shaped bottle, with a glass tube that reached nearly to the bottom, and two more tubes fixed into the cork top, one of which had a little bellows attached to it.

"So you're not dead, but you are a madman and a traitor," Lawton said.

"I can assure you I'm not mad. And just because I have a loyalty to something greater than my own country does not make me a traitor."

"The Kaiser, you mean?"

Foulkes shook his head. "Germany is merely a means to an end."

"And what end would that be?"

"The race, Mr. Lawton! The race!"

"What race?" said Lawton scornfully.

"The Aryan race." Foulkes turned around now, and Lawton saw that he was smiling faintly and holding a pair of scissors. "The children of the sun. The race that makes civilization possible. The race that has created everything good and beautiful in the world. That is responsible for every great step that humanity has ever made. Of course I would hardly expect someone with your lineage to understand that."

"My lineage?"

"You are half-Irish and half-savage, Mr. Lawton. An unhealthy admixture. No doubt it accounts for your . . . condition."

"I wonder what accounts for yours," Lawton retorted.

Foulkes showed no sign of emotion. "I've spent much of my life studying people like you. Black men. Yellow men. Half-castes and weaklings. And I can tell you we are not prepared to lose the flower of our race in a fratricidal war, and see our people overrun by niggers and Chinamen so that the sons of Judah can profit. Of course *they* never fight—they merely make it possible for others to kill themselves so that they can feast on the ruins. And this coming war will kill more people than any in the whole of history. This is why our work is so important."

"Harry?" Esperanza said.

"I told you to shut up!" Foulkes looked suddenly furious. "There are no equal rights in here."

"Is that what you were doing when you were murdering mad people at Everdale?" Lawton asked. "Defending civilization?"

"You have been thorough." Foulkes stepped away from the counter, holding a pair of scissors. "My wife chose surprisingly well. I didn't murder them. I was experimenting with transfusions—injecting patients with my own blood or the blood of other patients to see what effect it had on them. I'd already carried out some transfusions with rabbits at my home, and it was a logical development to continue these experiments on humans. Some of them died in the process—it was experimental after all. It wasn't until I met Dr. Weygrand that I heard of Landsteiner's categorizations and began to understand the negative consequences of mixing inappropriate blood types."

"And now you've turned Barcelona into your personal slaughterhouse."

"A laboratory, Mr. Lawton. Do be civil. For some of the most important scientific work of the century. We are doing what any sane country should be doing. I would have preferred to carry out this work in my own country, had we not allowed ourselves to be held back by sentimental humanism. What else was Everdale but a pointless sop to the conscience? You know one of my subjects used to smear his cell with his own feces?" Lawton tried to pull away as Foulkes began to cut the sleeve of his shirt and jacket, but the straps held him fast. "There was also a woman who murdered her own baby because she thought Satan had impregnated her. Why should such people be kept alive? What purpose do they serve?"

Lawton thought of his mother and remembered how often he had asked the same questions. "You might like to think of yourself as a scientist," he said. "But to me you're just one more murdering bastard."

"Of course you would think that," Foulkes replied. "Because you're a policeman. And the Irish are a sentimental race. Always fond of a drink and a song. But sooner or later governments will come to their senses." Foulkes pulled back the cut material to expose Lawton's bicep. "Nature always eliminates or dispenses with the weak and the superfluous. This is how some species survive and others decline. Nations and races are exactly the same. Even the Committee on Physical Deterioration recognized this, but they weren't prepared to take the necessary preventive measures. In the future other governments will be less delicate. There will be laboratories just like this, eugenics laboratories sanctioned by the state, entrusted with the defense and preservation of the race. And they will look on us as pioneers—people who were prepared to act when no one else would."

"You mean the Explorers Club?"

"Indeed. Though most of us had met before that—through the Institute for Racial Hygiene. That's how I met Dr. Weygrand—a true visionary. It's been a privilege to work with him."

"So the Explorers Club wasn't trying to reach the North Pole."

"We were looking for the ruins of Thule, Mr. Lawton. The capital of Hyperborea. Where our race was born."

"That explains the black sun and monk's robes."

"Correct."

"Have you ever thought that you might be the ones who belong in an asylum—or a freakshow?"

Foulkes stiffened. "There are 30,000 blind people in Spain, Mr. Lawton, and 37,000 deaf mutes, 67,000 insane, and 45,000 morally deformed. The police are useless. The officials are corrupt. In England or even in Germany our work might have come to the attention of the authorities. Here we are able to work unmolested, and I can assure you that one day these rooms will be a place of pilgrimage."

"And one day you will hang."

"I doubt it." Foulkes pressed on the vein just above Lawton's elbow with his thumb. "You have good veins. Dr. Weygrand will be pleased. I have to admit I wasn't enamored with the monster idea. My concern is science not politics. But Arenales believes his army friends will be sympathetic to our cause. And if his theater achieves its purpose and helps to bring about a more conducive and supportive environment for our work, then so be it. In any case we intend to be more discreet from now on. There will be no more bodies in the streets. And no more monsters."

Lawton heard voices in the corridor now, and a moment later the door opened once again and Weygrand appeared, accompanied by Klarsfeld and his driver. Weygrand was wearing a white coat and a bandage over his nose, and he stared coldly at Lawton's arm.

"We're ready to begin," said Foulkes. "Let's take a sample, shall we?"

Lawton tried to look around as Weygrand and Foulkes walked out of his line of vision, but it was impossible to move his head. He heard the sound of running water and drawers being opened and closed, before Weygrand returned holding a needle. Weygrand expertly slid the syringe into his vein and filled it with blood while Foulkes, Klarsfeld, and his driver stood watching. When the syringe was full Weygrand withdrew the needle and walked away. He returned a few minutes later, holding a rectangular glass plate like the one that Lawton had seen in the mortuary.

"Blood type A, Mr. Lawton. As I expected."

"I don't give a damn."

"Most degenerates have the same blood type. As do Jews and Asiatics. Dr. Foulkes believes your skull shape and facial features show Indian heritage, is that correct?"

"Go to hell."

"The Indians of South America originally came from Siberia you know, so there is a direct connection to the Lemurian Root Race there. Fortunately Miss Claramunt also has the same blood type, which makes the two of you an ideal combination for our next experiment. Would you like me to tell you what it is, Mr. Lawton?"

"I don't give a damn."

"You will look at me, Mr. Lawton!" Weygrand was standing directly in front of the chair now, so that it was impossible for Lawton not to see him. He stared down at the Austrian's feet as Weygrand explained what happened to blood that was extracted and left standing in the open air. After several hours, Weygrand said, blood began to change its consistency and formed three distinct layers. The bottom layer consisted of the red blood cells that distributed oxygen through the body. The second was formed by a combination of white blood cells and platelets, which helped fight infection and also contributed to coagulation. The top layer consisted of a mixture of water, salts, and proteins called plasma, whose function was not yet clear.

"One of our areas of inquiry is blood loss," Weygrand went on. "We've found that even when our subjects receive traumatic injuries it isn't the loss of blood that kills them. They die for some other reason. The anarchist Tosets, for example, had actually lost far less blood than some of our other subjects when he died. We believe the subject died of shock, due to circulatory collapse resulting from a lack of oxygen in the blood."

"A fascinating theory," said Lawton.

"It is," Weygrand said. "And now you are going to help us prove it. You see, we are investigating the possibility that plasma carries oxygen into the blood and that it may help treat hemorrhagic shock—precisely the kind of shock that our soldiers are likely to experience on the battlefield. This has been the main purpose of our experiments so far. Before the Russian, we used dogs to inflict injuries on our subjects. Now we shoot them—and then we give them plasma."

"What genius," Lawton said.

"More than you can imagine, my friend. So let me explain what we intend to do now. First we shall extract Miss Claramunt's blood. We will then leave it standing. When the plasma is fully formed we will separate it through a pipette and give you a direct plasma transfusion, using Acacia B gum as the anticoagulant. This is the first time we've ever done this."

"I'm honored."

"I'm glad to hear it." Weygrand's bulbous eyes gleamed. "Because in order to test our theory, we need a battlefield simulation."

"He means we have to shoot you." Klarsfeld said. "In the left shoulder."

"We will of course bandage you up," Weygrand explained. "As we did with the Russian. But as you can imagine it will be painful. And your chances of survival are not good. Even if you do, well . . ." He nodded at Klarsfeld's driver, who began to undo his straps while Klarsfeld pointed the parabellum at Lawton's head.

"Get up," Weygrand said.

Lawton did as he was told. He looked down at Esperanza, who was trying to turn her head in the wooden box.

"Take your clothes off," Weygrand said.

"The hell I will."

Klarsfeld sauntered over toward Esperanza. "You know what I did in the Congo when the natives didn't bring back enough rubber?" he said.

"I shot their wives and children. The same with the Herero when they refused to give us information. It worked every time."

Esperanza let out a whimper as he pressed the Parabellum against her right thigh. "Take your clothes off or we'll do it the other way around. And you can watch your lady friend bleed. First the leg and then the arm. Let's see how she reacts to shock."

Lawton stared back at the cold blue eyes and began to undress, until he stood naked in front of the chair. He was pleased that Esperanza could not see him, as Foulkes and Weygrand weighed him on a scale, and proceeded to measure his skull with a tape and the same kind of caliper that he had seen in Foulkes's study. Lawton had not undergone a physical inspection since his army medical, and he had been able to keep his underwear on. He had even felt some pride as the doctors examined his muscles and congratulated him on his physical condition. Now he felt like a trapped beast as Foulkes wrote down his details on a clipboard and commented on his brachycephalic skull, his apelike jaw, and degenerate ears. Klarsfeld and his driver watched with amusement as Foulkes photographed him from the front and side. Finally the humiliation was over and Klarsfeld's driver escorted him back to the chair and strapped him down once again.

Esperanza was sobbing now, as Weygrand and Foulkes returned to the counter. A moment later Foulkes crossed Lawton's line of vision, wheeling a small table carrying a bottle and tube. Foulkes ordered Klarsfeld's driver to gag Esperanza, and even after she fell silent, Lawton could hear her sounds of protest through the gag, and he knew the catheter was being attached to her arm.

"Time is eleven o'clock," Weygrand said. "Extraction of subject A has begun."

Foulkes was standing in front of Lawton now, looking down at Esperanza with the same detached fascination that he had seen in so many photographs. Klarsfeld and his driver also watched her in silence. At 11:20 Weygrand announced that the first bottle was full and Lawton heard him moving around beside her once again. "Subject has fainted. Pulse rate 40."

"Jesus Christ," said Lawton. "What kind of creatures are you?"

Foulkes glanced down at him with the same lofty indifference and then continued to regard Weygrand with a faintly reverential expression.

"We have enough for now," Weygrand said. "I suggest we return at three to perform the centrifuge on subject B, depending on the condition of our sample."

Foulkes waited till Weygrand and the others had left the room, and then walked in front of Lawton once again. "You know I've often thought it would have been better if the Irish had disappeared during the famine," he said. "And epilepsy is such an awful illness. All that dread and heartache—it's no kind of life, is it Mr. Lawton?"

Foulkes looked genuinely concerned now, and then he walked out of Lawton's sight. A moment later the light went out and Lawton found himself in darkness that was darker than anything he had ever seen, as the footsteps echoed down the corridor.

30

I t was impossible to make out any objects in the room, but even though Lawton could not turn his head he could hear the faint sound of Esperanza Claramunt's breathing. He tried to lift his bare feet, but the straps were bound so tightly that they began to cut into his ankles.

"Esperanza, wake up!" he hissed.

There was no answer, and then he heard a faint murmur.

"Esperanza?"

Again there was no answer. Lawton was shivering and trembling now, and he let out a low sound that was somewhere between a moan and a growl as he rocked backward and forward and strained against the straps. Once again his arms and legs were held fast. He was still tugging uselessly against the straps when he noticed that the chair had moved slightly from the rocking motion. It was only then that he realized that the board to which the chair was attached was not fixed to the floor. In that moment it occurred to him that there might just be something he could do. He began to rock backward and forward and side to side now in a more controlled and purposeful manner, until he felt the chair moving toward Esperanza's. Even that tiny movement required enormous effort and concentration, but it was enough to make him continue. Once again he called Esperanza's name and this time he heard an answering moan through the gag.

"I'm coming toward you!" he whispered. "Can you hear me?"

There was no answer, and he sensed that she was only barely present. He continued to rock the chair, pausing only to call her name or listen out for footsteps. It was clumsy and painstaking work, and it was made even more difficult by his inability to see or move his head. He was also conscious of the risk of overbalancing and tipping the chair over. At last he felt her chair alongside his own, and he was able to touch her bare arm with his little finger. He continued to rock and shuffle forward till his right hand was pressing against her left.

She felt cold and still as he groped for the buckle on the other side of her wrist, but his hand was held so tightly that he could only touch the metal with the outside of his little finger.

"Can you move your hand?"

Once again there was no answer, then he felt her fingers moving.

"I want you to reach for my strap. Can you feel the buckle?"

He heard what sounded vaguely like a noise of affirmation. As he had hoped, her wrist was not strapped down as tightly as his, and he felt her fingers crawling over his wrist like a spider's legs as she reached for the end of the strap.

"That's it!" he said. "Push it through now."

He felt her fingers and thumb fumbling with the strap, and then her fingers slipped away from him.

"Try again!" he said. "If you don't we're going to die here."

For a moment he thought she had passed out, and then the cold, delicate fingers worked their way back across his wrist and pushed the strap up through the metal loop.

"Good girl! Now open it!"

Lawton felt her struggling to ease the leather strap out through the prong. At one point she had nearly succeeded, then her fingers fell back and the strap sank back down.

"Come on! Push the damn thing!" he growled.

Once again she gripped the end of the strap between her thumb and forefinger and pushed it upward. For a moment he thought she would fail again, but then the strap came loose and he slipped his hand free. He almost tore the strap from his other wrist, before he pushed the box on his head back on its hinges and undid the strap around his chest. He reached down and unstrapped his feet and suddenly he was standing upright once again on his own two feet and ready to fight.

He stumbled toward the counter and used the wall to guide his way back toward the door, till he reached the light switch. He turned the light back on and went over to get his clothes. When he had dressed he leaned over Esperanza's chair. She was sitting with her eyes closed, and she did not open them when he unbuckled her straps. No sooner had he tilted back the wooden box and untied her gag than her head fell to one side. He slapped her lightly on the cheek till she straightened up and looked at him with a desolate expression.

"It wasn't Ruben," she said, in a tired, sad voice. "It was Arnau."

"This isn't the time for that. Can you stand?"

"I don't know." She pushed down on the arms of the chair and tried to lift herself up, and then sat back down again. "It's my legs. They're like water."

"Stay there for now." Lawton had felt briefly hopeful and optimistic but now he was beginning to feel trapped once again. The clock on the wall gave one o'clock, which left two hours before Foulkes and the others returned. He looked around for a weapon. At the far end of the counter he saw a lantern and a microscope, and in the corner beyond it he noticed a large can of paraffin. None of these objects were much use, and he began to look with growing desperation through the cupboards and drawers.

Most of them were filled with bottles, vials, rubber tubes, and an array of syringes, needles, and catheters, but another contained an array of scalpels and other surgical instruments. He was still looking through it when he heard Weygrand's high-pitched nasal voice. He grabbed a curved amputation knife and ran over to the light switch. He had barely had time to switch it off when the door opened and Weygrand turned it back on again.

Lawton was still pressed against the wall with the door turned toward him, and now he slashed downward with the knife. Weygrand shrieked and dropped his cane as Lawton reached around the door and grabbed Zorka by her collar. She opened her mouth as if to scream, but he wrenched her into the room and slammed the door shut, pressing the knife against her throat even as Weygrand reached for his stick with his good hand. Lawton brought his bare foot down on Weygrand's fingers, and kicked the stick away from him.

Weygrand was still holding his wrist, and a little puddle of blood was beginning to form on the floor. Lawton reached down and picked up the stick. As soon as he held it he realized why Weygrand had been so keen to retrieve it. The cane was heavier than it should have been, and he separated the stick from the silver handle to reveal a cane-pistol with a drop-down trigger, of the type that English gentlemen used in the last century to defend themselves on the streets. He had often heard of such weapons, but had never seen one, and now he pointed it directly at Zorka's catlike eyes.

"Do exactly as I say," Lawton ordered. "Or I swear to God I shall kill you both." He looked down at Weygrand. "Get up," he ordered.

"I'm bleeding!" Weygrand whined incredulously. "I need a bandage."

"Sit down." Lawton pointed toward the empty chair. "Miss Claramunt. Can you strap this bloodsucker's feet?"

Esperanza hauled herself to her feet with obvious difficulty, and knelt down to tie the straps around Weygrand's ankles. As soon as she had finished she turned away and retched.

"The she-wolf can take your place," Lawton pointed with his gun toward the vacant chair. Zorka meekly sat down and buckled the straps around her ankles as Esperanza limped over to the autopsy table and sat down.

"What are you doing here?" Lawton asked. "You said you weren't coming back till three."

"Foulkes doesn't like women to come into the laboratory while we're working," Weygrand said. "But Zorka wanted to see you."

"Did she now?"

"Dammit man, can't you give me a bandage?"

"A little bleeding won't hurt you. Just think of it as an experiment." Lawton turned to Zorka. "So you wanted to watch me? These things please you, do they?"

"It's not true!" cried Zorka. "He made me come. I don't know what they do here!"

"Of course you don't. Like you didn't know what was in that cigarette." Lawton wiped the knife on Weygrand's trouser leg and slipped it into his belt. "Do you have any spare bullets for this?" he held up the cane gun.

Weygrand shook his head, and Lawton looked through his jacket pockets. There were no bullets, but he was pleased to find his cigarette case and lighter. He lit a cigarette and filled his lungs. "Zorka told me that you really can read minds," he said. "Do you know what I'm thinking now?" Weygrand said nothing. "I'm thinking that it wouldn't be a bad thing to let you bleed to death. But I'd much rather see you dangling from the end of a rope."

Weygrand looked at him with a cowed expression as he walked over to the counter and took a roll of bandage from one of the drawers. "How many men are guarding the building?" he asked.

"Only one," Weygrand replied.

Lawton laid his weapons on the ground and quickly bandaged Weygrand's wrist. It was only now that he put his boots on, and knelt down to tie his laces. He picked up the gun and knife and walked over to Esperanza.

"We're leaving," he said.

"In her state?" said Weygrand. "She can hardly walk."

"He's right Harry," Esperanza said. "Save yourself."

"We're going together." Lawton stuck the knife in his belt and led her by the arm toward Weygrand. "Undo your straps," he ordered. "Anything else and I'll shoot you dead."

Weygrand leaned forward and unstrapped himself.

"Now her." Lawton nodded at Zorka, and Weygrand undid her straps.

"Stay just in front of me," Lawton ordered. "Otherwise it'll be the bullet for one of you and the knife for the other. Turn around." He prodded Zorka and Weygrand toward the doorway and they walked out into the corridor. Even before they reached the grille he heard voices shouting up from below and he paused and peered down into the gloom.

"Listen carefully," he said. "I'm going to get help. But you need to be silent now. Otherwise all of us will die. Do you understand?"

There was a murmur of assent and the voices fell silent before a woman called, "God bless you, Señor" in a soft, hopeful voice.

They walked on toward the closed doors, where Lawton unhooked Esperanza's arm and told Zorka and Weygrand to stand still. He was walking just in front of them now, with the knife in one hand and the pistol in the other as he inched one of the doors open. The chapel was silent, and he closed the doors once again and ordered Weygrand to kneel on the floor.

"Why?" Weygrand asked nervously. "What are you going to do?"

Lawton handed the pistol to Esperanza. "Hold this against his head," he said. "If he moves shoot him," he said. "And if I say anything I also want you to shoot him."

Esperanza nodded and rested the barrel against the back of Weygrand's polished black hair. Zorka looked at Lawton expectantly, as he pointed toward the stairs. "You're coming with me. When I tell you, call the guard in. Anything else and I'll cut your throat. Is that clear?"

"Of course, Harry. Whatever you say."

Lawton ignored the sarcasm and took her by the arm. The entrance to the chapel was slightly ajar, and he could not see the guard as he walked slowly and carefully through the pews, with his hand on Zorka's wrist. It was not until he reached the door that he gave her a nod.

"Señor," Zorka called. "I need you."

"Señora?"

Lawton heard the footsteps coming up the little step. The guard had barely stepped inside when he let go of Zorka's wrist and kicked the door shut. The guard tried to unhook the shotgun, but Lawton slashed him across the throat with a scythe-like motion. The guard let out a gargling sound and tried to staunch the wound with his hands, but his eyes were glazing over as he dropped to his knees and toppled over. Zorka had one hand over her mouth and she stared at Lawton with fascination as he wiped the knife on the guard's shirt.

The guard was carrying a 12-gauge pump-action Winchester, and Lawton unhooked it from his shoulder and rifled through his pockets for spare cartridges. He shoved them into his own pockets and inched the door open. There were no other guards nearby, but he could see two armed men walking along the far perimeter wall near the main entrance. To his left, the estate reached out across a wide strip of open ground behind the main house toward a citrus orchard that led into the wall and a fenced-in field where some horses were grazing. As far as he could see, the orchard offered the only way out, provided they were able to reach the trees without being seen.

Zorka seemed entirely docile now as he slotted the knife in his belt and pushed her back down into the tunnel, where they found Esperanza still leaning against the wall with the cane-pistol resting against Weygrand's head. Lawton took it from her and tucked it into his belt along with the knife, before nudging Weygrand with the shotgun.

"Get up," he ordered. "We're leaving." He looked at Zorka. "You can help carry Miss Claramunt. Take your arm away from her and I'll kill you. And if anyone tries to stop us out there then I'll kill the two of you first. Don't think I won't."

Weygrand's bulbous eyes flitted around desperately as Zorka put one arm around Esperanza's waist. Even then Esperanza struggled to get up the stairs, and she had to lean on the pews for support as they threaded their way back toward the doorway. Weygrand peered down at the dead guard as Lawton pushed him around the spreading pool of blood. "You can't kill them all," he said.

"You better hope they don't see us then," Lawton replied.

Lawton opened the door once again. There were no guards in sight, and he ushered the others out in front of him and pointed with the shotgun toward the orchard. In any other circumstances he would have run the short distance to the trees, but now he was forced to walk at Esperanza's pace as she stumbled forward with her arm around Zorka's shoulder. They had nearly reached the orchard, and he was beginning to think that they might make it after all, when he heard a shout from behind him.

He looked back and saw a guard standing at the corner of the outbuildings. In the same moment the dogs began to bark and two more guards came running toward them from the far wall. Zorka had stopped walking now and she had a faint smirk of triumph on her face, which quickly vanished as he raised the shotgun toward her head. Even as they neared the trees the barking grew suddenly louder. Lawton looked back and saw three more guards coming toward them, holding the two Dobermans by the leash. It was all going as badly as it could, he thought, and as he pushed Zorka and Weygrand into the trees there was no obvious prospect that it would get any better.

31

No sooner had they reached the orchard than Lawton realized that the trees were spread too widely to give much cover or protection. The barking was becoming louder and more frenzied, and guards seemed to be coming toward them from various directions. Lawton knew they could not outrun them. He looked around for a place to make a stand, and spotted a raised irrigation tank, whose low stone walls offered a potential defensive parapet. They had nearly reached it when he heard a sudden movement to his left. He swung around with the shotgun raised to his shoulder, and saw the guard standing about fifteen yards away with his rifle pointed toward them.

The two shots were almost simultaneous. Lawton saw a guard drop to the ground and Zorka also pitched forward, pulling Esperanza with her, and lay still with her face to one side. For a moment he thought it was a trick, but Esperanza crawled away from her with a little cry of disgust and Lawton saw that Zorka was not moving. He reached into his pocket for a cartridge, but Weygrand was running back toward the barking dogs now and shouting hysterically for help. He had nearly reached the edge of the trees when one of the dogs leapt at him. The dog seemed to tower over Weygrand as he screamed and tried to stay on his feet, but now the other dog came up behind him and bit his leg. Weygrand fell backward screaming and wailing as the two dogs tore at his arms and throat like lions taking down an antelope or a wildebeest.

Lawton knew they were attracted by the blood from Weygrand's wound. Esperanza was still kneeling on the ground, and she looked as though she were about to faint. Whether it was from the loss of blood or the horror at her situation he could not tell, but he reached down and hauled her brutally to her feet, and then hoisted her over his shoulder. During the war he had often had to carry wounded men away from the trenches, sometimes under fire, and Esperanza was lighter than any soldier. He ran toward the field, with one arm raised to stop her from falling and the other holding the shotgun. Almost to his own surprise, they reached the field he had seen earlier and he clambered over the low fence. He expected to be shot at any moment as they stumbled past the skittering horses, but to his amazement they reached the wall and he laid Esperanza back on her feet.

"Climb onto me," he said, bending down. "And then pull yourself over."

"And you?" she asked weakly.

He smiled at her. "I'm a sick man, Espe. I've lived my life. Go back to the city. Go to the British consulate. Tell them what you saw here."

Esperanza hesitated and then she stepped onto his back, holding onto the wall. Even as Lawton straightened up he saw the guards emerging from different parts of the orchard and fanning out on the other side of the fence. He was disappointed not to see Klarsfeld among them. He had five cartridges left, and he would have liked to have saved one shot for the German. He felt Esperanza step away from him now and he looked up to see her lying lengthways on the top of the wall.

"Drop!" he said. "You'll make it."

Esperanza gave him one last sad, grateful look, and then lowered herself over the wall till he could only see her hands. He emptied the shotgun and slotted in another cartridge. The guards were coming warily through the fence now, and Lawton knelt down and picked his target. He breathed in the smell of oranges and horse dung and glanced up at the peerless Spanish sky. He had spent the best part of two years sitting in a dark room like a prisoner in his own body, expecting nothing more from life than collapse and degeneration. It did not seem like a bad way to die, with the sun on his face and a gun in his hand, and it was certainly better than having his life sucked out of him in Randolph Foulkes's laboratory. Once again he heard the barking and he knew the dogs had finished with Weygrand. If the guards or the dogs did not get him, he promised himself that he would save one last bullet to make sure that no one took him back there.

He was just about to squeeze the trigger when he heard three shots from the orchard and the barking abruptly fell silent. Lawton stared toward the trees, and the guards also glanced back uneasily. For a moment everything was still and silent, and then two more pistol shots rang out and two of the guards dropped to the ground. Their three companions were still looking at the orchard in confusion when Lawton shot one of them down.

"Put your guns down and your hands up!" A hoarse rasping voice called from the orchard. The two guards dropped their guns and raised their hands.

"Step away!" the voice called.

Once again the guards did as they were told. They stared back at the orchard, as a man with white hair and a floppy worker's cap stepped out of the trees, holding a pistol in his hand, and Lawton recognized the terrorist Salvador Santamaría, who he and Mata had questioned in the Raval. Three more men and a woman emerged from the trees behind him. All of them were armed, and the woman was smoking a cheroot with one hand and holding a pistol in the other. Lawton was still staring at this incomprehensible sight when Georges Bonnecarrère came limping out of the orchard, holding a pistol and a stick to support himself.

The Frenchman stood by the fence, while his companions encircled the hapless guards and gathered up their weapons. "Monsieur Lawton," he said. "It seems I've arrived in time once again."

Bonnecarrère was leaning on the fence now, and despite his attempt at a smile, Lawton could see that he was in some pain.

"You're one person I didn't expect to see again," he said.

"The bullet hit me here." Bonnecarrère gingerly touched his left side just above the waist. "It went straight through me. I knew I wouldn't be so lucky twice so I decided to take my chances in the sea."

"A wise decision. But how did you find me?"

"After they bandaged me up I went looking for Miss Claramunt's informer. I thought he might tell me where you were. And I met Señora Tosets here and Señor Santamaría. It turns out they were already making . . . inquiries of their own, thanks to your intervention. This Montero was not the man Miss Claramunt thought he was."

"So I hear."

"It was Busquets who betrayed Pau." Rosa Tosets came up beside them now, holding a cheroot in one hand and a pistol in the other. "I'm Pau's mother. Ruben had nothing to do with that. He was working for the army. He was supposed to entrap Ferrer. That's why he played the revolutionary. And to think that bastard lived under my roof and married my daughter!"

"Busquets was Ugarte's man," Bonnecarrère said. "He helped him kidnap Tosets and some of the others."

"He won't be helping anyone again," Santamaría growled.

Bonnecarrère looked embarrassed now. "Busquets told us the shipment was coming to Arenales's estate. Of course I couldn't go to the police about this—not the way things are in the city. And I knew we didn't have much time. Señora Tosets and Señor Santamaría proposed their own solution and I was obliged to accept it. And now there is one more body in the harbor. When in Rome, one must do whatever is necessary. Especially when Rome is burning."

"We don't normally work with the French secret service either," said Señora Tosets. "Where's Esperanza?"

"She's on the other side of that wall," Lawton pointed behind him. "Just over there. Who else have you found?"

"Only Weygrand. What's left of him."

"And Foulkes? And the German?"

"Foulkes is alive?" Bonnecarrère looked at him in astonishment. Just then Lawton heard shots coming from the house, followed by the sound of an engine. "I'll explain later." He turned to Santamaría and Tosets. "There are some prisoners in the chapel basement. You need to get them out."

He ran toward the house and the outbuildings and slowed down as he reached the empty dog cage, with the shotgun raised to his shoulder. He turned the corner just in time to see the Delaunay-Belleville disappearing out of the main gate. Two guards were standing outside the entrance to the main house, exchanging fire with some men who were concealed behind some of the trees beside the driveway. They turned and raised their weapons as Lawton came toward them sideways on, looking down the barrel of the shotgun.

"Don't even think about it," he said.

The guards dropped their pistols and raised their hands.

"Who was in the car?" he snapped.

"The German and his driver!" one of the guards replied. "And the Englishman!"

"Where've they gone?"

"We don't know!" the other guard replied. "We don't know anything! We only work here, señor!"

"Who's in the house?"

"Just the count, sir. And the servants."

Lawton looked around now, as three men came toward them from the direction of the dog kennels, wearing crumpled jackets and flat caps and holding pistols.

"You're with the Frenchman?" Lawton asked them.

"With Señora Tosets," one of the men replied.

"So am I." Lawton turned back to the two guards and nodded toward the gate. I want you both gone now. Run. The first man who stops I'll shoot him."

The guards sprinted toward the gate, while Lawton walked into the building with the shotgun pressed against this shoulder. No sooner had he entered than the black servant appeared in the doorway of the dining room, and held up a pistol. Lawton shot him in the stomach, holding the shotgun at his waist and the servant crashed back into the room and crumpled to the floor. Lawton peered quickly inside and saw the two assistants from the laboratory cowering on the other side of the table where they had been eating their lunch. Both of them put their hands up. He nodded toward the front door and stood back to let them pass before making his way up the stairs with his back against the wall, loading the shotgun as he went. At the top of the stairs, he glanced around the corner before stepping into a wide reception area with a large fireplace on one side and a long tiled corridor running the length of the building to the other.

He walked down the corridor with the shotgun at his waist and his finger over the trigger, past the portraits of scowling aristocratic gentlemen who looked vaguely like Arenales. All the rooms were empty, but when he tried to open the door at the end of the corridor he found that it was locked. He leaned back and kicked it open. In the far corner of the room Arenales was still in his dressing gown, kneeling in front of a crucifix and a little altar. He stared back at Lawton and his eyes flickered toward the pistol that was lying on the bed beside him.

"You're not thinking of killing yourself, are you?" Lawton asked. "Don't you know it's a sin?"

Arenales shook his head and glanced at the pistol once again. "What do you want?" he asked.

"What do I want? Well I'm going to count to three," Lawton said. "If you don't tell me where Klarsfeld has gone I'm going to send you to whatever God you pray to. One—"

"Girona!" Arenales blurted out. "They're going to wait there till the strike is over and then catch a train to Paris. Then Berlin."

"Which road did they take?"

"They went inland—to avoid the city."

Lawton nodded and lowered the shotgun. Even as he turned his back he knew what he hoped would happen. He swung around with the shotgun, just as the count was reaching for his pistol. The count immediately pulled his hand away and began to hold up his hands, when

Lawton squeezed the trigger. The blast hurled Arenales back against the altar, and a silver cross fell onto his waist as his head slumped onto his bloodied chest. Lawton dropped the shotgun and walked quickly back down the corridor. He returned to the main entrance just as Bonnecarrère was coming around the corner, accompanied by Esperanza, Señora Tosets, Santamaría, and four men and a woman he had not seen before. All of them looked equally dirty and bedraggled, but it was not until they came closer that he saw that the woman was in fact a man wearing female clothes, and one of the men was dark-skinned, like an Arab or a Gypsy.

"We found the prisoners," Señora Tosets said.

"Good." Lawton turned to Bonnecarrère. "Did you bring your motorcar?"

"I did. It's parked in the forest further down the road. The others came in a cart. Why?"

"Klarsfeld and Foulkes have gone to Girona. They're trying to get to Berlin. Arenales said they went inland. He tried to shoot me, but he wasn't fast enough."

"They'll have gone through Montseny," Santamaría said. "Through the mountains."

"You know the road?"

"I do."

"Then you should come with us."

"Are you sure?" Bonnecarrère asked. "They have a head start and a faster car."

"They'll have to look for gasoline. And even if they get to Girona they'll have to wait for a train." Lawton turned to Señora Tosets. "Can you take Miss Claramunt back to the city? She's lost a lot of blood. She needs rest. A doctor should see her."

"Of course." Señora Tosets tucked her pistol into her skirt. "That room—the one with the chairs. Is that where they killed my son?"

"It is."

"But why would anyone do such a thing?"

"Miss Claramunt can explain," Lawton said. "Did you see the can of paraffin in the corner?"

"I didn't."

"Well I advise you and your comrades to burn that chapel to the ground. And then make yourselves scarce."

"With pleasure," Señora Tosets said. "Just make sure you get them—one way or another."

Lawton nodded. He picked up one of the pistols the guards had discarded, and walked back up the drive. It was only then, as he heard the birds singing all around him, that he realized how good—and how surprising—it felt to be still alive, and now that he had survived he was ready to follow Randolph William Foulkes all the way to Berlin.

32

Bonnecarrère's car was parked in a clearing just off the road, about a half a mile away from the estate. The Frenchman was unable to use the crankshaft because of his wound and he and Lawton stood back and watched Santamaría crank the motor into life. Lawton sat in the back of the car, while Santamaría climbed into the front next to the Frenchman. They drove away down the dirt road, through a forest of thick pines, until the road began to open up once again and he saw Barcelona and the Mediterranean to his right, with the columns of black smoke trailing up into the blue sky.

They had been driving for about half a mile when Santamaría told Bonnecarrère to turn left. They continued to drive down through the pine forest, until the dirt road began to flatten out and gave way to a macadamed surface. The macadam had been badly maintained. Much of it was badly eroded, and Lawton could feel every bump and pothole as they made their way through vineyards, cultivated fields, and a succession of small towns and villages that looked as though they had not fully entered the twentieth century. Many of them still had greased paper over the windows instead of glass, and towering churches overlooking mean little squares where dogs, chicken, and pigs mingled with people who looked as poor and wretched as their surroundings.

Most of these squares were patrolled by Civil Guards and Somaten militia, and even without stopping Lawton sensed their wariness and suspicion. Apart from the occasional mule-drawn cart, and peasants carrying twigs or bundles of hay on solitary mules, there was no other traffic on the road. Lawton was beginning to think they had lost the Delaunay-Belleville when Bonnecarrère stopped alongside a group of old peasants with burned faces and black caps who were sitting outside a little country bar. They stared admiringly at the automobile as Bonnecarrère pulled up in front of them. Lawton kept his pistol out of sight as Santamaría asked if they had seen a red motorcar passing through the village.

"Si, Señor," one of them replied. "Some foreigners bought gasoline here. They left about half an hour ago."

Lawton felt hopeful and also impatient as Bonnecarrère pulled away from the village. "Can't we go faster?" he asked.

"On these roads?" Bonnecarrère said. "I'm already breaking the speed limit. I'll break the car to pieces."

Bonnecarrère's face was strained, and Lawton knew his wound was hurting him, but the Frenchman stepped on the accelerator until they were driving over thirty miles per hour. Soon the road began to climb again through an undulating sea of pine-covered mountains broken by patches of cliffs and giant boulders. Santamaría said that they were now in the Montseny mountains. After a few miles the macadam gave way to a dirt road and the car began to slow down once again, and ground its way around a series of hairpin bends that made Lawton suck in his breath.

"There it is!" Santamaría pointed up ahead, and Lawton saw the Delaunay-Belleville moving slowly along the mountain road high above them. By the time they reached the same spot the car had disappeared, and they found their passage blocked by a herd of goats that completely covered the road. Bonnecarrère honked the Klaxon as the car ground to a halt, and Santamaría shouted at the goatherd at the front of the herd, who acted as if he had not heard. Finally he jumped down and pushed his way through the animals, waving his gun in the air, until the goatherd seemed to recover from his deafness. He flicked a leather switch on the end of his stick and made a series of incomprehensible cries and clucking noises till the animals began to move away from the road.

Santamaría jumped back on board and they moved away once again. There was still no sign of the Delaunay-Belleville, as the car crawled slowly up through wooded mountains that showed no sign of human habitation. They had been driving for another ten minutes when the road flattened out alongside a steep narrow gorge. A few minutes later they turned another sharp corner and Lawton saw the Delaunay-Belleville on the other side of the road about twenty yards ahead of them. The motorcar was slightly raised up off the ground, and Lawton saw smoke coming from the engine where it had crashed into a tree. He also saw that the vehicle was empty as Bonnecarré slowed down and Santamaría turned toward Lawton with a gap-toothed grin.

"We have them!" he yelled.

Lawton was about to tell him to get down when he heard the rifle shot and the blood spouted from Santamaría's ear. The old terrorist let out a howl, and then another shot hit him in the back of the head and his cap fell onto Lawton's lap as he lolled back like a drunkard. Lawton slid down into the space behind the front seats as Bonnecarrère wrenched the car to a halt. The Frenchman rolled sideways out of the car as another bullet hissed past the spot where his head had been. Lawton continued to kneel in the narrow space between the front and back seats with his head bent over, and another bullet smacked into the seat behind him. After everything that had happened in the last few weeks it was no surprise to find himself under fire for the first time since the war, and even though he was not a betting man he could not help feeling that the odds against his survival had suddenly increased.

He reached behind him for the door handle, as another bullet shattered the windshield, and slid backward out onto the road. Bonnecarrère was lying on his stomach with his pistol in his hand trying to shelter behind one of the front wheels, but there was no opportunity for him to shoot as the bullets threw up little candles of dirt just in front of him. Lawton heard a pistol as well as a rifle now, and he could see someone moving through the trees on the other side of the road, who was clearly trying to get behind them. He looked down into the gorge. About thirty foot below he could see a narrow stream, and even though the slope was steep, it was not vertical.

"They're trying to get round us!" he said. "I'm going after them!"

The Frenchman nodded. His face was glistening and taut with pain and he had still not fired a shot. Lawton could see underneath the car now as he wriggled back till his legs were hanging down over the rockface into the gorge. There was no obvious pathway, but the rock surface was sufficiently disfigured and disjointed to provide footholds and handholds. He lowered himself down until his head was just below the level of the road, and began to pick his way along the rock face, moving sideways away from the car and back toward the bend they had come from. Behind him he heard Bonnecarrère firing from the car, followed by another round of pistol and rifle shots from the forest.

Even as he moved along the rockface he knew he stood no chance if Bonnecarrère was hit and Klarsfeld and his driver came forward. More shots followed, and he continued to pick his way around the rock until the two motorcars were out of sight. He scrambled back onto the road and untucked the pistol as he ran into the forest. He continued to work his way slowly back through the forest, until he saw Klarsfeld's driver, leaning against a tree almost parallel to the tourer. The driver was holding a Luger in both hands, and he spun around as Lawton took a step forward and fired three times in quick succession.

The driver dropped to the ground, and Lawton heard the rifle and the ping of metal from the car as he turned deeper into the forest. He knew Klarsfeld and Foulkes would have guessed that something had happened to the driver, and he crouched down as low as he could so that he was almost on all fours, with his head flicking back and forth. There were no more rifle shots now, as he turned back in a wide loop toward the Delaunay-Belleville. The forest was absolutely silent, except for the crackle of his footsteps on the pine cones and twigs.

Suddenly he saw the stricken motorcar at the edge of the road, with a waning column of steam still hissing from the engine. There was no sign of Klarsfeld, but he saw the rifle lying on the ground a few feet away from the car and he heard a faint moan from the forest. He pushed his way through the trees and up a slight slope until he reached an overgrown outcrop of rock at the edge of a small clearing. The moaning repeated itself again as he inched his way around the rock and saw Foulkes sitting with his back against the rock. Foulkes's eyes were closed and blood was oozing through a wound in his head.

In the same moment he heard a sudden movement behind him. He spun around just in time to see the blade in Klarsfeld's raised hand. Even as it came down toward him he brought the pistol upward, but the point of the knife caught him in the arm and the gun fell from his hand. Now Klarsfeld was on top of him, pushing him back onto a bed of leaves and pines, as Lawton reached out with his bleeding arm. He managed to catch Klarsfeld's wrist and held it there as the German squeezed his other hand around his throat and dug his fingers into his windpipe.

Lawton could see his gritted teeth and flashing eyes as the knife bore down toward him. He was choking now and beginning to see black patches on the edges of his vision. The point of the blade was touching his chest when he twisted his head around and bit into Klarsfeld's arm. Klarsfeld swore and released his grip, so that Lawton was able to bring his right hand up and catch the German on the jaw. It was not the most powerful punch he had ever delivered, but it was enough to rock Klarsfeld's head backward. Before he could recover, Lawton grasped his knife in both hands and reared up, pushing the German off balance.

Now he was on top, and there was a look of panic and desperation in his eyes as Lawton turned the knife back toward him and pressed downward with his full weight, pushing the blade into his solar plexus. Their cheeks were touching now, and Lawton felt the same primal fury that he had sometimes felt during the war, as though he been transformed into one of the warriors in the Greek stories that Father McGuire had read them as a child. Like Achilles and Hector he felt a great rush of joy, pleasure, and exultation as Klarsfeld quivered and lay still. It was only when he got to his feet and stood rubbing his windpipe and panting for breath that he came back to himself and saw Foulkes staring at him.

"You've killed him?" Foulkes said weakly. "Well, he wasn't a great man. Useful, but not great."

Foulkes's face was drained of color, there was a film of sweat on his forehead, and he seemed to be struggling to breathe.

"They're all dead," Lawton said. "And there is nothing great about you. And you should know that your little killing house will have been destroyed by now. Burned to the ground with everything in it."

Foulkes let out a long sigh. "You bloody Irish fool. You have no idea what you've done."

"I think I do," Lawton said. "And there will be no pilgrimage. No one will even remember you or think of you—except as a criminal and a madman."

"I could have saved lives—and not just in the war," Foulkes said.

"You won't even be able to save your own. It's over now. And you are going to the gallows."

"I'm not going anywhere." Foulkes raised his hand and pointed the pistol at Lawton's chest.

In the aftermath of the fight, Lawton had completely forgotten that Foulkes might be armed, and now he stood with his hands by his sides and cursed his stupidity.

"You know what they used to call me?" Foulkes was staring at some point in the distance just above Lawton's shoulder. "The last of the great Victorians."

"They didn't know you."

"I was greater than they knew." Foulkes said bitterly. "You know the sun really is black today. Or is it the sky?"

Lawton glanced up at the sun, but it was the same yellow ball it had always been. He looked back to find Foulkes pointing the gun barrel into his own mouth. Before he could stop him, Foulkes fired and his mouth exploded in a splash of red. His head jerked back and then tilted to one side as the pistol slipped from his fingers. Lawton knew the investigation really was over now. He stared down at the bloodied jaw and the reflection of the trees and sky in Foulkes's sightless blue eyes, and felt only a vague disappointment that Foulkes had cheated the hangman. He was just about to take the pistol from his hand when Bonnecarrère came round from behind the boulder with his pistol in his hand. He stepped past Klarsfeld and looked at Foulkes.

"He's dead?" he asked, lowering the weapon.

"Very much so," said Lawton. "And good riddance."

"Then I think it would be better for both of us if we get away from here."

One of the tires on the Peugeot had been punctured, and Lawton replaced it with the spare, while the wounded Bonnecarrère sat watching and gave instructions. Both of them agreed that it would not be sensible to drive back to Barcelona with a corpse in the front seat, and Lawton left Santamaría by the side of the road and cleaned the seat as best he could before taking his place. Finally they drove back down the mountain and followed the road back to the plain. The villages were busier now, the peasants and farmers were coming in from the fields, and some of the villagers and militiamen stared curiously at the bullet holes and broken lights as they drove past. They did not stop to explain themselves, and Lawton hoped that they would not need gasoline.

It was nearly seven o'clock when they reached the Collserola once again and began to make their way down to Barcelona. Lawton could still see columns of smoke curling up from various points in the city, but they seemed to be dwindling and there were less of them than before. Even as they entered Gràcia, he heard the distant pop of gunshots, but it was soon clear that the authorities were fully in control of the city, as they drove past cavalrymen and mounted Civil Guard on street corners and intersections, and soldiers in khaki and white kepis standing by the wreckage of barricades, manning artillery pieces or sitting on the pavement.

In the Mayor de Gràcia, they passed a line of men and women being marched down toward the port by a military escort. Further down the Passeig de Gràcia, customers were sitting in the outdoor cafés, and Lawton saw an impeccably dressed couple walk their dog past a corpse that was lying facedown on the pavement.

"I need a favor," Lawton said. "I don't want to stay in Mata's apartment tonight. But I haven't any money—not till the banks open."

"*Pas de problème*, my friend. You can stay at my hotel. Consider it a gift from my government. We fought together as members of the Entente—and we won!"

"We did."

Lawton felt relieved now as they drove on toward the Plaza Catalunya. The square was still swarming with soldiers and horses, and dozens of prisoners were sitting in a circle with their hands on their heads.

"I shan't be sorry to get back to my country," Bonnecarrère said. "But I think you may need the help of your own government if you are going to get back to yours."

33

That night Lawton ate supper at the Hotel Internacional, at Bonnecarrère's expense. He fell asleep to the sound of horses' hooves and military commands coming from the Ramblas. In the morning he woke up to find that Bonnecarrère had already checked out, but he was pleased to find that the Frenchman had left him an envelope with some pesetas and a note "From the Entente Cordiale." After breakfast he went out to buy cigarettes and get his suitcase from Mata's house. Once again crowds were flowing up the Ramblas, and the carriages, trams, and bicycles were moving up and down the street on either side of them. Though the fires were no longer visible the smell of smoke continued to pervade the central thoroughfare as he walked past the newspaper kiosks and looked at the headlines on the events of the last week, and the battle in Morocco in the Wolf Ravine, in which two thousand Spanish soldiers had been killed.

Mata's newspaper bore the headline TRAGIC WEEK! above a picture of Barcelona with smoke rising up from all around the city. Lawton bought a copy of *El Diluvio*, and sat down in a café to read it. Already the events of the last few days seemed distant and unreal, as he drank his coffee and smoked his first cigarette of the day, with the sun on his face and the birds once again chirping in their cages. Like all the other newspapers, the front page carried a long article on the disturbances of the last week. The article noted that it had been approved by the military censor, and it listed eighty buildings burned and destroyed, and more than one hundred dead and wounded. Hundreds of arrests had already been made, the paper said, and more were certain to follow, as the authorities sought out the terrorists and agitators who had brought chaos and destruction to the city.

The newspaper also reported that one of the city's most celebrated journalists, the poet Bernat Mata, had been shot dead near the cathedral; that His Excellency the Count of Arenales had been murdered and a chapel on his estate burned by an anarchist mob; that the captain-general Santiago had called upon all citizens of Barcelona to work together to ensure that these terrible events were never repeated. Afterward Lawton walked over to Mata's house to get his suitcase. He was relieved to find that his wife and children had not returned. For a moment he thought of writing them a note, but he knew that he could not find the words to describe what had happened. After picking up his case he posted Mata's keys through his letterbox, and headed back out into the city to the post office.

He had hoped to send a telegram to Mrs. Foulkes, but the telegraphist said that the lines were still being repaired. To his surprise, the telegraphist said there was a telegram for him that had arrived before the strike and got lost. Lawton stood outside the post office and read:

```
Dear Harry,
    It's long time now and I don't hear from you.
I hope you have no problem? Remember to take
medication. Everything fine here. I miss you.
Lotte.
```

For a moment Lawton could not think who Lotte was, and then he realized that the telegram came from the widow Friedman. Whether it was the strain of the last few days, or the realization that someone actually cared what had happened to him, Lawton felt genuinely moved by this simple message. Of course her name was Lotte, but he was so used to thinking of her as another man's wife that it was only now that he remembered the tenderness and concern that she bestowed on him and he felt suddenly grateful for it. He was pleased to think that she would be waiting for him as he walked back down the Ramblas to the consulate.

He found Smither standing in the center of the room, dressed in his tennis whites with his tennis racket, practicing his forehand. The vice-consul smiled hopefully as Lawton came into the room.

"Harry," he said. "You've come for the ashes?"

"I won't be taking them," Lawton said.

"Why on earth not?"

"Because the ashes in that jar are not Randolph Foulkes."

Smither's mouth fell open, and he sat down at his desk as Lawton lit a cigarette and told him what had happened during the last few days, right up to the gunfight in the mountains. He told him about Lieutenant Ugarte, about Foulkes, Weygrand, and Klarsfeld, about the blood transfusions, his kidnapping and escape, and the help he had received from the French secret service agent Captain Georges Bonnecarrère. He did not mention everything. There was no need to tell a representative of His Majesty's Government that he had shot the Count of Arenales. By the time he had finished however, Smither was staring at him as though he had just fallen out of the sky.

"Good lord," he said, shaking his head. "Good lord. So Foulkes was the Monster—and a traitor to boot?"

"He didn't see it like that."

"And you're sure this . . . laboratory has been destroyed?"

"Very much so. It caught fire accidentally. And everyone associated with it is dead—except for Lieutenant Ugarte. And right now, I need your help."

"Oh?"

"I need to get out of the city."

"Right-o." Smither did not look displeased at this prospect.

"Today."

Smither frowned. "That could be a little awkward. They're still repairing the railway lines."

"Then perhaps His Majesty's Government would be good enough to put me on a ship," said Lawton. "Because I'm sure you'll understand that I don't want to have any more conversations with Barcelona policemen."

"Of course." Smither glanced sadly at his tennis racket and picked up the telephone. "Good-o. The exchange is working again. Let's see what I can do."

Within an hour, Smither had booked a ticket to Marseille on a steamer that evening. Lawton remained at the consulate for the rest of the day. In the evening Smither escorted him to the port. Even as Lawton looked around the harbor where Bonnecarrère had nearly been killed the night before, he still found it difficult to believe that he had survived, and he half expected Ugarte or Bravo Portillo to come after him once again.

"Well, Harry," Smither said. "I wish you luck. This has been a strange affair."

"It has." Lawton shook his hand. "And perhaps you could speak to Mata's wife when she returns and tell her what happened? Tell her she can write to me if she needs to. Tell her her husband was a brave man."

"I will."

Lawton thanked him, and watched his white trousers disappear into the dusk. It was not until the ship had pulled away from the harbor, and he watched the faint wisps of smoke rising up against the purple sky, that he began to relax. Behind him the seagulls followed the ship's white trail as he looked back at the statue of Christopher Columbus with his pointing arm, at the gloomy silhouette of the Montjuïc fortress, at the streetlamps that had come back on again. It was a beautiful city, but he would not mind if he never saw it again. The next morning he arrived in Marseille and took the train to Paris, and the following day he took the train to Boulogne, and caught the ferry to Dover. Soon the white cliffs appeared out of the mist once again that he had seen in so many pictures and postcards. Before leaving for Spain he had never actually seen them with his own eyes, and now he found something reassuringly permanent about them. They marked the entrance to the only place that laid any claim to be his home, the sceptered isle that Mata had described, a country of restraint and moderation, of wise, sensible governments that did not do stupid or mad things.

It was true that it was the country of Randolph Foulkes, but England had rejected Foulkes's schemes, and inadvertently forced him into his depraved exile. All that was over now, and he looked forward to collecting his payment from Foulkes's widow and, more surprisingly, to seeing Lotte Friedman once again. Even as the ship pulled into the dock and he came down the gangway, he saw the two men standing in long coats and derby hats waiting on the pier. He was not certain whether they were detectives, Special Branch, or something else entirely, but he knew they were waiting for him, and as they sauntered along the pier toward him, he realized that Smither had found a way of sending a telegram after all.

On the first Monday morning after the strike Esperanza Claramunt got up to go to work as usual. Her mother said that she still looked unwell, but she was already tired of sitting in bed, listening to news of the world from the neighbors and comrades who came to wish her well. Rosa Tosets had told her not to talk about what had happened at the Arenales estate. Even her own mother knew only that she had been held prisoner with the Irishman in a place she did not know, and that the Invincibles had rescued her.

From these visits she learned of the street battles she had not been involved in, and the names of some of those who been killed or wounded. She learned that Arnau Busquets had been found floating in the harbor with a bullet in his head; that Ruben Montero had vanished and no one knew where he was. She also heard the political news. The state of emergency remained in place and the Regionalist League—Mata's own political party—had called on the government to extend it. The Archbishop of Barcelona had called on all the people of Barcelona to reject the forces of godlessness and anarchy. The Radical Party had denied any responsibility for the church burnings and blamed them on the anarchists.

On Sunday afternoon Flor Tosets came with her mother and her two young children to see her. Señora Tosets said that the number of dead and wounded was much higher than the figures in the newspapers. Some bodies had been taken away by the army, she said, and no one knew where they were buried. Already the movement had begun to demand the authorities release the names of the dead and called for an amnesty for the prisoners who had been arrested during and after the Tragic Week. Señora Tosets also said that the police were searching for Ferrer as one of the organizers of the strike.

Esperanza asked Señora Tosets about Lawton. No one had seen him, she said, or the Frenchman, but three foreigners had been found dead in Montseny, only a few miles from Sant Celoni. The authorities claimed that bandits were responsible, and even though the bodies had not yet been identified, all of them had been driving in a red Delaunay-Belleville.

"The Irishman did well," Señora Tosets said.

Esperanza was relieved that Lawton had survived, but she was disappointed that she had not been able to thank him and say goodbye. Later that night, she dreamed that she was trapped in a chair in total darkness, in a room filling up with blood, and she woke up shouting to find Eduardo braying in sympathy. Her mother came in and calmed them down. For the rest of the night she had slept with a candle burning, and her brother in the same bed, and she took as much comfort from him as he did from her.

Now she felt the weight of the world once again as she walked out onto the Mayor de Gràcia to take the streetcar downtown. Everything was working again. The wrecked trams had been taken away, the barricades were mostly cleared, the army had returned to its barracks, and the trams and carriages moved back and forth along the Passeig de Gràcia as though nothing had happened. She could still smell smoke and ashes, and the sight of the passersby going about their daily business made her wonder once again what had been the point of it all.

She got off the tram at the top of the Ramblas and walked along Pintor Fortuny before turning down toward her school. The children were already beginning to arrive, and they were talking excitedly to each other as if they had all been through a great adventure. They fell silent at the sight of Director Vargas, who stood gloomily by the main entrance.

"Miss Claramunt," he said. "I'm surprised to see you."

"Why?" she replied. "Is the school still closed?"

"Come with me."

Esperanza followed the director into his office, where he shut the door behind him.

"Miss Claramunt, I regret to inform you that your employment here is terminated with immediate effect. You will receive a week's salary. But you must leave the school immediately."

Esperanza stared at him coldly. "May I ask why?"

"We have received information from the authorities, about your . . . activities," Vargas replied.

"From Lieutenant Ugarte?"

"The source is not important. You understand after the events of the last week that things cannot go on as before. Rational education is one thing, sedition is quite another. As you may know, there is a warrant out for Don Francesc's arrest. If our school is to stay open we must disassociate ourselves from—"

"Ferrer had nothing to do with the strike," Esperanza said. "And Lieutenant Ugarte is a murderer. Teaching children to think for themselves is not sedition."

"Well, that is your opinion, of course."

"You are a coward," Esperanza said. "In a country of cowards. And this country will never change until people like you no longer decide what happens in it."

Vargas nodded, as if had expected something like this. He unlocked a drawer in his desk and handed Esperanza an envelope. "You may leave now, Miss Claramunt. Perhaps you would do better to stay out of politics if you have any concern for your mother and your brother."

Esperanza was tempted to refuse the envelope, but the thought of her mother and Eduardo stopped her. "Can I say goodbye to the children?" she asked.

"No you may not."

Vargas opened the door and ushered her out into the corridor. He continued to escort her past her own classroom. It was not until she reached the entrance that she stopped and looked back at the faces of her students pressed against the classroom window. She raised her hand to wave at them and then clenched it into a fist. Vargas was still staring at her as the children let out a cheer. She would have liked to tell them that one day they would grow up in a republic—not the Republic of Lerroux and the Radicals—but a republic of justice, where the rich no longer ruled, and cardinals and bishops no longer sent the poor to fight. But now Vargas shooed them away from the window, and she wiped her eyes and walked back home through the streets of her conquered city.

Even before his return to England, Lawton had wondered what he was going to say to Mrs Foulkes. He had intended to see her as soon as he arrived, but his initial interrogation by the Special Branch officers in Dover proved to be only the first of many. For the next two weeks he was ordered to remain in London. Almost every other day he was summoned to Scotland Yard or Whitehall for interviews with officials from the Ministry of War, the Foreign Office, the Directorate of Military Intelligence, and other ministries that were not even named.

All of them wanted to ask him about Barcelona and Randolph Foulkes. Some of them questioned him about Bonnecarrère and the French secret service, others asked about Weygrand, Klarsfeld, and Foulkes's German connections. He was also questioned by two army doctors, who asked him detailed questions about the experiments that Foulkes and Weygrand had conducted, while another army officer took copious notes. How had they extracted blood? What instruments had they used to perform transfusions? What equipment had they used for storage? What anticoagulants had they used? What were their experiments intended to achieve?

One of the doctors asked him to draw pictures of bottles and tubes, and was clearly disappointed that he had given the order to destroy Foulkes's laboratory. Both doctors were incredulous when he described the yellow substance that had been extracted from Esperanza Claramunt's blood, and asked him repeatedly how this had been done and how long it had taken to achieve the transformation. Lawton answered these questions as well as he could, but by the end of the interview he sensed that the two doctors did not entirely believe him.

At times Lawton sensed that he was under suspicion himself. On the morning of his third day back in the country he emerged from Lotte Friedman's café and realized that he was being followed by a plainclothes official, who made no attempt to conceal himself. Maitland said the authorities were nervous about German spies, and that it was only natural that Lawton would come under scrutiny for a while after what had happened in Barcelona. Maitland was as astounded as everyone else by what Lawton told him, and said he deserved an OBE or some other medal for what he had done, but what Lawton wanted more than anything else was payment.

On the second Friday in August he was summoned to Whitehall once again, where an official he had not seen before explained that his debriefing was over. The official also said that any attempt to disseminate or even mention the transfusion and storage procedures that he had observed in Barcelona would be considered a breach of the Official Secrets Act, and Lawton was instructed to sign a document to that effect there and then. Nor was he allowed to mention Randolph Foulkes in any public forum. There was no mention of an OBE or any other award.

The official did not say whether these instructions applied to Foulkes's wife. That same afternoon Lawton called Mrs. Foulkes on the number that Maitland had given him. Her voice sounded flat and slightly slurred, as though she was under medication. She criticized him for not having called her before in a tone that made him feel suddenly anxious about his payment. The next day he caught the same train that he had taken with Maitland the previous month. As the train moved slowly through the hedgerows and meadows, the oast-houses and coalmines, he thought of Barcelona and its burning skies once again. Even in August, England was greener than Catalonia, and the countryside exuded a sense of timeless order and serenity.

Since his return he had read that nearly two thousand people had been arrested on charges of rebellion during the July riots. He had also read little snippets of news on Spanish military operations in Morocco; of sniper attacks from Moorish tribesmen or Spanish artillery bombardments of Moorish positions.

There was no mention of Randolph Foulkes, and now as he looked out at the neatly ordered fields, he wondered how he was going to tell Mrs. Foulkes that her husband was a murderer and a traitor who had drained human blood in order to help the German army win the next war. Would he be breaching the Official Secrets Act? And would she even believe what he told her? On arrival at Hastings he caught a cab to Graveling once again. Soon the redbrick house appeared in front of him, and he braced himself and told the driver to wait for him. The maid ushered him inside, and he was not surprised to hear that her mistress was abed.

He followed the maid upstairs to the bedroom, and waited while she knocked lightly on the door. Mrs. Foulkes called them in testily. She was leaning up in a dressing gown with the curtains half drawn. A newspaper was lying on the bed next to her, but she looked drained and her face was creased, as though she had just woken up from a nap. She gave him a sour look and gestured languidly toward the chair by the window.

"We'll have tea, Amelia," she said. The maid nodded and left the room. "I'm glad to see you back safely, Mr. Lawton."

She did not look glad at all. Lawton wanted to smoke, but sensed that it would not be appropriate.

"I'm sorry I couldn't come before, ma'am," he said. "I was obliged to leave Barcelona in a hurry. Because of the riots. I wanted to contact you earlier but there were certain details that needed clarification."

"Well I would also like some clarification. Especially after this." She handed him the newspaper and Lawton looked at the headline: ENG-LISH SCIENTIST KILLED IN SPAIN. The article reported that the scientist, explorer, and author Randolph Foulkes had been killed in a terrorist bomb in Barcelona, and went on to list his achievements. Lawton was still reading it when the maid returned and poured two cups of tea.

"You haven't seen this?" Mrs. Foulkes asked, as the maid left the room.

"I don't read the *Times* ma'am."

"A lackey from the foreign office brought Randolph's ashes home last week," she said. "He confirmed what you said—that Randolph was killed in a terrorist outrage. But until yesterday I'd heard nothing from *you*. Regarding our other matter."

Lawton did not know whether the ashes really did belong to Foulkes or the tramp who had taken his place, but the Foreign Office had clearly made its own decision about what Foulkes's widow was allowed to know.

"As I told you in my telegram, your husband was killed in the Luna Bar bombing," he said. "But I have since discovered that it was not an accident. Your husband was deceived by two confidence tricksters in Vernet-les-Bains, a mesmerist named Dr. Weygrand and a woman named Zorka—who went under the pseudonym Marie Babineaux. They hypnotized your husband and got him to make out the payment that you mentioned. They then staged a terrorist outrage in order to kill him, and killed the perpetrator in order to keep him quiet."

"Good God. Have they been caught?"

"The perpetrators are both dead, ma'am. Chief Inspector Maitland has made a formal request to the Bank of Sababell to have your money returned to you. I believe it will be."

Mrs. Foulkes nodded. "This Weygrand was German, you say?"

"Austrian, ma'am."

"Same difference. Poor Randolph. That wasn't how he expected to die. The Foreign Office also brought his possessions with the ashes. But there was no manuscript there—he always took his writings with him. Did you see it?"

"I didn't, ma'am."

"Pity. His publisher called me today and said that he would be interested in posthumous publication. A pioneer, he called him. A great man. Do you think my husband was a great man Mr. Lawton?"

She no longer seemed drowsy now, and her face bore just a trace of irony that he had not seen in her before.

"I couldn't say," Lawton said awkwardly. "I never met him."

"He wasn't much of a husband," she said. "He wasn't kind."

"I'm sorry to hear that."

"Not to people. But he loved animals. We had a dog once. A red setter. It lived for fourteen years. Randolph showed more tenderness toward that animal than he ever showed to me. When the animal died he actually shed a tear. Only one. But that was the only time I ever saw him do that."

Lawton could not think of anything to say to this, and he hurriedly sipped at his tea.

"I sometimes felt there was . . . a darkness in him," she went on. "Something I couldn't see. Couldn't reach. I'm sorry. I'm rambling. I thank you for your diligence and professionalism, Mr. Lawton. Chief Inspector Maitland was right. I underestimated you." She put down her cup of tea. "I'm tired now. I've not been well."

She handed him a check with a thin, bony hand, and Lawton glanced at it just long enough to see that it was nearly double what he had been promised.

"Thank you, ma'am. That is most generous."

Mrs. Foulkes leaned back with her eyes half-closed. She looked as though a heavy weight had just descended upon her, and it was obvious that the conversation was over. Lawton placed the empty cup on the bedside table and stood up to leave. He glanced out of the window and saw the maid standing by some rabbit hutches at the end of the yard. One of the hutches was empty and a large white rabbit was sitting on the grass on its hind legs staring back at him, as if it recognized him. For a moment he stared back, and then he turned back to Foulkes's widow to say goodbye. Her eyes were closed now, and he left her lying in the gloom and shut the door softly behind him.

EPILOGUE

O f all the seasons, Lawton liked autumn best. Even in London he liked the cooler days, the long sunsets, the changing colors on the leaves in the streets and parks. The autumn of 1909 was unlike any he had ever known. It was not just the Indian summer that stretched into late September, bathing the city in a warm golden light even as the first leaves began to turn, or the pleasure that he took from his own survival. It was not even the pleasant days he spent with Lotte Friedman, which felt almost like a courtship.

At the beginning of the month he had his first seizure since returning from Barcelona, while eating supper in Lotte's kitchen. One minute he was looking at the newspaper report describing how Francesc Ferrer had been arrested in a cave after more than a month in hiding, and then he saw himself walking once again beneath the burning sky of Barcelona and he felt the ground moving beneath his feet.

He came to himself to find Lotte Friedman wiping blood from his mouth, while her children peered from the doorway with expressions of fear and wonder. In that moment he could not stand to live like this any longer. The following day he went to see Dr. Morris and told him that he was ready to pay for surgery at Dr. Horsley's clinic. Within a week Morris had managed to secure him an appointment at the National Hospital in Queen Square for an initial examination.

For a few days Lawton felt a surge of relief and hope that his torment might end, and then he saw himself transformed into a slack-jawed half-wit, a useless mouth, with Lotte or some nurse spoon-feeding him as he eked out his vacant days in his apartment or an asylum. As the golden autumn continued to unfold, these dire possibilities filled him with a determination to make the most of the time he had left, and to leave Lotte and her children with some pleasant memories of the man he had been. He bought two new gramophone records: Caruso singing *Aida* and Eddie Morton's "Somebody Lied." He treated Lotte Friedman to a silver bracelet and a new hat. He took her and the children to the circus and the park, and bought them ice cream, toffee apples, and cotton candy.

In the last week of September he took Lotte to the cinema for the first time in her life, to see a science fiction film called *The Airship Destroyer* at the Cinematograph Theatre. The film told the story of an attack on England by a German airship fleet. Even without sound, the audience gasped as the bombs fell on English towns and country roads, and everyone clapped when the handsome hero finally shot them down with his homemade missile and ended the film with his beloved swooning in his arms. Lotte came out of the theater looking anxious and said she was worried about what would happen to her children if there was a war.

Lawton replied that it was just a story, but he knew that she was not the only one who was anxious. The newspapers were filled with rumors of war and invasion, of German spies filtering into the country in their thousands, of simmering crises in the Balkans, Morocco, and the Ottoman Empire that could blow up at any moment. He sensed that the world was being pulled toward some vague catastrophe, and the knowledge only reinforced his determination to make the most of the time remaining to him. On the day before his appointment at the London hospital, he and Lotte went to see *The Arcadians* at the Shaftesbury Theatre.

Afterward they walked along the river toward Embankment Station. Lotte was wearing her new hat and bracelet, and she looked younger and prettier than he had ever seen her as they walked arm in arm through the drifting leaves. Ahead of him Lawton could see the Whitehall buildings where he had only recently been questioned, and as he looked at the barges moving slowly back and forth and the streaks of gold reflected in the dark turbid waters, he had the disconcerting sensation that he was seeing everything around him for the last time. He heard Big Ben strike five and he imagined each solemn toll reverberating through all the corners of the Empire as the refrain from the Chorus of Fear passed through his mind: *"To ev'ry race/In ev'ry clime/I set the pace, and call the time/From Camberwell to Candahar/But I quite forgot Arcadia!"*

They had nearly reached Embankment when he heard a voice yelling, "Read it here! Ferrer executed! Read it here!" Lotte looked at him in surprise as he pulled away from her arm and quickened his pace to the station, where he fumbled for change and bought the *Standard* with the headline FERRER EXECUTED written in large black letters. He stood holding up the newspaper, oblivious to everything else around him, and read that the anarchist teacher Francesc Ferrer I Guardia had been shot by firing squad the previous day at the Montjuïc fortress in Barcelona for his part in the July riots. Ferrer had been convicted by a military court of helping to organize the rebellion, and despite protests and pleas for amnesty across Europe, the Spanish government had remained firm.

According to the paper, Ferrer had refused a priest and the blindfold, and told the firing squad: "Aim well, my friends, you are not responsible. I am innocent: long live the Modern School!" Lawton stared at the owl-like face, and remembered the man he had last seen sitting in a deckchair outside his home. The execution followed the assassination of Lieutenant Jorge Ugarte, the paper said, an officer from the Spanish political police, who had been shot dead outside his home by an unnamed female assassin. Lawton thought of Esperanza Claramunt and Rosa Tosets, as Lotte Friedman came up to him and looked at him with concern.

Lawton stared past her, past the pedestrians walking back and forth, beyond the boats moving along the river and the drifting clouds and he saw Barcelona once again. He saw the cavalry moving down the Ramblas.

He saw Ferrer sitting in his deck chair and he wondered whether he had been looking over the sea when the bullets struck him. Lawton remembered the scripture that Ferrer had quoted to him: watch therefore, for ye know neither the day nor the hour. Ferrer had not known his hour, and nor did he. He could not know what would happen when Horsley operated on him. He did not know whether Horsley would cut out the bad part of his brain or leave him a vegetable.

Perhaps the world was always like that: sleepwalking toward catastrophes that the present could not even imagine. But his generation knew what was going to happen. Everyone knew that war would break out—the war that Foulkes and Weygrand had predicted would kill millions and shatter thrones and empires, but no one knew when. And even as he stood there, on a fine autumn afternoon in the greatest city in the world, it seemed to him that he could hear the thunder of the great guns, and he saw the flaming cities with their roofless buildings and their blackened stumps of walls, and the lines of soldiers—more than the world had ever seen—marching toward the front like an endless swarm of ants.

And somewhere beyond the light puffy clouds, behind the pallid blue of that English sky, in some country he could not yet name, he saw pitiless men wearing white laboratory coats standing in a barred room in front of a black sun, while human beings just like them lay on operating tables with their mouths taped up, crying into their gags for their mothers and fathers. Could such things really happen? There was nothing to say they could not. Now a breeze rustled the pages of his newspaper, a chill Hyperborean wind blowing down from the north, whistling through cemeteries filled with white crosses, through forests stripped of trees, and battlefields piled with the bodies of young men, and he shivered and folded the newspaper.

"Are you alright, Harry?" she asked.

"I'm fine." Lawton took Lotte Friedman's arm and drew her closer to him, and as they walked back down into the underground, he felt grateful for the time they had had together, and for whatever time they had left.

AUTHOR'S NOTE

I n historical fiction, any references to real persons or events are entirely deliberate, regardless of the liberties that may be taken with them, and this novel is no exception. That said, readers not familiar with this period of Spanish history might appreciate some sketching out of the people and events referred to. The urban insurrection known as *La Semana Tragica* (The Tragic Week) is one of the key events in early twentieth-century Spanish history, which took place in Barcelona between July 26 and August 2, 1909. It was the culmination of a decade of intensifying political and social conflict that followed the collapse of the Spanish empire in 1898.

According to the two-party political system established following the restoration of the Bourbon monarchy in 1874, local political bosses known as caciques bought and manipulated elections locally, while the Liberal and Conservative parties effectively took turns in government according to the ritualized system known as the *alternancia pactada* (agreed alternation). In the aftermath of 1898 this system came under pressure from Basque and Catalan nationalists; from a militant trade union movement strongly influenced by anarchism, and increasingly confident socialist and republican parties.

This confrontation was particularly sharp in Barcelona, the largest industrial city in Spain, and a city with strong separatist and anarchist traditions. In 1901 the conservative Catalan nationalist Regionalist League triumphed in local elections and became the dominant Catalan party for the next two decades. The prospect of Catalan autonomy alarmed the Spanish army and government, and resulted in the incident that Mata refers to early on in the novel, when junior Spanish army officers ransacked the offices of the satirical Catalan magazine ¡*Cu-Cut!* in 1905, in response to a cartoon insulting the Spanish army.

Instead of punishing the officers, the Spanish government passed the Law of Jurisdictions, which placed a swathe of offenses in military courts. In response Catalan nationalist parties formed a new coalition, *Solidaritat Catalana* (Catalan Solidarity) in 1906. The rise of separatism in Catalonia coincided with a political struggle between the city's powerful anarchist movement and the Radical Republican party.

Under the leadership of the fiery journalist Alejandro Lerroux, the Radicals gained widespread support in the city's working class districts, particularly in the Raval and the Parallel. In the same period a city with a long history of anarchist bomb outrages experienced a dramatic increase in terrorist bombings. As the novel suggests, the perpetrators of these outrages were never clear, and the controversy was such that in 1907 the Barcelona city council contracted a retired Scotland Yard detective, Inspector Charles Arrow to form a new anti-terrorist Office of Criminal Investigation. The "twentieth century Sherlock Holmes," as he became known in Barcelona, soon found that he was not being given the support he required, and that his presence was resented by the local police.

As the bombings continued, Arrow's office became effectively irrelevant. In 1908 an anarchist and police informant named Joan Rull was arrested by the Spanish police and put on trial for most of the bombings of the preceding few years. Though the trial concluded that Rull and his family were planting bombs in order to justify Rull's continued employment as a police informer, some observers—including Inspector Arrow—believed that more complex political motives were behind them.

Rull's execution in 1908 failed to resolve these debates. His bombing campaign was something of an aberration at a time when the new anarchist coalition *Solidaridad Obrera* (Workers Solidarity), was rejecting bombings and assassinations in favor of an anarcho-syndicalist strategy of trade union organization and direct action, with the ultimate goal of a general strike.

In July 1909 the conservative government of Antonio Maura took the decision to call up the Catalan reservists following another military reversal in Spain's conflict with Rif tribesmen in Morocco. The escalation of the war was greeted with widespread opposition across Spain, but the protests were particularly virulent in Barcelona. When the anarchists, the trade unions, and the socialists called for a general strike, the Radical Party was obliged to follow suit. The strike quickly degenerated into a week of chaotic and confused violence that fell somewhere between an anticlerical riot and a spontaneous revolutionary insurrection that surprised the organizers of the strike as much as anyone else.

Lerroux's Radicals were instrumental in turning the antiwar protest in an anticlerical direction, which resulted in the burning of more than eighty churches and religious institutions. The uprising was put down with considerable violence by the Spanish army. Between 100–150 people were killed by the security forces, though the real figure may have been higher. Nearly two thousand people were arrested and charged with armed rebellion. Dozens were imprisoned and five individuals were tried and executed.

The most famous victim of the Tragic Week repression was the anarchist educationalist Francesc Ferrer I Guardia. Ferrer was not directly involved in the preparations for the strike, and was not in Barcelona during the Tragic Week itself, but the Spanish government and army believed him to be complicit in the attempted assassination of King Alfonso XIII in 1906, and seized the opportunity to execute him, despite widespread protests across Europe.

The Tragic Week was a catalyst in Spain's road to civil war. That same year, the reactionary government of Antonio Maura fell from power, following criticisms of the heavy-handed repression in Catalonia, thus bringing to an end the system of "agreed alternation." The rebellion and the repression also led to the formation of the Confederación Nacional de Trabajo (National Work Confederation) the following year, which rapidly became the most powerful national anarchist organization in Spain. In 1909 Inspector Arrow returned to England with his payment.

Inspector Manuel Bravo Portillo went on to become the chief of Barcelona police, and a key organizer of the *pistoleros* (gunmen) hired by Barcelona employers to assassinate scores of anarchists and trade unionists during World War I, before he himself was assassinated in 1919. In the aftermath of Tragic Week, Alejandro Lerroux fell from favor with the Barcelona working classes, and moved his political base to Córdoba. Under the second republic he became prime minister three times, and went into exile following the outbreak of civil war.

Lieutenant Ugarte is entirely imaginary, but the Brigada Social did exist, and was largely responsible for the "Inquisitorial" response to the Corpus Christi bombing of 1896.

As the novel suggests, the transfusion experiments carried out by Weygrand and Foulkes were indeed ahead of their time. Despite improvements in blood transfusion techniques during World War I, blood was mostly used to treat battlefield injuries through "direct" patient-to-patient transfusions for much of the war, rather than through the use of stored blood. In 1917 Captain Lawrence Bruce Robertson, a doctor with the Canadian Army Medical Corps, persuaded his British colleagues to conduct "indirect" transfusions for the first time, using the new syringe and paraffin tube methods that had been developed in American hospitals—and which Foulkes and Weygrand use in the novel.

That same year an American military doctor named Oswald Hope Robertson built the world's first blood bank following America's entry into the war. Robertson stored blood mixed with a citrate and dextrose solution in glass bottles in ammunition boxes packed with ice and sawdust, thereby making it possible to store blood for up to twenty-six days and move it to casualty clearing stations to be used in transfusions to patients. In 1917 the British surgeon Geoffrey Keynes, a lieutenant in the British army, designed the first portable transfusion kits, consisting of a wooden box, a storage bottle, and needles.

Between them, these three men saved thousands of lives, and laid the basis for the further development of blood transfusion and blood storage techniques on the battlefield. The experiments with blood plasma described in the novel are also anachronistic. Though Captain Gordon R. Ward of the British Royal Army Medical Corps suggested injecting patients suffering from shock with plasma during World War I, his advice was not followed.

It was not until World War II that plasma was used on a large scale by the American army on the battlefield, and also in the United Kingdom, as a result of the American "Plasma for Britain" initiative. This program was overseen by the African American scientist Charles Drew, who developed a method for "banking" dried plasma while completing his doctorate at Columbia University in the late 1930s. Following the American biochemist Edwin Cohn's discovery of the process of blood fractionation, serum albumin—a derivative of plasma—was used by the American army during World War II for treating battlefield shock. As a result of research carried out by one of Cohn's colleagues, Dr. Carl W. Walter, plasma transfusions were carried out using plastic bags and tubing, rather than glass or rubber, and these became standard procedures during WWII and the wars that followed.

The "pre-Nazi" beliefs and characteristics of Weygrand, Foulkes, and the Explorer Club were not as unusual as they might seem. Dozens of groups proliferated in Germany and Europe in the last decades of the 19th century and the first decade of the 20th that combined paganism, Wotanism, Runology, occultism, German romanticism, antisemitism, racism, and a quasi-mystical fascination with mythical Aryan homelands. Perhaps the most famous exponent of these views was the Austrian writer Guido von List, who predicted that the Central Powers would win World War II and create a global Wotanist empire.

List died in 1919. Had it not been for World War I, he and the other exponents of "Ariosophy"—wisdom of the Aryans—would have mostly likely faded into complete obscurity. Instead these movements went on to influence the Nazi Party and the SS, and some of their ideological descendants are still with us even in the twenty-first century.